THE PATIENCE *of a* DEAD MAN

1/10/20

Sarah —

Thanks for reading!

— Michael Clark

THE PATIENCE *of a* DEAD MAN

MICHAEL CLARK

This is a work of fiction. Any resemblance to actual persons, living or dead is entirely coincidental.

Don't fall asleep! Stay in touch:

https://www.michaelclarkbooks.com/
https://www.facebook.com/michaelclarkbooks
michael@michaelclarkbooks.com

CONTENTS

PROPERTY MAP

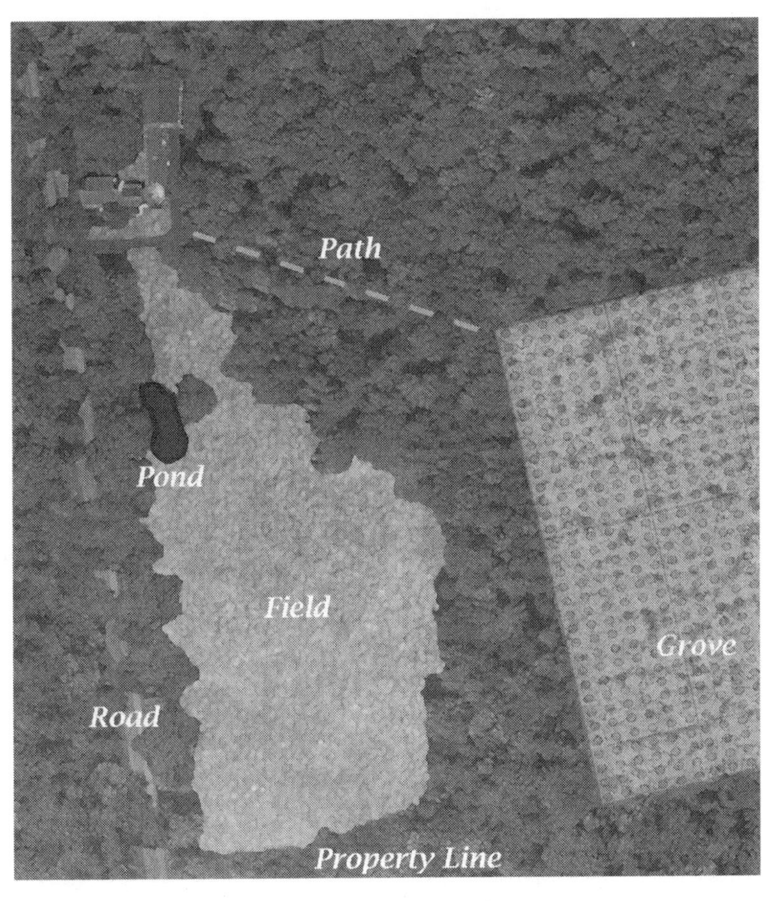

HOUSE PLAN: FIRST FLOOR

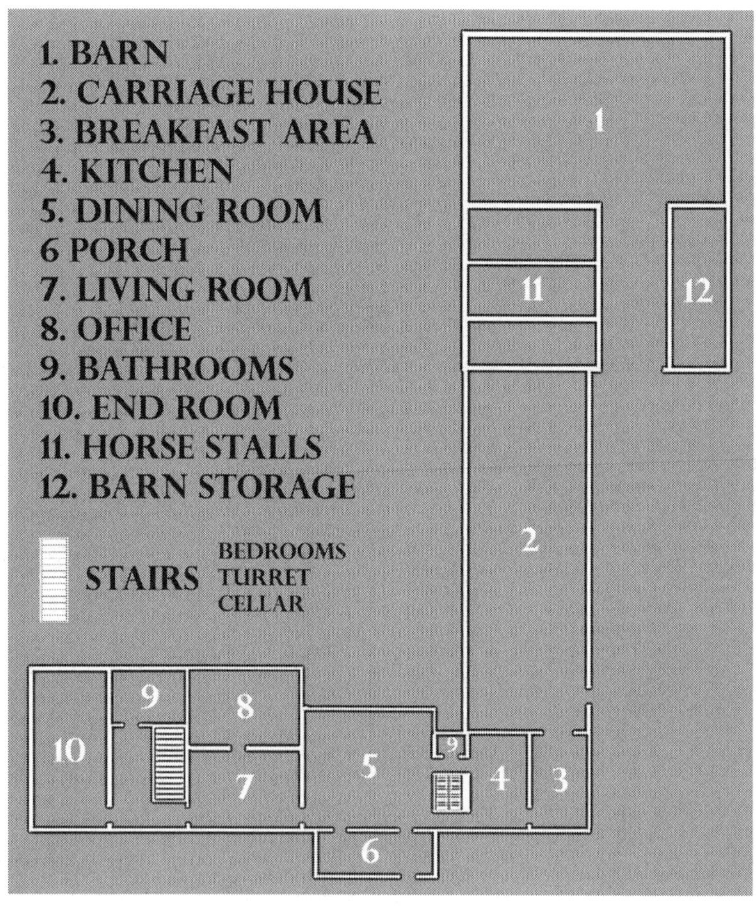

HOUSE PLAN: SECOND FLOOR

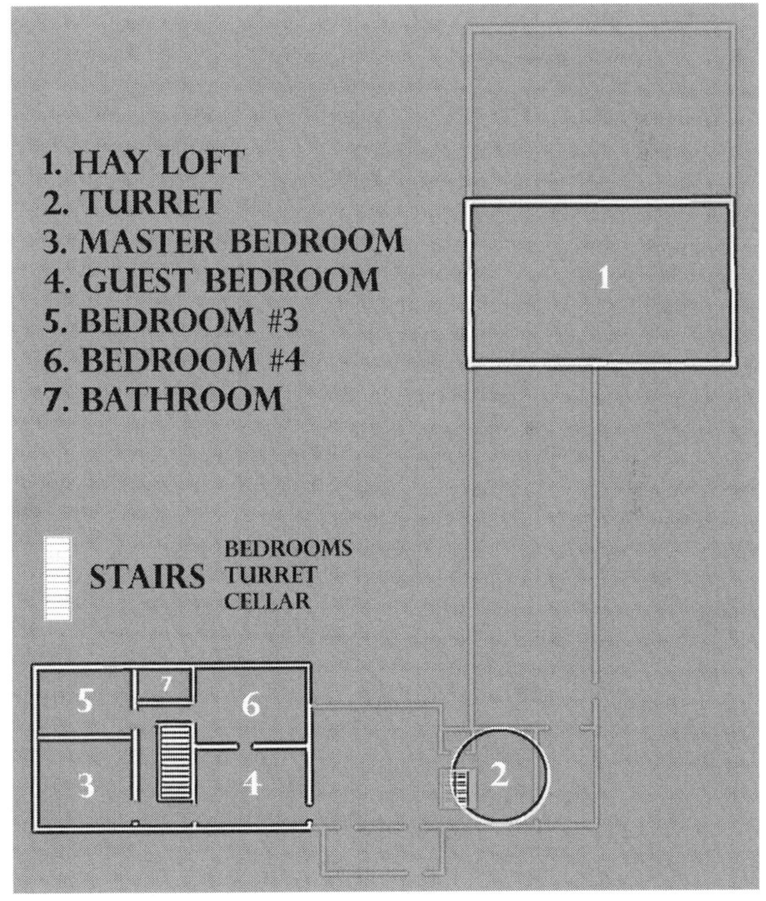

CHAPTER ONE

Henry's Demise

November 29th, 1965

The sun was low in the sky on another perfect New Hampshire day. Henry Smith had just washed and brushed his favorite horse, Fiona, just inside the old red barn. He led her back to her stall and made sure there was plenty of hay to munch on, and then tossed the bucket of soapy water outside into a patch of lawn. The workday was over. Farming was not nearly as stressful as his previous job as a banker, but it was much more physical. Because of the daily exercise on the horse farm, he hadn't had a night of insomnia since the day he and Annette moved in, and his heart was on the mend to boot.

Things were different here, in a good way. The air, the noise, and the way time passed were off the clock; life was much simpler away from the city. The animals all had their timely needs, like food and water and sleep, and they, along with the sun, did the timekeeping for you. It was remarkable how accurate their body clocks were. If by chance you tried to sleep in, the geese would show up at the front door honking at 7 A.M. sharp looking for their breakfast.

Every minute on the farm was about working *together*. In a

little more than a week, he would take Fiona to Concord to be auctioned off. His little horse breeding hobby had taken off; he was beginning to gain a reputation not only around the town but also the state as a competent, up and coming horse breeder. This hobby had become more than enough to pay for their happy lives in Sanborn, without even tapping into the banking nest egg of their previous life.

He shook the excess soap and water off of his hands and wiped them on the back of his jeans. It was getting close to dinnertime, so he headed for the side door to the house. Just before he turned the knob, something caught his eye…something out beyond the pond, way out in the field. He let go of the knob and walked toward the front of the house—maybe it was nothing. He stood there for a few seconds, scanning the tree line where he thought he might have seen her.

It had looked to Henry like the woman they would see from time to time at the corner of the property, cutting across the field into the woods. Dusk was an odd time of day for a walk for anyone, never mind someone that could not possibly live nearby. The closest neighbors were more than a mile away. Henry knew them, and this woman did not look familiar.

Henry and his wife Annette had even speculated that the woman could be a friend or relative of…well, *somebody* nearby, but they really didn't know; they were grasping at straws looking for answers. The truth was there *was* no explanation why the woman made frequent appearances way out here for the past few years. All of the neighbors had their own meadows full of wild grapes and blueberries, not to mention pumpkins. Why come *here*? It would be a heck of a walk home.

Tonight was a cool November evening, just after Thanksgiving, and they had all enjoyed a nice family weekend together, all in all. Both kids (and their spouses) were able to make it to New Hampshire for the holiday. Now that the extended family had eaten their fill of farm-fresh vegetables and free-range turkey and gone back home, it was time to select the annual Christmas tree; Annette had even reminded him to keep an eye out for one just yesterday. Now, as he stood staring at the field and the forest, he thought: *Why not kill two birds with one stone*?

Henry went back to the barn, grabbed the hatchet and set off down the front lawn past the stone wall and the pond headed out toward the far left corner of the field. Just past the now seasonally bygone garden, was the meadow, and beyond that, the woods. The horses grazed out here for about half of every day. As he walked across their beautiful piece of property, he reflected on how fortunate they were to have it and to live here. One hundred yards later, he turned left into the forest.

He had known about the overgrown grove since they bought the place, but he was still enamored by it. *Damn shame. If this grove had been tended to over the years, I'd have my tree already. I'd have my pick. I'd just saw it right down, and after a relatively short drag back to the house, I'd be done. I could even sell a few to the neighbors and the townspeople.*

The grove was an abandoned Christmas tree farm that started about thirty yards into the wild forest, fully on Smith property. The Christmas trees gone wild had become towering spruce and of course, too far gone for holiday use. They were all at least forty feet tall, more or less, and grew in perfectly symmetrical rows.

In and around the grove in odd spots were random wild spruce that could pass for Christmas trees if you looked hard enough. The ones in the middle of the aisles were so out of place it was obvious. The ones just outside the grove were slightly harder to spot because of the chaos of Mother Nature. Trees could be in clumps, and therefore hard to inspect from all sides, and nobody wanted a Christmas tree that looked uneven like it had been in a windstorm.

Henry made his way through the first few yards of the wild forest, and as always, all at once, the chaos of random trees ended, and the grove opened up in front of his eyes. He was fond of this place. It gave him a chill for no particular reason. It was hidden, and then it was in your face. And if you were here, it was yours and yours alone to enjoy, kind of like being lost in the hallways of an empty mansion. It was peaceful and quiet. He rarely had the time to make it out here, however. *Who had time for leisure walks on a fully-functioning farm?*

He angled his path to cut through the forty to forty-five rows of grove, moving diagonally to the right, deeper into the woods. *Where was she?* She was making better time than he was—probably because he was doing double duty trying to find a suitable tree to please Annette. Maybe he could meet the trespasser some other day; the tree was more important given the coming sunset.

He passed more rows than planned, and before he knew it, he could see the man-made symmetry coming to an end at the border of the congested wild forest. More and more rogue trees had claimed odd spots in the last rows; it was a near-even mixture of man and nature. At the edge of the grove began wild plants such as scrub brush, briars, poison ivy and several species of vines. The forest floor here wasn't just spruce needles like the rest of the grove; leaves from all sorts of trees had drifted over the years, leaving piles of natural mulch.

The briars were thick, and behind them, undisturbed forest. Nestled inside the briars and brush were two high mounds of leaves that had collected for years, perhaps decades. They seemed artificially high as if they covered something. At first, Henry thought it might be a section of stone wall, but the stone wall in this forest also happened to be the property line, and he was sure he was still a ways from that.

The sun was sinking, ticking down the last minutes of the day, and Henry had to squint his eyes to choose a pathway through them to the mounds in the brambles. He chose carefully, albeit slowly, making his way forward, folding over the bases of the closest thorns with his boots to disarm the long gangly arms. He wished he'd brought his gloves, but it was too late for that now.

As he closed in, he realized the two piles were each nearly

waist-high. A section of gray stone peered out from under twisting vines that had caught years of falling leaves, revealing something several shades lighter than anything naturally occurring out here.

Gravestones, he recognized. *Thirty-one years living here and I didn't know I had...neighbors.* He looked down at his hatchet, wishing it was a pair of pruning shears. The briars proved well prepared to protect their long-held secret, but Henry's curiosity was powerful. He forged ahead, hacking and flattening the bases of the sharp plants so that getting back out wouldn't be the same battle it was coming in. Even though he took great care, he got hooked a few times on his clothes and his skin.

The hazardous patch was larger than he had estimated; roughly twenty feet from the starting point to the main objective, and time was now a serious factor—the sun would be down in minutes. The Christmas tree plan was definitely off now, even if he happened to stumble into the perfect one on the way out. Dinner could very well be on the table already, and he hadn't told Annette where he was going; this excursion wasn't supposed to have taken this long.

As soon as he broke through the last of the thorns, he put down the hatchet, dropped to his knees and began to clear the dead leaves and ivy. He took care not to disturb the stones themselves in case they were weakly anchored. They were crooked from years of heaving frosts but remained steady as he worked. There was a large one on the left and a smaller one on the right.

His mind buzzed with questions, not the least of which was *how the hell did I miss this*? It was twilight now, the sun had set, and only the glow from it beneath the horizon remained as a light source. He would have to call it quits soon, or it would be hard to find his way out in the dark.

There was so much moss on the headstones they were illegible. Concentrating on the left one, Henry scraped gently at the space he estimated the epitaph would be, taking care not to dig too hard into the marble or granite itself; the stone might be soft. After three or four moments of gentle effort, he had cleared the top two engraved lines. The first, in smaller letters, read: "Here lies." The second line, where the person's name should appear, was taller than the first—but he couldn't quite make out the inscription.

Then, a twig snapped. Henry looked around, attempting to focus in the dark; *it must be her; time to meet the stranger.* Henry had his doubts but hoped it was true. He looked back, down the near-perfect aisle of spruce pestered by the forest. It was all shadows; night had fallen. He squinted and took off his glasses, trying to catch a better glance. Someone approached.

She stood there in the dark—the mystery woman in the long dress. All he could make out was her silhouette; her pale white hands were holding what might be a bouquet, and her hair was pinned up, worn away from her neck. It was as unkempt as the woods behind her, strands and bunches pushing out in odd directions.

The rest of her features were lost in the dark, but he knew it was her. Why hadn't he taken the time previously to introduce himself before this awkward moment? *Nobody should be in the middle of the woods when night falls, blueberries or no blueberries. Were there even any blueberries left this time of year?* He searched the ground for his hatchet.

"Hello," he said. "My name is Henry Smith. We're neighbors, aren't we?" The woman stood still and silent, and he couldn't judge her reaction without seeing her face. He stood, and his knees cracked. His back needed an extra moment to straighten.

"What's your name? Do you live around here?" She must be a Simmons, Henry thought. That family has a reputation for being slightly…off.

Making contact was not going smoothly, but he wanted to break the ice with small talk before asking her to leave, so he took a step forward, continuing the effort. He continued his approach as he talked.

"Did you have a nice Thanksgiving?" Still no response. "Where do you live, down the road? Are you one of the Simmons clan?"

She stood silently in the shadows. *What's her deal?* Halfway to her, he opened his mouth to continue the spiel and then held his tongue, suddenly at a loss for words. She was ten feet away. There was a glint in one of her eyes from the twilight, but the rest of her face was still cloaked.

And there was a smell.

There are many unpleasant odors on a farm, but Henry recognized this as the smell of something unmistakably *dead.* Like the time a mouse died inside the wall of their bedroom. It was decay, and it was coming from her.

She was shaking slightly, as if upset. Henry hesitated while he reassessed. Her shoulders were pulled back, and the flower arrangement she was carrying dropped to the forest floor. The left hand shifted across her body and passed something to the right hand that Henry could not see. Then her right arm turned outward, and the silhouette of Henry's hatchet became clear.

He looked down around his feet in a panic, knowing he would not find his dropped hatchet; she had it now. *How the hell…?* His hopes sank as he realized the time for talk had passed; this was not a neighbor or even a living person—the smell was not only strong; it was overbearing. This was a being with an agenda he couldn't pretend to imagine.

She dropped the hatchet into the spruce needles and lurched forward, reaching him nearly immediately, grabbing his face. All Henry heard was a small pop, but he felt nothing. A gray static washed down over his open eyes, as his nervous system shut down; *lights out.* Gray turned to black; he barely had the time to regret leaving Annette behind…unaware.

CHAPTER TWO

The Divorce

January 3rd, 1971

Tim Russell took a breath, then took the pen from his lawyer Frank Turnbull and signed near the bottom of the page next to the "x" written in yellow highlighter. He slapped the pen down on the desk in nervous frustration and sat back, exhaling as much stress as he could before shrugging his shoulders. *Is it over?*

"That's it, buddy…you have officially beaten the Devil," said Frank with an excited smile. He was trying to pump Tim up, but he was also privately celebrating the windfall he would collect for the full day in court. Calling Tim's now ex-wife Sheila "the Devil" was a phrase that he had coined about a year and a half ago in the middle of the divorce process. It was an awkward attempt to relate to Tim (and male clients like him) and make them feel better about parting with their money at a rate of which they had never dreamed. Usually, the angrier they were, the more they ended up paying. Tim didn't laugh. Apparently, people divorcing didn't have much to laugh about, so he shrugged it off and enjoyed his joke alone.

"Woo-hoo, I won," Tim said in a monotone voice with a touch of exhaustion and sarcasm. He was certainly not feeling victorious.

Nobody really wins, one of his friends told him that at the very beginning of the whole deal. *Nobody wins; only the lawyers.*

Frank kept on: "It's over, buddy! Now go home, take a few days off, and get your courage back. Wait for your tail to come out from between your legs, and then, when you're feeling up to it, get back on the market and get yourself some *strange*! You know what I mean? You're a free man! Just don't get married any time soon."

Tim was thirty-eight years old but still hip enough to figure out Frank's slang: "Strange" meant either a strange new woman or more offensively, *specific parts* of a strange new woman. Frank was a full-fledged male chauvinist pig. Tim took a mental pass at the boorish advice. Getting some *strange* was the farthest thing from his mind. Dating came with consequences. All he wanted to do was get away from everyone and everything (except for his two daughters), as fast as possible.

He wouldn't have dreamed of calling a shark the likes of Frank to represent him if the divorce had a chance at being amicable…or at the very least, straightforward and honest. He changed his mind a year back, however, when he realized Sheila was playing dirty. One day while trying to withdraw money from their joint bank account, he was told by the teller that the account had been closed. Right then he realized he'd better look for some legal help, and in calling around, learned she had secretly lawyered up months ago.

He had no idea she was unhappy in the marriage. He thumbed through the Yellow Pages in the phone book and chose a lawyer with a prominent ad on the second page. Upon calling him, the attorney gave an opening spiel and explained the process. Tim decided to meet with him. As soon as the lawyer took his name, he paused. You said your name is Timothy Russell?"

"Right," Tim replied. A moment of awkward silence followed. Finally, the attorney cleared his throat.

"I won't be able to help you, and I'm afraid I'll have to leave it at that, I hope you understand."

Tim was dumbstruck for a second or two. *What's happening?* Finally, he realized; Sheila had already secured his services.

The specter of betrayal crawled up his back like a spider, and much of the confusion and many of the questions of the past couple of months suddenly began to make sense. Sheila had been vague and distant recently…she seemed confused, and told him she thought she might want a divorce. Tim worked long hours, so he chalked it up to some sort of weird phase between them; now he knew the truth. He was being lied to; she had a full-blown plan already. Right away the pieces of the puzzle began to fly together; he wasn't in the dark anymore, and now it was just a matter of catching up to her level of disconnect.

The *apologetic unhappy wife that was heartbroken things weren't going to work out* was really just manipulating the situation, moving Tim around like a pawn while she plotted the next move. She had even suggested that they go through a mediator, for God's sake. Her dishonesty was now transparent, and the Sheila he thought he knew, was dead. In her place was…an enemy. *She probably has a boyfriend already too*, he thought. A short time later, he found out he was right. The guy didn't seem to stick around for long, though, and Tim celebrated bitterly with a six-pack the night he found out. At least that cheating asshole wouldn't be around his kids for very long.

Tim tossed aside any chance of mediation; she had already stolen their money and hired her own attorney behind his back, after all. He decided to hire the type of lawyer that liked to fight and liked to win; so he called Frank. It wasn't that he wanted to go on the offensive; it was more about girding his loins. Sheila was months ahead of him emotionally. He hadn't realized how bad things were at first, and then she kept him in the dark intentionally for who knows how long. He didn't need a lawyer to mediate; he needed a lawyer to end it as quickly and efficiently as possible, and Frank Turnbull, the crass bastard, might be able to keep Sheila the liar honest.

Tim and Sheila Russell had owned a successful general contracting business together. They started out small with handyman projects, eventually moving up to kitchens and bathrooms, taking any work they could get, building their reputation slowly. Sheila was the bookkeeper for only the first two years. Now that they were no longer a team raising a family and running a business, Tim resented this fact. *Two fucking years, then two kids—and then her boredom set in. Nice work, mom. Now it's all but gone.*

Eventually, the business graduated to building houses. During that stretch, Russell Construction had grown to six full-time employees they could comfortably keep on the payroll through the winters and slow periods. The divorce cost him most of the company assets, and the business was now a shell of its former self.

Much of the equipment had to be sold off, and the employees let go (except for his "number two" man, first hire and best friend, Johnny Upson). By law, Sheila got her half as well as a hefty child support payment. She also got to live in their house for up to five years. Sometime within that timeframe, it was agreed that the house would be sold and they would split the proceeds. This left Tim with no choice but to rent a studio apartment and very little capital to run his business.

Tim got his half of the assets, but living on *half* just because the stay-at-home-mom got bored was a tough pill to swallow. Sure, taking care of the kids was hard work, but he would have switched roles with her in a second if he could have; especially since she used some of her "mommy time" to find a new boyfriend.

Today was supposedly the day the divorce would be final. They had a basic set of "Permanent Stipulations" drafted between them, but there were some details left unsettled. Here at the conference table in one of the courthouse meeting rooms, his mood went sour, despite the light at the end of the tunnel. He caught himself getting sucked into a vortex of negative thoughts and quickly snapped out of it. "Primary Physical Custody," it said on the courthouse papers. That meant that the kids would live with her, but he would have rights to visitation. It was all against his will, but that was his life now, and that was what he would have to learn to live with.

Tim and Sheila had been married for twelve years, and their family consisted of two daughters: Olivia, age 8 and Vivian, age 6. During most of the married years, Tim spent sixty to seventy hours per week on the job. What happened to them was the same age-old scenario that keeps many couples from surviving their thirties: the husband feels the need to "climb the career ladder" and the wife is on board with the idea, but they both realize too late that the plan had way too much emphasis on tomorrow…and not enough today. *All work and no play makes Jack a dull boy.* They had grown apart. Apparently, they were not the soul mates that they and everyone thought they were—*victims of cliché.*

Now, the little ceremony in front of the judge was over, and now so too were the negotiations for every stick of furniture and possession they owned. This process had started more than six months ago and very frustratingly still wasn't finalized; Tim wasn't fighting, so Sheila kept asking for more and more; including dumb things, like folding chairs. *Petty bullshit*, thought Tim. *Who wants to fight over part-time furniture?* The lawyers from both sides scribbled on their working copy of the *Permanent Stipulations*, bouncing between the two conference rooms; the one Tim was in, and the other with Sheila. At one point she sent her lawyer in for one more thing…half of the dining room set that was originally typed up as going to Tim.

"Are you kidding me?" said Tim. "What the hell am I going to do with three chairs?"

"Satan just has to have those chairs, buddy. Want me to make it difficult for her and ask for half of the bedroom set?" Frank could smell another billable hour.

"She's going to bust my balls until the eleventh hour, right? Screw it. Give her the dining room set, but if she doesn't sign after that then I'm not signing today, and I'm just going to leave. We can do this some other time. Do your job, Frank. Stop the madness and get me out of here."

Frank recognized that Tim was spent, and dispensed with the "devil" talk for the time being. He scribbled a few more notes and left the room to deliver Tim's ultimatum. Frank's money train was leaving the station, at least for today. Sheila took the dining room set and signed the papers—they were done. Tim got up from the chair, grabbed the few papers he had before him, and got ready to leave.

Things hadn't always been bad between Tim and Sheila. He'd thought it was a low period, a valley, and that they would come out of it sooner or later like they always did. They were a team, a family. He smiled cynically; *nobody ever thinks it will happen to them*, he thought. *What a waste; what a shame.*

Tim, was, however, a bit of an optimist, and began to try to look at the bright side, the silver lining. As a small consolation, he could now do things he had all but given up while with Sheila. *Big things! What a rebel,* he told himself, with a heavy dose of sarcasm. For instance, he could...*cook with mushrooms*—or *work on his golf game.* Or perhaps *leave the bed unmade for weeks at a time.* With the death of the marriage, all the little pet peeves were gone with it, like how she used to put all of his stuff away in places he would never find; or how towels were not meant to be shared with other family members. *They're all gone now,* he thought. *Enjoy freedom.*

In truth, standing on the edge of the proverbial cliff (the rest of his unplanned life), was exciting. There was no long-term plan anymore, only *today.* Today and whatever *new plan* he decided on. "Life begins at divorce," he had heard someone say, but the true meaning had never really registered. He would now test that out, like it or not. Not knowing what was going to happen, or where his life would lead, was both scary and thrilling at the same time.

CHAPTER THREE

The New Goal

March 7th, 1971

Two months later, once Tim had had his fill of all the mushrooms Sheila had deprived him of, and after he had not so much as shifted a pillow on his bed, he began to sense (for the first time since...maybe boyhood) the forgotten feeling of boredom. His adult life had always been too busy to be boring; he liked his line of work, and when he wasn't working, he was with family or doing house chores. Boredom was something he didn't think he would ever feel again.

This lack of mental stimulation camped in his skull for several weeks until one evening; it cracked and crumbled away at the rare spark of inspiration. He and Johnny Upson, the only two remaining employees of Russell Construction, had been downsized due to lack of business. There would be no more house building; there weren't enough employees to finish large projects in demanding timeframes. They were back to kitchens, bathrooms, and handyman projects. Tim hadn't taken the setback very well; his heart wasn't in it. He wasn't motivated to repeat the last twelve years building the company back to where it had been just before the divorce. In another twelve years, he'd be fifty years old. *I've been there and done that. I know I could do it again if I had to, but—I want something else.*

Johnny was a monster when it came to output. If you were going to redo a kitchen, you were better off standing aside and letting Johnny do the whole thing because you'd only get in the way. In fact, if Johnny wasn't given enough work to stay busy, he would grow impatient, followed by antsy…and finally, he would begin to get angry. He was the opposite of the typical clock-watcher, so Tim found himself naturally giving extra leeway and backing off, letting Johnny work. *I'll tire him out like a pet dog if that's what he wants.*

Johnny's competence left Tim as the sales guy and part-time gopher, which was far more monotonous, but unfortunately vitally necessary to keep the money train rolling. Manning the phones was Tim's least favorite task; it was like watching paint dry. Now that his nuclear family had been destroyed the phrase *unfulfilling waste of time* came to mind. *Who am I doing this for?* His sense of purpose had been stripped away in the divorce. He didn't know what to do, but he knew it had to be different; something with more meaning—more satisfying—but he didn't know what *it* was—*so much freedom. My life is a blank canvas again. What to do?*

Thank goodness his divorce hadn't been ten years earlier. Those were much leaner times. If Sheila had dropped the bomb in his mid-twenties, he would have had no choice but to probably just go to work for somebody. Sheila had gotten their Amesbury house in the deal, and wouldn't have to sell it for at least the next five years. The courts didn't like to see homeless kids, and she, like practically every divorcing mother, had won "Primary Physical Custody."

Tim's biggest chunk of the settlement was the proceeds of the sale of their summer cottage on Lake Kanasatka up in New Hampshire. Sheila had never really liked the Kanasatka cottage; it was more of Tim's thing, and he only found this out after she asked for the divorce. Just like that, it was sold off and gone, and with it, a slice of Tim's soul.

"Living well is the best revenge" was his current favorite saying, just edging out "Life begins at divorce." He liked the quote the moment he heard it and even looked up the person who wrote it. The man's name was George Herbert, an English poet from the 1600s. *Wow, just inventing that phrase is the best revenge*, thought Tim. It had become historic; timeless. *The other person must have felt like shit...forever.*

If he were honest with himself, he had to admit the only shred of "living well" he had accomplished so far was gorging on mushrooms: *Not exactly total victory just yet.* There was a silver lining, however; the divorce was fresh; it was still early in the game for him, and the blessed boredom had given him time to think. He now felt as though he had been forced out of New Hampshire prematurely, and this feeling became the basis for the next big thing.

Suddenly he felt a direction, and he couldn't even sleep the first night; he got out of bed and started making notes. The idea was to buy a fixer-upper in New Hampshire, where there was plenty of land, and real estate prices were nothing compared to those surrounding Boston. Even better, he didn't have to research school systems or stress over a spouse's veto. *Now, how to make it work?*

After hours of careful thought, he decided that career-wise, he could continue to be the "sales and service" man for Russell Construction from anywhere, as long as there was a telephone. If he had to meet with people, it was just an hour and a half drive. He could set everything up for Johnny and let him knock himself out; win/win. Excitedly, he got on the phone, let Johnny in on the plan, and made a few other business calls to fill up Johnny's month. Then he dialed zero on his rotary phone and asked the operator to find him a real estate agency in Laconia, New Hampshire.

His next few non-visitation weekends were spent driving up to the Lakes Region to grab newspapers and real estate magazines. When he didn't find anything immediately, he expanded his search to times when he *did* have the girls. He even convinced his daughters that they were in for a treat…they were going to a hotel! A hotel on Lake Winnipesaukee in March: *Ooooh boy, so fun. Maybe they'll want to ice-fish.*

The plan was to find a house with some property, refurbish and sell it, but first, he needed to speak with his accountant to see how much havoc the divorce had wreaked on his financial well-being. Tim hated going to the accountant. His name was Stanley Brown and looked as if he might be one hundred years old.

Since Tim was self-employed, that meant he had to gather up all of his papers, ledgers, and receipts and make the drive all the way up to Gloucester every quarter, where he would sit across the desk from Stanley…and wait, and wait *and wait.* It was always agonizing, and in the end, it was never good news. To Tim, it was like waiting on death row.

Stanley would hunch at his desk, poring over the numbers and papers, while tapping on the adding machine. He had a cup full of sharp pencils and highlighters, and he wore bifocals worn down near the tip of his nose. He was surrounded by stacks of files and folders on all edges of his desk that reduced his workspace to roughly two square feet. The piles blocked Tim's view, and for all he knew, Stanley might be finishing a crossword puzzle. While Stanley muttered, Tim's eyes would wander the room, waiting endlessly—reading notes taped to the wall, client names on spines of binders and the diplomas hung behind the desk. It was nervous tedium followed by a swift kick in the balls—and the wallet.

This quarter's moment of truth approached. Tim had learned to read Stanley's body language. When he was about to finish, he would unconsciously clear his throat, then rip the paper off of the adding machine and staple it to the paperwork. This particular year would not…certainly *could not* be a good tax year for Tim. Legal fees and a divorce settlement on top of poor sales meant he would be buying a bottle of Jack Daniel's on the way home; there was just no way around it.

"Uh…Tim, is this everything? Any savings accounts I don't know about, perhaps? Off the record?"

"That's it, Stan. Look, just hit me with the bad news. I'm fucking tired, excuse my language. I know it was a bad year, and I know Sheila gets half of whatever's on your paper there. I'm exhausted, and I'm getting to the 'just shoot me' stage. Just tell me what I owe before I throw up on your desk and jump out the damn window."

Stanley looked at Tim aghast as if he had never heard a curse word before.

"Look, Tim, I…"

"Don't worry. I'm not really going to kill myself, Stanley, but I might have a heart attack because of *you* if you don't rip the band-aid off and tell me! The suspense is too much—in fact; it's always too much in here. Every freaking quarter I'm in here chewing my fingernails down while you peck away at that thing. There's got to be a better way; you're killing me." And there it was; the end of Tim's rope; it had been one hell of a year.

"I…well…if you don't like this process, I… Tim, you aren't going to like this at all. If you have another year like this sales-wise, you might have to seriously consider bankruptcy. You've got some revolving debt here that concerns me, and your income is down almost sixty percent."

Tim's mini-tirade was over, and Stanley's shrewd reply shocked the anger away and replaced it with a chilling feeling in his bowels. *Bankruptcy?* He knew today would be a shitshow, but he had no idea it would be this bad.

"I know. I had to lay almost everyone off a few months back. The economy hasn't been great, plus the divorce…I—I also took some mental health time. But I'm back now, and I'm lining up the work again. We are only two employees, so things will be very different, but I have some new goals, and I'll get this turned around."

"And pay off this debt, too? It looks like an uphill struggle from this side of the desk. Tim, you're not my first client who has gone through a divorce. I've seen dozens of small businesses go under. Sometimes it's the best option; bankruptcy, I mean. It might even lower your child support payments."

"No. I've been my own boss since…well, forever. This is it. I can't change careers. And I might have an idea on a new venture."

Stanley looked over his bifocals at Tim as a librarian would at a whispering child. "A new venture, you say? Well, unfortunately, after Sheila's half, and the end-of-year taxes, this is what I see as your bottom line." Stanley turned the paper around and handed it to Tim.

Tim saw the number, and it was worse than he thought. His stomach did a somersault, but his brain had taken too much pain and decided to go numb. Three years ago, Tim and Sheila had been millionaires on paper. Now, most of the equipment had been auctioned off, the Kanasatka cottage was liquidated, and Sheila had the house. He wouldn't see a dime from that for perhaps five years.

Millionaires! Not cash-in-the-bank millionaires, but they lived well. They had even flown to Disneyland with the kids that summer and gone on a separate *mommy-daddy* trip to Bermuda that fall. Despite all that paradise, Sheila managed to get bored just two years later. Tim felt the numbness slip to anger with this last thought, so he decided to get moving.

"Okay, Stan. Thanks. What do I owe you for today?" He pulled out his checkbook, wrote the check for the accountant's fee, and walked out. *Fuck me.*

There was nowhere to go but forward. The cliff of excitement that he wanted to fly off to start his new life was the only option. His first looks at New Hampshire real estate had been at shorefront properties on some of the many lakes in the region. He hadn't given up on the "lake" part of the dream yet, perhaps because of all the good memories on Kanasatka; there was just something romantic about it. Evenings by the fire, fishing for pickerel and those little pine-scented pillows sitting on the coffee table were heaven on Earth.

But, after the nightmarish meeting with Stanley Brown, he realized that he had to be more practical. He realized it didn't really matter if it was a lakefront property or not because he would be turning around and selling it to someone else as fast as possible once it was refurbished. This first house would not be his forever, no matter what.

The bottom line on lakeside cottages was they were more expensive to start with, so he made a decision. There was no time for dreaming and reminiscing; every dollar he had was on the line, not including the cost of construction materials he would need to fix the new place up. He needed a property that could double or triple his money, and this eliminated not only anything lakeside, but also several entire towns in the region. He quickly crossed off any property in Gilford, Center Harbor, Laconia or Wolfeboro and began to concentrate in towns slightly less picturesque.

Two weeks later, about twenty minutes out of the way of the summer rentals and touristy places, he found the house with the pond.

CHAPTER FOUR

Welcome to Sanborn

April 3rd, 1971

Sanborn, New Hampshire was technically part of New Hampshire's Lakes Region but didn't really have much in the way of lakefront property. In fact, the lake it barely touched (Lake Winnisquam) was one of the smallest in the area; however, if you wanted to go to any of the other nearby lakes (not just Winnipesaukee but Squam, Wicwas, Kanasatka, etc.), many were within a half hour's drive. Downtown Sanborn had all of the charm of Moultonborough, which was the town in which Tim & Sheila had owned their cabin. Both "downtowns" were tiny, consisting of a town hall and a post office and not much else. It felt like home, even though it wouldn't be his for very long.

The chosen house was an old horse farm, an hour and fifteen minutes from the kids. He could cover that easily when visitation weekends came up, plus he could spend those visitation Fridays back in Massachusetts touching base with Johnny, meeting with clients, potential clients, delivering proposals, estimates, and the like. *This plan is very doable;* he thought to himself.

He drove up rural Route 14 for two miles past the center of Sanborn, and then took a left onto his new address; *Lancaster Hill Road.* Lancaster Hill Road was a long dirt road cutting through a forest that went on and on eventually ending up near the town of Meredith. While traveling the road, occasionally the forest would open up into a meadow for a quick few seconds before the trees closed back up around you. It was like driving through a tunnel of foliage. He noticed immediately that he hadn't passed many houses, and that the road had grass growing down the middle where tires never touch.

About a mile and a half in, as he passed one of the gaps in a wall of maples, he saw out in the distance a woman in an old-fashioned farm dress walking through a field. She turned her head when she heard his truck, but Tim missed that as the gap had passed and he was on to the house, anxious with anticipation. This would be his first visit. *Howdy neighbor*, he thought and drove on.

Lancaster Hill Road was full of potholes, and his pickup truck bounced its way forward and side to side at about fifteen miles per hour. Eventually, on the right, the tip of the paved driveway sloped up steeply for about thirty feet, right between two large maples. About all you could see from the road was the tongue of the driveway sticking out between the two trees unless you knew what you were looking for. If one had time to observe before entering the driveway, there were openings that revealed the white house behind, but they didn't reveal much of it even at just fifteen miles per hour. It was April, and the leaves were just beginning to fill out the trees. By June the house would be nearly invisible from the road. Tim steered his truck between the two maples and applied more pressure to the gas pedal to make it up the short hill. Suddenly, there it was.

To his immediate left was the beginning of the white farmhouse, not twenty feet away. It faced a pond and an open field to his right; he approached from its side. He took a look back around through the rear window, surprised that the two trees did such a good job hiding the house from the road, which was only thirty feet behind. The listing said the house was four thousand square feet and came with twenty-three acres, a barn, and a pond. About half of the twenty-three acres was field and the other half forest.

Because the house had appeared so quickly on his left after clearing the two trees, he had to slam on the brakes so that he wouldn't sail past the first section of the building. He didn't want to ruin his first impression, preferring to take a long, slow look at the potential. It was a farmhouse built in 1860 and L-shaped. The front of the house was the long left side of the letter. Tim was driving in from the top. The "L" took a left up ahead at the turn in the driveway, around the front of the house to the barn. The front lawn was overgrown and as wild as the field. It began at the house, was split in two by the driveway, and continued another fifty feet to Tim's right, down a small decline that ended at a knee-high stone wall.

Just after the stone wall, the lawn continued another fifty feet to a frog pond that might be able to entertain one small boat (if that) for fishing purposes, but two would be a crowd. There were two weeping willows, one on each side. The branches of the trees were very long and hung down to the ground, each looking like a mushroom cloud. Beyond the pond, even further to Tim's right was the field, which looked as if it might have had multiple purposes in the past. Part grazing pasture, part cornfield, part garden, perhaps. It went for about two hundred yards from there until it hit forest and the property line.

Tim continued to sit in his pickup with the engine idling,

taking it all in. He could see that the field bordered Lancaster Hill Road for a good distance. Thinking back, he wondered if the woman that he had seen in the pasture had been on his property. *Whoops. THIS property,* he corrected himself. It was far too early to consider it *his* although he had to admit he did like it already. He had liked what he had seen in the listing, and it was so-far-so-good in person. *Slow down, Timmy, you'll come off as a 'motivated buyer.'* He hadn't even looked inside. What if it was completely trashed, or full of mold? *Never mind that; hey lady, get out of my wild blueberries!*

He studied the meadow and the woods beyond it. The distance from the road to the forest, or the width of the field, was about a hundred yards. He wondered what exactly twelve acres of forest looked like…and how much of these woods came with the property. Since the divorce, he had toyed with the idea of going hunting again. After he met Sheila, he abandoned the sport. She loved animals and hated the taste of venison, so like the mushrooms, hunting went away. Another freedom to reclaim! *Living Well Revenge Train*, full speed ahead.

He turned back to the house. It sat as still and silent; *emotionless*, if that made any sense. The paint was peeling, and the exterior was weathered. The windows were empty; there were no curtains or shades, making the house look like a vacant shell, somewhat cold. *We'll see if we can put some life back into those eyes*, he thought.

According to the real estate agent, it had been empty for three years. That seemed like a long time, so Tim asked why, and also about the previous owners. It had last been owned by a widow who had passed away in her sleep. A sixty-year-old dying in her sleep seemed a bit young to Tim, but *hey, when your time's up, your time's up.*

So much for healthy living and fresh air, but…that must be the reason. That's why this place is so cheap. She died here, and she lived alone. They must have discovered her days, weeks—I don't even want to know. Potential buyers begin to balk when a place hasn't sold after being on the market so long. They don't want to be the suckers who say "yes" to a money pit. When it's mine, all of that will be erased. Tim took great pride in his work and knew the selling power of a fresh coat of paint, not to mention all the other bells and whistles he would install. The news of the woman that died upstairs was not a deal-breaker.

The house began with a big conventional ranch-like structure and a front door. It had a second story to it where the bedrooms were. Then the house continued as one-story. The one-story portion of the house featured a living room and a formal dining room. In front of the dining room, a porch jutted out from the building. Inside the porch was another front door to the house. This one story-portion ended, and another two-story box began; the bottom floor held the kitchen and a breakfast area, but the second story was a one-room octagonal turret. The turret was ringed with windows and had a 360-degree view. The overall condition of the exterior was "needs improvement" in Tim's best judgment. The previous tenant, the widow, was probably not up to hammering, painting, and fixing. It would be a big job for anyone.

Tim put the truck into gear and pulled forward slowly as he examined the details. He began to take a mental inventory of what would need to be done. *A roof for sure, steps need leveling, siding, paint*—The driveway turned around the side of the building and headed to the left. As he pulled around, the first thing that struck him was the big red barn at the end of the driveway, perhaps seventy feet ahead. He was surprised he hadn't seen it from the end of the driveway but reasoned that it was probably because the turret blocked his view.

Connecting the barn to the house (and the bottom part of the "L") was a long carriage house that had been converted into a utility room. This particular carriage house was used in the old days to park not one, but two horse-drawn carriages. It looked like whoever had converted the carriage house had used the original garage doors on the outside of the building to keep the old-time look going. The doors themselves were simply nailed onto the outside wall, a facade for cosmetic appearance only. There was also a normal-sized side door.

Parked just in front of the barn and waiting for Tim was the real estate agent, Holly Burns. She had shown Tim two of the last three properties he'd seen. She was an attractive, sandy-haired thirty-something, and yes, Tim had noticed, but he had not attempted any flirtatious come-ons. He was enjoying his freedom, still very gun shy about taking part in a relationship, reminding himself that everyone and everything has consequences. She opened her car door and stepped out.

"Good morning, Tim. How was the drive up?"

"Peaceful and traffic-free as always," he replied. It was so true. *No Boston traffic up here. I love it.* He had spent countless hours of his earlier life stuck in traffic on Routes 93, 128, 1, 2, 3… the Central Artery ("The Distressway")…you name it. Those were his younger years. *You never get those hours back.*

"Yes, it is quite different up here," she said with a smile.

He might have been dreaming, but the way she said it seemed…seductive.

Pump the brakes. You're an overconfident chauvinist. Nothing she said was meant to be taken that way. He attempted to correct himself, and turn down the "caveman"…but admitted that it might be because Holly's girl-next-door looks were actually smoking hot. *He'd grown accustomed to her face*…to quote the song from *My Fair Lady.*

Keep it professional, he commanded. Even so, he caught himself, sneaking looks.

"Yeah, I think I've found where I want to be, and that's up here in New Hampshire. You just have to help me find a place to hang my hat. So what's the story with this place?"

"Okay, we'll talk as I show you."

She began to walk toward the side door in the carriage house part of the building. It wasn't a new door, but it hadn't been part of the original house. She inserted the key and pushed the door open. A musty smell escaped the building, and Tim passed through it. They were in a large utility-type room that could be used for just about anything; *hell, it could be a racquetball court if the ceiling were higher*, he thought.

Since the original purpose of the room had been to park carriages, it was away from the main living area of the house. It looked like it could be a playroom for kids perhaps, or maybe storage or something; it was just a big empty room with very basic mat-like carpeting. Once inside the room they headed left through an oddly-placed sliding glass door (obviously not 1860 original) and into the main part of the house.

"This is the breakfast area, and as you can see, it is connected to the kitchen." Tim noticed that there was no dividing wall except for a counter that separated the two rooms. Inside the kitchen was an old stove and beyond it on either side, two passageways to the next room, which looked to be the formal dining area.

The old stove was against the kitchen wall between the two passageways, and behind the wall were two staircases; one down to a small cellar and one up into the turret. Tim noticed he could stand in the breakfast area near the front wall and look all the way down the length of the house to the end room (at the top of the "L"). He looked up at the ceiling, realizing he was directly underneath the turret. He looked over to the passageway on the right. There was a bathroom across from the entrances to the two staircases.

"I have to admit, I can't wait to see the turret," he told Holly. "Believe it or not, I don't think I've ever seen one from the inside."

"Oh, it's pretty cool. It's a good place to sit and drink a cup of coffee, or a beer, or just sit and think." Tim took the initiative, and they made their way up the stairs to enter a smallish circular room with a single piece of furniture remaining: a desk. The turret was very sunny and offered a 360-degree view of the property. From this perch, you could get a good look at the pond and the field behind it—to the left, the forest. To the right, he could see across to the one-story portion of the house and into one of the bedrooms. To the rear, there was a small, shadowy backyard.

Tim felt a little cut off from the rest of the house up here, and it gave him a slightly uneasy feeling. He felt as though his senses were dulled, and he couldn't hear anything going on in the house below. *It doesn't really matter*, he supposed. You'd see a visitor coming up the driveway after all. *Of course, it's quiet up here. That's why they built it.*

His momentary discomfort with the turret did nothing to discourage his interest in the property. The confidence in his decision to follow his dream came right back. *This is the house.* They descended the stairs and took a left into the formal dining area. It was a big room that had wide pine floorboards. It was also dimly lit. The addition of the front porch robbed the room of the light the other rooms at the front of the house enjoyed. There weren't any sun-catching windows in here at all. Then Tim noticed that one of the windows in the back of the room was boarded up.

"What happened here?" he gestured.

"I'm not sure," Holly responded. "The house has been empty for a while, and there's nobody to watch it 24/7. That window has been boarded up since I've been showing the place. I guess that somebody needed a place to stay for the night."

"Bad neighborhood?"

Holly smiled. "No, not really. It might have been kids. I'm only guessing. Forget I said it."

Toward the front of the house was the second front door that led onto the porch. Included with the purchase would be an old dining room set with table and chairs left behind by the previous owners. *Screw you, Sheila! I got my dining set! Another omen.*

"I've seen some furniture on our tour. Is this a furnished house?" he asked.

"Well I wouldn't say it is completely furnished, but there are some things that were left here. Most of them are not in great shape unless you're a handyman that likes to refurbish things." Holly's words hit Tim a little funny. *Was she flirting?*

"I might know a guy," he said and let her comment go with a mental note attached. They continued: Immediately after the dining room was a living room with a fireplace and bookshelves built into the wall. The shelves were still full of old books. He took a close look and saw a World Atlas from 1925.

This room was half as deep as the dining room because there was another room behind it in the back of the house. He stepped through the doorway into what might do well as an office. There was nothing fancy in here, just a pair of windows looking out into the backyard. He peered out and saw clearly that the house had almost nothing of interest out there; the attraction of this property was the *front* yard. There were some tall pines providing too much shade over a postage stamp of a lawn covered with years of fallen needles.

He turned and walked out of the office back into the living room with the books. He was facing the front of the house and could see the pond in the distance out of the window. To his left was the portion of the house he had already seen. To the right, he stepped through a threshold into a foyer or *entryway*. To say *foyer* made it sound grand and cavernous, but it wasn't grand by any means, just 1860 functional. *Let's just call it a foyer*, he thought.

As he faced the last room on the first floor, the front door was to his left, and the stairway to the bedrooms ascended to his right. At the top of the stairs was a narrow balcony accessing the four bedrooms and the bathroom. Tim looked up.

Somewhere up there was the room that held the reason the house had been on the market for so long. Someone died up there, left unnoticed for far too long. He didn't know all of the gory details, but his mind wandered as Holly waited just behind in the living room. He could picture the body, followed by the worms and beetles, and finally, bones. And that would be *his* bedroom, most likely. *Desperate times call for desperate measures*, he thought.

Before they started up, he finished the tour of the first floor with a couple of quick glances. Straight across the hallway was the room by the road. It was basically another catch-all room that could be turned into several things; it could be a fifth bedroom; it could be a den, whatever. Tim was almost sure at least while he owned the place that this room would be closed off to save on the heating bill. The house was just too big for him and his visitation-only daughters. In the back of the house and under the stairs was another bathroom. He skipped taking a look for the time being and went up.

The upstairs hallway was, like the dining room, pretty dark for ten in the morning. There was one small window at the front of the house as the only light source. He reached the top of the stairs, standing in front of another bathroom directly between the third and fourth bedrooms at the back of the house. He walked into the third bedroom overlooking Lancaster Hill Road and peered out the window at the horizon.

"That's Mount Kearsarge," said Holly. Tim could see in the distance a hill that seemed just a little taller than the other hills. It was not a rocky peak, or a real mountain in his opinion, as some of the mountains further north. "That's twenty-plus miles away," she added.

It sure didn't look that far to Tim; *maybe ten miles?* He had no idea. *Been living urban too long*, he thought. He noticed that Holly stood close to his arm as they huddled around the window. He unintentionally caught a whiff of her perfume, or shampoo or something wonderful, and started to daydream. *Damn, she smells good, but hold on. Don't get ahead of yourself. You just got your freedom back, don't give it away so quickly; remember the consequences. Besides; she probably has a boyfriend anyway, and this flirting is just part of her selling charm.*

Tim blinked twice and cleared the hypnotic scent from his sinuses. They took a right out of bedroom number three and walked along the balcony to the master bedroom. This bedroom shared the view of Mount Kearsarge from the side window, but only in the late fall and wintertime. One of the "guardian maples" at the end of the driveway was in bloom, obstructing the view. A freestanding full-length mirror stood in the corner, left behind. It was the only piece of furniture in the entire upstairs.

The master bedroom was on the corner of the house. It was the same room he had temporarily parked in front of when he had arrived, surveying the property and making mental notes. It was also most likely the room the widow had died in, to be found (he wasn't sure and didn't want to know the number of) days later. This room, like the others in the front of the house, looked out across the front lawn to the pond and beyond. Out in the distance, he glimpsed a red kite flying over the trees. He scanned the meadow but couldn't locate the person flying it.

"Holly, I didn't see many, if any, houses on Lancaster Hill Road on the way in. How many other houses are out here?"

"Good question. You have the second house on the road; you might have missed the first one right at the beginning because it is set back from the road a bit. Go another half-mile past this place, and there are two more farms, and then Lancaster Hill Road turns into Abbott Road halfway between here and Meredith. So to answer your question, there are three houses around here and not much else; just woods and fields."

"So looking out in front of us here, past the pond, it's nothing but field and woods for a mile, and behind us is just the backyard and a small field and about a half-mile of woods as well?"

"Yes, I think that's right," agreed Holly. "I can double-check for you. I live about twenty minutes away and spend most of my time around Winnipesaukee. This property is my first and only listing in Sanborn."

He took his eyes off her to look back in the direction of the kite, but it was gone. *Where's he standing...in the middle of the woods?* He dropped his follow up question in favor of another that he was surprised to hear coming out of his mouth.

"And…this is where it happened, right? This is the room?"

Holly dropped her eyes and looked at the floor, nodding uncomfortably.

"I'm not exactly sure, but it would sure make sense. This is the master bedroom, and she lived alone. I'm not aware of the details, though, to be honest. Are you afraid of ghosts, Tim?" She was smiling slightly, daring him to say yes, but also probing to see if this discussion might interrupt the potential sale.

"Haha…no. No, I'm not," Tim answered sheepishly, like a teenage boy that watched too many scary movies. "I don't know why I asked that. I don't really care, but…here we are if it did happen here. It's just weird, I guess. The scene of the crime, so to speak."

"It is a little eerie. A few years back I drove down to Fall River and visited the Lizzie Borden house—the girl that chopped her parents up with an ax back in 1892. It's just a bed and breakfast really, but when you see the actual…places…there is a weird vibe. But just to be clear, the woman that died here wasn't murdered. You said 'scene of the crime,' I don't want you to think…"

"Oh, no, no, no. I said 'so to speak' after that. Poor choice of words on my part. I'm sorry; we're off on a tangent here. I don't believe in ghosts; I don't care about ghosts—I just…well, to be honest, I wonder, *but don't really want to know*—how many days she laid in here, everything quiet, nobody aware…it's creepy, right? Morbidly fascinating? Am I talking out of both sides of my mouth?"

"*Morbidly fascinating.* That's it—the same reason I paid to sleep in the Lizzie Borden house. Yes, I get it, Tim, and I have always had trouble putting it into words. I'm going to borrow that phrase if you don't mind!" They laughed, not only because they had found something in common, but also because the conversation—and the setting—had them a bit nervous.

Across the hall from the master bedroom was the fourth bedroom, which Tim imagined as a guest room. It was perhaps the sunniest room in the house because there were no trees to block the windows. It had a straight-on view of the pond, and also a window facing the inside of the house, looking directly across at the turret. Beyond that, Tim could see the top of the barn.

The indoor tour was just about over, but Holly had more. "Don't forget that this property comes with twenty-three acres. Come outside and check it out. If you like *morbidly fascinating*, then I might have a similar surprise. It's fascinating, but not morbid."

"No more dead people, I hope."

"This one is *not* about dead people, but...well, it's hard to explain. It's better if I show you."

She led him back through the house, stopping only at the porch they hadn't yet looked at, and the cellar, which was a tiny dugout of a room that only occupied the space underneath the kitchen. It had a low ceiling and housed the furnace and not much else; definitely 1860 original. It smelled slightly musty but nothing terrible. Holly and Tim left the house through the side door they had entered near the barn, right next to where their cars were parked.

"You've got a nice big barn here," said Holly. It was, Tim noticed, like the house; in fair to poor shape, and she was right, it was big. It had a large set of sliding doors that were unfortunately rusted open halfway. If Tim ever wanted to close them, it would take several cans of *3-IN-1* oil and a lot of determination. They were open wide enough to drive a car in, but not two cars side by side. In fact, even if the doors could open that wide, the passageway in the first half of the barn had horse stalls on either side leaving just enough space in the middle to groom a horse.

Above the barn doors was the hayloft door, and inside the building behind it (and over Tim's head), the hayloft itself. The hayloft door came complete with a rusty winch and pulley *post* for lifting bales into storage. Inside the dark barn, the hayloft went halfway to the back directly over the stalls and ended suddenly with no back wall and only a ladder to get up or down.

The back of the barn was dark and had a workbench in the back left corner and not much else. Over everything was a cavernous ceiling under a cupola. Tim didn't have to wonder if the cupola had bats. It was broad daylight, and the bats circled overhead. He wondered if they were up there all day long.

"Do they come with the property?" he said, pointing to the bats.

"Uh, yes they do, sorry about that. You might want the bats in the summer, though. Some say the New Hampshire state bird is the Black Fly, and the bats eat them."

Tim laughed. *She's pretty funny*, he thought. He took another look at his potential tenants and walked out. *We'll save that project for last, or maybe never.* Outside the barn on top of the cupola was an old iron and lead weathervane in the shape of a horse. It was riddled with bullet holes, most likely the result of bored hunters trespassing on the abandoned property. *That's probably an antique,* he thought.

Tim and Holly walked the driveway and crossed the front lawn making their way down to the pond. Four Canada Geese were there, preening feathers in the sun. There was a gap in the stone wall that served as a sort of gateway to the water. Once past the opening, the geese took off; obviously the humans were getting too close for comfort. Tim continued, and as he got about ten feet from the pond, the ground began to squish under his feet. Suddenly he realized that the pond might be more of a small marsh. The cattail weeds suddenly seemed a little taller, and he wondered what sorts of things swam in that water. It was not what you would consider a *swimmin' hole* unless you were a frog, snake, spider, or water bug. The smell of the stagnant water was distinctive; a raw mixture of algae, frog's eggs, goose dung, and compost. He imagined when the seasons changed, he might lose some sleep to horny bullfrogs calling out for a mate.

The two willows on either side of the pond were special characters. One of them was about fifty feet tall, he estimated; the other, maybe thirty-five. They looked like two big mops and were near full bloom already. Most of the branches reached the ground to form a curtain. He walked up to the larger of the two and parted the branches; it was like entering a room, somewhat closed off from the outside, and you could see out better out than you could see in.

Once they were done in the pond area, Holly led Tim into the field beyond. *Wow, I'm getting the ten-dollar tour*, he thought. *Does she show everyone this much I wonder, or can she tell I like the place*? He looked at her hand, and he noticed that she wasn't wearing a ring. *Good.*

"This used to be a garden or a pumpkin patch," she said. "That or corn. And I think the horses and cows may have grazed out there, too." She continued toward the forest. "Are you ready for the fascinating part?" Tim looked around the field. An old pumpkin patch was certainly not his idea of something interesting. He couldn't imagine anything near this place that might be considered "fascinating," unless…*oh no.*

Maybe Holly was a real country bumpkin, and she enjoyed things like cow patty fights, or cow tipping, or squirting people with milk directly from the source; stuff like that. *That* would be a letdown. If she were that kind of girl, then he might have to fake enjoyment from her so-called *fascination.*

"Have you lived around here your whole life?" he asked, hoping to hear that she was a little more cultured than that.

"Yeah. I was born in Laconia, and I still live there."

Uh-oh. "Did you…ever work on a farm like this?"

"I did for about a week when I was a kid and, not that I was very helpful to him or anything, but after the week was over the farmer paid me with five one-dollar bills. I never went back. I hated it, too; very hard work."

That's better. "So what did you do after that?" Tim asked.

"Well, eventually, I went to UNH, and I studied Business Administration. I never really used it, though, in my professional life."

Whew. Holly wasn't a hayseed that found enjoyment in things like churning her butter. "UNH? Very nice." He was a bit out of breath, walking over the uneven field. Tall grass hid rocks and mole trails and an occasional woodchuck hole. The conversation tailed off for the time being.

They reached the edge of the field, somewhat near where Tim had seen the kite a half-hour before. Holly took them into the wild woods, off-trail. He followed her and couldn't help but continue to check her out. Athletic, early-thirties, no ring—*Hmmm. Dilemma time.* How had he not noticed her beauty the first two times she had shown him properties? He had been out of the dating game for a while now, and the very hint of intimacy reintroduced itself to him. *Hi, I'm back, and I missed you so much.*

Ten yards into the woods she stopped him. "Okay, wait right here for a second." So he did. She looked at him; studied him actually, and he looked back blankly as if there were a question mark floating over his head. She was obviously waiting for some sort of reaction, and he didn't understand. She smiled. "Nothing yet?"

She started walking again, this time backward, and much slower. She watched Tim with every step deeper into the woods. Whatever it was she expected him to see; he hadn't. He looked high; he looked low. *One more pause, one more step, one more second of eye contact.* She was enjoying this, which was good on one level, but on another, he was beginning to feel foolish. *Nice job Tim, now she thinks you're a moron.*

She began to count the steps out loud. "One, two, three, four…" *I literally cannot see the forest for the trees,* Tim berated himself silently but kept the stupid grin. When Holly said "two," he stopped entirely; enjoying her amusement and her pretty smile as she walked backward. *How did I miss that the first couple of times?*

Suddenly his eyes shifted focus; stopping dead had helped, and in one miraculous second, he understood what she was talking about. At first, it wasn't there, and then it was; like looking at a bunch of colored dots on paper and suddenly seeing a hidden picture. About thirty yards inside the tree line, the wild woods gave way to an overgrown, man-made grove. It was perfectly invisible from the field, or even ten feet outside because the wild trees in front had camouflaged it. *An overgrown Christmas tree farm*, he thought.

If you turned to the left or right, you were smack in the middle of a perfect row. Between every row was a near undisturbed bed of dead, brown spruce needles. It looked like nature's bowling alley lined with spruce trees. To Tim, it was like standing in a giant, dark cornfield.

Holly seemed excited to see his reaction. She was right, it was a weird feeling in here, and certainly a *fascination*, but he wasn't sure why. *Oasis? Sanctuary?* No, that's not it. Wait—*Secret*. Perhaps that was at least part of the description he was looking for. Maybe it was the irony of beauty abandoned. The sunlight had trouble penetrating the canopy, which blocked most of it even at eleven o'clock in the morning. Everything was quiet. Tim suddenly felt like he had to pee. He squashed the thought.

Holly seemed to be enjoying the atmosphere. "It's cool, right? Creepy, maybe? I didn't want to try to describe it to you. I didn't think I could do it justice. By the way, I don't usually tour wooded parts of properties, but the last guy that looked at this place insisted on walking the grounds. I thought he was overdoing it a bit at first, but he might have been a hunter looking for some good land, I'm not sure."

She continued. "I thought I would be bored while he led the way; after all, woods are woods, and nearly every property I have listed has a piece of forest with it. Halfway out here I realized I might be getting myself into some trouble. He wasn't much of a talker, and I couldn't really read him, so I had no idea what he was thinking, and of course, I didn't know him very well. Then we found the grove, and he started talking more, and I forgot all about my concerns. The grove surprised him too, but I don't think it added any value for him. In fact, it probably hurt; there isn't much deer food in these rows. Obviously he didn't buy it, or you and I wouldn't be here right now."

"Yeah, this is definitely...unique. It's a mood or something. I like it," said Tim.

"Right? I think about this place from time to time. I dreamed of buying it myself, but I could never restore it." He stood quietly for a few seconds, taking it all in; the atmosphere, the perfect rows, and Holly's company. He felt seduced—not by Holly, or the sales pitch, but by the property itself. *And that's the clincher*, he thought.

Holly didn't take him much further into the woods. He left, not knowing how far back the grove went. *Maybe that's better, for now*, he thought. *Save it for later and leave some mystery—that is if you even get the house. It's not yours yet.* With that uncomfortable thought, he began to bother over the possibility it could fall through, and he might not get the property. He'd place a bid.

As they walked up from the pond, he ended the small talk with, "I suppose we need to look at the numbers then?" to which she recited the basic terms; the bank was asking $45,000. He could probably swing that, but it would be tight. Perhaps he wouldn't upgrade everything he had originally planned and save some cash there. All he had to do now was take the leap...open his arms wide and swan dive off the proverbial cliff; put up or shut up. He started with a proposal of $40,000.

CHAPTER FIVE

The Previous Owners

Annette Smith was a former nurse and social worker, and the wife of Henry Smith, a successful investment banker from Boston. She and Henry had given up city life a few years back after Henry suffered his first heart attack at age forty-two. She literally nursed him back to health; guiding him in fixing bad habits, helping to change his diet, and convincing him to leave Boston. Henry had done well at the bank before the Depression had hit, but the daily stress had become unbearable. They decided to get out while the getting was good.

They had both always loved horses, so in 1933 they decided to search for an available farm. *Hopefully, we can find a place with room for at least four horses*, Annette aspired. They began their search in Essex County, Massachusetts and worked their way north from there. Eventually, they found and fell in love with a large white farmhouse on Lancaster Hill Road in Sanborn, New Hampshire.

Annette was a smart cookie. She had attended college, graduating in 1930. In those days it was no mean feat for a woman to graduate from a University, never mind one like Radcliffe. She was free-spirited and a think-outside-the-box kind of person, but she was also all about family, and had many practical, real-life dreams and desires. One of those desires was to settle down and have children, so in 1932 (at the age of 24, which was a late start for a woman in those days) she married Henry. Henry was fifteen years her senior, and this was his second marriage. His first wife had died several years back of tuberculosis. There were no children.

Once they had moved to New Hampshire, Annette volunteered part-time at St. Mary's Nursing Home not only to stay current with the nursing profession but also to maintain her social skills. She was self-aware enough to realize that talking only to Henry and horses all day-every day might leave her wanting for conversation. Henry's horse hobby started strong like just about anything he chose to set his mind to and became a sort of second career as he worked toward becoming a reputable horse breeder. His heart problem seemed to all but disappear after Annette convinced them to leave the big city. Two years later they were blessed to have their first child, Julia, in 1934, and then two more years later another: Henry Jr.

Time passed all too quickly. Julia got married and moved out in 1953 and Henry Jr., in turn, followed suit in 1957. The horse business not only took off but grew enough so that they had to hire two employees just to keep up with the demand. They ate the freshest home-grown produce almost every day. Annette canned much of it for the winter months. They even cut their own Christmas trees from the property when they found a nice, wild one; the old grove in the forest had grown out decades before, and those trees were too big. It was all a very happy and fulfilling life until one night right after Thanksgiving 1965 when Annette found Henry lying in a heap on the lawn by the barn.

November 29th, 1965

Annette called Henry for dinner, but he didn't come; that was very unlike him. She put down her dishtowel and headed out the side door that exited the house right in front of the barn. Henry lay in the grass near a spilled wash bucket. He was unresponsive, already gone. He was also a full quarter of a mile from where he had been slain, but there was nothing left to suggest he had even gone into the woods.

She did her best to revive him to no avail. The ambulance arrived twenty-five minutes after her call, but he was already gone, and as much as she wanted to blame somebody, she couldn't blame the paramedics. He had been at risk of a heart attack for years, despite her success in turning his unhealthy habits around. It seemed as if the old vices had done their damage, and it came as no real surprise when the official autopsy results came back confirming this.

Annette was stricken with grief, and since her parents were both dead, her sister Marjorie took time off from her family to comfort her as well as help with the farm temporarily while she began her incredibly painful life adjustment. Marjorie could only afford to stay for two weeks, however, and seeing her leave so soon was perhaps the loneliest moment of Annette's life. Suddenly the farmhouse that was way too big for two people seemed like a mansion for just one. After the first two days of solitude, she felt like she might as well be living on the moon.

Her loneliness went away three days later, however, when she saw her first ghost.

CHAPTER SIX

Fresh Cut House Keys

April 17th, 1971

Tim powered the truck up the ramp of his driveway right between the two maple trees, headed for a parking spot in front of his barn. Buying the house had gone much better than he had anticipated.

Tim had been helped by the youngest-looking banker he had ever seen. The man (*boy*, really) had hair greased tightly to the sides of his head and wore bifocals with circular lenses. He couldn't have been more than twenty-five years old. Tim thought he looked like the character Alfalfa from the old TV show *The Little Rascals*. He got right to the point and offered forty thousand dollars for the house in Sanborn that had been empty for three long years.

Alfalfa acted as if he couldn't recall which property it was—as if the bank wasn't even aware that it was a liability on their books. After he feigned looking it up and refreshing his memory for five minutes, he turned to Tim and deadpanned that the offer was too low. Tim immediately got the impression that Alfalfa would have given the same response if he had started with an offer twice as high. Perhaps the boy had learned to negotiate at a used car dealership, or maybe by watching a game show like *The Price is Right*.

"I'm pretty sure it's worth forty thousand dollars," he replied. "How many offers over that have you refused in the past three years?"

The kid commented under his breath while shaking his head that he would have to check with his boss and excused himself. Tim watched him walk the length of the lobby, past a row of desks full of busy bankers and enter a restroom. Five minutes later, Alfalfa came out, drying his hands on a paper towel. He tossed it into a co-workers wastebasket on the way back to Tim and sat back down, once again shaking his head in false disappointment.

"Yeah, I was right. We're not going to be able to accept that offer. The house comes with twenty-three acres, you know, but I do have some good news. He said we could do forty-four thousand."

Tim could smell a first-year student when he saw one. *Probably the bank president's son,* he thought.

"Is your boss's office in the men's room?"

He stood up and began to walk out. Immediately the president himself burst from his office across the lobby to head Tim off at the door. Apparently Alfalfa was on a short leash and was being observed; there was no way the president could have even known why Tim paid the bank a visit.

"I'm sorry, can I help you, sir? My name is Charles Trudell, and I'm the bank president. I happened to notice that you were here for a very short time and that things may have ended somewhat...abruptly with Charles here. We're a bit short-handed at the moment, and I just wanted to see if we had met all of your needs today." Tim noticed that both the bank president and Alfalfa shared the same first name.

"Well, I stopped by to see if I could take the Lancaster Hill Road house off of your hands, and I was prepared to offer you thirty-five thousand dollars."

The president turned to Charles Jr. with *you almost screwed this up* written all over his face. Alfalfa kept his mouth shut about the five thousand dollar discount Tim had just awarded himself with the hope Tim would never let it be known to his boss…and father.

"Oh, I see. Well, as I'm sure you know; that property has gone unsold for three years. It was once a beautiful home and a beautiful addition to the town of Sanborn. Everyone is simply sick that it has fallen into disrepair. What are your plans for the property should you be the buyer? Will you raze the house and put up something a little more modern?

Tim could tell from the Lion's Club pin on the man's suit coat that he was deeply involved with the local community and probably did not want to see a modern eyesore constructed in his quaint little country town.

"No, I'm a contractor myself, and I intend to restore the house and resell it in a year or two."

Charles Trudell Sr.'s eyes lit up, very pleased with Tim's answer. The president accepted his offer on the spot and shot Alfalfa several dirty looks as the papers were signed.

Sold, to the divorced bachelor in the red shirt for thirty-five thousand dollars.

His new life would begin soon. He was elated.

Tim cruised slowly down the driveway along the front of the house, head on a swivel once again, re-examining all that was now *his. Well, mine and the bank's*, he corrected himself. *Take it all in; the clock starts now. Start pounding those nails; you need the money. Restore and resell ASAP.*

He was stopping by today late in the afternoon to drop off some materials and then head down to Massachusetts to meet a client. He planned to start day one of the refurbishment first thing tomorrow morning.

Something caught his eye out past the pond at the far end of the field. It was the same neighbor-woman he had seen on the day of Holly's grand tour. She was standing still, knee-deep in the grass, looking away. *Hello again,* he thought. *Help yourself to my blueberries, or whatever you're doing out there. Are blueberries even in season yet? I know you've had the run of the place for the past three years or more, and I'll be too busy to make blueberry jam anytime soon, so knock yourself out.*

He turned left around the side of the house and parked in front of the barn. From a small bank envelope, he pulled two freshly-cut house keys. The metal was bright, sharp, shiny, and new. He hoped they had been cut correctly or it would be an exasperating twenty-minute drive back. He walked around front to the main front door underneath the bedrooms, inserted the first key, and turned. It worked, and he was in.

There was a lot of work to do, and it was time to make a plan as to where to start. He decided to save the exterior work for the summertime when the sun rose early and set late. For no particular reason, he made up his mind to start in the heart of the house, which was the living room with the bookshelves. This room seemed like it would be restored relatively quickly, as it wasn't in terrible shape.

The wide pine boards of the floor were in decent shape, as they were probably hidden by an area rug for most of their years. What Tim needed to do was properly winterize everything, and that meant a complete gutting of the outer walls. This room had two front windows that needed replacing as well as old fashioned plaster that needed to be torn out in favor of much warmer modern drywall and fiberglass insulation. He would also check to see if more electrical outlets should be installed while he had everything apart; they were not even part of the original construction in 1860. Any outlets he had were added later. Other than that the room looked like an easy start; the bookshelves looked good, and the fireplace was fine.

There was no furniture left in the room, so there was no heavy lifting. The bookshelf was, however, full of old books. To revamp the room, Tim needed to start with a completely blank canvas, so he began moving anything not nailed down to a temporary storage area on the floor of the formal dining room. As he cleared the bookshelves, he couldn't help but take note of some of the titles while trying to imagine who the previous owners had been that had once called this place home. On the top shelf were the old standbys: a World Atlas, a set of encyclopedias, some old novels, and a book on Boston. *I'd set the kids up with a table out by the road and have a yard sale, but we might not see two cars all day,* he thought.

The middle shelf was more interesting. If Tim ever decided to dive deep into who had lived in the house, he may have hit a rich vein. Amongst several novels by popular authors, he found a nondescript black hardcover that turned out to be a handwritten journal. He cracked it open and turned to a random page.

> *Thursday, February 17th, 1966:*
> *Today, from the turret above the kitchen, I sat and waited for the boy to come to the field to make his snowman. I waited until noon when I thought he would come, but he did not. I even waited an extra hour and rechecked the calendar to make sure I had the correct date. He never showed, and now I wonder if my current theory is off?*

Since when do kids plan their snowman-building? Tim wondered. *And if they do—who waits an hour to watch it happen?* Confused, he clapped the book shut and moved it with the others onto the floor of the dining room. It took him about thirty minutes to empty the room of its contents. Once everything was out, he realized that he might need a new hearth—this one was cracked.

Now that the room had been cleared, Tim decided to call it a day. Phase One was finished, and tomorrow would begin Phase Two, actual demolition. Depending on how things went, he might even start Phase Three, the reconstruction of the walls.

After he checked to be sure the front door was locked, he went through the house to the kitchen, planning to leave through the side door right next to his truck. He hadn't seen this part of the house in the two weeks since Holly's walkthrough. Everything appeared as it had on that day as he headed through to the breakfast area where the sliding glass door looked into the carriage house room. Before he reached the slider, he caught a whiff of something funky.

Tim backtracked, sniffing like a dog, glad that no one was there to witness the spectacle. He got halfway through the kitchen when he heard something, so he stopped in his tracks and listened. It was a splashing sound—footsteps in water. He counted six or so.

It came from beneath him…*the cellar.* Tim remained still, listening. Six footsteps were enough to eliminate the possibilities it might have been a squirrel or his imagination. When his patience ran out, he tiptoed the rest of the way to the cellar door as quietly as possible. As he stood before the door, he eyed the doorknob, gathering his courage. Behind the door, the footsteps splashed again, six more times. He pulled his hand back and held his breath listening until he began to see stars. All he could hear after that was the sound of his own suppressed panting.

After a moment of doubt and weighing his options, recalling all the money he had bet on himself, along with the disturbing fact someone had lain dead in his bedroom for far too long, he opened the door. The stairway began in the darkest corner of the kitchen and continued down into pitch black. The light switch was a foot inside the door on the right-hand wall. He reached in and flicked it on.

The floor was under an inch of water. It smelled like a marsh… no…like the pond. The last of the ripples on the surface of the water bounced off the bottom of the stairs. Tim crouched on the second stair, craned his neck under the floor dividing the two rooms and looked around. The cellar was equal in size to the kitchen above; a single naked bulb provided all of the light. The furnace took up roughly a third of the space and was surrounded by shadows the bulb would never reach. Nothing moved.

He went back quickly to the living room and grabbed a hammer, then returned to the top of the cellar stairs. After a final precautionary look, he descended. The hammer was just in case the cellar door closed itself or was closed upon him; it was more of a paranoid precaution than a belief in the supernatural. As he descended the stairs, it felt as if he passed through a thermocline; the temperature was borderline chilly. He looked around for any faucet or drainpipe that might be dumping water periodically, but there were none. He walked the room, tapping things with the hammer to scare a potential rodent or wild animal; once more, nothing.

A twinge of buyer's remorse pecked his brain, and he immediately squashed it. *Don't worry; I can fix that,* he told himself, already trying to put the exactly twelve footsteps he had most definitely heard…out of his mind. Finished but unsatisfied, he climbed the stairs, flicked the light off and closed the door, attempting to will his blood pressure back to normal. The water in the cellar was a setback and a pain in the ass, but not the end of the world. Every house had its problems. Every house had its problems. *Every house had its problems.*

He walked to the sliding glass door once again, ready to lock up and drive back to Massachusetts. He would spend the last night in his Haverhill apartment, gather the last of his things there and complete the move to Sanborn tomorrow. Things he had in storage would have to come later. As he reached for the door handle, he heard a noise from deep inside the house—footsteps *again,* this time coming down…as far as he could tell, the staircase below the bedrooms. *Six, seven, eight, nine, ten, eleven.* The hairs stood on his arms as he braced for confrontation.

He backed away from the slider and looked down the entire length of the house, through the kitchen, dining room, living room, hallway—all the way into the last room by the road. He waited, reluctantly. Tim knew most staircases had roughly a dozen steps. These stairs were hidden behind the living room wall. If he was correct, whoever had stopped on the eleventh step was just behind the doorway.

"Who is it?" he bellowed, hammer in hand.

No response. Tim questioned himself; perhaps being alone in a large house was something he wasn't used to, especially a house that had been empty for so long, and had such a mysterious past. *No*, he corrected himself; *the footsteps had happened—all seventeen of them.*

Impatiently he rapidly walked the length of the house, hammer raised, remaining as close to the front wall as possible. The unseen stairs remained silent. He rounded the threshold and faced them. *Empty*; as was the hallway above. He tensely called out:

"Come down."

The hallway was cold, and the dimly lit balcony above was the last place he wanted to go. Right now an hour and a half of highway with a beer in the cup holder were all he wanted. After ninety seconds of listening and waiting, and he started up noisily, in a sort of panic mode. The hair stood on the back of his neck as he knew deep down that if he found someone up there, it would not be a drifter or burglar.

In a frightened sprint, he barged into each bedroom, ready to swing the hammer. He was done with the entire upstairs in less than twenty seconds, and when he had finished, he stood in the hallway between the two front bedrooms monitoring each doorway and the staircase below. A drop of sweat rolled down his forehead and into his eye, and he wiped it away, panting.

Enough was enough—he had to leave now, and process these happenings later. If he kept checking out every last squeak on his way out, he'd never get out of here. He was upset; something had robbed him of feeling satisfied with his purchase, and the completion of the first day on the job, but it would have to wait.

The house had taken care of itself for three full years, surely one more night was not going to change anything.

He heard a creak or two on the way out, but no footsteps. He ignored the small noises and locked up. Once on the highway, beer between his legs, he wondered; if he *had* heard more footsteps, would he have checked them out?

CHAPTER SEVEN

First Full Day

April 18th, 1971

Tim returned the next morning and went right to work, refreshed, and ready to confront any noises that might interrupt his day. He chalked up yesterday's uncontrolled panic to nerves and lack of sleep. The footsteps were something he didn't have time for or even want to think about. He got a lot done working straight through the day, stopping only to eat a sandwich he had purchased at a gas station on the way up. The sun had set more than three hours ago now, and he was about to call an end to another day.

He had managed to rip out the old-fashioned lath and plaster wall in the front of the living room, re-insulate it, add an extra electrical outlet, replace the two windows with some pre-mades, and sheetrock it all. He could look at that wall proudly and declare it done. *Check that box...*and as always after every day on the job, there remained about a half-hour of cleanup.

He was hungry and tired but also motivated and encouraged. The first thing he checked upon arrival this morning was the cellar to see if the water level had risen, and was elated to find that it had all drained away. In fact, the floor was barely moist, just like most any cellar. He started work on the living room with extra pep in his step.

Now that today's work was done he thought he might head into town to grab a burger and a beer, silently celebrate the day's success, then come back and crash on the mattress upstairs. Maybe he would call Holly the real estate agent tomorrow and tell her how things were going and see where the conversation went from there. *Why not?* He had struggled with the decision and thought it might be better for his professional life if he didn't…but she kept popping into his mind…a *very pretty curiosity.*

Just as he filled his last dustpan of crumbled plaster, the phone rang. Wow, his very first phone call. The line had only been activated this morning. Only Johnny and the girls (meaning Sheila) knew the number, so he looked at it, puzzled; it was a little late for anyone to call. He walked over and answered, but there was nobody on the other end. *Perhaps, my first telemarketer,* he reasoned.

He placed the receiver back in the cradle and returned to cleaning up. No sooner had he touched the broom, something moved upstairs.

Thud-thud-thud-thud-thud-thud-thud-thud.

The same footsteps he had heard yesterday. He grabbed the hanging painter's light and peeked around the corner, looking up the staircase to the upstairs bedrooms. He tried the light switch at the bottom of the stairs, but nothing happened. *Why didn't I check the damn bulbs first thing?* In his haste to get a jump on his construction goals, he had put all his energy into the living room. He had even taken the bulb out of his backup painter's light to use in the living room lamp. *Mental note: Shopping list; light bulbs—Way to set yourself up, Tim.* Now he would face the footsteps after sundown, and this time there would be no comfortable joyride home; *this* was home now. He realized immediately it would be a long night.

The glow from the painter's light made shadows of everything up the staircase. The banister had a long tall double that expanded and contracted as Tim searched with his eyes. The light barely reached the ceiling of the second floor. There was no movement along the banister. His heart beat rapidly; he was full-blown afraid. Confrontation was one thing, *let's get it over and done with*—but this was akin to being hunted. He paused silently with his shoulder against the threshold and waited in frustration again. Ten seconds, twenty seconds—

THUD-THUD-THUD-THUD-THUD.

The footsteps were sudden and loud in contrast to the silence; he jumped, completely startled. They were different this time; it took him a second to realize, as his eyes searched the upstairs wildly…that they came from behind; the kitchen area. He spun, feeling vulnerable and surrounded; *were there two?* Or did he (or she?) somehow get to the other end of the house without taking the only possible staircase? He lifted the light high, hoping it would carry into the breakfast area, but it only managed to illuminate the dining room.

If someone was there in the darkness, there were plenty of places to hide: The kitchen, bathroom, cellar, turret, carriage house, and barn, just to name a few. He was not in a good position to pinpoint their whereabouts, given that he was limited to the length of the painter's light cord. Again, he waited with limited options, listening in all directions, a sitting duck. *The next truckload from storage in Massachusetts includes the baseball bat and the rifle.*

The house had been empty for three years. Someone at some point had broken the back window in the dining room. Could there be homeless people, or squatters, or gypsies out here? He realized he didn't know much about Sanborn. Perhaps they had been here before and used the house for shelter whenever passing through.

You wouldn't hear footsteps from two different rooms. You've been in the center of the house all day long. If they had snuck in, it would have to have been this morning before you arrived. Not probable, he told himself. And they just stayed quiet all day long and waited for dark? I don't think so. He dismissed the desperate theory.

Stuck in a compromising position, he decided it was better to act. He snapped the painter's light off in an attempt to lose the watcher or watchers. It was a bad idea; his eyes were not prepared, and it only blinded him for several seconds. Even after his eyes had recovered somewhat, and the moon began to illuminate the room, his vision was still worse than it had been. The doorway to the dining room was now just a dark hole; he had sacrificed the ability to see through to the kitchen. If someone was stalking him, he had just given up precious warning distance. He moved from his position to the back of the living room in an attempt to even the odds; perhaps they would no longer know exactly where he was, now that it was dark.

From this viewpoint, he could only see the doorways themselves; still a failing plan of action. In frustration he snapped the light back on, blinding himself temporarily again. Rather than blink, he let the light burn his eyes as he focused on the doorway to the dining room.

The footsteps again; thud thud thud thud thud thud thud.

Definitely the kitchen side of the house; very faint this time. He held the painter's light over his head and pushed around the threshold, attempting a look for the source. The short-range beam only carried halfway through the kitchen. Deep in the black of the breakfast area, two eyes shone in the ambient light.

They were about three feet off the ground, unblinking. Tim braced himself, finally able to focus on his tormentor. He strained to see more detail, but the dark would not permit. Neither moved; the tension brought his heart into his throat. *I'm not prepared for this.*

As he prepared to call out, the eyes moved in the darkness, swaying slightly side-to-side as they walked forward.

He stopped well short; thin and pale; a boy of approximately eight years, wearing overalls, a farm shirt, and leather shoes. The room grew noticeably colder, and Tim realized *it was because of the boy.*

He stepped closer again, remaining in the shadows, seemingly interested by Tim. His eyes were lifeless, yet Tim gathered from his body language he was trying to decide whether or not to approach any further. The better light revealed more details; his skin was bone-white, and his hair was stringy. Was he alone? An orphan, perhaps? *What's your story*?

The boy took another two steps, closing the distance, now just the width of the dining room away. A smell reached Tim's nostrils. An odor of must and dampness, similar to the cellar. Tim reached out verbally:

"Where are your parents?" he spat nervously. He knew there was no good reason why a boy should be in his house alone. There was no response as he studied Tim's face. Suddenly he began to walk backward. *Is that it?* He continued the slow backpedal until he had passed the limits of the painter's light. The shining eyes were the last thing Tim saw before they faded, gone. Tim listened for the sound of the sliding glass door, but it never came.

Enough was enough. Tim bolted taking the nearest exit, out the front door and into the night, slamming the door behind him. He needed his truck, which was back around the side of the house, and near the place he had seen the boy. The house was completely dark except for the painter's light he had left. He rounded the corner made his move for the truck, grabbing the door handle and hesitating momentarily, bracing for an unexpected surprise, but all was quiet. He yanked the door open, started the truck, and threw it into reverse.

You're running away, a grown man like you, with not only your pride and confidence at stake but also your ability to provide for your daughters. One night, and you've already quit. Don't ever tell anybody this story, Tim. Don't ever tell anyone you're in the poorhouse because you're afraid of ghosts.

He backed the truck up fast, just in case somebody or something decided to rush him from his blind spot, and spun around in the driveway's bend. On the way out, he kept his eyes on the front of the house, and also in the rearview for any last chance attack from behind; *nobody's coming.*

Suddenly ashamed of himself, he slammed on the brakes at the end of the driveway and paused, gritting his teeth. This house was all he had. He was leaving his entire future as he knew it. He bit his lower lip, put the truck in park and opened the door defiantly, albeit terrified. Standing on the lower lawn halfway to the pond, he stared into the lit living room; still no movements or noises since the encounter.

You don't want to believe it, but you know you just saw a dead kid in front of your very eyes. That was no homeless person or gypsy. Nothing alive smells like that.

He might have shamed himself into going back in to explore, but self-preservation thought better of it and designed him a *Plan "B."* He hopped back into the truck and left, driving down Lancaster Hill Road until the house was out of sight. Ten seconds later and now fully ashamed, he pulled over, shut the lights off and cut the engine. Getting out, he locked the truck and walked quietly along the dark road toward the house. It was impossible to be completely quiet; the dirt sounded like coffee grinds under his feet. He hadn't grabbed a jacket on the way out, and as of now, he felt the chill of the April night as soon as the adrenalin wore off.

He crossed the spot where the wild forest became his pasture. The trees lining the road blocked the view of the house, now about two hundred yards away. He felt his way across the gulley on the side of the road, over the stone wall and into his field where he had a clearer view. The moon illuminated the field, and he watched the house for signs of movement. About all he could see was the light from the lone bulb in the living room, and nothing appeared to disturb it or cast any new shadows. He stayed for five minutes to be sure.

Tim hated to admit it because he had never believed in ghosts, but he knew he had just seen his first. *Thirty-five thousand dollars and it's haunted? …HAUNTED? You've got to be shitting me.*

When the five minutes were up, he stood in the field—cold and without a plan. He didn't like his options. Despite nothing visibly going on at the house, he was ashamed and flat-out afraid. What to do? Go to a hotel? He imagined bumping into Holly somewhere and being asked how the new house project was going. *Fine, thanks for asking, but I don't ever sleep there.* It wouldn't be his proudest moment, that's for sure.

He could…go to a bar, smooth things out a bit…and then what? *Go back in? Sure, Tim, things will go much better closer to midnight.* Indecision was a rarity for him, and he was rapidly becoming upset with himself.

Just then, his eyes still fixed on the house; a light went on in the turret.

It was dim and flickering, unlike the steady beam of the painter's light—*a candle.* A chill crawled up his body. *He's back, and damn it—he plays with matches.*

Now he would have to go back to protect his investment; he couldn't just let the house burn down. *Life begins at divorce?* Starting over? Turn your back now, and you won't have a house for the girls to visit. What poison would Sheila plant in their heads after Daddy's failure?

With hairs raised on his body like a frightened dog, he walked back to the truck.

As he shut his door quietly, a thought occurred: Whoever was in the turret might be aware he had faked leaving the property. With this thought and the fact that he couldn't see the road in front of him, he turned the headlamps on and drove back, fully announcing his arrival. Deep down, he knew he wouldn't be able to approach the house undetected. He pulled up the driveway and past the two trees. Forty feet in front of him and one story up, the candlelight danced on the ceiling. His heart pounded. *I'm back.*

And I'm betting my life again; instead this time it isn't my financial life. Please, please, please...let's be friends.

He pulled around to the side where he had before. *Here I am. And I'm not going to run this time.* He opted for the side door, rather than walking around to the front because it was closer to the turret. All was dark; he didn't even have a flashlight.

Check that; change of plans—no side door. It's too dark; too many turns, rooms, and angles. If the boy wants to run at me, I won't see him coming. I would only smell him, or worse—feel him.

Tim went back out and circled to the front door where he had fled like a rabbit only fifteen minutes before. He was tense and sweating, even though he had been cold moments ago.

He opened the door; the illumination of the painter's light came from the living room on the right and only barely leaked into the hallway. He could see up the first six stairs but after that nothing but darkness. He went into the living room and fetched the painter's light. In the dining room were more extension cords, so he bravely stepped in and got them as well, rigging everything for his long-distance house check.

He climbed the turret stairs slowly, praying that nobody would unplug the painter's light from the outlet in the dining room. The candlelight above him moved on the ceiling. There had been no candles in the house when he had moved in that he was aware of, certainly not the turret room. *Where the hell did it come from?* He decided very quickly it was the least of his worries.

As his eyes cleared the top of the stairs, he swiveled his head defensively to cover all angles. Thankfully nobody worldly or other-worldly was here waiting. Outside the windows was nothing but black of night. The candle's flame and the painter's light were reflected off of every window, ruining the view of the yard below. He knew that the opposite was true for everything inside the room, putting him in a fishbowl.

Accepting his exposure, Tim turned to the main attraction,

the candle itself, lit seemingly just for him. It sat in the middle of the old desk that had been left behind, held upright with what appeared to be an antique iron candelabra. Both sat atop a nondescript hardcover book.

He lifted the candle and moved it to the surface of the desk, then picked up the book. It was the journal, or diary that he had seen on the bookshelf yesterday when he emptied the living room before starting work. The last he knew, he had set it down with the other books on the floor of the dining room. Opening to page one, he intended on taking it much more seriously than he had the previous afternoon. Apparently his first impression had been wrong…and someone was not so subtly *suggesting* that he take another look.

CHAPTER EIGHT
Annette's Inspiration

Thursday, December 16th, 1965

Annette sat in the turret with a cup of tea. Things were difficult without Henry, and she missed him terribly. There was a lot to do on a horse farm, especially alone. She was left with several horses that were considered works in progress, which was Henry's expertise, not hers. Very soon she would begin selling things off at a discount because she knew nothing about horse breeding.

Annette's sister Marjorie had left three days before. The two weeks she had been able to afford Annette had been immensely helpful, albeit brief. So many unpleasant, yet necessary tasks were seen to; the care of Henry's body, the funeral arrangements, the life insurance…and so forth. The painful transition from life with Henry to life without Henry had begun. Today had been a long day. The horse chores, on top of her own duties, were just too much for her and her broken heart.

She had briefly considered selling the farm and moving closer to one of the kids (she never decided which one), but it just didn't feel right. Annette had always had a bit of an independent streak, and she did love it here. Moving away would not help the pain of losing Henry. Henry Junior had helped out, staying for a week, but he had young children and had to get back to Cambridge; he promised to visit more often. Julia came out for the funeral but now lived in Illinois with her family, so her visit was even shorter and more complicated to arrange.

Annette knew that if she got too lonely, she could always volunteer more time at the Sanborn Nursing Home. She had always felt a duty to help the elderly, and why not? Maybe they could help her, too. The patients there were also lonely and had had their share of personal loss, so there was much in common. Mutual therapy.

As she sat relaxing, she realized it was 3:30 pm and sunset was only about forty minutes away this time of year; another lonely day just about over. There was a foot of snow on the ground, and nothing left to do but prepare her dinner and get to bed. She wasn't eating much lately. No matter how hard she worked, the appetite just wasn't there anymore, at least not yet. She had lost ten pounds off of her already thin frame, but it was nothing to worry about according to her doctor; she was simply grieving.

She attempted to enjoy the last of the day's sunlight and the beautiful view of the farm as she waited for the upcoming orange light show. It was then that something moving by the pond caught her eye.

Directly between the two naked weeping willows, beyond the pond and almost in the pasture, ran the little boy. She had seen this boy well, for...a few years, perhaps...exactly how many, she could not recall. All these years, and yet she had no idea who he belonged to; the neighbors were so far away! He was a little young for such a distance in her opinion, but...a thought occurred to her; if she had been seeing him for a few—or maybe several years, then how old *was* he? And of course, *who* was he? He trudged through the snow, making his way toward the woods, deeper onto her property and away from the road. The wind blew, and the hair on his forehead moved with it. To her surprise, he was not wearing a coat.

She grabbed her sweater quickly and descended the turret stairs, leaving the house in a run, making her way down the snowy lawn toward the pond looking for the boy, but she had lost him; he was nowhere to be seen. The wind picked up, and the naked willows shifted as if alive. She had to blaze her own trail through the deep snow because she hadn't been down to the pond since perhaps October. All the while running, she looked left, hoping to reacquire him. In the time it took her to get up from her chair in the turret, descend the stairs and leave the building, he had presumably covered four times the ground he had while she was watching him, which seemed practically impossible.

She stopped and turned, scanning the tree line, the pasture, back to the pond area. No sign. The pond itself was frozen over, and its surface was unblemished. Her breathing labored due to the effort required in snow of this depth. She arrived at the approximate spot she had seen the boy and examined the smooth surface, looking back at the turret once more for point of reference. There were no footsteps here; and no sign anyone had crossed the field at all, even though the snow had a thin crust a rabbit's weight would have broken. Annette again regarded the forest along the field opposite the road. The trees betrayed no secrets.

This was not the first time she had seen the boy on her property recently, and she had begun to speculate. This sighting confirmed a new theory which sparked a feeling of excitement. She had always believed in spirits and the afterlife, and for the first time since Henry's death, she felt her mind shift to something...inspirational. A woman looking to fill a great hole in her life due to the loss of her husband had just found herself a mystery, and perhaps something of a project to occupy her time.

CHAPTER NINE

The Birth of the Journal

Friday, December 17th, 1965

Annette got into the farm truck and drove into town with one goal in mind. She pulled into Newman's Stationery and parked. On the wall by the pastel paper stock was a shelf of blank journals. She chose the most common-looking plain book and grabbed two of them just in case they went out of print. She paid and left.

CHAPTER TEN

Long First Night

April 18th, 1971 (same night)

Tim's nerves were fried after the candle and journal episode. He was proud of himself, however. He had reentered the house and faced his fears. He hadn't choked when the chips were down, and that renewed his spirits somewhat, but it was far from over. It wasn't even midnight yet, and he was still on high alert, wondering what could possibly be next. The threat of another uninvited visit kept things tense.

Tim brought the journal and candle down the turret stairs, ready for whatever awaited. Thankfully, there was no ambush waiting on the way upstairs. He chose to make camp in the master bedroom where there was nothing but a mattress sitting on the floor in the corner. He knew the previous owner had died in this room, but he figured it better to keep close watch than let her wander about—if she was even a part of what he had already witnessed.

He reminded himself to make moving all of his stuff up here from storage in Massachusetts a priority; *that, and buy a ton of LIGHTBULBS.* There were many things in storage that could have been put to good use tonight if they had only been here—he would not repeat this mistake. *Better to have it and not need it than need it and not have it.*

Tim settled in as best he could for the night. He left the master bedroom still dragging the extension cord behind him, passing the two dark bedrooms at the top of the stairs and brushing his teeth in the upstairs bathroom. As he brushed, he had a thought: If something wanted to get him, the top of the stairs would be a great spot for an ambush. Depending upon which direction he was going, he was vulnerable from either bedroom, from the stairs, or from the bathroom itself.

It was mentally agonizing to pass the dark rooms; he thought he saw the boy inside one of them for a second, but stood his ground and raised the light; once again proving it was only his imagination. Later in the bedroom, he noted that there had also been no odor, or temperature drop—sure signs of the boy.

The painter's light was now plugged into an outlet in the master bedroom. The process of moving it from the downstairs had been harrowing. He had to put himself into darkness once again, climbing the dark stairs and finding the outlet in the barely moonlit master bedroom using his fingertips. The final ten seconds had been agony. Another sweat had broken out on top of all the drywall dust caked on his skin, and he *really* needed a shower, but there was no way he would put himself behind a translucent curtain, naked—*not tonight.*

Once the bathroom rituals were complete, he crawled into bed with the journal. Things got quiet quickly. He realized he felt the same up here as he did in the turret…deaf and blind to the goings-on in the rest of the house. It would be hard to hear something happening in the kitchen up here. He did his best to let this thought go, as it was out of his control and opened the journal to the first page.

Friday, December 17, 1965
My Journal
By Annette Smith

Today while I was having tea in the turret, I saw the little boy on our property again. This time he was running through the snow just past the pond. I'm always so busy I never think to go outside and flag him down to ask him who he is and where he lives. He's always poking around. It seems like he's been around for a while, too. Has it been years? Time flies—I couldn't begin to guess with any accuracy. I wish Henry was still around; I could ask him.

Since we are so isolated from our neighbors (I barely know them), it's a bit shocking to see a boy his age so far away from his home, out on his own. These country folks are a little more naïve than we city folks, however. Or maybe they know more than we do in certain ways…it's hard to say.

Anyway, I left the turret to catch up with him and finally pick his brain. I exited the house very quickly and crossed the lawn to the pond area, but he was already gone! He also left no footprints so; I am either losing my mind or—I can't believe I am about to write the words—I may have a ghost.

I actually hope he IS a ghost. If he is, well then, he must need help and, I would love to help. Yes, I am so heartbreakingly lonely that I would befriend a ghost. I wonder if seeing this little boy coincides somehow with Henry's death here at home.

Tim's first thought was not about the boy, but of the "previous owner" dying on the property (and in this very room). Now there was a journal entry stating *both* of the previous owners had died here...*owners*—plural: the wife *and* the husband.

So...who's the kid? Annette, the person Tim assumed, had written the journal...seemed to think he might be a ghost, too... *and that makes three.* He would call Holly tomorrow and re-ask all of the relevant questions, plus some new ones, paying closer attention this time.

His thoughts then returned to tonight's special guest, the boy. *So I'm not the only person who's seen you...* At least Tim knew he wasn't losing his mind, and that was a good thing. However, those other people died somewhat suspiciously.

He paused in thought; had the boy delivered the journal? Tim agreed with Annette that he was somewhere in the range of seven or eight years old. Do ghosts stay fixed at the same age when they die? Would a seven-year-old be aware of the contents of a journal written by an adult? Was the boy capable of striking a match? In short: *How many ghosts do I live with?*

He didn't read much further. The house had been quiet for close to three hours now, and his heart rate had slowed back to normal. He was exhausted. If something wanted him dead, or out of the house, it could have had him by now. He crashed hard with the journal on his chest and the painter's light still on. He didn't have much to lose, anyway. *Come and take whatever you want.*

CHAPTER ELEVEN
Roofing

Monday, April 19th, 1971

Tim awoke at 6:15 the next morning. It took him a second to come to, still exhausted, waking slowly to the memory of where he was—*his new house, his new...haunted...house.* His first complete thought was of the ghost boy, and that shook the cobwebs away completely. The butterflies in his belly woke with him as he surveyed the room, heart suddenly back to the races. His second thought was of the day's agenda. The original plan was to pick a wall and redo it, but things had changed. He was going to have to drive down to Amesbury and haul as much stuff as he could back here. And then in the distance, he heard a pounding noise.

He rose, still dressed in yesterday's dirty clothes. Fight or flight, he had to be ready at a moment's notice; he didn't want to have to run out of there in his underwear. Tim searched for something to wield before investigating the banging, grabbing the only thing in the entire upstairs—the hammer. The rest of his tools were downstairs, but he figured the hammer was probably still his best bet, at least until he picked up his stuff in Amesbury. Well, maybe the crowbar would work better, but either way, *good luck whacking that ghost, Tim.*

Somehow, the heft of the hammer granted him confidence, and he didn't really mind that it was false; any confidence at all would do. He supposed the hammer would simply pass through a ghost harmlessly if he swung at them, but realized he knew nothing of the supernatural laws of physics. *Were* there really any, or just invented crap you saw in the movies? He had felt the cold when the boy was around, so perhaps the stories were true.

He crossed the hallway to the opposite bedroom, the sunny one that looked across the roof to the turret. The top of the barn was behind and to the left, about seventy-five feet away. He could see only the near side, but the noise was definitely coming from that direction. He descended the stairs quickly while cautiously glancing into each and every room on his way out.

Once the house was completely checked from the upstairs through the dining room, he went to his tools. So far, nothing was amiss—no more journals, candles or signs of ghost activity. He grabbed the crowbar, hefting it for a quick second before sticking with the hammer. The carpenter's level was longer but much too fragile. A baseball bat would have felt great in his hands right now.

He hastily scanned the kitchen and breakfast area, skipping the turret, the kitchen bathroom and the basement, exiting swiftly through the carriage house and side door. The pounding was louder out here, and there were interruptions in the racket when whoever was making the noise paused to grab a fresh nail.

He approached the barn slowly and confirmed that the hammering was coming from the right side of the roof; the one blind to the rest of the house. The barn was attached to the carriage house, so walking around from the left side was impossible. The right side of the barn was up against the forest, so walking out to get a view from a distance was also impossible. Tim walked to the front of the barn and looked up. With no clear vantage point, he followed front wall and as quietly as possible and turned left around the corner. Wild shrubs, vines, and thorns made passage unpleasant but not impossible. He looked overhead once again at the edge of the roof, but he realized there was no way he was going to get a look at the roof's surface this way.

He was about to backtrack to the driveway when he heard a metallic rattle followed by scattered rolling. Six nails plopped one after the other in front of him in the tall grass by his feet. He bent down and picked them up, examining closely. They weren't the typical modern-day roofing nails he used on the job, but were square-shaped, tapered to a point on two sides and made of iron. They were rust-free and brand new in appearance, even slightly oily, yet they were without a doubt old-fashioned. He decided that the time for silence and sneaking was now over; he trudged his way noisily through the weeds and brush back out to the driveway. When he was thirty feet out from the barn, he called out:

"Hey, who's up there?"

The pounding stopped.

"Come on, say hello! Who are you? Let's talk!"

Nothing happened. Tim tried his best to back away further to get a look, but there was no possible angle. At least, once again he had not been attacked or threatened; this boosted his courage. He considered the possibility that whoever was up there might have even tossed the nails directly at him as a sort of offering, or sign. They landed so perfectly close he couldn't have missed them, and after all, he had already been gifted the journal the night before. *How many ghosts do I have?* He wondered again. *Surely little boys don't fix roofs.*

Undeterred, Tim went into the house, climbed the turret stairs, opened a window, and lowered himself out onto the roof while the hammering continued. He had to be careful as he made his way because the shingles were old and some were loose or in disrepair; the roof *was* on his list of projects; now he might have to make it a priority. He ambled precariously over the top of the carriage house and started up the steep left side of the barn's roof. Tension rose as he approached the peak; the pounding continued, much louder and much closer.

As his line of sight cleared the summit, the hammering ceased and…anticlimactically, yet almost expectedly, the roof was empty. In checking around later, it came as no surprise that there were no ladders anywhere on the building, and the roof where the noise had originated was in as poor condition as the rest.

I need to get through that journal somehow, he dreaded. Tim hadn't read a book in thirty years, and he was up to his eyeballs in adult problems. He began to feel pressure building; there were not enough hours in the day.

CHAPTER TWELVE
Tim's Questions

Monday, April 19th, 1971 (same day)

Holly Burns, the real estate agent, had just arrived at her office when the phone rang.

"Hi Holly, this is Tim Russell at the Lancaster Hill Road house; how are things? Would you happen to have a minute?"

Holly was just about to sit down and organize her day, starting with some paperwork at her desk. It hadn't yet been ten days since Tim had signed the papers and closed on the house, and she had all but attributed the flirty vibes and mixed signals between herself and Tim as the heat of the moment. He was barely divorced, and maybe still gun shy, or worse—damaged goods. It was best not to force some things.

The current phone call was interesting, however. By coincidence, today's plan included a check-back courtesy with her latest customer to see how things were going, followed by a reminder that she was always looking for referrals. It was something the boss suggested all of the agents do. *Just doing my job*, she thought (even though she seldom made these phone calls). She knew Tim would no doubt be busy with the fixer-upper and needed time to settle in, but he had been nearing the end of his grace period. She was beginning to lose hope, but this phone call might be promising.

"Hi Tim, how are things going? Kicking up some dust over there? Ready to re-sell yet?"

"Haha, sure Holly, I'm just about finished. Just one more coat of paint in the living room and we can put it back on the market."

"Well, you aren't calling to ask if I can hold a paintbrush, are you? Because I'm busy that day, no matter what day it is."

"You sound like some people who have worked for me. Hey, honestly, I was calling with some questions, but I can call back if it's not a good time."

"Yes, yes, I have time, I just walked in. Coincidentally, you were on my list of call-backs. I just wanted to say congratulations and see how things were going. I'm even going to mail you a tin of cookies fresh from Lakes Region Realty later today. They aren't really fresh, though. My older customers like to dunk them in milk. Don't blame me, though; the owner makes us send them."

"Do birds like them? I'll smash them up first, of course."

"I would do the same thing. My name is on the card inside, but I swear I didn't bake them."

"Say no more; you're off the hook." Tim paused for a second to segue into the meat of the phone call.

"...but the reason I'm calling... I was wondering...we talked about it a little bit, but...how much do you know of the history of the house?"

Buzzkill thought Holly. Not only was this *not* looking like a flirty phone call anymore, but perhaps he was about to call her out for holding back on information; some detail she might have left out, or worse—*Buyer's Remorse. Not you, Tim... I even showed you the grove!* Holly was every bit the professional and never misled anyone intentionally, so she put on her counselor's hat and braced for his questions.

"Oh, sure...well, I told you about the Smith woman who died

on the property, but…you have more questions? What's on your mind?" She did her best not to sound defensive.

"Yeah, I guess so. I found a journal on the bookshelf and read some of it. Apparently, Annette Smith's husband Henry died here as well. Not that it bothers me a whole lot, but I haven't read the whole thing, and it got me to thinking…do you know anything else about their deaths? Not that you would hold anything back, but are there any other details? I mean…she was only sixty years old. That seems a little young, and now there's the husband. I don't know, I'm sorry; I just wanted to ask you first. Does the house have some sort of history that everyone knows about but the new guy?" Tim was easing into the full story. He couldn't just blurt out that he'd seen a ghost boy on the first night, and then heard what might be a second ghost roofing the barn the next morning.

"Well, to be honest, Tim, I purposely avoid studying up on this type of thing. I don't know any of the stories, or whether or not there might be any 'gory details.' If the house has a history, I'm not aware of it, and I haven't heard any comments from my colleagues over here. Of course, we do work out of Laconia, and that's twenty minutes away from Sanborn. Maybe some of the Sanborn locals know something we don't. That house is over a hundred and ten years old.

"If you don't mind my honest opinion, however…personally, it doesn't bother me if somebody died in my house. Somebody did actually, but I don't know the details. And before him, I don't know, and honestly, I don't want to know. Many houses in this area have had people die in them. In fact, *most* of the houses have. It doesn't sound strange to me that your house, built in 1860, may have had *several* people die in it; there may have been some births, too. I'm a little surprised; you don't strike me as someone who usually cares very much about this sort of thing, either. What's this journal you're talking about?"

Holly already had an idea of what he might be talking about, but she didn't want to be the first to say. She honestly knew nothing of the house's history but had gotten a vibe one day while giving a tour. She hoped Tim would not be too ashamed to open up and confirm her suspicion.

Tim paused; the ball was back in his court. Holly was right in that he wasn't the kind of guy that normally cared about people that had passed away, and he agreed with her philosophy. If people wanted to know this sort of thing they could do their own research at the town hall or the library, don't blame it on the real estate agent. The phone line between the two of them was silent for a full second.

"There was a journal left on the bookshelf in the living room, and I've only read a page or two. Holly, have you ever gotten a phone call like this after the sale?" He was still hiding the real story, along with his pride.

"No. Not about dead people; this is a bit of a surprise coming from the contractor who plans to rebuild the place all by himself. What's in this journal? Is it spooky or something? Maybe you're just not used to living in a pre-Civil War era building, not to mention the condition that one is in. How old was your house in Amesbury?" She did her best not to bruise his ego.

"Uh…my house in Amesbury was pretty old too, 1800's as well, actually. But I don't think that's the problem. The journal was written by Annette Smith, the woman that died in my bedroom—and she writes about a ghost she regularly saw on the property. Now, I don't believe in that stuff, but…I…to be honest, I've seen a couple of things myself, and one of the things I saw she wrote about."

He exhaled deeply as the last word fell out of his mouth. He waited for the giggle or the disbelief in Holly's voice. There was nothing but silence on the other end until:

"You *did*?"

He hadn't planned on letting the entire cat out of the bag, but the conversation had progressed quickly, and once he got rolling, he passed the point of no return. His hopes of asking some basic house history questions then turning the conversation to flirtier matters now seemed a long shot. She asked pointed questions and picked his locks faster than he had anticipated. She did, however, seem to take him seriously when he stuck his neck out and confessed: "*You did?*"

No matter where the conversation went from here, he was sure of what he had seen (and heard…and smelled), and he was proud that he hadn't fled his investment; even pursuing the ghost on the roof the next morning…albeit in broad daylight. He even had some physical evidence: six brand new/antique nails in his pocket, a candelabra, and a journal.

"Okay, …yes. I hate to say 'yes,' but there's no doubt in my mind. I know this opens me up to ridicule, but I've seen some weird things, and I even have some physical proof, part of which is the journal."

"What do you mean the journal? Didn't Annette Smith write it? And you said it was on the bookshelf when you moved in?"

"Yes. It was on the bookshelf. Then I moved it to the dining room floor. And last night before I went to bed, someone lit a candle in the turret. When I went up there to put it out, the journal was lying underneath it."

Tim didn't know it yet, but he had just lit a fire beneath Holly's office chair. She and her grandfather, back when she was a little girl, had made a fun little hobby out of 'ghosts.' Not real ghosts, but ghost stories and scary movies. It started with a Saturday afternoon movie on TV called "The House on Haunted Hill," made in 1959.

Little Holly had walked into the living room while Grandpa Walter was watching it. She was about eleven years old at the time, so Walter got up, turned the volume down and warned her; "Honey, this is supposed to be a scary movie with ghosts in it, you might not want to see it." She told him she didn't really care because she "liked ghosts." This was no lie; she was a fan of Nancy Drew books and had recently finished "The Ghost of Blackwood

Hall." There were no "real" ghosts in the book, however; it was all a big hoax, but the book was creepy in several chapters, and she enjoyed feeling the goosebumps when things got scary.

Grandfather and granddaughter watched the movie together, and after he was sure Holly hadn't suffered any nightmares as a result of the movie, he let her watch more. This started a tradition between the two of them; horror movies turned to ghost stories, and the two of them spent their days away from each other looking for scary things to share and talk about the next time they met.

Holly was enthralled by Tim's story. "What? *Did you go up there? In the turret…alone?* Okay, tell me slowly now. What happened? Is the journal the only physical evidence? Tim, so that you know, what I said is true. I don't care about people dying in homes. They die, and they rest in peace for all I know, and I really don't want to know. But…I've been a sort of ghost…um… hobbyist since I was young. I love scary books and movies and the like.

"My grandfather and I were both into the whole genre, you know, movies, ghost stories and such. I can't say I've ever seen a real ghost, however, and I don't think he ever did, either. He even told me once that he didn't believe in ghosts, except for Jesus. Maybe he was just calming my nerves so that I wouldn't have any nightmares; I don't know. He enjoyed a good scare—not one of those cheap scares that only startles you. We spent a lot of time looking for creepy stuff. Oh wow, Tim, I'm sorry, I'm rambling. When you said that, I got a real chill up my spine."

She was talking a mile a minute, audibly excited. Tim sat back and let her take the floor. He wasn't a huge horror movie fan, but maybe they could find something in common given his current situation.

"The way it goes in fiction is, 'dead people that come back as ghosts are unhappy for some reason.' Some people like sad stories, or comedies or science fiction, but I love ghost stories. And…*oh shit.* I hate to cut this short, but my boss is signaling to me. We're having an impromptu office meeting. Great timing on his part, right? Hey Tim, I want to hear this story of yours. How about I buy you a burger tonight? Do you know the Bunkhouse Bar?"

Well, that escalated quickly, Tim smiled to himself. He had stuck his neck out and reeled in a date! Heck, he was even asked out. As he hung the phone up he had an ironic thought—*might his ghost problem get him laid?*

CHAPTER THIRTEEN
First Date

Monday, April 19th, 1971 (same day)

When they met at the restaurant, she was not wearing work clothes. Holly had finished her day two hours early in order to go home to dress for a casual date: jeans, a simple blouse, a light jacket, some perfume, and light makeup.

Tim too had driven a little faster down to Amesbury to load up as many items in storage as he could for use in Sanborn. He was also sure to stock up on light bulbs, batteries, flashlights and anything else related to illumination at the hardware store. Then he sped back to the house and unloaded everything while keeping his eyes peeled for...*roommates*. After that, he went upstairs and showered for his date—curtain half-open, baseball bat leaning against the outside of the tub, back to the wall. *Showering with a baseball bat; the things we do for love.*

While at dinner, he told her everything, from the boy, to the roofing nails, and of course the journal left for him in the turret. "Did you bring it?" She asked. He had forgotten.

"I'm going to shoot myself, but no. I *did* bring the roofing nails, though—I put them in my pocket early and forgot everything else while watching my back. *Damn!* I can get it to you tomorrow. There's a lot to read, and I haven't had time. I haven't gotten much sleep; I guess I'm not thinking clearly.

The first time I found the journal, in the living room, I mean, I opened it up to somewhere in the middle, and I wondered what the woman was talking about. I thought she was talking about waiting for a *normal* boy to build a snowman, but now I think it was probably the ghost boy I saw. I'm not sure why she seemed to know when he would show up, though. Maybe it was a pattern he repeated from time to time.

"That's just about all I know; that and the time he walked through the snow and didn't leave any footprints. I've been there just over two damn days! I've barely cracked the book. I guess I'll just have to grind through it. There are no bookmarks, highlights...anything." He reached into his pocket and pulled out the roofing nails.

Holly was fascinated. Her face showed an intense, nervous focus. She was afraid for him, yet naively excited at the same time. For Holly, fear was to the average emotion what cayenne pepper was to a spice rack; it was more powerful than the others...you felt it more. Fear and love, of course.

They ate in what seemed like fifteen minutes, but it had really been an hour and a half. Holly had asked Tim out on the date, but he insisted on picking up the check. Before the bill arrived, Holly made her second proposal of the day.

"Tim, I'd love to try to help you figure this all out. Do you mind if I stop by right after this to grab the journal? That is if you're not going to read it tonight? We have a Xerox at the office, and I can make us a duplicate. We can both read at the same time—compare notes."

Tim knew given the context of the evening that this was not a proposal-in-disguise for a one night stand, but the unofficial date had gone extremely well in his opinion, and it seemed like it would lead to other opportunities down the road. *Let the tension build a little; it's better in the long run. Besides, there are dead people in my house. Sex? Who are you kidding? You don't even dare shower at night.*

"Uh, sure… that would be great! Very helpful, too, thank you; I'll show you the candelabra, and the spot I found it in the turret. Perhaps if you're lucky, you'll even see what I saw."

Holly's jaw dropped, and she looked at him as if suddenly realizing what she was getting herself into. *Be careful what you wish for.* Tim wanted to tell her he was dreading the return but felt if he did, it might sound like he was asking for an invitation to sleep at her place. At least by inviting her in to get the journal and tour the highlights of last night's festivities, he could use her company to check out the entire house before bedtime.

With that, they got up and left in their two cars, but not before agreeing to park her car at the end of Lancaster Hill Road, and then ride the last mile or so to the house in his truck. He wanted to approach the house slowly, keeping engine noise to a minimum. Holly's VW Beetle had somewhat of a loud muffler, and Tim's truck was slightly quieter. When they had made the switch, she climbed in. Nervous energy filled the air, and neither said a word as Tim pushed on. He broke the silence as he stopped the truck just before the property line.

"I'm going to shut my headlights off now and drive slowly. Depending on what we see in the next fifty yards or so, we'll decide how to proceed. I spent a good amount of time today unloading lights and lamps, so at least we'll have more than just a painter's light. Two of the lights in the house are on timers and were set to go on at 8 pm if I set them up correctly. I've also got a flashlight in the glove compartment and a baseball bat and a rifle in the box in the bed of the truck."

"What are the baseball bat and the rifle for?" Holly asked. She was a country girl born and raised; rifles and guns were part of her upbringing. She didn't appear opposed to their presence, so Tim reconsidered what she was saying: *You can't shoot a ghost.*

"Oh, right. Well, I guess I'd rather have a false sense of security than no sense of security." Holly looked back at him as if he had two heads. He put the truck in gear and crept forward, crossing the property line. The house was still mostly obscured by the trees lining the road and the willows surrounding the pond. He drove on by the light of the moon without headlights, keeping the wheel steady.

Every so often they could see light from the house flicker through the leaves. *Good*; the timers were working. He almost wished the trees weren't blocking his view but remembered they were also serving as cover if that really mattered. Sixty yards from the house and dead even with the pond, a ten-foot gap in the trees opened up. From this vantage point, while stopped, he could see nearly the entire front of the house.

Tim let the engine idle quietly. He was pleased with the timers; that was the good news. He had put them in two rooms; the living room and the master bedroom, and both rooms were completely illuminated. He could see anything this angle could offer, which meant for the living room just about everything, but for the master bedroom, it meant only the ceiling and part of one wall.

The bad news was twofold: First, the living room and the master bedroom were not the only rooms with lights on. The turret was once again alight with a flickering glow.

Second, there was a woman in the master bedroom.

Holly gasped. "Who is that?! What is she doing in the bedroom?"

"I think that's the woman I've seen in the field," Tim replied.

His pulse quickened. *Thank God she didn't show up last night*, he thought. *There's no way you would have stayed.*

Holly interrupted his thought: "Is there any chance she lives around here, and she's crazy or something? Maybe that was her kid last night?"

"You know more about my neighbors than I do, Holly, and you know they don't live close-by. Oh and, I didn't light the candle that's burning in the turret right now. I might have another delivery up there."

"That light up there is not yours? Tim, stop; if you're messing with me, I want to know. No bullshit, please!"

"I'm not messing around, I promise you. I'm just as shocked as you are, wondering if the whole town is in on some sort of practical joke!" They locked eyes and Holly saw he was telling the truth.

The woman paced with purpose, all business, or worse… *angry*; he couldn't tell.

"Tim, I'm freaking out. This is the creepiest thing I've ever seen! Let's go back!"

"Wait, do you mind if I can at least see what she's up to? I don't think she knows we're here. I don't think they want to hurt us or we wouldn't have had such a nice date tonight. Besides, don't worry, I've got a baseball bat." He smiled at her, attempting to make her feel at ease. Holly exhaled, calmed down a bit and managed a nervous smile. *She got the joke even in a moment like this.* "We'll wait until she's gone and then put the candle out. What do you think?" Tim still felt as though he couldn't ask her to stay overnight; plus, his house could burn down.

She looked him in the eyes, speechless. Then she looked at the house. The woman was still moving about, ranting, perhaps. It was impossible to tell exactly what she was doing.

"She might not have been in the house at all last night, Tim. Maybe she doesn't even know you're here yet—and she doesn't look harmless in the least. Let's go, please. I think I could deal with the boy; I'm not sure, but *she* scares me."

Tim had been on the fence, but Holly pushed him off to the safer side. He would have to trust the candelabra, or whoever lit the candle to protect the house from burning down. He reached down to put the truck into gear, but the engine died. He immediately turned the key to restart, and the only sound was a series of clicks. They both looked at each other in silent panic but said nothing. He exhaled slowly, rested his forehead on the steering wheel, and tried again. Not even a click. *Of all the fucking clichés…*

"Okay Tim, get the gun," she said.

"All right. Let's get out quietly together, get the rifle, leave the truck, and run back to your car."

"What's that, like a mile? Are you sure? What if we just—*Oh, I don't know.*" Holly was in shock.

He turned his head and looked out the windows, then grabbed the flashlight but left it off. Instead, he held it like a club. "Are you ready?"

"Okay, but do it quietly!" she reminded him.

Tim grabbed the handle and pulled. It was stuck. He checked the door lock which would push and pull freely, but the door handle itself remained fixed. "How's your door? I'm stuck." He began to feel the beginnings of claustrophobia—blood rushed to his head.

Holly tried as well, with the same result; the door wouldn't budge. Tim tried the window crank, but it too was frozen. *Someone had them trapped.*

"I can't sit here and wait for whatever she's got planned." He removed his jacket and wrapped it around the flashlight. Making noise didn't matter anymore; escape was paramount. The ghost seemed to know they were there and had them hostage while she…*paced?*

He finished wrapping the coat around the flashlight and told Holly to shield her eyes, then wound up and swung. They both expected an explosion of glass, but instead, the flashlight met the window, cracked it and bounced off as if it was backed with cement. He hurt his hand, expecting follow-through; instead the hand bent painfully, and he dropped the flashlight.

He ate the pain as best he could, perhaps more for Holly's benefit than for the woman in the bedroom. "Son of a bitch!" Stars flew beneath his closed eyelids as he shook his hand, rubbing it, feeling bones and tendons for damage. A trickle of blood dripped between two knuckles.

"Are you okay?" she asked, alarmed. "Let me see."

"*Oh, man,*"... His eyes were shut tight as he winced, and for a few short seconds, he didn't care what the woman in the window was doing. She seemed oblivious to the commotion going on sixty yards away, and continued to move about the bedroom, pacing and perhaps talking to herself—or someone else out of view. Holly, eyes hardly leaving the spectacle upstairs, wondered why the woman had not begun to approach them.

Tim shook his hand in pain again, loosening the tightness. It was only a jammed finger; he would be fine. He studied the spider-webbed, but still intact driver's side window. The broken safety glass was impossible to see through, and not one pebble had fallen onto the road outside. He poked his finger gently at the center, and six shattered chunks fell easily out onto the road. Making silent progress, he placed his whole hand flat and pushed gently. Several hundred pieces crumbled and landed on top of the growing pile with minimal noise.

Relieved, he quietly cleared the whole window and prepared to climb out. As soon as he attempted to lift himself off of the seat, something grabbed him by the neck firmly and pressed him back into the seat. He held his breath, expecting the pressure to choke him out.

A palpable weight held him in place; he was pinned, although not violently so. The pressure backed off at a certain point well short of dangerous. He struggled, still unsure of his safety, grabbing at his throat, but remaining silent. Holly saw this and drew in a lungful ready to release a scream of her own, but was forced back into her seat the same way. All was quiet.

They battled the invisible grasp, but the holds tightened the more they fought. Holly wisely surrendered and felt the grip lessen. She tested it again ever so slightly only to feel renewed tightness.

"Stop fighting, it helps," she instructed.

Tim listened and relaxed, feeling the pressure yield. The two of them panted, sucking air for several seconds before exchanging glances.

"Are you okay?" she whispered. Tim nodded, still panting. He relaxed and shifted his weight slowly, still feeling the clutch—a reminder to go slow and easy. *You're not in charge,* he told himself. He eased off and waited nervously.

"How are you?" he asked her.

"I'm scared."

"Is she coming down here? If she does, we might be in trouble." He looked back up at the master bedroom, and thankfully, they witnessed her pass the window once again, still wrapped up with her mysterious agenda.

"I guess we're supposed to watch? What the hell does she want? What's she doing?" Holly was frustrated.

"I don't know. I would say she wants to show us something, but it looks like she's just pacing back and forth. I would have guessed she was angry, and I'm fine with her up there." *And on another note, this is one heck of a first date.*

At that moment, the woman walked away from the window and did not return.

"She's not coming back this time?" said Holly.

Tim felt nervous butterflies. Tim and Holly, in their immobile state, were helpless. They were fish in a barrel if the woman was coming for them.

"I don't know. It looked like she might have gone into the hallway. It's dark; I lost her."

"Is she coming to get us?" Holly was wide-eyed and worried.

"I would guess 'no'…" he lied.

They could do nothing but wait. Tim didn't mention it out loud, but he was privately paying more attention to the dark road in front of the truck, praying he would not see the woman emerge suddenly.

All at once, the two lights Tim had hooked to timers blinked out. The turret remained lit. The night became darker. Tim checked his watch: 9:37 pm.

"What time are they supposed to go out?" she asked.

"I set them for 8:00 pm until 5:00 am," he replied, wondering what would happen next.

As soon as he finished the sentence, the grip on his throat relaxed. Holly sat forward and drew in a slow breath. Their hands went to their necks instinctively.

"Let's get the hell out of here," said Tim. He turned the key once more to the sound of …*nothing.* He exhaled in defeat. *No, no, no.* In his opinion, their best bet was that run to Holly's car, but he held back. "What do you think?" he asked.

"I don't know. I'm scared, and I want to leave, but the idea of walking down that dark road doesn't make me feel much better." At that moment, the light went out in the turret.

The house was now completely dark, and the only light on Lancaster Hill Road was that of the quarter moon.

"Oh shit, Tim, this is messed up. We don't have *any* options, let's run!"

As soon as the words left her mouth, the turret candle sparked to life again, followed by the familiar dim flicker. *This is communication*, Tim recognized.

"Hold on. At least we haven't been hurt. You said yourself that there's usually a reason some ghosts can't 'rest.' Maybe there's something we're supposed to see."

"In there? With her somewhere nearby? Are you sure? Tim, it's too dangerous. We've already been…choked, who knows what's waiting inside? What if it's evil?"

"All right, let's try the car idea. Let's get out of the truck and walk toward your car....slowly. I'll do the same. I don't want to run and make more noise than necessary and attract attention. Let's keep our eyes on each other for the first few steps."

They tried the doors, and they opened; s*o far, so good.* Once they were both outside the truck and maintaining eye contact, he hand signaled: *Ready? Slowly. One...two...three...four...* They began to walk, strangulation free; but as soon as they passed the tailgate, the squeezing began again, this time not so suddenly. It was a slow, deliberate pressure that increased slightly with each step. Holly stopped immediately and felt the pressure subside. Tim took two more baby steps just to be sure. The grip tightened, leaving them with only one option.

"Okay, we don't have a choice. How's your throat?"

"It's fine, but I'm scared." She was stressed, not happy with the next step.

"I'm sorry about this whole thing. If I had known things would get physical, I wouldn't have let you come. Last night I only saw and heard things."

"I know. I wanted to come. It's not your fault. It's just that...six hours ago, when I was getting ready to meet you at the restaurant, I thought you were going to tell me about things you *thought* you saw...little creepy subtle things like, maybe I'd be able to hear a couple of footsteps, or creaky shutters, or something. You know—the first half-hour of a horror movie? And instead... I'm scared to death."

"If it makes you feel any better, I'm really glad I didn't have to do this alone." He reached for her hand, and she let him take it. "Ready to get this over with?"

"Not really, but as you said, we don't have a choice. We're either going to choke to death running for my car, or we can take what's behind door number two. Where is she, anyway? Can you see her?"

"I don't know. But I supposed she could have killed us already if she wanted to. Just be prepared for a face-to-face. Maybe we'll get lucky, and she'll tell us what she wants."

"Wishful thinking. I know a bitch when I see one," Holly said, disbelieving.

Together they walked hand in hand very quietly the sixty yards to the beginning of the driveway and the two giant maples. As they made their way up the slope, Tim watched the windows for ghostly white faces.

He weighed their options; either take the much closer main entrance near the staircase or go all the way around the corner to the side door by the barn. He didn't even have the key to the porch entrance with him. He made a move for the closest entrance, and Holly yanked his hand firmly but quietly in protest, pulling him away.

"That's near where we saw her!" she mouthed. Tim had been of the mind that the woman upstairs was gone for the evening, but Holly was right to think cautiously. Tim was also reminded that Holly, the real estate agent—knew the house as well as he did. He nodded to her, and they walked on. Once they rounded the corner of the house, the barn stood in the shadows, big door half-open looking like a great dark mouth.

He unlocked the side door quietly and stepped in, flicking on the flashlight. The interior of the carriage house brightened in the path of the beam. Slowly and quietly, they opened the glass slider to the breakfast area and checked every shadowy corner on the way in. They stood where Tim had first seen the boy's eyes shining the previous night. He attempted without the flashlight, to see down the long path of doorways that ran the length of the house but beyond the dining room was pitch black.

His first thought was to hold off shining the light anywhere near the staircase in case the woman was still upstairs. He changed his mind; however, fearing if he did not take a look, she could be as close as the living room undetected. Much too close for comfort and safety. As the light painted the walls at the other end of the house, Tim couldn't help but wonder if this kind of thing happened each and every night regardless of human presence.

Satisfied that there was no imminent danger in the lower level, they went to the turret stairs, purposefully ignoring the silent cellar door, and began the climb to the glowing room. Holly was close behind, holding his hand; neither wanted her yanked back into the darkness. He sensed déjà-vu as his head passed the floor, and his feet neared the top of the stairs. The light on the ceiling was in perpetual motion as the candle burned, and there on the desk sat the same candelabra. This time, however, it was not on top of the journal, but right in front of it, book open to a specific page.

Holly looked down at the journal, aghast. She was long beyond certain that this was no elaborate prank. She instinctively touched her neck again, feeling where the ghostly grip had restrained her and asked Tim for the flashlight so she could read.

> *Tuesday, January 18th, 1966*
> *Today from the turret, I saw the woman in the dress out in the distant pasture again. Not that I think she is a living person now, of course. She can't be after wild blueberries or grapes as Henry and I first suspected, as the season for fruit has passed. She wears no overcoat in this January freeze. She walks with purpose from the far tree line, out into the pasture and into the woods that lead to the grove. I see her take this path regularly.*
>
> *I don't know why; perhaps I was bored or something, but I decided to tempt fate and ask her some questions; maybe see if I could help her find comfort…or just talk, the way I do with the ladies at the nursing home. I threw on my overcoat, put on my boots, and made my way outside as quickly as possible to catch her before she…disappeared. I only lost sight of her for a second as I ran down the stairs but quickly reacquired her as I made the transition from*

indoors to out. She does move swiftly and doesn't seem to be slowed by the snow as much as I am. I'm not surprised, as I imagine we may not share the same laws of physics. I called out, but she was steadfast and focused on her destination...either that or she didn't hear me. I made it past the pond, still calling out, "Miss! Excuse me, Miss!" She was now a few yards from the woods and the grove, but there was still a good hundred yards of field between us. It was a windy day.

I had to stop running, as I was exhausted from the trudging. Panting, I drew in a deep breath preparing for one last attempt to call her attention. It was then that I was pushed from behind, my body thrown to the ground. Before I knew it, I was face down in the snow, weighed down as though someone was on top of me. It was hard to breathe, and I couldn't scream; if I could, it would have only been muffled by the snow. I had no idea what was going on above the surface. I could breathe somewhat but feared I might be slowly smothered if it were to continue long enough.

After what seemed like a minute, the weight released me, and I picked myself up. The woman was gone, and my face was red and numb with cold. I went back home crying, defeated and scared. I had been assaulted on this beloved property that I have so painfully decided to call home still.

Must I share my home with this woman who now poses a physical threat to me? Can I avoid her safely, or will we have chance meetings where I end up on the ground? Can it happen inside the house? Was she even the one to knock me down, or was it someone else...unseen?

As I have little to do here but to maintain the property and think for hours on end, I have always felt deep down that the woman in the field doesn't look...happy, to say the least. It is usually so peaceful here and so enjoyable. She is the only thing I have seen here with the opposite demeanor. The boy is distracting...but not a physically disruptive presence. Perhaps the woman wants nothing to do with me. I suppose if this is true, we may be able to coexist. She's in my house, on my property, but then, maybe the exact opposite is also true.

Yes, the more I think of it; at least until I learn more, it is best to keep my distance from the woman in the field.

"I told you I didn't like her..." said Holly. "...and it looks like I'm not the only one. Tim, I don't like the fact that 'the woman in the field' was actually 'the woman right here in this house' not ten minutes ago. You can't stay here tonight. And that's...not a come-on. I don't want to be re-selling this house next month. Let's grab the journal and take it back to my place. You can sleep in the guest room."

The topic was apparently not open to discussion, not that Tim disagreed with her. *I accept your offer of a good night's sleep—ghost-free with a chance of breakfast.* Holly blew out the candle and picked up the journal. Tim led them down the stairs, hoping they'd be allowed to leave. As soon as Holly was in her car leading him back to Laconia, he had to smile; *this is one hell of a first date.*

CHAPTER FOURTEEN

First Date Aftermath

It was getting late, but Tim was relieved and excited. The cold air blowing in the broken window kept him awake. It was so good not to have to brave another night alone; his eyes were bloodshot tired. At the same time, he knew he had to put his best foot forward at Holly's house; they still barely knew each other. He hoped she wouldn't hear him snore.

Her house was built in a cute little Cape Cod style. He would learn later that she too was divorced, three years before. She married a man that ended up spending too much time and money at the pubs, and when things went sour, she won the house in the settlement. Holly called it a "starter marriage," as it had lasted less than two years and there were no children. She held the front door open for him.

"How are you feeling?" she asked.

"I'm frazzled. I feel like my brain was in a blender. I'm on the hook for $35k with that place, and I can't just abandon it. I hope this Annette woman can point us in the right direction, but I'm skeptical because she died on the property and the ghosts are still there. She might even be one of them, for all I know. That wasn't her, was it? I'm kind of freaking out, I guess. How about you?"

"I'm okay but…I'm still in shock. I don't think I'll have the right words to describe tonight for quite a while. It seems like a dream—or a nightmare. That was life-changing; I'm going to look at things differently from now on for sure. And to answer your question, no, I don't think that was the woman that wrote the journal. Her clothing was definitely not something from this century. And…wow; I might have financial concerns coming up too. I'm not sure I can sell houses from now on in good conscience. I'll need to do more homework—let people know, from a moral standpoint, at least. I'm so sorry, Tim."

"I don't blame you, Holly. No one could have known."

"Yeah, I know, but…that's a dangerous situation you're in now. Let's think out loud. What's the meaning of the open book? Maybe Annette was on to something. The woman ghost is dangerous. Why else would it be left open to that page if it wasn't something we could understand?"

"Who was she? Annette, I mean. Do you know any details?"

"Honestly, no, but I will definitely take a closer look into her death and her husband's death as well. I'll check tomorrow and let you know."

She opened the journal, skipped past the sighting of the boy in the snow, and read on aloud.

> *<u>Saturday, December 18, 1965</u>*
> *As I wait for the next sighting, I will pass some time explaining myself, just in case this journal goes unfinished. I am Annette Smith, and I have lived in the house on Lancaster Hill Road since 1933. My husband Henry and I have lived here for 29 years without a supernatural occurrence, or so I had thought. He died a little over a month ago outside by our barn, his second heart attack, and I miss him terribly. We have two grown children that have moved on to have families of their own. For now, I do not see a reason to include their names or contact information, so I will leave them out of this, for the time being at least.*

As I stated, I had never thought we were being haunted, but now, looking back, I'm sure I was wrong. If you're reading this, you have most likely read the first page with the sighting of the little boy. It may not sound like much, but I can tell you that I'm completely sure beyond the shadow of a doubt that he is a ghost. Maybe you're asking yourself if perhaps the wind had filled in his footprints with snow as I was leaving the house to search for him—all I can say is…no. I was there. The wind was not strong, and I have had other sightings over the years. More years than I had even realized! I'm ashamed to admit how many years off I was. I should have noticed that he never grew up, but honestly, I never paid much attention to who he was. It could have been two or three different little boys over the years for all I knew or cared. I was busy! And it's not like we saw him every day; sometimes there were weeks or even months between sightings.

For years we had seen the woman in the plain long dress (an old-fashioned dress to be sure, but then again we do live in New Hampshire). She would walk in the distance across the pasture near the property line from time to time. We had theories about her, like; she wanted some of our blueberries, or just had a favorite walk that happened to use one of our trails. We didn't mind at all. Take the fruit; you're welcome to it. We came from Boston and were used to seeing people at all hours of the day in all sorts of places. Honestly, we were so happy and relieved to be living in NH, and we had (and still have) more property than we could ever put to use; it's the Christian thing to do if nothing else.

We had also seen a red kite flying near the same spot from time to time. It seemed normal at first, but then one day,

Henry wondered out loud why he had never seen anyone flying it. After that, we even ventured out to try and find that someone once or twice, but as soon as we looked away for any reason or the kite flew behind the trees it would be gone. One day as I took a long winter walk by myself I found a snowman staring at me from just inside the tree line near the grove.

If you're reading this, I assume you have seen the grove. If you haven't, walk straight out past the pond about two hundred and fifty yards and make a hard left into the forest. The grove starts maybe thirty yards in from there. We believe it used to be an old Christmas tree farm. I imagine that back when our "neighbors" the ghosts were living people, and the Christmas tree grove was maintained properly that the pasture was larger. Perhaps even today, the little boy that flies a kite still stands in the same spot he used to, even though some wild trees have grown in his way.

In the coming days (and pages) I hope to find these things out, and I will report it here. These are certainly odd or jarring things if you've never seen a ghost. If you haven't seen one of them yet, perhaps save reading this journal for the day you do, or, for whomever you sell this house to.

"What the hell! I've been there less than a week, and I've seen everything she's written so far. She said she'd been there since 1933? Did I win the ghost lottery or something?" Tim was frustrated.

"Slow down; we're only about four pages in! Who knows what's next. I want to know how the hell she put up with it all. How could she sleep with them running around? She must have been either very strong or…maybe a hippie. They're peaceful and tolerate everything, right? She kept a journal, so maybe she was into it."

Tim chuckled and then yawned; he was running on fumes. Holly continued skimming.

"Annette Smith. I vaguely remember that name."

"What's tomorrow?" Tim asked. "I've forgotten everything. It feels like a Saturday because I went on a date."

"Oh, was that a date? Or were you with another woman before our business meeting?" she deadpanned.

"Well, you invited me back to your house, didn't you?"

Good one, she thought. Tim's overtired but still joking.

"I do this all the time for clients who I sell haunted houses to." Holly laughed at her own joke. She was tired, too, and after all of the stress of the evening, the laughter felt good. He laughed back. *She's funny*; that had to be a good thing. They paused to catch their breath; what a night. "Tomorrow is only Tuesday," she frowned. "What do you have planned?" The laughter died.

Tim exhaled. "Oh, boy. I'm refurbishing an old house that I depend on for my financial future." He put his face in his hands.

"Tim… That's not safe. What if she shows up? Even Annette wrote we should steer clear. I wonder if she was the one to open that page up for us."

"You think? She got smothered out in that field, just like we did in the truck. And do you think Annette is in a state of 'unrest'? If I were her, I'd rather be at peace with my late husband—I mean, she said she missed him, right?"

"Maybe you're right, but shouldn't you take a little time off? Maybe wait and see if we can figure this out?"

"I… I don't think so. I don't have tons of time or money at this point. I took a lot of time off waiting for the closing and all of the paperwork. I have to go back. If I see her, I'll keep clear. I was making all kinds of noise in there the other day replacing the front wall in the living room—saws, hammers, the whole works. She didn't bother me then. Plus, I've seen her only out in the field. Never in the house…well, until tonight."

"Yeah, that's what I'm talking about! You don't know where she'll be!"

He stopped to think. Stress made itself a nice thorny nest between his ears. "I guess I'm going to have to take the chance," and then his brow furrowed even more. "*Oh, no.*"

"What?" she asked.

"I…have my kids for visitation this weekend; my ex is going away." His face reddened and any remaining humor drained from his face. She let him think for a few seconds. *Avoid giving parental advice on the first date.*

"All right, well, you don't have to figure that out yet. Friday is still four days away," she offered.

"We…we haven't gone into our personal lives very much yet Holly, obviously, first date and all, right? This is usually not stuff you talk about right away, but my personal life sucked for the last three years. It was an ugly divorce. The kids were used as weapons and props, manipulated by their mother. She managed to put some things into their heads from time to time about Daddy having better things to do and things like that. She fought me at every turn, even though she was the one who wanted out.

"I realize this is all he said/she said crap, but at the end of the day; there is a little bit of pressure not to make waves and keep the peace even though the divorce is final. It's just not worth the hassle. Mountains turn into molehills very quickly in Sheila's world, and it's because she wants them to. In the end, the kids end up paying for it, and more often than not it ends up being expensive. I'm sorry to tell you all this, but my good judgment fell asleep a couple of hours ago. I'm just burnt."

"Yeah, you're damaged goods, Tim—too much information. Actually, I'm kidding. I kinda get it. My ex had a similar situation going on for a little bit. We'll see what happens. But as far as this weekend goes, if worse comes to worst, you can always get a motel and take the kids to Funspot for the day. You'll be a hero. Tell them you had to fumigate or something. They can go report that to Mommy when she picks their brains about your humongous new house."

We'll see what happens. Tim took note that Holly didn't give him a complete pass. She had been in a similar situation with another man, and it didn't go well. He'd have to morph his previous life into his new life carefully and not let the ex-Mrs. Russell interfere all too often. But Sheila knew how to push his buttons, and it would not be easy. He couldn't count how many times she had used the phrase "for your children" in the last three years. That and several others like it.

"Thanks, Holly. I like that motel idea, but maybe I'll just stay away during the nighttime, maybe get some work done at the house during the day while the kids play close by or something. Sorry, lots of thoughts—information overload. Two very busy nights in a row, but I want to tell you—I had a lot of fun tonight. Thanks for the invite."

Holly's adrenaline had subsided, and she was tired too. It was late, but she stopped everything for a second, walked over and kissed him on the lips, then nonchalantly went to the linen closet and got him a towel. She brought it upstairs to the guest room, and Tim followed.

"Here you go. There's an extra toothbrush in the bottom drawer of the bathroom vanity."

"I'm glad I didn't go through that alone. I'm glad you were there…to help me out. If I had gone through two nights in a row of that alone, I might begin to doubt…just about everything I guess—even *reality*. At least now I know I'm not going crazy."

She smiled at his kind words. "I had a nice time, too. I would say 'fun,' but the part in the truck wasn't much fun."

He laughed and touched her elbow, moving in for another kiss. She lifted her head, and he stepped into it. They kissed, although short and sweet, respecting the original plans. She didn't want to be too inviting in her own house, and he didn't want to push his luck. It *was* a successful date; no need to get greedy. They said a very pleasant goodnight.

CHAPTER FIFTEEN
Back to the Grove

April 20th, 1971

Holly was up early for work. Tim woke slowly as he always did, remembering where he was. Despite the ghostly encounters, he had especially pleasant memories of the previous evening. He rose and stripped the linens from the bed (to show he was making no assumptions about staying over again) and laid the quilt back over the bed. Then he went downstairs and sat on the couch waiting for Holly to emerge from her bedroom.

While he waited, he searched the room with his eyes. The house was modest, yet cozy. She had a fireplace in the living room and wall-to-wall carpeting. There was a shelf built into the wall over the television full of books and photographs. He was semi-relieved to see that there were no pictures of Holly with another guy, although he was somewhat ashamed for thinking this way. *How old are you Tim…fifteen?* Most of the photos seemed to be family-related: Parents, perhaps a sibling or two, and maybe a niece or nephew; but the visual tour ended suddenly when his eyes fell upon the journal on the coffee table.

She emerged from the bedroom dressed for work. "Good morning!" It was slightly awkward, staying overnight yet sleeping separately for Tim, and he felt useless sitting on the couch with nothing to do. Thankfully she was smiling. "I'm sorry, I don't have much in the way of food in the house. I need to go shopping; I've been so busy. I usually grab a coffee on the way to work, so I can't even offer you that unless you want to stop…"

"Oh no, don't worry about it," he replied. "I can grab something later. I might be dead right now if I didn't sleep over, so don't worry; you have nothing to apologize for."

She laughed a little bit and then looked at him with a measure of concern. "Tim, be very careful today."

"I will."

"Stay near the telephone. I will check in with you, and I'll take the journal to work and start making copies when the boss isn't looking. Those toner cartridges aren't cheap, and we'd better get reading. *Anything* Annette learned over the years could help us. Do you want to lock up here when you're ready to go? I have to run."

"No, I'll walk out with you. Hey, are you doing anything tonight? Do you want to get some dinner again?"

She smiled. "Yeah, I was hoping you'd ask. I asked last time, after all, right?"

"You did because your boss was waiting for you to get off the phone. You didn't give me a chance!"

"Oh, so you called to ask me out? I thought you called because you were angry. I sold you a haunted house!" Tim prepared to refute her claim but saw she was smiling, teasingly.

"Nice try. You're a real firecracker, aren't you?" said Tim.

"I might be… Think about what kind of food you want to eat; I know the area pretty well. Just watch your back today; I don't want to eat alone tonight."

"I plan on being alive. Oh, and don't get caught making copies!" He took hold of one of her arms and kissed her. She smiled as she drove away. He followed her to a fork in the road about a mile from her house where they turned in separate directions.

Tim enjoyed the drive from Laconia back to Sanborn, despite the cold April morning blowing through the shattered window. Funny thing about love—even the cold spring morning didn't bother him. It wasn't exactly *love* yet, of course, but it was the best thing he'd felt in a long time. It didn't even matter that their first date had been so dangerous—in fact, it might have even helped—a good healthy thrill never hurt a romance.

As he drove on, Tim marveled at how easy it was for two people to get along when they both *wanted to*; as simple as that. A relationship like that had no petty fights or pet peeves—no manipulations, cold shoulders or grudges. It had been a long time since he and Sheila had cooperated on anything, and if they had ever been so cooperative, he couldn't remember. Their relationship had slowly deteriorated; it didn't just happen overnight. All it took was one night out with Holly to remember how things were supposed to be; it was very refreshing.

Post-divorce, he didn't even fear *death.* Divorce was itself a death of sorts, and he had lived through it. He survived something he had always feared and never thought would happen to him—*betrayal.* It wasn't easy, and in the painful process, he had been forced to part with much of what he had loved: Living with his kids, most of his money (meaning freedom to live his life the way he wanted to) and the comforts of home. He lost an entire lifestyle and was forced to start over alone in a studio apartment, and he got through it emotionally. Now, not many things scared him. *When you've got nothing, you've got nothing to lose.*

Now, as he drove from his new girlfriend's house on the way to his new house it was clear he had hit bottom sometime in the past already—perhaps it was the day of the divorce—and was on the way back up. He had his name on a new piece of property, and a sweetheart of a woman risking trouble at her work by copying the journal for him. Even if she wasn't copying it just for *him,* but for the *two of them*—that was just as pleasant a thought.

Tim realized he had begun to care again. His fear of death

had returned; Holly might be someone to makes plans around. He would have to be careful at the house.

He stopped at a diner and had a quick breakfast, beginning to think of the day ahead. There was much to do. When breakfast was over, he climbed back into the truck and noticed that despite his good mood, his energy ebbed the closer he got to the house. *Duty calls, but at least it's daylight.* As he coasted down the bumpy road, he kept his eyes peeled for the woman and the kite. He exhaled as he reached the sixty-yard mark, not even realizing that he had been holding his breath. It was the spot he and Holly had been accosted the night before, now memorialized by a shiny pile of shattered glass glistening in the sun. *Mental note: Fix the truck window.* He slowed and then stopped to observe.

While the truck idled, his eyes surveyed. All seemed in order. Satisfied, he drove on and up into the driveway, much slower and with more caution than ever before. His eyes scanned the windows as he passed, once again looking for faces peering *out.* The daylight, however, produced too many reflections and hid the house's contents.

He lowered his head and looked up at the turret, then turned left at the bend in the driveway, backed up into the elbow, and pointed the truck out toward the road. Now he was ready for a quick escape if need be. Grabbing the truck's flashlight, he got out and went in the side entrance. There he paused, listening. Hearing nothing, he proceeded.

Tim felt as though his original tour of the house had been *good*, but after the festivities of the past two evenings, he decided to give some of the lesser-explored parts the fine-toothed comb treatment. His time spent in the carriage house up to this point had been in passing only. Now, he paced the walls examining baseboards, corners, and windows, not really looking for anything in particular, but getting to know the house better.

The two windows across the room from the side door looked out on the tiny back lawn dotted with tall pine trees that had gone wild. It was a small, dark, sunless dreary patch of land, and looked as though no one had ever spent time out there and enjoyed the space. It was the ugly sister to the expansive front yard with its view of the pond, pasture, and forest. From the carriage house window, he could see across the entire back of the house almost to the road. If it weren't for the overgrown shrubs and a lone pear tree up against the building, he could have.

He entered the main body of the house, passing the breakfast area and kitchen because they were smallish rooms in which he had already spent significant time. The basement was a different matter; he had only been downstairs twice and had never explored some of the shadowy corners. He grabbed a hammer from the toolbox in the dining room, flicked on the stairway light and headed down the wiggly staircase cautiously. The floor was dry (thankfully), the ceiling was low and about the only thing down here was the furnace and a well-worn winter snow shovel that the previous owners—*Annette and Henry*—must have used.

He followed the cold, moist walls, which were built of stone between upright beams. The stones were held together with white cement or mortar filling the cracks between the rocks. The low ceiling left the naked light bulb right in the way at eye level. *It would be very easy to take that out with my head,* he thought. The bulb did all it could to illuminate the room but could not reach around the furnace. He clicked on the flashlight and peered behind the old mass of iron and piping. The spiders had the run of the place back there; he would have to clear gobs of webbing.

Behind the furnace, one of the upright wood support beams in the wall stuck out from the stones and blocked his view to the other side, so he went around. The furnace was closer to the wall on the right side, so he was forced to turn sideways and shimmy in. The cobwebs deep in the corner were again dense, and when he had them cleared out, he found a small stack of firewood or lumber scraps at the end of the nook. He pulled the boards out and tossed them into the center of the room, then turned the flashlight back around to see what was left. Remaining in the shadows was a toy drum, and a rocking horse stood on its end. *Must have belonged to the boy,* Tim shuddered.

One of the runners on the horse was broken off by a third; perhaps the child's father had intended on making a new one and hadn't gotten around to it. Tim cleared the corner of toys and went back in for one last look. Peering around the back of the furnace, his light shone on the previously unseen side of the support beam. Leaning against it was a rifle.

He grabbed the rifle from its dusty hiding place and backed out carefully into the open room, being careful not to knock it. Once under the light of the naked bulb, he took a closer look at his find. It was surprisingly long and fixed with a bayonet. The metal on the side was stamped "1861 U.S. Springfield" along with an engraving of a small eagle. The steel was corroded and pitted badly, probably because it had been kept in the often-damp (and sometimes soaking wet) cellar for over a hundred years.

The stock was warped and swollen, and the butt plate had broken off due to repeated soakings. The word "Millie" carved into it by what Tim guessed might have been a pocket knife. He ran his finger over the carving; *wife or girlfriend*, he guessed. He was no historian; in fact, he was embarrassingly ignorant on the subject. Wasn't the Civil war sometime in the 1800's? Could this be a Civil War rifle? His school days were so far behind he'd forgotten just about everything.

He brought everything upstairs. Once back in the kitchen, he set his finds down in the breakfast area and continued with the already worthwhile inspection. The formal dining area had little in the way of new things to offer, so he went to the back windows. The right one was broken and boarded, so he peered out the left one and saw the overgrown boredom of the backyard from a different angle.

The front porch revealed nothing new. It was a "three-season" porch, which to Tim just meant it was too cold to enjoy most of the year. He skipped the rest of the house, having explored the remaining areas thoroughly. Once the home examination was finished, he felt a bit more at ease. It probably didn't mean a thing in terms of safety since ghosts might come and go at any minute, but he found comfort in the fact that he had gotten to know all of the nooks, crannies and hiding places a little bit better. He checked his watch; he hadn't yet pounded a nail, and it was almost 10 am.

He chose the back wall of the office behind the living room as the project du jour, continuing with his strategy of fixing the outer walls first. Just as the other day in the living room, he ripped out the old lath and plaster and replaced it with modern-day materials. At noon the phone rang, and he looked at it suspiciously; the last time he answered the phone nobody was on the other end, and just after that the boy showed up.

To his relief and cheer, it was Holly. "Are you still alive? What's happening?" she asked.

"Still alive. I'm glad you called. I got kind of a late start, but I've torn out the back wall in the office and put it back together."

"Anybody *there* today? Any sightings?"

"Nobody; I was a nervous wreck coming down the road, so I gave the house an informal sweep before I started work. I found a couple of antiques down in the cellar. Stuff nobody's seen in probably a century. They were way behind the furnace. I'll show you later. How's work for you?"

"Well, the morning has been slow, but the good news is my boss is out of the office, and I was able to copy the entire journal; three hundred pages." This was a huge help. Now they could divide and conquer. Another pair of eyes reading Annette's work might even prove to be life-saving.

"Thank you! Were you able to read any of it while you were copying?"

"Not a lot. Today was more about not getting caught. I was dodging coworkers, too; I didn't want them to ask what I was doing. I did gather, however, that Annette did some legwork on trying to find out who used to live there. I couldn't read it thoroughly. Annette may end up saving us lots of time, let's hope. We might be able to build on what she learned." Tim started to daydream about a house without ghosts but stopped before he started counting his chickens.

"We still don't know much more about Annette's death, right? It sounds like you've been busy with the journal."

"Oh, yes I did check into that a little bit, but I don't have much to report. I asked one of my coworkers who used to be friends with one of Annette's kids. Her death shocked everybody. She was young and in good shape. She just went to bed and didn't wake up, apparently. I'm not sure how long it was before they found her—Oh, and as for the journal, I'll help you get through it, but you're going to read too, Mr. Russell. All hands on deck! Think of it as a chance to get your house back."

"Okay. I know, I will. Are we still on for tonight? Did you pick a restaurant?"

"Yeah, I know a place if you like Chinese food. As for sleeping arrangements, you were a perfect gentleman last night, so I think I can trust you. You are cordially invited to sleep in my guest room again, and you can owe me for saving your life again."

"Well, thank you, that's mighty nice of you," he replied with a touch of sarcasm. "I have *another* favor to ask, though. Do you mind if I shower at your place before we go out? Although the chances might be slim, I would prefer not to have to come running out of the house naked if somebody interrupts me."

Holly pretended to be put upon: "Oh wow. I give you an inch, and you take a mile. Is there anything else I can do for you?" Tim had several dirty replies lined up, but it was still too early in the relationship for sex jokes.

"That'll do for now, but I do thank you for your hospitality and sweet maple syrup charm."

"Sounds good, Mr. Russell. Call me when you're done for the day, and I'll stop work at the same time."

As Tim returned the handset to the cradle, something in the corner of his eye flashed. He crouched down, then ran to the window, heart racing. He peered out; it was the boy, running across the lawn very close to the house and onto the driveway. Tim watched as he disappeared into the woods at the bend.

He stood up straight and paused, nervously, indecisive. *What to do?* He *should* let it go. On the other hand, the office wall was finished, and it was either start another project or work toward solving this mystery in broad daylight. There wasn't much time to decide. The boy didn't try to hurt him the other night; he'd follow safely and keep his distance. Tim untied his apron quickly and ran through the front door. It was cool out; spring-like. When this was over he would have a story for Holly, and perhaps a piece of the puzzle that even Annette hadn't encountered.

He jogged swiftly and quietly up an old footpath he didn't know existed. It began at the corner of the driveway and made its way up a slight incline into the woods. He could tell already he was most likely on his way to the grove. The forest was near-silent; barely a breeze stirred the air, and the birds were suspiciously absent. The boy was nowhere to be seen. Two hundred yards into the forest, Tim was surprised once more as the grove suddenly opened up in front of him.

It must have been the different route that tricked him; he knew it might be coming up but was still surprised by the abrupt *unveiling* of the camouflaged rows and aisles. He was entering the grove lengthwise this time; from the very ends of the aisles, not cutting across the middle. He broke his run and stopped altogether, *adjusting.*

He listened for footsteps or any clue that would lead him to the boy. It wasn't apparent from his vantage point how many rows of the grove went right or left, although he guessed there could be many more to the left as the woods went deeper. Relying on impulse, he turned left and walked as quietly as he could along the edge of the wild forest so he might reacquire the path easily should he need to escape.

He padded silently on a soft bed of spruce needles, grateful he did not have to trudge through piles of noisy leaves and acorns that maples, elms, birches, and oaks drop. One row passed, then two. In the third row, down the aisle roughly eighty yards away, the boy stared.

He faced Tim, seeming to know he had been followed. From this distance, the features of his face were indiscernible; it was nearly impossible to make out the details; eyes, nose, mouth. He could only see two shady spots that were the boy's eye sockets. He looked like a skull.

They stared at each other for what seemed like an eternity. Tim was too spooked to stand still for long, and nervously raised a hand. *Howdy, neighbor.*

The boy didn't move. It took all of Tim's willpower to remain.

He approached me the other night—checked me out good. Why not now?

They remained at a standoff as Tim scrambled for another idea. A moment later, the boy made a move; turning and walking slowly to Tim's left, keeping his distance; cutting across rows.

Tim followed. He crossed the first row, losing him for a second, then reacquiring in the next aisle. The boy waited for him to cross, staring, then moved on.

Another row of trees passed, and the blank stare waited again as Tim crossed. On the third turn, the boy failed to emerge, and Tim found himself staring down an empty passage. He poked his head back, but saw nothing, then looked down the third and final aisle again; still no boy. There *was* something there however that hadn't registered the first time he looked. Way down at the other end of the aisle was what appeared to be a mound of leaves. Normally a pile of dead forest debris would not call for a second glance, but Tim had a feeling. *It means something to him.*

Before considering a chilling walk to the pile, Tim tried two more times to find the boy again, feigning and hesitating amongst the rows to no avail. The temptation to approach the mounds was the next logical step, but he wasn't ready for such bravery. Perhaps just seeing where the boy had been headed, along with the mysterious pile (and the rifle!) was enough for one day. He had plenty of new information to work with. He'd best catch up on some journal reading before going on a big-time ghost hunt, especially alone. *You're gonna catch hell already when you tell Holly what you did,* he thought.

He turned back to the way he'd come in and found the tiny path that led to the driveway. His first few steps walking away from the grove made him feel as if he were being watched. He stopped suddenly and turned back to look…just an empty row. He'd had enough of the grove for today. After a few walking steps, he decided it would be much better to run.

The figure in the black dress stood in the back of the hayloft and watched as Tim emerged from the path in the corner of the driveway. He was running, checking behind himself twice…as if he had seen a ghost. He even took a third look before entering the house through the side door.

As if…he had seen…a ghost?

CHAPTER SIXTEEN
Second Date

April 20th, 1971 (evening)

Tim and Holly met at her house where they both showered (separately) and got ready for a Chinese dinner at a restaurant called Eastern House. They made small talk, as Holly requested they save the juicy conversation for the actual date. They took her car because Tim's side window was still broken.

She brought the Xeroxed copy of the journal inside with them but left the original at home. Both of them were in good spirits, no pun intended. Tim noticed that she was smiling a lot, which was always a good sign. The previous night couldn't have been any stranger…she might be something really special. He felt a wonderful excitement, and he sensed the feeling might be mutual.

He teased her, "If you liked last night, you're going to love the second date. Last night was boring compared to what we have in store tonight." She faked as if she were about to spin around on her heels and walk out, but then spun back around comically and sat down.

"Oh, boy, I can't wait! Last night was getting choked in your truck, what is tonight going to be?" The last line came out a bit on the loud side. Tim thought he saw a couple of heads pause conversation at nearby tables for a quick second.

"Hey hey, not so loud, you're going to ruin my reputation, I'm new around here," Tim said. She blushed and covered her face slightly.

"No, no, just kidding. Nobody heard that I'm pretty sure…"

"Me and my big mouth; how are things? Any 'occurrences'?"

Tim paused and got serious. He would tell her the truth, no ifs ands or buts…but the truth might land him in a little trouble. He hadn't anticipated the question so soon, so bluntly. "Yeah…I saw the boy again." Her eyes widened as her jaw dropped.

"Where was he? Did you get the hell out of there?"

"No…I…followed him. But of course, it was broad daylight."

It was a preemptory deflection on his part, attempting to cover up the fact he had followed the boy, with the nonsense that the daylight made it safer. She focused her glare a bit but said nothing, and waited for his explanation. *This had better be good.*

"As soon as you and I hung up, I saw him run by the living room window outside. He went up a path in the corner of the driveway up into the woods. I hung back, trying to stay a safe distance, and kept my eyes peeled. The woods opened up into the grove, except I was looking down the rows lengthwise. I could see down the whole aisle, like a hundred yards, or however long it is. He was way down at the other end, staring back—but I couldn't make out his face or read his emotions. He started to cut across the rows, and I followed on a parallel course, staying the same distance apart, and suddenly, he was gone. At that point, I just got out of there. But I was much, much closer to him the other night—this was nothing compared to that."

She sighed, pleased at least that he didn't have to be a macho man and attempt to approach the boy. "At least you got out of there, but please, please, please, don't be a hero! We've really got to read about these ghosts first!"

Tim thought he heard the conversations hush somewhat again

at the surrounding tables when Holly said the word "ghost." *Uh, oh well.*

"Tonight after dinner we'll be very romantic and read some of that journal," he agreed, passive-aggressively.

"I can hear the sarcasm. Are you a stubborn man, Tim Russell?" she asked.

Ooh. That's a loaded question if I've ever heard one, thought Tim.

"If I say yes, is it a deal breaker?" he replied.

"Right now I'd have to say honestly probably not."

Tim swooned a tiny bit.

"Well then, I'll be honest too, and say 'maybe sometimes.'" He reached over and squeezed her hand. They were quiet for a moment enjoying the *rush.*

"I saw something else today, too, but I'm not sure it was anything."

Holly's glazed eyes cleared momentarily. Her smile disappeared.

"What did you see?" Her look made him feel his change of topic was ill-timed.

"Uh…it might be nothing, but I think the kid led me to something in the last row of the grove. It looked like a pile of leaves, but I didn't want to go check it out yet. I just wanted to get out of there."

"Oh, so you do have some limits. That's good to hear. You said you wanted to get out of there…why?"

"I was creeped out! Look, just because I slept overnight there and followed the boy into the grove doesn't mean I'm not afraid; I am!"

"A pile of leaves creeped you out?"

"No. The boy did—that and the fact that he disappeared. Plus the grove is damn creepy, too! You and I were looking for words to describe it that day of the tour. What did we say?"

"Creepy. I've always thought it was creepy, but I *liked* creepy then. Now I'm not so sure."

"Okay, well that's part of what I was afraid of. The whole atmosphere, not to mention the actual dead boy I followed up there. Anyway, I felt he was trying to show me the pile of leaves. He disappeared, and that was the next thing I saw."

"Well, it will be interesting to see if Annette knows anything about it WHEN WE READ THE JOURNAL, right?"

After a few more minutes talking about the rifle, they had a pleasant two-hour meal, drank some wine and talked about things in their lives *not* related to ghosts, even though Holly had brought the journal copy into the restaurant. They didn't open it; contrary to Holly's good intentions, *life goes on* was the mood at the table. When they were through, they went straight to Holly's place as planned. It was safer, and there was a chance they could get some studying done.

CHAPTER SEVENTEEN

Annette's Good Work

Saturday, January 22nd, 1966
Last night I heard the little boy running around. I've never heard that before. It was terrifying trying to ignore the sound after I had checked out the premises. At first, I was upstairs and heard him moving around downstairs. I thought an animal had gotten into the house, so I went down and grabbed the fireplace poker. When I made it down to the kitchen, I heard the same footsteps upstairs where I had just been. It was shocking and unnerving, and I thought for a second I might be losing my marbles. There were obviously no raccoons in the kitchen, so I cautiously made my way back up. The footsteps started again as I crossed the living room but stopped as soon as I touched the first stair. I pressed on, and after I got back in bed I heard him once more, back downstairs. I didn't get much sleep last night. I miss Henry so much.

It makes me wonder why we've had so many sightings since Henry's death. As I have already written, we did see them on-property from time to time, but we didn't even know they were ghosts. Now they're in and around the house at just about any time. As a result, I have become suspicious of his death. I know he worked hard and had a history of heart problems, but it seems more than coincidental that he died, and then they just started showing up—all the time.

Let's see: what do I know? Allow me to think on paper and organize my thoughts. First, I believe that most people do not die and come back as ghosts; otherwise, we would see them everywhere, all of the time. Therefore, the people that do come back as ghosts must come back for a reason. Assuming Heaven is for angels and Hell is for demons, ghosts must exist in some sort of unrest. "Unrest" to me means unhappiness or perhaps injustice, or maybe a task left incomplete. So why would a little boy be in a state of unrest? Emotions are simple at young ages. If my theories are true, then a little boy would have very few tasks left to complete, but he might be unhappy or could be a victim of something unjust. My guess: he was murdered. Common sense tells me a natural death would not result in "unrest," and this boy seems frozen forever at eight or nine years old. So I feel some duty to look into that further.

As for the woman: I never see her with the boy. Figuring out her problem might prove to be more difficult, as adults can have a range of emotions or a boatload of incomplete tasks. Perhaps it is because she can't find the boy. Perhaps she is not even related to the boy (not my current theory, but it is possible). And what is her story? Was she murdered, too? If that's true, how did she die? Why did she knock me down into the snow? Was it even her that knocked me down in the snow?

To this day, I have not seen either of them up close. Perhaps I won't ever see her in the house, and that's fine with me. However, all of this activity has helped me decide to do some deep digging on the previous owners.

Monday, January 24, 1966
I could barely wait for this Monday morning and for the Town Hall to open so I could start my research. The rest of the weekend was relatively quiet, ghost-wise. I did, however, have trouble getting to sleep last night anticipating that I would begin to hear footsteps again. Thankfully I didn't.

What I found in the town records gives me goosebumps and also tells me I have made the right decision to look deeper. The owners before us moved here in the year 1894 and stayed for 39 years. Joseph and Rebecca Hobson. Before the Hobsons lived here, it was Robert and Katherine Miller, and they lived here from 1863-1894, a total of 31 years. Before that, I don't know. This is the part that gives me chills. The actual records were there, but they were illegible. It is hard to put into words, but...they were deliberately and violently smudged. It looked as if someone had taken a charcoal pencil and scrubbed the page from right to left from top to bottom. The pages also looked as if they had been soaked in coffee and dried that way, with no attempt at cleanup. They were brittle, and I had to use great care with them, even though they were unreadable and useless anyway.

I showed the damaged records to the clerk at the desk, but of course, she had no answers. I suppose in the back of my mind, I know. Some dead soul doesn't want anyone to know who lived here or what happened. I suppose my next step is the library.

Tuesday, January 25, 1966

I know the house was built in 1860 and the smudged records end in 1863. So I went to the library and began scouring the microfilm of the Sanborn Crier newspaper for those years. I made it through 1860 and 1861 today just skimming, and I didn't see anything that caught my eye. This is proving to be a little more time-consuming than I thought it would be. Some of the work around the house went undone. I'm tired and a little discouraged.

Wednesday, January 26, 1966

To my horror, I woke this morning with my journal laid out on my chest, opened to my January 19th entry (the day I decided to start my investigations). I know for sure that I did not bring the journal with me to bed; I had left it in the turret like I always do. When I woke, the house was silent, and the sun was just coming up, and there it was. I do not think that the page it was left open to was a coincidence, but rather a message. That day's entry expressed passion and desire to explore the occurrences in the house today and... years past.

Now the motivation is not only my own, but I may have also motivated someone else. This could be the answer to my previous question; why are there so many ghosts around here nowadays? Well, because YOU, Annette, are taking an interest! Help us!

I feel I'm being pushed in a direction by someone who used to live here and is no longer of this world. Somebody other than, I presume, the little boy, who would know nothing of things like town records, would he? The underlying message of the open book left on my sleeping body is terrifying to me because I feel I do not have a choice anymore. What have I gotten myself into?

Wednesday, January 26, 1966 (night)
Today's trip to the library was more productive than yesterday's. I was able to finish 1862 and 1863, and my research may have brought me my first clue. In the obituaries section of May 12, 1862, I read that a soldier from Lancaster Hill Road was killed in preparatory exercises for the war, right here in New Hampshire. He had been shipped back to Sanborn from Concord for burial at Tower Hill Cemetery. His name was Thomas Pike. I guess whoever destroyed the records in the town hall might not know how to deal with microfilm? Tonight I will perform an experiment. I will write five names in this journal, each across two pages. Then I will close the book and leave it on the desk in the turret. I'll also leave a pen. It sounds so silly to write these words.

Holly sat on her couch with Tim and turned the next several pages. Page one said "John" only. The next said, "Sherman." Following these pages were: "George," "Brown," "William," "Lincoln," "Thomas," "Pike," "Daniel," and "Boone."

"Hey, she thought we might be haunted by the ghost of Daniel Boone," Tim kidded. Holly elbowed him and continued reading.

Thursday, January 27, 1966
Writing this makes my pulse race. I woke early this morning with a purpose. Thankfully no book had been left on my person or anywhere in the bedroom. I rose and headed straight for the turret, fireplace poker in hand, mindful of my surroundings, and anything that might be...amiss. I am distrustful of the ghosts...they're everywhere nowadays! I opened the door to the turret stairs and ascended cautiously, listening carefully as I went. Of course, there on the desk lay the journal, and it was open to "Thomas Pike."

Instinctively I looked behind me, as it seemed someone might witness my discovery. My eyes searched the pond, and the field, but saw nothing. I turned to the left looking over the roof and to the barn, still nothing. I relaxed somewhat, picked up the open journal, and sat down. Examining the pages, there were no marks of any kind. The pen I left for—Thomas—lay where I had placed it, untouched. I had left it purposely on top of the journal, and yet it was ignored. Was this a sign that communication between us will be painfully limited?

After getting some things done around the house and buying some groceries, I stopped at the police station and asked where exactly Tower Hill Cemetery is (other than being on Tower Hill, of course). For your information (you the reader of this journal) it is on the north side of town, on Old Range Road which is off of Tower Hill Road. It is a small cemetery surrounded by trees and easily missed if you aren't looking for it. It is only about a half-acre, and the stones are all extremely old.

I found the grave of Thomas Pike along the back row, under the limb of a pine tree. There are only about two hundred or so stones in the whole yard, and I looked at all of them. I learned in the library that a Civil War soldier's headstone frequently has the outline of a badge around a simple epitaph.

I am now surmising that I have at least two ghosts on-property (the boy and the mother), and perhaps one more that I haven't yet laid eyes on by the name of Thomas Pike.

I have also learned that someone else did not want me to discover Thomas Pike or anyone else that lived here from 1860-1863. Best guess is the woman (wife?).

The boy and the mother, both visible presences, are never seen together.

Holly sat back and exhaled heavily. "That's a pretty good start. What compelled her to stay there? I mean…to do that alone… hippie or not, that's a very brave lady."

"Do you have something against hippies?" Tim asked. "My mother is a hippie." He looked her in the eye straight-faced. She elbowed him again.

"Nice try. And for the record, I don't have anything against hippies. I admire their…mellow and open-minded demeanor."

Tim laughed. "You're funny."

He too wondered what gave Annette the courage to go through it all. She could have just sold the farm and downsized.

"I agree with what you're saying. It would have been so easy, minus the financial commitment, if there was one, to just cut and run. I'm sorry Annette died, but I'm glad she stayed for my sake. This could all be very helpful, but on the other hand, …the ghosts are still here. We…I…need to be careful."

They read on for another fifteen minutes, but it was getting late. Annette's journal went on to mention a couple of what she called "minor" occurrences over her next couple of weeks in late January/early February 1966. Tim had to shake his head in disbelief that they were now categorizing audible ghostly footsteps as "minor," and that reading about this sort of thing had become boring. *99 out of 100 people would wet their jammies if they heard footsteps in the hallway,* he thought.

Holly yawned and leaned into him, looking up at his face. "It's getting late, and ghosts or no ghosts, we both have to work tomorrow…" Tim smiled awkwardly. *Ah yes.* He purposely put the comforting thoughts of sleeping with Holly out of his mind. He also refused to calculate the odds of that happening. *Remain calm.*

"You're right. Just point me in the direction of the towels and sheets again, and I'll set up shop." He thought his term for preparing the guest room ("setting up shop") was appropriately... *neutral.* He didn't want to drop hints for sex or sound as if he didn't want sex at all. This was her house; it would be her call when she was ready.

"They're in the hall closet," Holly replied, and then she hesitated, dropping her eyes, before looking back up. "Tim...I want you to know that ghosts aside, I'm enjoying hanging out with you. We've had a nice couple of dates." He waited for a half-second before responding.

"I'm enjoying it, too. That's very sweet of you to say. No pressure, it's fun. First week...lots going on...I'm sleeping over prematurely—I get it. Thanks for allowing me a safe place to get some rest." Tim spoke sincerely with no come-ons as a grateful guest. She smiled, but said nothing and waited where she stood. He walked over and embraced her, looking for lips. They kissed for a good minute, and when they separated, their eyes were glazed over.

Holly faux-frowned as if to imply *it's time to say goodnight.* She looked down at the floor again and ran the fingers of her right hand through her hair, taking a step in the opposite direction.

"Goodnight," he slowly turned away and began to unfold the bedsheets.

"Goodnight," she said and closed the door across the hallway. After brushing his teeth, he finished setting up shop and clicked off the light. His eyes slowly adjusted as he relaxed and stared at the ceiling, gathering his thoughts. *Tomorrow: another day of looking over my shoulder while I try to get some work done. I'll start in the room by the road. If I get lucky ghost boy will—*

Holly reappeared, standing over him, and tapped him on the chest. "Come on," she said motioning. He didn't need to be asked twice. He got up and grabbed his pillow, quickly realizing she would already have one for him in her room. She took him by the hand, and he dropped the pillow back on the guest bed. For a second, he thought he might keep it to hide his excitement, but quickly realized he didn't have to play the gentleman anymore.

CHAPTER EIGHTEEN
Observations

April 21th, 1971

Tim opened the side door and stepped into the house, fully alert. It had been roughly eighteen hours since he had locked up and left; who knew what might have happened inside these walls in the meantime? In a normal house, you walk in, pick up your tools, and start hammering. In this house, you listen and check your surroundings.

The truth was, however, that ghosts or no ghosts, he was in a very good mood due to Holly's surprise invitation the night before. He was so mellow he almost didn't care if he saw a ghost…*almost*. Now it seemed he had something to be excited about and look forward to daily. It wasn't just one good day, but the promise of many good days to come. He felt renewed, and despite the ghost problem, *happy*. In the back of his mind, he wondered if Holly might be considering this a relationship as he was. He couldn't help but think again about the word *cooperation* and how it wasn't normally regarded a romantic word unless you've been divorced. *What a pity.*

As he had begun to plan the night before, today's house project was to rip out the walls in the room nearest the road, directly beneath the master bedroom. He started with the noisier tools. It made Tim nervous about running the Sawzall; a high-powered saw used to cut into almost anything. As it screamed its way through the old walls it was equivalent to turning your back and going deaf. He kept the cutting sessions short by using quick bursts, stealing glances all around in between. It was nerve-wracking work—as if he was advertising easily predictable opportunities of vulnerability. His t-shirt was soaked with sweat mostly due to nerves; work would have gone twice as fast without the additional concerns.

On two occasions while cutting, he caught a whiff of something rotten, as if a mouse or squirrel had died in one of the walls. He stopped the saw and sifted through chunks of plaster on the floor looking for the culprit so he could toss it outside; it reeked, and he didn't want to lose his breakfast. A housefly caught the same whiff and landed on the window, hungry. Tim crushed it with a drywall knife. He sifted a few minutes more and pulled out another section of plaster. Finding nothing in the rubble, he opened the windows to air out the room and carried on. The smell eventually dissipated.

When five o'clock came, Holly called, letting him know she was finished for the day, wanting to know what "the plan" was. She didn't have to ask twice; he was more than ready to drop the tools and celebrate. She was relieved to hear he had been able to work all day without ghostly interruption. They chose a fancy restaurant in Gilford called *O'Steak*, and nobody had to talk about the evening's sleeping arrangements.

What Tim did not know, however, was that the dead woman in the dress had watched him the entire day, from the morning on. She began by lingering in the kitchen, observing from afar. She learned the pace of his work, timing the noise of his machines and the silence that followed. She used the racket to advance because he became alert when things were quiet.

She got close, even watching from the doorway at one point,

anticipating the moment he would pick up her scent, retreating before he could track it down. She didn't mind his presence in here as long as he didn't get too curious; the house was more interesting with people in it.

When the phone rang in the living room near evening, she descended quietly and observed the conversation while his back was turned. He didn't catch her smell this time. He also didn't hear the flies, of which there were relatively few today.

This new man, like the previous owner, was barely aware of her daily presence. None of them knew of her agenda, and that's how it would stay. There was work to do to correct past mistakes, and with persistence, she could be forgiven. The search, the guilt, and the solitude were almost...no, not almost. They were all too much to bear.

CHAPTER NINETEEN
Sneak Attack

Thursday, April 22th, 1971

Tim and Holly enjoyed another near-perfect evening followed by more sex. They had so much fun they procrastinated too long and didn't get to Annette's journal. The ghosts could wait; things were going extremely well—to the point of overconfidence. Besides that, there just weren't enough hours in the day for everything, and the temptation to live in the moment after being alone for so long was too great, ghosts be damned.

When Tim unlocked the side door on Thursday morning to begin work, the phone was ringing deep within the house. He burst through the door, looking right and left for potential danger, and jogging through each room just as cautiously. When he arrived in the living room, he grabbed the noisy phone.

"Hello?"

"*Tim?!*" The female voice at the other end made it sound as if she was surprised he answered.

"Yes?" He couldn't recognize the voice after just one word, but he heard the urgency.

"*Where have you been?!* I've called several times. I almost had to call off your visitation this week. I've got a situation, and I need you to be there for your daughters, or I'll have to make other arrangements."

Oh no.

It was Sheila, and as always, she was ready, willing, and able to disrupt his life in the name of her agenda, using the girls as pawns. She had no right to change his visitation unilaterally but acted as if she did, and Tim had no doubt she would cross that line one day. His only recourse would be to take her to court, which would cost a pretty penny, and he didn't have the cash to fight that battle right now.

"What do you mean you've called several times? And what gives you the right to cancel my visitation? What's the matter? I was in town, grabbing some breakfast." He lied in self-defense; he much preferred her out of his personal life. Letting her know he had a new girlfriend would result in trouble; she would do anything in her power to sabotage his happiness. If she knew he had someone, the girls would be suddenly available every weekend. If he said no, she would tell them, *Daddy's too busy for you.* On his normal visitation weekends, she would line up birthday parties and sports leagues to reduce the quality of their time together.

"I've called you four times in the last hour! Judy Larson was right here with me the entire time, you can ask her. Is there going to be a problem with communication up there in New Hampshire going forward? You need to be available to your children. You should have bought a place closer to us; we don't understand why you would do such a thing. Moving so far away wasn't in their best interests." She liked to add a liberal dose of false panic to the tone of her voice.

"Did you say you started calling me at about 8?" he asked. Sheila would call at all hours in the name of "the children," even though she was really just keeping tabs. She was always plotting to make his schedule wrap around hers. They had been separated for a year before the divorce was final, and Frank Turnbull had told him to "dot the i's and cross the t's" at least until the divorce was final; this meant; *try not to make waves to keep the divorce "affordable."* Apparently Frank had lost some paying customers to bankruptcy. Thanks to Frank's sketchy advice, Tim did his best to accommodate her, and Sheila got used to having him on call. Now that the divorce was over, Tim occasionally caught himself still acting the trained monkey.

"Yes, I've been calling since at least 7:45. The girls are very upset that you weren't answering."

"Did Judy Larson sleep over, or something? Why's she there so early? Why did you involve the girls? Did you have to wake them up to tell them I'm not home?" Tim knew that they were most likely still asleep. Because Tim had called her out, Sheila changed the subject, deflecting. To her, Tim's new habit of questioning everything was obnoxious.

"They asked. I need you to come get the girls tonight. I have a seminar at the bank, and if you can't come and get them I'll have to call a sitter tomorrow, and she won't work for less than twelve hours pay, so if you want them before 8 P.M., you'll have to pay the difference."

What a load of horse shit, Tim thought. His blood pressure spiked. He had been slow to learn in the beginning that everything out of her mouth was about control—the very opposite of *cooperation*. Paying for her sitter was a new one. He would never help pay for that; it set a dangerous and costly precedent. He would be in effect enabling Sheila's last-minute schedule changes.

"So what's the problem? I don't know what time you need me to be there, or anything. All I hear is your last-minute crisis, and how I'm supposed to drop everything and bail you out."

"I told you I need you there tonight at 5 pm! You're self-employed, Tim. You're the boss; you get to make your own hours."

She had NOT told him that, but he knew, as did she, that nobody was recording the call, and there was no rewind. Despite all of the progress he had made in dealing with her antics, she still knew how to change everything on the fly, and he saw red.

"That's the first time you've mentioned a time at all!"

"Judy is sitting right here, she heard it too, and—"

Tim had been through all of this before. Sheila was good at her craft. Judy Larson might not even be there, and even if she were, she would only be there to back Sheila's story. *Oh, if he could only turn back time and not marry her*—With no excuses at the ready to call her bluff, Tim caved, mostly because he missed his daughters.

"I can be there at 5." Tim knew that if he told her he couldn't come, the kids would most likely stay with Judy and her oddball family. The girls did not like the Larson kids, the husband, or Judy herself. As soon as he said he could pick them up, he cringed. *You chose poorly.* He'd been caught unprepared again and didn't have an excuse ready. She turned up the heat, and he didn't think it through.

Even though he felt like he'd been suckered, there was a silver lining. He would see his kids earlier than planned, and they would be there an extra day. One of the days would be ad-libbed and spur-of-the-moment, but it wouldn't be the first time, and at least there were new places to explore up here in New Hampshire.

Olivia and Vivian (also known as "Liv and Viv") were coming… *(Oh no).* They were coming to Daddy's haunted house up in Ghost Country. He had been so pulled into Sheila's vortex he forgot about everything else. To make matters worse, he had unintentionally sabotaged his evening with Holly, who had slipped his mind completely. Tim had learned long ago, as almost every man does, that you can't use *that* as an excuse…no woman wants to hear she'd been forgotten. Worlds had collided; New Tim had allowed Old Tim to do the talking.

Now he would have to ask forgiveness after their second night of intimacy. It didn't look good. It didn't *sound* good. She might not believe him. He dialed the telephone. After exchanging pleasantries, he got to the point.

"I… uh…I…messed up. I'm going to apologize up front, but; I…got a phone call from my ex-wife just now, right as I was arriving. I got ambushed; caught off-guard. She needed me to take the kids tonight, spur-of-the-moment. I had to tell her—"

"*Tonight?*" Her tone was short.

"Yeah," he exhaled. "Sheila surprised me...and I fell for it. She had a prepared story that she needed an answer to on the spot. I wasn't thinking straight. I said yes too soon. She caught me off guard, and then..." Tim started to repeat himself.

Holly sighed. "Uh-oh. My ex had kids, too. I know what's going on." She let her statement hang in the air.

Tim continued: "Look...maybe we can do something. Eat dinner together or something—that is—if you're up for it. I'm already divorced, so most of the *keep-the-girlfriend-out-of-the-picture* stuff is over. This shouldn't be a problem going forward."

Tim's words rang true despite the unpleasant surprise. He was being honest but was still clearly under the spell of an opportunistic ex-wife, and that was a bit of a turn-off. The good thing was there were no signs that, because he had gotten her in bed, he was backing off. Her ex, Roger, had been a pain-in-the-ass with his kids. She stayed "hidden" at his request for over a year while he went through his divorce. They were not some of her best memories.

Roger blamed everything on his ex. He told Holly that if she found out, she would make trouble, and she might win a certain type of custody he would not be happy with. Holly spent many a weekend in limbo, alone in her house or working extra while he sat at home watching TV, ignoring his kids. He was a selfish man. To make matters worse, as soon as his divorce was final, she married him; this she chalked up to youth and inexperience and a touch of brainwashing. It took her two years to wise-up and get out.

"So... what's your plan? Where will they sleep?" He could practically hear the frown on the other end.

Tim sighed. "I don't know; I just hung up. It JUST happened. Then, I realized what I had done, punched myself in the face and called you." She raised a concern:

"Are you sure you want to introduce me to your daughters so early on? What if we don't make it? Then they get to meet the next girlfriend, too. You don't want to be 'daddy-can't-get-it-right,' do you?"

Tim smiled. She had a way with words. "*Daddy-can't-get-it-right* would be bad. No, Holly, I fell into a trap; I'll be ready next time. I'm not yanking your chain."

"All right, I'll give you a Mulligan; but I don't think we should mix with the kids quite yet. Where would I sleep? Where are THEY going to sleep? I'm picturing the three of you all in your bed because of the ghost situation. Are *you* going to be all right? Are *they*? You'll sleep in a hotel, right?"

She was right; it was too soon for Holly to meet his daughters. Everything that went on in the house this weekend from "Who are daddy's friends?" to "What color was the wallpaper?" would be pulled out of the girls by Sheila in third-degree fashion. They didn't deserve it, but Sheila could give a damn. If they slept in a hotel, that would add more questions to the grilling. He would at least start the weekend at home. These ghosts seemed to be well-behaved so far, and the girls were heavy sleepers. *Ha ha...go ahead and rationalize, Tim. You're between a rock and a hard place. Hopefully, the girls don't get choked.* Thanks to Tim's poor handling of Sheila's phone call, the honeymoon phase was on hold, and the pressure was on.

CHAPTER TWENTY
Visitation

Sheila's phone call considerably shortened the amount of work he could do that day. All of his Friday plans were now Thursday plans. He gave up and drove down to Massachusetts to visit his one remaining employee, Johnny, who was installing a kitchen in Topsfield. While he was there, he made some Russell Construction phone calls (a total of three), lining things up to keep Johnny busy for the next two weeks.

"You're here early. I was expecting you tomorrow," said Johnny.

"Yeah, Sheila called with one of her national emergencies, and I'm picking the kids up tonight." Johnny shook his head. He had seen it happen before. He had witnessed his friend and boss battle through his divorce and had seen some of the darkest days: The initial shock of betrayal, the layoffs, and the day he had to move out of the house away from his daughters.

"So…no school tomorrow?" said Johnny, squinting one eye quizzically. Tim hadn't even thought of that. He rolled his eyes, and Johnny knew Sheila had dropped a doozy of a carpet-bomb phone call on Tim's head.

"Man…you need to take a class or something on how to prepare yourself! She got you *again*!" Johnny knew all too well. Tim changed the subject.

"I'm going to need to get those beds you were talking about. They're in storage, right? Somewhere in Salisbury?"

"Right. The one on Newbury Road. Here's the key to it; number 217. Use them for as long as you like; I don't even think we need them back. How are things going up there?" Tim was a bad actor, and his body language betrayed him when he followed it with the word:

"Great."

"Is it in worse shape than you remembered? You want me to come up on the weekend and help you out?"

"No, no, no, I can do it. I just lost a day because of Sheila, and I'm a little behind otherwise, but I'll catch up."

He didn't mention his date nights with Holly, which were contributing to the slowdown, *but were so worth it.* He also didn't mention the ghosts. The absurdity of these words hung in his mind. The original plan, back before he signed the papers to buy the house, had been to work late into the evenings, alone, no interruptions. Eighteen hour days—work like a bastard on the cheap and sell the house in a year. He didn't anticipate he'd be dating so soon and had budgeted zero time for a new relationship. *I'll file that under "good problem."* He also hadn't budgeted any time for dealing with ghosts—*the bad problem.*

"You looked stressed, man. Grab one of those 'Cow Hampshire' women by the hair like a caveman. I heard they like that. I heard they still churn their own butter too, you know?" Even though Sanborn life was not that different from Methuen life (where Johnny lived), he loved to portray Tim as a *nouveau-hick.*

Tim ignored Johnny's comment, which was strangely out of character, and Johnny picked right up on it.

"NO *WAY!* You're already scoring up there. Who is she? Is it the girl at the hardware store or something? A farmer? Some maple syrup-making wench? A real cow? Who the hell could you meet so fast? The real estate lady? She was pretty hot. What was her name?"

"Holly."

"Holly! Wow! It's her, right? Good for you, boss! Did you make her breakfast? Chicks like that."

"Shut up, Johnny. No, I didn't make her breakfast. We slept at her house." Tim wasn't used to taking dating advice from Johnny; in fact, at one point, it had been the other way around.

Johnny's eyes bugged out. He began clapping for Tim, a standing ovation. Tim ignored the digs.

"...Yeah, she's cool, but I messed up with Sheila today on the phone—taking the kids early. I... had to break some plans we had made."

"Oh no, no, no, no" Johnny dropped his hands and hung his head disappointedly. "When are you going to take your balls back, man? She still owns you. Enough is enough! Kids or not... they'll always love you no matter what she tells them as long as you do the right thing. Call her bluff. Slow the conversation down and *think*." Tim sat there and listened to his third lecture of the day: First Sheila, then Holly and now Johnny. They were all right, except for Sheila.

"Yeah, I hear you, Johnny. I'm pissed at myself, and I don't even want to talk about it anymore." He had taken enough punishment, most of it from himself. "Hey, I've gotta go. Are you all set with your work schedule for the next two weeks or so?"

"Yeah. I'll finish up here and start on the Mills house on Tuesday. After that, you let me know." Tim nodded as he looked down at the doorknob, grabbed it; but didn't turn it. Taking a breath, he turned back around.

"Johnny...do you believe in ghosts?" Tim had been tossing around the idea of asking Johnny through the whole conversation. He had nothing to lose. He knew Johnny was deeply religious, so there might be a chance. Even if Johnny laughed in his face, he didn't really care. They were boss and employee, but they were also close friends.

"What did you say?"

"Have you ever seen a ghost?"

Johnny hesitated. He had so far been the macho man of today's conversation, and Tim could be baiting him right now to try and turn that around. It might be a ball-busting move that the two of them often played off of each other over the years. Johnny looked directly at him. Tim had a straight face. *Where's he going with this?*

"No, man. Hell no. What are you talking about? Is this a riddle or something?"

Tim sighed and squirmed a bit, a bit disappointed with Johnny's answer, now wondering where to go from here.

"Johnny, I've got ghosts." He readied himself for the razzing, but Johnny didn't laugh, which surprised him.

"What do you mean?" Johnny was all in on Tim's next words.

"I…I've got a little kid running around…maybe some other stuff. No kidding—and no doubt about it." Johnny's eyes bored directly into Tim's for several seconds, making sure this wasn't a joke.

"Okay boss, I lied. I thought you were baiting me. I have seen a ghost—and it messed me up. My grandmother stuck around for a while after she died. I'll tell you about it sometime. It wasn't fun. She wasn't the same grandma I remembered. What do you need… help or something?"

"Why? Would you know what to do?"

"No, not really, unless you know why your house is haunted. We knew why my grandma was—still around. We knew her so well and knew her all through her final days—her sickness, the crap she went through with my grandfather, all that. We had to put some things together to get her to go away. We had to figure it out. Ghosts don't just come up to you politely and ask for help; they're …different. Things change when you die, I guess. I can't say I'm an expert and I know what to do, but another set of eyes couldn't hurt if you need me up there. I'll just tell Maria you need me overnight."

"I'm good for now, Johnny. But that's a tempting offer; I appreciate it.

"There's also a woman out in my field, and maybe another one we can't see. I know that sounds messed up, I know, I know—But there's a journal that was left behind by the previous owner who also saw them. She left some helpful notes." Johnny's face lit up in surprised disbelief.

"'*We*'? Did you say '*we* can't see' one of the ghosts? Did Holly see them too?"

"Yeah, she saw one and was witness to the one we can't see. She hasn't seen the boy yet."

"Wowwwww. So you've got a whole family up there? Less than a week and you've seen all *that*?"

"Yeah… It's nerve-wracking, to say the least, especially the night I stayed there. Besides that, it's—a huge pain in the ass, robbing my time—and now the girls are coming over." Tim was in a daze, thinking aloud. His thoughts trailed off. "So, that's it? With your grandmother, I mean? Just figure out why the ghosts are sticking around?"

"As I said, I'm no expert; I'm just telling you what happened with my grandma. It did work with her, but I wasn't the frontman figuring it all out. I was just a kid. Do you want me to tell you the whole story?" Tim looked at his watch.

"Yeah, but I can't do it right now; I've got a bunch of things to do before I pick up the kids. I may call you about it later if you don't mind. I imagine it won't be a pleasant trip down memory lane for you. I appreciate it."

"No problem, boss."

Tim left. He ran his errands, picked up the beds from Johnny's storage in Salisbury, stopped at the hardware store for some things, and when that was done, it was time to get the kids. After a long work week, he was always happy to see them, even though this particular long work week was only four days. He pulled onto their street in anticipation of the dreaded handoff. He hated pulling into the driveway because he would have to talk with Sheila, and that was usually something like a bill they were supposed to split or some controlling instructions about the girls' recent health or behavior.

"Olivia shouldn't be allowed to watch TV because she lied and said her homework was finished" or "Vivian has a cold and shouldn't be outdoors." Things designed to hamstring whatever plans he had made; things he nodded in agreement to in Sheila's presence but ignored later. When the handoff was over, and he began backing out of the driveway, the fun began.

"Are you guys ready to see the new house?" Tim said excitedly.

"Yeah!" they replied in unison. They were at the age where they weren't yet know-it-alls, and hanging out with dad was still cool. He was glad that they were only about two years apart; they leaned on each other through the divorce, whether they knew it or not.

The three of them had a nice time catching up with stories of school and work on the way back to New Hampshire. They talked about the Plexiglas patch-job window on the driver's side door first; Tim told them he locked his keys in the truck and had to break in. After that, they talked about the recent happenings at home and in the news. When they were a half-hour outside of Sanborn, thoughts turned to dinner.

"What do you guys want to eat?"

"Pizza!"

Easy enough. Tim took pleasure in spoiling them when they were together. They got the pizza, the dessert, whatever they wanted. And when dinner had ended, he headed for Lancaster Hill Road. *Home Sweet Home* it was not, at least not yet. *Make room for us, Pike family, if that's who you are*—His anxiety grew the closer they got. The girls were all eyeballs, excited to see daddy's new digs.

"Wow! It's bigger than Mom's house! There's a pond! Hey, where's our bedroom?"

"You're going to love it. It *is* unfinished though, still kinda messy in there. I just barely moved in. I'm working on it. It will be even better next time!"

"Yaaaaay!" said Olivia.

"Yaaaaay!" mimicked Vivian.

He gave them the fifty-cent tour, but they really didn't care much about anything except for their bedroom. He wanted them to sleep near him, so he put them right across the hall, in the front of the house; the "sunny bedroom," as he had come to refer to it. He didn't care if they woke up early because of the sun. *Just be sure to wake up.*

Strangely enough, he felt safer with the girls in the house, like their love and company had some power over the ghosts. He knew this was full-on naïve and had nothing to do with their safety, but he also felt it was far from meaningless.

They went back to the truck together to unload it. *"Hey, I need you guys to hold the doors for me"* was the excuse. That's about *all* they did as he dragged the bedding upstairs single-handedly. He had them shower while he assembled the beds and tucked them in at around nine o'clock. After that he took his own time showering and brushing; *shortening the night.* When he was about ready for bed, which was close to ten, he walked downstairs to the living room (with the hammer) and called Holly.

As the phone rang on the other end, Tim realized he had not set himself up very well. All of the lights in the downstairs were off, including the living room. He had never reset the timers after Thomas Pike had shut them down three nights ago. Now the room was dark and the lamp was across the room from the phone, just out of reach. He stood near the doorway of the staircase, resting his shoulder on the doorjamb, looking through as many dark doorways as he could. He was standing in the same spot that he had seen the boy in the breakfast area on the first night, but this time, there was no painter's light in his hand.

Holly picked up, "Hello there. How's the family?"

"Hi, Holly. Wish you were here, but I understand why you're not. The kids are in bed. I put them across the hall from me. They were excited to see 'their room,' and now, it's 'Tim can't sleep time.'"

"Yeah, I bet. I don't envy you. Listen, I'm going to put the phone next to my bed. If you need anything, please call. I'm twenty minutes away, but maybe I could help in some way. In fact, call me every couple of hours if you want—and if you don't have time to call and things are…happening, just get the hell out of there. I'll leave the door open."

That's nice, Tim thought. He took a few steps toward the kitchen as he held the phone to his ear, watching—double-checking.

"Thanks, I appreciate that. I think we'll be all right. I hope so, anyway. What are you doing tomorrow? Do you want to meet us for lunch? I could just say you were the real estate lady."

She thought about that for a minute. It seemed she might be moving toward becoming part of the family already, and they hadn't even been dating a week; *too much too soon.*

"Um… I have some stuff that I should catch up on, and I have a showing at 11 A.M., so you go on ahead. We can talk in the afternoon and see what's happening."

Tim heard the hesitation as he turned left toward the dark office, exploring the space as much as he could without pulling the cord out of the wall. He couldn't see anything in there, so he walked back to the light coming from the upstairs hallway. He let the idea of tomorrow's lunch go.

"Okay, sounds good. We'll catch up. And I'll bring the phone upstairs and put it in the bedroom." He couldn't wait to unplug down here and head up. He should have moved the phone earlier because now he was nervous, wishing he was closer to the girls, even though they were mere feet away in the room directly over his head.

She said goodnight and Tim hung up. As soon as the receiver hit the cradle, he remained still for a moment and let the silence of the house close in. He listened. The girls were upstairs, but he felt alone because he was the only one in the house that knew the whole story, and he was the only one in the house *responsible.* Without looking down at the cord, he crouched and unplugged the phone from the wall, backed out of the room, and headed up.

He looked in on the girls, then went back to his bedroom and dragged the mattress closer to the door. He set himself up so that he was literally no more than two feet from the hallway and twelve feet from the girls. Both bedroom doors were open. He left his jeans, t-shirt, and shoes on as he had the other night…just in case. He clicked off the light and attempted to relax, but with his ears perked it was nearly impossible—at first. Thankfully the house was quiet, and despite his nerves, he was exhausted. Having the girls with him brought some comfort; the empty house seemed a little bit more like home. Despite all his worries, he fell asleep in minutes.

CHAPTER TWENTY-ONE
The Two Stones

Friday, April 23rd, 1971

The sun woke Tim, and he opened his eyes, trying to remember the dream. The details were fuzzy, but he thought it might have been about the house, and something else he couldn't recall… *yet.* It took him another second to get his bearings, and when he did, he remembered that the kids were here. A twinge of anxiety pushed him out of bed quickly. His watch said 6:30 A.M. and, pending the girls' situation, he was at least excited that it hadn't been a long, torturous ghost fest.

His shoes hit the floor as he pulled the blanket off, and as he did so, he noticed his arm was bleeding. There was a long scratch down the right forearm that took a short break in the crook, only to continue along his bicep another two inches. The bleeding hadn't even stopped. He looked down at his front and saw that the front of his t-shirt had dots of blood in four different places, with two small pulls in the cloth that had opened into tiny rips.

Before he delved any deeper into his situation, he crossed the hall to the girls' room to check on more precious cargo. Thank God, their heads were peeking out from under the covers, and they were still asleep; he checked their breathing just to be sure. His heart relaxed. He picked up the blankets from the bottom of the bed and checked their bodies—no blood.

He crossed back into the master bedroom to check himself in the full-length mirror. It looked as if he'd lost a fight with a housecat. In addition to the wounds on his arms, he had a nice four-inch scratch across his nose and left cheek. Still baffled, he went to the bathroom and cleaned up as much as possible before the girls woke up. As he closed his eyes to splash his face with the warm water, he remembered part of his dream. There was a pair of headstones in between two perfect rows of trees.

He tried to concentrate and remember more, but nothing came; the complete answer to whatever had happened to his body remained hidden. He began to think, nervously.

The two perfect rows—must be the grove. The two stones… must be under the pile of leaves. Did I go out there? My arm hasn't even clotted yet; did I just get back?

He was shaken with the possibility—or probability, more like it…that he had sleepwalked out of the house all the way to the grove. Nevertheless, he finished cleaning his wounds as best he could, put on a couple of strategic band-aids, changed his clothes and headed to the kitchen.

The downstairs received his full-attention sweep, and thankfully, all was clear. After sneaking back upstairs to retrieve the telephone, he plugged in downstairs and called Holly. She was awake, awaiting his call.

"So you survived!" she proclaimed.

"Yes! We did, but—something happened. I think I sleepwalked…into the woods."

"What? Tim, that's scary! You left the girls alone?"

He hadn't even thought about that, and it bothered him. He had been awake just five minutes, but he should have immediately realized that he had left them alone. But why did he leave? Had he been baited outside?

"I…did. And I don't think it's my fault. I'm freaked out; I've never sleepwalked in my life."

Holly didn't know what to say at first.

"Uh…that's not…um… Do you remember anything? Where did you go?

"I only remember one thing; I was in the grove, and I saw two gravestones. I can't remember anything else. I'm all scratched up—as if I walked through some thorns. My arm was still bleeding a few minutes ago."

"Two gravestones? Was it the dream, or are they really in there somewhere? Might it be symbolic?"

Good point, he thought. A pair of headstones. What could that mean? He and Holly. Olivia and Vivian. He forced the thought out of his head.

"I don't know if it was the dream or not. I guess I need to check it out…sometime."

"No! Don't you dare, at least while the girls are there, and certainly not alone!"

"Holly, how long have you been awake? What's going on, are you a morning person or something? Why do you have all the good questions and answers? I'm exhausted. Help. Please."

"I'm not a morning person; I'm just *wicked smaht.*" She exaggerated her New England accent in an attempt at humor; it didn't work. A moment of silence followed. Tim still seemed upset, so she changed the subject.

"What are you up to today? What's the plan?"

"You know, I woke up and saw a little blood, but I wasn't *completely* freaked out yet. I was even elated when I looked in and saw the girls sleeping safely, but now I feel terrible. This place is one hell of a head trip. It's overwhelming. I'm even scared, to be honest—but call me stupid; I can't give up. And call me stubborn, but I also can't tell Sheila about this or visitation will be all but over."

Holly knew Tim was right, and he wasn't just playing

alpha-male. Some would say it was a simple "life or death" decision to pick up and leave, but it wasn't. If he chose "life," it would be…no life at all. He would be penniless and unable to come up with the level of child support ordered, which would have to be changed, and that would open up a new host of problems. First, it wasn't good for the girls. Second, it would take away his entire lifestyle of working for himself, setting his own hours, calling the shots. Working for someone else just wasn't in his blood. Third would be the field day Sheila would have trashing his reputation with anyone and everyone, including the girls—for years to come.

Alternatively, if he chose the "death" option… Well, it might not necessarily mean *death* at all. It might just mean "risk."

The biggest risk is not taking any risk at all—

Nothing ventured, nothing gained—

No risk it; no biscuit.

It was dangerous, wishful thinking, maybe—or perhaps foolish rationalization. The previous owners were both dead, and they didn't die normally, like, in a hospital—they died on-property; right there on Lancaster Hill Road. Hell, the whole place might be a graveyard for all they knew…the way things were going, anyway.

"I hear you. I know you're not a macho-man, and I agree; however, it is dangerous over there. Annette and her husband died on your property, and yes, it's too early to abandon ship, but we have to be smart and think it through." Tim took several seconds to respond.

"I have a scratch across my face. A pretty good one, too. The girls will see it when they wake up. I'm going to have to make an excuse."

Holly wanted to get in her car and come over and make breakfast for everybody…restore a sense of normalcy…if it only made sense in terms of their relationship. Unfortunately, real estate agents don't just pop in for waffles and sit down to eat with single dads; even young girls know that. It was too soon to be introduced to his daughters, and they'd probably be in their pajamas, which might make it awkward for them.

"Tim… Take a breather, have some breakfast, and relax. Nobody else got hurt, and you didn't see any ghosts. Eat your breakfast, and just have a nice day with the girls. You don't have to be anywhere or do anything."

"Okay. Yeah. I will. I was going to make banana pancakes. And guess what? I'm starving. I must have burned a lot of calories roaming the property all night."

Holly laughed to make him feel better. He wasn't quite as down now. He was recovering; making light. His humor was returning.

Tim mixed the batter, cracked the eggs, and lit the burner. He even whistled a little bit, even if it was slightly forced, doing his best to push the darker thoughts back and enjoy the day. In minutes the kitchen was full of the sweet smell of banana pancakes. He had even picked up some real New Hampshire maple syrup made just up the road at Abbott's farm. It was one of the tiny little jugs, not a quart or gallon. *That shit was expensive, and the kids probably like Aunt Jemima better, anyway. Somehow they infuse the flavor of butter right in the factory, something the average maple tree can't do.*

They ate and made small talk. The girls asked about the scratch on Tim's nose, and he told them he bumped into a post in the cellar while looking at the furnace. After breakfast, the girls went upstairs to get dressed while Tim did the dishes. For ten minutes he cleaned everything up and went back to the bedroom to check on them. The girls were already gone when he got there, so he checked all the rooms and closets in a bit of a panic. On his way down the stairs, he noticed the front door was slightly ajar indicating the possibility that they were outside.

After exiting and scanning the pond area, he jogged left towards the turn in the driveway and around the side of the house. The barn faced him as he stopped and listened, but there was no sign of them. His nervous stomach turned as he perked his ears and pivoted toward the path in the corner of the driveway. *Please no. Not on day one. You didn't go up that way. Not ever, if I can help it.*

"Liv! Viv!"

There was no sound but the chirping of robins. He decided to check the barn. As he approached, it occurred to him he didn't know it nearly as well as he knew the house. The massive doorway swallowed him like a great mouth, and the musty atmosphere dampened the outside noises. He passed the long-empty horse stalls after which the space of the barn opened up to the width of the building, creating pockets of shadows to the left and the right that the light could not reach. Bats circled high overhead as always. He had never been this far inside. *Probably would have been a good idea to check out the whole thing before buying, right?*

"Olivia? Vivian!" His controlled demeanor was about to come to an end. He would scream soon, even if it frightened them. He turned and walked into the dark corner on his left. His eyes had to adjust as he inspected the bygone mounds of hay and the nearly bare bench along the wall. Most of the tools that had once adorned it were long gone, perhaps as part of an estate auction, or pilfered by trespassers. He opened a drawer and found nothing but spider webs and an old nail. The second drawer held a mason jar half-filled with an assortment of orphan screws.

"Liv! Viv! Where are you? I'm worried! Enough! Game over!" The barn remained quiet for three more seconds as he waited, listening. Then, he heard a giggle, from the loft over the barn door above and felt relief wash over him.

"You guys! I hear you up there! You had me going! Hey, be careful up there, I don't want you to fall." The girls were under an old, filthy horse blanket that undulated wildly as Olivia attempted to restrain Vivian and keep her quiet for a few more seconds in a last-ditch effort to continue the game.

Crisis averted, Tim ignored the girls for a second and opened the third and final drawer in the tool bench. From the depths of the drawer, he pulled an old-fashioned, well-worn hatchet. It had a claw on the back for pulling nails opposite the corroded, but still sharp blade. He had no way of knowing, but this was the same hatchet Henry had brought into the forest to cut a Christmas tree that fateful day in November 1964.

The woman in the dress would take it while he looked at her gravestone, just before she killed him. Henry must not be found in the grove; that would not be good. She didn't want anyone near the two stones…that would only attract more attention. Unfortunately for Henry, he had gotten too close. Once he was dead she threw him effortlessly over her shoulder and put him back near the barn where he always washed the horses at the end of the day; the barn that she and her family had raised more than one hundred years ago, just before the happiest years of her life came to an end.

Tim examined the hatchet briefly, then put it back in the drawer and closed it. He abandoned the bench and quietly climbed the ladder to the loft. Once up there, he crept silently toward the old blanket with the two wiggling lumps underneath and attacked, tickling them. "Come on, let's go have some fun!"

They left the house and started the day at a place called Funspot, an arcade with pinball machines, go-carts, batting cages and the like. Twenty-seven dollars of game tokens later they left, and Tim took them on a drive around Lake Winnipesaukee. Visiting the lake was anticlimactic for the girls after all the stimulation at the arcade, and it was deemed "boring" by Vivian because they couldn't go swimming. For Tim, it was nostalgic—rare good memories from his former life. In a way it was like visiting the grave of a loved one; he felt something, but it was a poor substitute for the way he had felt back then.

They spent the rest of the day driving up to Moultonborough and checking out their "ex-cottage" on Lake Kanasatka. The girls were bored and didn't care much; they were too young to remember most of the time they had spent there. All it did for Tim was stir up more of the same old memories he had felt earlier in the day around Winnipesaukee. He treated them to some penny candy at the Old Country Store before surrendering and calling it quits.

When they arrived back at the house, Tim did his best to stay close to them until he had checked the house out. He tricked them into following him by telling them he might have seen a mouse and needed help looking for it.

He wished he'd brought the TV up from Massachusetts to keep the girls in one place while he put the groceries away, but he hadn't. It had rabbit ear antennas, and if he was extremely lucky it might have only picked up a channel out of Manchester, but that would have been better than nothing. They finished the night playing a painfully slow (for Tim, anyway) game of Monopoly, eating some chicken nuggets, and getting ready for bed.

Tim had spent odd minutes of the daydreaming up ideas of how to prevent another night of sleepwalking. In the end, he settled on installing a screw eye hook in the baseboard next to his mattress and tying a string between the screw eye and his wrist. The string would be silent and wouldn't wake the girls like a length of chain might. The whole idea (installation and all) was pretty quiet, which would prevent the girls from waking up and asking what he was doing.

He kissed them goodnight and returned to the master bedroom, tying a strong double square knot around his wrist, which was about the only knot he knew short of tying his shoes. Remaining fully-clothed once again, he checked his front pocket to make sure the jackknife was there for the morning when he would have to cut himself free.

CHAPTER TWENTY-TWO

A Change of Clothes

Saturday, April 24th, 1971

The early morning sun woke him once again, and he raised his still-restrained left hand to see the rope secured just as he had left it. Before celebrating, he examined his shoes and clothing for signs of *travel.* His work boots were mud-free thank goodness, and as a bonus, he even felt rested. *Thank God*, he thought as he cut himself free to look in on Olivia and Vivian. They were safe and sleeping—a tremendous relief. This day was off to a much better start.

It was only 5:15 am and too early to call Holly, but he was done sleeping, so he went quietly downstairs to make some coffee and begin preparing breakfast. Every other minute he would cross through the two rooms between the kitchen and the bottom of the stairs to listen and make sure the girls were safe. Also, every five minutes or so he would go all the way up to the second floor and look in on them, full-on paranoid for their safety.

After three cups of coffee and close to twenty trips back and forth, he heard them starting to wake and talk to each other. He fired up the front right burner to prepare this morning's anticlimactic spin on yesterday's breakfast: *Blueberry*...pancakes.

The kids were now up and about, and like kids in general, no matter how little they weighed, they seemed to sound like Frankenstein when they were upstairs. They weren't even above him, but all he could hear was *thud-thud-thud-thud-thud-thud*. He stepped away from the stove and peered down the length of the house to the bottom of the stairs to make sure it wasn't the boy.

Vivian rounded the corner first, closely followed by Olivia. Their hair was mussed, and Olivia was yawning. As they approached through the living room and into the kitchen, something seemed odd, and at first, he couldn't place it. Then he realized; last night the girls had gone to bed in their glorified t-shirt nightgowns that Sheila had provided. Olivia had *Barbie* on hers, and Vivian had *Bugs Bunny*.

Now they were wearing full-length formal nightgowns.

Tim, in his shock, knew right away he was looking at clothing from days-gone-by.

"Daddy, what are these? I don't even like it! It's too much clothing! I feel all hot!" said Vivian.

"Yeah, these are weird, dad. Mom's gonna hate them. Did you put this on me?" added Olivia.

Tim felt the blood rush to his head as his temper flared, not at the girls of course, but at whoever or whatever had come so close to his daughters in such an intimate way. He hid his emotions as best he could.

"What? Yeah! Don't you like them? It's what they wear in New Hampshire! I thought I might surprise you."

At ages six and eight, they were too old to be changed and dressed by their father, but in this situation, he was forced to lie. Telling them he didn't know where the gowns came from was obviously not an option.

"Then why didn't you just give them to us before bed?"

"Well, I didn't think you'd like them because I didn't get to tell you about the history of New Hampshire yet."

"Booorrring," said Vivian. She pulled a stool up to the counter.

He walked over and grabbed her face, pretending he wanted a kiss but really checking for marks of any kind. Then he faux tickled her to see if she winced. Nothing, thank God. He did the same thing to Olivia, and she shooed him away. Tim's stellar mood was gone, and breakfast was now a distraction.

"Do we have to wear them every night?" said Olivia.

"Why wouldn't you? I'm telling you, it's the thing to do up here. Everyone wears them." In the back of his mind, he was afraid the ghost would change their clothes every night if he let them go back to regular pajamas. He might have to stay awake to *confront*, and that didn't sound like the best plan of action.

"But don't worry, you can go change them right now before the pancakes are ready. Go, go, go! You have two minutes!"

"Pancakes again?" complained Vivian.

"Not just pancakes! *Blueberry* pancakes!"

They ran out of the room, not very thrilled, but very gullible and cute.

After breakfast, he went upstairs to look around while the kids went out to explore. He told them to stay within view of the front windows and to not go down to the pond because the water wasn't clean and was full of frogs and maybe even snakes. That would be enough to keep them away; neither daughter was a tomboy, and they both *hated* frogs. The first thing he did when they left the house was go to their bedroom and examine the gowns.

Olivia's was on the floor, and Vivian's was on the bed. The fabric was uneven and frayed in spots, clearly not made by an automated machine in a modern-day factory. They smelled slightly musty but were otherwise in decent shape. He wondered why a ghost-woman with a ghost-boy would have two female nightgowns for his girls, but there were so many things that already didn't make sense—The Barbie and Bugs Bunny t-shirt nightgowns were nowhere to be found.

He looked out the front windows of the house, and the girls were in the driveway playing hopscotch on an imaginary court.

He tossed the gowns on the bed and went back downstairs to call Holly.

"Listen to this; the girls woke up in some nightgowns that I've never seen before, and I think they're from the 1800s."

"What do you mean? Like somebody changed their clothes in the middle of the night?"

"Right; I couldn't give them a complete physical check-up without scaring them, but they didn't appear to be touched, or marked or anything like that. I'm beyond pissed. That's just too close for comfort."

"Yeah, I understand. Did the girls say anything, or remember anything?"

"No, they think I changed their clothes. And they think I'm weird. And if they tell Sheila about it, she's gonna ask questions. I'm hoping they forget by Sunday night."

"Tim, honestly, who cares what Sheila thinks? That's the least of your problems. She can go to hell! You've got somebody changing your children's clothes in the middle of the night!" Holly was right, and he knew it.

"I know; I'm overly worried about what kind of crap I'm going to get from her. I've been brainwashed, but I'm working on it."

"So what are you going to do tonight? Where will you sleep? I mean...you can bring them here if you want. We could make up a story. I'll be the real estate lady, and we can say we had to test the house for radon gas or something."

"I appreciate the invite, Holly, but...the girls will figure it out, and I know that's not really what you want. They'll ask questions, I'll have to tell them stories I may need to retract down the line, and I'm a terrible liar; I'll forget. I'll give it one more try tonight. I'll sleep in the girls' room, in between them. I mean, they weren't hurt, and we haven't been threatened or anything. If I wake up and try to start walking, I'll wake them up, and they'll wake me up."

"Well, the invitation still stands," Holly said. "If you guys need to come over, come over. If it seems dangerous, don't risk it. If you hear things at 3 am, and you don't feel safe, get out of there!"

"Thanks, Holly. That gives me some options. I hope to get through tonight and return the kids tomorrow. After that, we'll catch up on reading that journal and figure out better how to deal with this. But like you said; if things get hairy tonight I'll head over, possibly without a phone call."

"Okay, I'll leave the outside light on and a key under the mat. I'll leave the guest room set up, and the couch pulled out and ready to go. I'm going to read some more of the journal tonight, too. I read last night a bit; I just forgot to tell you. Nothing major to report, unfortunately."

"Thank you…you know I appreciate it."

CHAPTER TWENTY-THREE

The Giant Bed

Saturday night, April 24th, 1971

"Dad, what are you doing?" asked Vivian.

"I'm setting up a giant's bed!" Tim had pushed the girls' beds together, dragged his mattress across the hall, and piled it on top of the other two. They now had a towering queen-sized bed. Tim compared it to the one in "The Princess and the Pea," and the girls bought in and helped him set up.

"Where are you going to sleep, Daddy?"

"Right here, with you guys!"

"Why?" said Olivia.

"Why? Because this bed is awesome! You don't want me to sleep on the floor, do you? You have all of the mattresses in the house!" That was a good enough excuse. He kept them up until 9:30, which was a bit on the late side, but he dragged his feet on purpose, hoping again to shorten the night. They goofed around while showering and brushing teeth and had a lengthy pillow fight. Eventually, it came time to turn out the lights.

Tim planned to sleep in the middle. He knew their wiggling would most likely allow him little or no sleep, but he couldn't bear the thought of one of them being quietly stolen from the bed because he wasn't close enough to feel it happening. The whole story about the girls waking him up if he sleepwalked was a pipe dream and really just for Holly's benefit. The girls were such heavy sleepers they would never even see him leave.

CHAPTER TWENTY-FOUR

Night Sweats

Early Sunday, April 25th, 1971

Time passed slowly. It was just after one o'clock in the morning, and Tim had not slept, on-edge, and unable to relax. Something was bound to happen. Something had happened *every night.* He wanted to stretch out and turn over, but he also did not want to wake them or turn his back.

The room was dimly lit by the moon coming through the pulled shades. Both girls were sleeping and had kicked him a total of three times in addition to normal tossing and turning. He had closed the door to the bedroom before joining them in the bed which, at the time had seemed like a good idea, but now he found it only made him try harder to hear things through the door. The first hour was uneventful except for the development of a crick in his neck.

At approximately fifteen minutes past one, he heard footsteps downstairs walking back and forth, ...and then moving away until he could no longer hear them. Ten minutes later he heard them again, meandering in a pattern he could not discern from behind the closed bedroom door; fading, returning—yet methodically approaching this end of the house. It was definitely not a child; the footsteps were too calm and measured.

His heart raced when they seemed (as best he could tell) to pause at the bottom of the stairs, just beneath him on the floor below. *Listening?* A moment later, they began to ascend. Measured and cautious like a hunter, they approached as Tim counted in his head. He remembered the word that Holly had used on the phone: *dangerous.*

His count paused at eleven, meaning there was only one more step until the footsteps were on the same level as he and the girls. He pulled them in closer, lifting his already sore neck to hear better. It was quiet for so long that he began to hope it was over; they had disappeared. *They all end sometime, right?*

The silence broke when the banister near the bathroom groaned as it was used for support.

Odd.

Individual footsteps became a quiet shuffling as they approached, and the same floorboards that creaked under Tim's weight every day sang out.

Aren't ghosts supposed to be weightless?

The hair stood on his arms, and he squinted, feigning sleep in case the door flew open; but he could still see. The shuffling continued outside, and then paused, perhaps for a look into the empty master bedroom. *It won't be long now.*

Forty seconds passed. The muscles in Tim's neck ached. He adjusted his arms underneath each daughter, in anticipation. He imagined her (if it was her) just outside, waiting, listening, with the patience of a cat. *What next?*

Abruptly, a soft scraping began, like a fingertip along the door. It was all he could do to remain still. His eyes remained fixed on the doorknob. Then it stopped.

He forced his head back into the pillow to relieve his neck, no longer able to endure the position. The stress of remaining alert added to his pain, and he did his best to redistribute his weight without waking the girls. The hallway remained quiet as he silently stretched. Another minute passed: *Was she gone?* The sheets were soaked with sweat.

Just then, a light flared to life on his left, settling to a glow. It came from behind the window shade. As quietly as possible, he retracted his arms and separated himself, taking care, despite their deep sleeping habits, not to wake them. When he had escaped the sandwich, he walked to the window and moved the shade—the turret was illuminated by a candle. Suddenly it blew out, leaving the turret in darkness.

He let the shade fall back while he collected his thoughts. There was nothing to plan; the three of them were cornered. He stood motionless at the foot of the bed, listening…waiting. Hearing nothing, he peered out the other two windows. Nothing moved outside.

He listened, and began to consider opening the door to look; perhaps he should check the entire upstairs for the girls' safety, but he reconsidered. Nearly ten minutes had passed since the footsteps stopped; assuming they were gone was a dangerous wager. Not only was he afraid, but he couldn't leave them. Anything outside the room was a risk he couldn't take. A horrible thought of the door slamming shut behind him crossed his mind. If it became locked or impenetrable somehow with the girls on the other side, he would rather die.

With no real plan of action, and tension turning into fatigue, he returned to the bed, being careful not to call attention to the girls, or anyone that might be listening. The house was quiet, and it had been for a long stretch—but still, his heart rate had not slowed. Vivian snored, and Olivia breathed deeply.

A tense quarter-hour later, his body could not take any more exhausting emotion. He said a short prayer for the stress to subside so he could rest. He had been on edge since the girls arrived and it was beginning to take its toll. A short while later he began to drift off; physically and mentally drained. The last thought in his head was his own voice justifying the nap, allowing him to sleep because the ghosts had not opened the bedroom door, and probably couldn't, or wouldn't, anyway.

CHAPTER TWENTY-FIVE

Formal Introduction

He fell into a deep sleep and dreamed of the house. In the dream, it was night, and he was a raven flying high, circling over the turret. Even though it was dark, he could see everything for miles, including the entire property. As he flew, the circles widened, starting over the house, soon expanding to the pond, the woods, and finally the grove.

The raven banked his wings, shifted orbit to the grove and scanned the man-made rows.

He selected a spot and dove, landing on the same mound of leaves he had seen the other day at the end of the last row. It was more than just a pile of leaves; it was a heaping compost of vines, thorns, and brush, all covered by leaves, and he hopped over it like the bird he was.

Still dreaming, Tim realized the two gravestones he saw during his sleepwalk were the foundation; and presumed the vegetation covering was there by design. This was the second time he had been intentionally led here. *What's the message?*

The raven pecked at a canopy of dead leaves that lay on supporting thorns, uncovering one of the stones. The other stone remained hidden by the mulch. From this vantage point, he could see the face of the first stone:

Here lies
Elmer Pike
Abandoned by his father,
Sufferer of his mother's broken heart.

As soon as he'd finished reading, he caught a whiff of something gone-by. The raven took off immediately, which surprised him. It had seemed, up until this point that the bird went where he willed it; now he realized he was just a passenger. He had barely finished the epitaph when he was taken away, leaving no time for the larger gravestone.

The bird flew directly this time; no more slow orbits; he was on his way back with a purpose. As he was about to collide with the outside wall he braced, then realized he was back in the bed with his sleeping girls. The odor was strong. As the memory of the raven dissolved and his consciousness returned, he heard a series of gentle clicks, two or three; the first sounds he had heard in some time. He was not yet fully awake, and the stupor held for another moment. He tried to place the source of the clicks. It was a familiar noise, and yet it escaped him. His eyes opened slowly as he, at last, placed the sound; the trying of a doorknob, followed by the whine of a hinge.

The dream blurred as the adrenalin commenced. Something was amiss, or needed attention; the pungent odor was overbearing. Ultimately Tim remembered it all, and the scene came roaring back.

The bedroom door was open.

Just into the hall, stood the last thing he wanted to see; as still as death and just as silent, face shrouded in shadow, stood the woman in the dress. He had no way of knowing how long she'd been there. Her arm extended into the room, still clutching on the doorknob. The hall window lit the side of her face. Tim stiffened and sat up slightly, pulling the girls in, holding his breath, trying not to wake them.

She was covered in *flies*, and the stench was coming from *her*. This was not pond water or marsh; this was decay, like the dead mouse in the wall the oth—*dear God.* He gagged, and the girls stirred, crimping their noses as they somehow slept through it. *Don't wake up. Not now.* He understood now why the raven had rushed him back. The woman stared motionlessly. Nothing moved but the flies.

Finally, she moved, releasing the knob from her grasp. She took her eyes off Tim and let the arm drop to her side. He strained to see her face to read her emotions, but the poor light would not reveal. He might catch the outline of eye sockets and pursed lips, but no details. She moved again, suddenly oblivious to her audience, and rolled her neck as if it was stiff.

She finished the head roll looking down at the floor seemingly lost in thought. Her head wagged left and right, still working a neck problem that would most certainly never go away. Then she pulled both palms up to her face as she inhaled…*crying?*

He prayed she would not wake the girls during this *display*; the tension was palpable. *What's the point?* She could just as easily leave as she could murder them all right now. *She's unbalanced.*

Then, as suddenly as it had begun, her little moment alone came to an end. She straightened and turned her attention back to Tim, eyes fixed on him as they had been when he awoke from the dream. He tensed, far preferring to be in the audience than to participate in the production.

Here it comes, the moment of truth; I love you, Olivia. I love you, Vivian—

In effect, he said his goodbyes and braced. But...one last chance; he would attempt to whisper; try to talk his way out of her crosshairs without waking the girls. This was it; time was up.

Then—footsteps, downstairs.

Thud-thud-thud-thud-thud-thud-thud.

Focus broken, she turned away from Tim and turned toward the stairs, presumably to try to see the landing below. Leaning over the rail, she listened...waiting. She looked back once more at Tim, then away. *She's waiting for the kid*, he thought. *She's not running to him; wants to surprise him. Catch him.*

She remained motionless, like a hunter seconds from the kill. The footsteps approached, slower now. She sprung and took off down the hall. Several flies circled and dissipated in her wake. Tim heard the front door open as the woman chased the footsteps out of the house. Silence returned.

Tim waited thirty seconds then left the bed, afraid to breathe, for fear of being heard. He was drenched in sweat, and his heart raced. He tiptoed to the bedroom door, and carefully peered around the doorjamb down the hallway to the top of the stairs to see—three dark bedrooms and a bathroom. There was no sound but the gentle breeze, and he quickly ran downstairs to close and lock the front door as if it made them all safer.

He sensed no more sound or movement in the house, and the girls remained asleep, *thank God*. He climbed back up the stairs and looked out the hall window to the front lawn and beyond, thoroughly exhausted. He imagined the chase would eventually end in the last row of the grove...sooner or later. Exhaling, he took off his soaked t-shirt, wiped his forehead, and checked his watch. A quarter past four. *Almost sunrise.*

Feeling safer than he had in hours, he reflected: Why did she let me see her like that…the head roll/neck stretch? The crying… The palms to the face? Can she feel pain? The flies… The stench! Why do ghosts need to open doors?

He felt as though he was trying to put together a jigsaw puzzle while missing half of the pieces.

CHAPTER TWENTY-SIX

Happy Anniversaries

Late morning, April 25th, 1971

With nothing else to do, and sensing the danger was over, Tim crashed heavily, completely exhausted. After the encounter, he had changed his t-shirt and laid a bath towel where he had soaked the sheets. After crawling carefully back between the girls, he physically collapsed, asleep in seconds. It didn't matter how many times they kicked him; there were no dreams this time, at least none that he remembered.

Hours later, he sensed the sunlight through his eyelids, but it wasn't enough to wake him. Minutes later, he heard a ringing in his ears, as if from a mile away. He felt as though the ringing might mean something, but his body was still too tired to cooperate.

"Hello?" it was Vivian's voice...downstairs.

Tim sat up straight, squinting; sun in his eyes. The shades were up. *The girls must have done that,* he hoped. He was alone, and that scared him enough to shake the cobwebs—*back on duty.*

"Yes, but he's asleep. Who are you?" Vivian continued. She was on the phone.

"Viv! Who is it?" he shouted from upstairs as he worked his

way urgently to the edge of the bed and stood up, moving to the doorway. *At least it isn't Sheila.*

"It's the real estate lady. Her name is Holly!"

"Okay, hold on, I'm coming!" He was halfway down the stairs.

When he rounded the corner into the living room, Vivian was there, phone to ear, dressed for the day.

"Where's your sister?" he asked semi-urgently.

"I can't tell you; it's a secret!"

"Vivian, I..." just then he heard a commotion in the kitchen—pots and pans clanging.

"Olivia?"

"Don't come in here, Dad! It's a surprise!"

He sighed heavily, relieved. They were probably trying to make him some breakfast.

"Oh, okay!" Knowing where they were and that they were safe was all the relief he needed. He decided to address the *mess-to-be* in the kitchen after talking with Holly. "Don't start a fire in there!" He rubbed the top of Vivian's head and hugged her as she passed him the phone. His mood suddenly lightened, and he let the tension of the night melt away for the time being.

"Hello, Holly. How are things?" He would have been a bit more personal, but Vivian was still in the room.

"How am I? How are you? Do you know what time it is? *Eleven-thirty!* Did you forget to call, or did something happen? Something must have happened. What happened last night? Tell me what happened!" He was touched that she cared.

He paused for a second to organize his thoughts; a lot had happened after all. His mind wandered, picturing the woman in the hallway, hand on the bedroom doorknob, and the light of the moon behind her.

"Well... You're not going to believe it. It *was* one hell of a night. *Is it really eleven-thirty?* That's not good."

He told Vivian to see if her sister needed any help, then went into detail, quietly recounting all of the night's festivities; from the sleeplessness to the raven-dream with the oddly-worded epitaph (for "Elmer"), to the horrifying stare-down in the bedroom doorway and the footsteps that probably saved his life. Holly was taken aback and remained silent for a few seconds.

"Oh, my God. You're so lucky you're all okay! The girls didn't even wake up—*that* would have been a fun story to explain to Sheila. Can you imagine? You're bringing them home tonight, right? You can't let them stay another night until we have this all figured out."

They were sobering words, and they hit him like a ton of bricks. He was *not* the master of his house, the renovations were behind schedule and would continue to be so under these conditions: Not to mention; the house was just plain unsellable. The back of his neck began to tighten; it was all too depressing when you heard the facts plain and simple.

She sensed gloom at the other end of the line. Perhaps she should have pulled her punch just a bit and made it less hopeless sounding.

"Tim, it's not too late to see if we can figure this out. I read a good-sized chunk of the journal, and I learned some things. On top of that, I didn't see any reference to the name "Elmer." *You* figured that out or were chosen to see that, or whatever. Annette just calls him "the little boy," at least as far as I've read. Maybe if we're getting closer to getting rid of these *ghosts*—I still can't believe I'm saying that. I'm sorry, you must be exhausted. I didn't mean to hit you with a ton of bricks. We'll get there!"

Her pep talk brought him out of his despair.

"You're right; I can't spend another night here because I'm freaking exhausted. I can't even think straight, and I'm a nervous wreck. Maybe things will calm down when I'm not so worried about the girls."

"Exactly, nothing is good when you're tired. We'll get you rested, and that will change the whole game. You need a break. Why don't you just take it easy today? You don't have to entertain them every single minute. Play some board games or something. It sounds like the girls are preparing you a brunch of sorts for you. Just eat it, and kick back. That's what you'd be doing if you were still married most likely anyway—am I right?"

"Yeah sounds good, I do need a break. And a good night's sleep sounds even better."

"I didn't say it was going to be all about sleep, at least not at first. If you want to use the bed you have to pay the toll." Holly's words kindled his spirits, and he was near back to being his happy self.

"I'm no lawbreaker; I will gladly pay the toll. You can tell me how expensive it is later."

"Good. Done deal. I'll see you at two. Stay safe until then!"

Tim sat on the couch a few moments longer, collecting his thoughts. He was exhausted; physically, yes, but more so mentally. He'd been tired tons of times but it had never gotten in the way of his motivation—his drive. In the current situation, with ghosts parading through the property daily, hampering his progress and safety, he was damn near beat down.

He rubbed his eyes, beginning to smell the banana pancakes (as interpreted by an eight-year-old) in the kitchen. They would most likely be well-done on the outside and gooey on the inside. He would have to pretend to enjoy them; part of being a dad. Just then, he remembered something from the night before.

The light in the turret.

He popped up and made a beeline for the staircase, accessible only through the kitchen. Olivia protested when she saw him enter.

"Daaaad! It's a surprise!"

"I know! I can smell the surprise!

She was at the stove, which was chest-high for her, and it looked a little dangerous. Tim wondered for a second if he was a "cool" dad for letting an eight-year-old use the stove, or just another idiot parent that would need help and a lot of luck keeping his kids alive until they became adults. She had a spatula in her hand and was staring at one very lumpy pancake in the middle of the pan. Tim walked over and reduced the burner's heat by almost two-thirds.

"Dad, stop! I'm making them!" Olivia protested.

"Honey, you have to cook them slower, or they will burn. It smells delicious. I didn't look in the pan; I still don't know what you're making."

"Yes, you did!'

"No, I didn't. Hey, what time did you guys wake up?"

"I don't know, you don't have a clock yet, but it was a long time ago. We got dressed and then watched the neighbor. I think he was looking for frogs."

"Honey, there aren't any frogs yet in April. Wait; what neighbor? And *where* did you say you were?"

"Your little boy neighbor. He wouldn't talk to us. We went down to the pond, but he wouldn't say anything. He ran away into the woods. And a goose hissed at us."

"A goose…what? How close did you get? I—I don't even know my neighbors yet—please, don't play with him…or any of them—until I say it's okay."

"He wasn't too close. It was like from me to the table. But the goose scared us…" The distance she was referring to was about ten feet. Tim's heart skipped a beat.

"Okay, I want you guys to stay within my sight, or where we can see each other for the time being. No more hiding in the barn, no more going down to the pond, and *absolutely* no going in the woods. Not until I get to know this place a whole lot better. There are even some floorboards that might need fixing, so stay close even inside, all right?" He was fibbing about the floorboards, but they didn't need to know that.

The girls agreed, and Tim headed to the turret as Olivia continued to stare at the pancake. On the way up the stairs, he reminded her to flip it. This time it was broad daylight upstairs, and the climb was not as harrowing. Even so, he still felt butterflies as he neared the top.

On the desk lay...*the journal?* The journal was supposed to be at Holly's house. He picked it up and opened it. It turned out it was *not* the journal at Holly's house, but another, nearly identical. The handwriting was Annette's. The inside of the hard front cover had the word "Anniversaries" written in bold red ink. The first page had the header "January 1" and then seemed to list all of the happenings that Annette had witnessed on January first...over four different years.

January 1
Saturday, January 1st, 1966
No sightings.

Sunday, January 1st, 1967
Possible footsteps upstairs; not certain.

Monday, January 1st, 1968
No sightings.

Wednesday, January 1st, 1969
No sightings.

He didn't know yet what the new journal meant, but he felt a surge of confidence. Someone, most likely Thomas Pike, was helping him. *Consistently* helping him, and he was only just beginning to realize it. He might have deduced this sooner but for all of the setbacks, interruptions and lost time. Last night had been the worst, and yet Thomas came through once again. Without a doubt, these were not random dreams or sleepwalking sessions or turret candles, but a grand plan to tell him something. It couldn't be the woman; bad things had always happened when she was around; threatening things. Her appearance alone *screamed* evil, with the stench—and the flies—He sensed her malevolence; for a moment last night he had truly believed he was going to die. He recalled the epitaph:

Here lies
Elmer Pike
Abandoned by his father,
Sufferer of his mother's broken heart.

Surely his father didn't commission the headstone if he had "abandoned" the boy. And the next line: "Sufferer of his mother's broken heart"; what did that even mean? It sounds selfish on the part of the author, like something Sheila would say. Obviously the kid couldn't have written it, and it's all about her.

The new journal gave him renewed hope that even as things seemed to get tougher in the house, there could be an answer; he just had to figure it out. Mr. Pike seemed to think it possible that he and Holly could get the job done (whether his intentions were good for them or not); perhaps Tim needed to reciprocate and have some faith in the man that had waited a century to put his plan to work. It was either that or quit on the house, and he still wasn't ready to go there yet.

He chose to believe the new journal meant that they had qualified for "stage two." He and Holly had passed a test and were ready for the next step. He looked out at the woods as he processed the information:

Why not give us both journals at once? Because the information in them must be guarded; given out as needed.

Guarded—from whom?

Take a wild guess, Tim. I'll give you a hint. She's weird with kids, and she smells like roadkill.

With so much on his mind, Tim decided he was too tired and in no mood to invent an activity for him and the girls that Sunday. They piled into the truck and drove to the Radio Shack in Laconia and bought a small black-and-white TV so the girls could watch closeby in a nearby room while he worked.

They set up in the spare room under the master bedroom. He saved any noisy activity such as sawing and drilling for the commercials. After a quick lunch of macaroni and cheese, he realized it was almost time to drive them home. They would be safe, and he wouldn't have the added burden of worrying about them. They didn't even have any stories to bring home to Sheila that he couldn't lie his way out of. He felt a large measure of relief; it could have been much worse.

5 pm finally came, and he had to struggle to keep his eyes open on the highway, even on the trip down to Massachusetts. Once the kids were dropped off, he found a payphone and called Holly. She picked up on the first ring. No games, no grudges, no unjust punishment for spending time with his kids. Holly was a sweetheart.

"You did it. You all survived. How are you feeling?" Holly asked.

"I'm dying, but I'm relieved. I'm going to need to stop for coffee at least once before I head back. How are you?"

"I'm good… You won't cry for me, but I could also use some sleep. I was up late last night reading."

"Did you read the journal?"

"Yes, I did, about three-quarters of it."

"Oh, that's great news. It's been bothering me; I just couldn't get to it! Thank you…I could kiss you."

"Oh yeah? Says who? You have to ask me first," she flirted.

"Okay, I'm asking. Can I kiss you?"

"Maybe. How long until you get up here? And you're coming to my place, right? Not your place…for *anything*, right? I have everything you might need right here. You could use a break, I imagine?"

"Well, I didn't want to invite myself, but I will gladly accept your invitation. It's just not very, uh, relaxing at my place lately."

"Oh? That's too bad; I can't imagine why. You are cordially invited to my house but bring some energy. I mean…I'm *tired*, but I'm not *exhausted*."

Tim grinned.

"It's nothing coffee can't fix."

"Oh, good. Get your coffee, and then get your buns back here. And a word of advice: if you want to stay awake, don't stop to pee. It'll help during those last twenty miles."

Tim laughed at her joke. He laughed at the whole conversation, really; they were excited to see each other. Suddenly a thought crossed his mind like a lightning bolt.

"Oh, my God… Holly, I'm losing my mind—I told you about the journal today, right?

"Uh, no, I just told you about the journal, about how I read a good chunk of it. Wow, you *are* tired."

"Well…you have no idea, and I can't believe I forgot this, but that's not what I'm talking about. Thomas Pike dropped off another journal last night just before my encounter with the Mrs. He left it in the turret again. I saw the light after I heard someone at the bedroom door, then went through the night of hell, and I forgot about it until after our phone call this morning. I went up there not sure of what I would find, and there it was.

"It's a little different than the other one. Annette breaks everything down by date, I think. I only read the first page. Like, January 1: 1966, 1967, 1968, and 1969, all on one page. It might be helpful."

The line was quiet for a second or two.

"Another journal? I'm not even done with the first one, and you haven't read more than three pages of it! Oh, no…"

"Yeah. We're in deep now. Somebody likes us, but I'm starting to think that I'm okay with it. Out of curiosity, what time did you stop reading Journal number one last night?"

"I don't know…wait…maybe I do. I went to the bathroom and saw the clock. It was 1:32 A.M."

Tim thought for a second.

"That is right around the time I saw the light go on in the turret. I wonder if it had something to do with your progress or the fact that I was being harassed right then."

"That's creepy… I prefer to think that nobody was watching me read the journal in my own house!"

"I'm sorry, I'm just thinking out loud. What do I know, anyway? Forget I said it. I'll be there in about an hour. Hold tight. At least it's good that we might have a ghost on our side…right?"

"I don't know. I'm sitting in my house alone as we speak and I don't want to think about this right now. Just come here and don't take too long. *I should have never sold you that house!*" Tim hoped she was just trying to be funny.

"Haha…right. Sit tight; I'm on my way."

CHAPTER TWENTY-SEVEN

Old Shoes and Tired Feet

Tim knocked on Holly's door at 8:18 P.M. She came to the door in her bathrobe, looking like she was ready for bed.

"You don't have to knock, Tim. Just come on in. We know each other well enough now, right?"

"Sure, well, I…didn't want to assume anything."

"Mi casa es su casa."

"Oh. Do I get a key to your place, then? Can I have my own drawer for some of my clothing? And can I hang my toothbrush next to yours?" He was teasing, trying to get a rise out of her. He placed the two journals on the end table by the couch.

"Hey, slow down, I just said you could come in the unlocked door, let's not push it!" She could bust balls, too. He couldn't remember if he and Sheila had ever done that.

"Okay, thanks. I appreciate the hospitality, even with the added snark. You're funny. I think I like it."

"Perfect. Come on in. I made you something."

Tim stepped inside and saw that her table was set for two. There were even a candle and a bottle of wine. *Jackpot*, he thought. For the first time all week, he felt a sense of relaxation; Holly's place was like home. The weight fell off of his shoulders, if only just for the evening.

"Oh...wow. What did you do? Wine and everything? I'll pour!"

"I've been waiting for you to say that for over an hour...but truth be told I didn't wait; I already had a glass."

"Well, it's your wine...I don't blame you! Let's celebrate."

Holly felt the same vibe that Tim did. It had been a long time since she had set her living room table for a date—way too long. The last time was with Tony, and Tony didn't even appreciate this sort of thing. Tim was a breath of fresh air compared to him.

She sat him down after both glasses were full, and brought in the simple dishes she had prepared—a stir-fry with white rice. She was no gourmet, but she did enjoy preparing good food. Tim seemed to like it, and that was another success on this mini-reunion. She had missed him over the weekend. He had made an effort to stay in contact with her multiple times, as though they were connected, which was just what she was looking for. Good people didn't grow on trees, never mind attractive good people. She seemed to be lucky enough to find a good man that had been cast aside by a foolish woman.

It had been a few years since Tony. She could *attract* men certainly, but the talent pool wasn't that large in the Lakes Region, and finding someone who wanted more than just sex wasn't easy. Once in a while, she would almost lose hope and begin to doubt her chances. At times like this, she harkened back to something her old college roommate had told her.

The roommate's name had been Adriane, and she was from Brazil. They had become good friends, and one night, after Holly's boyfriend of two years had broken up with her unexpectedly, Adriane told her an old Brazilian idiom that stuck with her to this day:

"There is always an old shoe for tired feet."

At first, she hated the comparison, and let Adriane know it by poking her arm gently.

"I'm not an old shoe! Don't you have more romantic sayings? Play me some Bossa Nova or something! That's much, prettier!"

Adriane smiled and pointed out that *new* shoes (or *beautiful* feet) wouldn't help a person feeling bad about themselves to feel any better. An old shoe needed to feel there was hope for everyone, including an old shoe. It wasn't the sexiest, most romantic saying she had ever heard but she begrudgingly warmed up to it and years later even realized there was an English equivalent: *There's someone for everyone.*

Holly and Tim ate and talked, catching up on the details of the weekend. The food was good, and the wine made it better. She got a little tipsy and was sure Tim was, too. *Hard to hold your wine when you're tired,* she thought. Unfortunately, she began to see his eyelids grow heavy near the end of the meal. He was still chatty and happy, but she knew his relaxed state would soon become an all-out crash; especially after all he had been through this weekend. She looked over at the untouched journals, and a feeling of guilt set in. It had been such a long weekend without him—reading the new journal was the last thing she wanted to do—and sex was the absolute *first.*

She interrupted him gently and told him to go shower while she cleaned up. Tim protested and offered help, but she insisted. From the kitchen, she kept tabs on the status of his shower as she washed the dishes, and when she heard the water shut off in the bathroom she continued the kitchen cleanup for another seven minutes, attempting to time it perfectly. Whatever mess was left after the countdown was over could wait 'til morning. She heard the bathroom door open as she turned the lights out in the kitchen, then went upstairs to intercept him before he could put anything more than a bathrobe on.

CHAPTER TWENTY-EIGHT

Lots to Talk About

Monday, April 26th, 1971

The alarm went off at 6:45 am, and as always, Tim had to concentrate for a moment to remember where he was. His sleep had been deep and worry-free—no need to protect anybody (including himself) from nighttime stalkers. He did feel something in his first twinge of consciousness that he hadn't felt in a long time: *joy*. It was akin to a child waking up on Christmas morning and realizing today was the day. Even though it was a weekday and he had to go to work in a haunted house all alone, he didn't *feel* alone—in general, anyway. All was right in the world because he had found someone to share his days with, whether they were physically together or not. But still, he wished for more.

"Ohhh… I need a weekend or something."

"Unfortunately, that was yesterday," she replied.

"Life is cruel. What are you doing today?"

"Working, of course. I've got a pretty tight schedule too, for a Monday anyway."

"Ahhh, damn. Heigh-ho, heigh-ho, it's off to work we go. What are you doing tonight?"

"You."

It took a second for it to sink in. *Holly said she was doing* you. Already Tim couldn't wait for 5 pm.

"You're dirty. I'm a *gentleman,* and I don't talk like that, but let me do the cooking tonight. I'll prepare one of my two specialties. By the way, do you have a grill?"

Holly smirked. "I'm sorry if I offended you, but don't worry, I'll clean up my language. Yes, I do have a grill, but it's a charcoal grill, so no propane. It was my ex's…and it sits in the garage as he left it, several years ago. What's your specialty, hamburgers? Please, tell me that *both* of your specialties do not require a grill because we might starve to death in the winter."

He played offended. "No, they do not both require a grill. You'll eat fine in the winter, don't worry, I only wanted to grill my special *side dish* for you, unless you hate grilled marinated asparagus. By the way, I know my way around a kitchen. I worked in a restaurant while in high school, and I like to eat. I can cook just about anything, Smarty-pants, but I have two specialties, and I don't use that word lightly."

Good answer, she thought. *Tim grills his side dish.* "Please let the *chef* know I didn't mean to offend him and carry on."

Tim jumped in his truck after kissing her goodbye, knowing full well that they hadn't even cracked the second journal. I'm just too fucking busy, and it's going to have to wait. I'm not a teenager in a horror movie with two choices: leave the summer camp, or die—I'm a busy adult with kids, an ex-wife, and a new girlfriend… and they all require my time. On top of that, I have to take care of myself, and that means fixing the damn house. Hell, the eighteen-hour days aren't even happening, and I'm up to my eyeballs. I'll get to your cryptic mystery soon.

He had even unintentionally left both journals back at Holly's place. That was probably the safe thing to do if there was anything to his hunch that Thomas Pike might be keeping them from the fly-covered mother of his child. *I'll keep the playbook at Holly's house, Tom, don't worry.*

The same old knot in his stomach turned as he passed between the two trees that marked the beginning of the driveway. He cursed at the house out loud in defiance: "You're a piece of work, you know that? I'm not going anywhere. I've got nowhere *to* go." As the truck rolled past the front door, he felt a hint of déjà vu… something familiar, something he hadn't felt since—*yesterday, come to think of it.* The last time he was here. It was the feeling that he wasn't alone; that he was sharing the house with someone, like a roommate who was always home. *He's quiet, and he doesn't bother me, but I can't truly relax.*

He scanned the property fruitlessly looking for the cause, but of course, didn't see anything or anyone. *That would be too easy*, he thought. As he pulled around to the side door, he cut the engine, and as the vehicle went silent he immediately heard the pounding.

Tim got out of the truck, heart thudding in his chest and called out. The noise came from the roof of the barn. *He's back.*

With no vantage point, and no other options, he called out:

"Thomas! Thomas Pike…is that you? Hey! Come on out! Come to the edge of the roof!" The pounding stopped, and he waited nervously. What might he be getting himself into? He could only picture a mummified corpse-like creature with sunken eyes and wispy hair, but nobody came to the edge of the roof to chat. Now that the hammering had ceased, the silence was deafening. *Don't you need my help, Thomas? Don't ghosts want justice, or rest, or whatever? Give it to me straight. Skip the clues and the puzzles. Make it easier for both of us. C'mon man, what do you want?*

"Hey… Are you sending me journals? If you are, I haven't had time to read them yet. Can you be more direct? Is there a better way for us to communicate? Let me see you. Come to the edge of the roof—look down."

He braced himself again as "be careful what you wish for" ran through his mind, but the roof remained silent as if he were alone, and for all he knew, he was. Maybe he ruined the opportunity by speaking out. *Too late now*, he thought.

"All right, Thomas, well… I had a dream the other night, and I'm not sure if you had anything to do with it, but I saw a couple of gravestones out in the grove—stones that looked like they were covered up on purpose. I'm going to go check them out right now. I don't know what else to do. I can't afford to leave this place. I'm hoping you'll help me out if this is a bad idea—you know if that lady shows up or something. Who is she? Is she your wife?"

Still no answer from the roof.

"Okay, I'm heading out there. And like I said, I haven't had time to read either journal. Holly read part of one of them, but I'm tired; not thinking things through very well right now, if you know what I mean. I had my kids this weekend, and your ex kept me up all night—Wait that sounds bad, sorry. I mean…your ex haunted us all night, I heard the kid running around, and I saw her crying. Come on. Come with me. Come help me out."

He headed up the trail that began at the elbow in the driveway, hoping for something to tell him to stop, but nothing happened, so he kept on. The sunny, warmish April morning dropped a few degrees to the temperature of twilight under the tree canopy, and after three minutes of steady walking while listening for any sounds or warnings, the grove opened up once again. The chill in his belly returned, and he felt vulnerable. Holly would hate this recklessness. He looked back again to see if Thomas had followed him, but once again, disappointedly he had not.

Tim turned back to the grove and began walking along the same path he had a few days before when he followed the boy. He wasn't here today, at least not yet, so Tim walked briskly, head on a swivel, counting the rows, anticipating confrontation.

When he got to number thirty-two, the perfect rows came to an end, and so did the nearly unblemished bed of dead brown spruce needles beneath them. He looked deeply into the wild woods; outside the grove was uneven ground, dead foliage of all varieties, and thousands of trees born from seeds that were planted randomly by nature. This end of the grove was much darker than the other side near the field because he was much deeper in the woods now than when he took the tour with Holly.

He broke his gaze with the wild forest and looked down the last tree-lined alleyway. Way down near the end he could make out the mounds of vegetation covering the gravestones. *Here we go,* he muttered to himself, preferring a proactive approach toward solving this mystery rather than letting the pace be set by someone else. *Better to be proactive than reactive.*

With each step, he checked all directions. To the left was the wild forest; open to possible approach. To the right, there were forty or more rows of grove, followed by about thirty yards of wild forest that ended at the meadow by the road. There was also the forest behind him to keep tabs on, and he didn't even know how far back it went. If it wasn't for the little footpath, he imagined it would be difficult to find the barn from here. If you went through these woods looking for the barn and missed it, you might go on for a mile or more; he wasn't sure. Now that he thought of it, he realized he had no idea how far east he was from the barn and that if he had to run out of here, he had better not miss that footpath.

Onward he continued. The woods were silent except for a faint breeze whispering through the trees. Ahead, the mounds at the far end of the row were becoming clearer. The forest had done a good job of reclaiming the headstones, even if it may have had some supernatural help. The vines had the stones in a chokehold, and thorns stood guard all around. Five years of fallen leaves had all but erased Henry Smith's clearing efforts from the day of his death. Only a small section of the bottom half of one of the stones was visible, looking like an exposed bone from a wound that had healed incorrectly.

A sense of dread fell over him as the forest seemed to get quieter—here it felt as though someone had pulled the plug on his confidence and optimism. The dark specter of depression crawled up the back of his neck and held him by the back of his head, sapping all of his recent joy. Last night was completely forgotten. *It's just not going to work out up here. I've been a fool.*

He stared at the exposed bit of stone as if it had called to him. It peered out from a tiny cave of vines that had caught some unlucky falling leaves, trapping them, robbing them of what would have been a normal decay cycle on the damp forest floor. The top of the stone had been overcome by the rest of the vines, which also seemed to have gathered every available dead leaf that had blown their way.

The thorns made further approach slow, difficult, and dangerous for Tim. He'd have to return another time with the proper tools for a closer look.

Then he felt a new chill and caught a whiff of something that could only be dead. The scene in front of him; the mound of vines and leaves covering the gravestones…flashed. The forest became dark. It was now night. The memory he had in the bathroom the morning after he sleepwalked had returned. The blanket of vines that had been covering the two stones was now pulled back completely, most certainly for his benefit. He looked down at his arms and body and noticed that he was wearing the same t-shirt and shorts from the other night. This, in fact, *was* the other night.

He tried to make out the epitaphs on the two stones even though he had already learned Elmer's, but he was too far outside the perimeter of thorns to make them out. He then felt his body move forward even though it was against his wishes; this was a replay. With his second step, he found the thorn that had ripped into his arm and winced, feeling the pain he hadn't noticed on the night when it had actually happened.

Tim attempted to will his way out of the situation and escape the vision, or dream, or whatever this was, but soon gave up the effort, realizing the futility. His sleepwalking body carried on without hesitation, penetrating the circle of thorns, scraping and catching them painfully as he relived his steps. The briars bit through his t-shirt and drew blood, leaving stains in the exact locations he had found them the morning after.

He grimaced again, wishing that he could have been awake for the ordeal the other night and done a better job of navigating the thorny hazard; then again, he would never have come out here given a choice; he would not have left the girls in the dead of night. This trip out to the dark grove would not have happened at all.

Half a hundred cuts, scratches and gouges later, he reached the headstones and knelt, attempting to read in the poor light. The mildew that had set into the marble surface made it all the more difficult. He tore at some of the bigger chunks of moss with his fingers as he tried to clear the words on the larger stone. *Who are you?*

The larger gravestone sat at an eighty-degree angle having settled unevenly, the victim of a hundred frosty winters. The ground under his knees was especially sunken as if perhaps the coffin beneath him had collapsed and the dirt had fallen in. He kneeled in the depression and grabbed the flattest stone he could find to use as a tool to scrape at the moss and the mold that had made so much progress under the shroud of debris.

His left knee moved and began to sink into the loose earth as he scraped. He heard a muffled snap underneath him, his body weight fell. Suddenly his thigh was half-buried; he shifted his weight to the other leg and repositioned, and finally there it was—the epitaph, or part of it, anyway. It read:

HERE LIES
MILDRED WELLS

As soon as he was finished reading the name, the forest flashed once again, and Tim was blinded for a quick second by...sunlight. Just as quickly as it had come, the night faded away, and Tim found himself just outside the field of thorns. He looked around quickly in all directions to be sure he was safe. The two headstones were still obscured under the compost of vines and leaves. His leg had almost disappeared into the soft grave, but it wasn't as if something had *grabbed* him from beneath—he hadn't even felt like someone else had been there with him…it just wasn't a properly prepared gravesite, at least—that was his hunch. Perhaps the burial had not been done by a professional, or worse…perhaps the grave had been *dug up* at some point.

He regretted not being able to have read the entire epitaph, but at least he would have some news for Holly…that is, after the scolding she would give him after being reckless again. He paused to reflect: This corner of the grove was in all of the messages he was receiving. *Ground Zero for him,* Tim thought.

As fast as he could, he quietly and cautiously left the grove and headed back to the house. The first thing he did when he got back was to phone Holly to share the news and…confess.

"Tim, do I need to chain you to the floor? You keep going out there unannounced, and it makes me nervous! I need to be able to trust you or…or—I don't know what."

"Well, I figured it was just the two of us, Thomas and I, and I wanted to talk to him in the driveway, but he wouldn't show himself. It was an attempt to call his bluff and get him down off the roof, but I guess he…doesn't work that way. And I thought he would protect me or warn me or something if it wasn't a good idea. He wants something from me, or, I mean *us*."

"Yes, I know what you thought, but it doesn't make me feel any better. Look, I know you're a grown man and all, and you're gonna do what you're gonna do, but…please hold off on any more adventures until we're caught up. We didn't really—have time to do that last night. Tonight's the night; it has to be. I learned a lot from what I read. A few things stood out, and most things were just subtle background info, but even if you only learn one thing and it saves your life, it's worth it. Things are happening so quickly; let's not leave ourselves in a dangerous situation."

"I agree, so...what about dinner? We could..."

"We'll order takeout. I don't want to put this off any longer; quick and easy. At first, I just wanted to use you for sex, and I didn't care if you lived or died, but now I'm starting to care for you a little bit."

Tim grinned. "Poor you. I'm sorry to burden you like that. Well, I guess you fell under my spell. So...by 'takeout,' do you mean you want to get a bucket of fried chicken or something?"

"Ew, gross. No. No fried chicken. We'll get a pizza or something, or a Greek salad. I know a place. And for the record, never take me anywhere the food is served in a bucket. No, thanks."

"I was kidding about the fried chicken. I don't consider it 'date food.' I don't think I've ever had a girlfriend that likes it. What time tonight?"

"I had one of my appointments cancel at four, so I'm just going to call it a day around then. I'll be in Franklin before that, which is the next town over from you. I'll stop by. But Tim...seriously... stop with the little side adventures to the grove. You're scaring the crap out of me."

Tim looked at his watch: 11:17 am *What? Already?* How long had the flashback lasted? It was beginning to look like today would be another low productivity day.

"No more trips to the grove, I promise—Time's flying today. I haven't even started on the house yet. I like your plan for the afternoon. Come get me when you're done."

"Good! Get busy and stop exploring."

They hung up, and he went to work in the room by the road on the first floor, the same one he started when the girls were there. He worked like a maniac for more than three hours straight, trying to make up for lost time while making sure to take an occasional walk down to the kitchen and back, checking for *Mildred Wells.*

At around two o'clock, after a short break for a sandwich, he returned to the room at the end of the house to check his work. The walls were done, and he could now either demo the back wall in the hall bathroom or do a thorough cleanup to prepare for Tuesday morning. He decided on the latter. He coiled the cords on his saws, swept up the plaster dust and tossed the old lath boards into the back of his truck for a run to the town dump. In the process, he routinely glanced out the front windows, which were partially obscured by the limbs of one of the big maples. She was there, out beyond the pond.

He ducked to see better under the boughs of the maple. Way out in the pasture, very close to the property line, walked Mildred Wells. *Now I can refer to you by your name.* She moved right-to-left, out of the woods from the far property line, cutting the corner of the meadow and back into the woods toward the grove.

A panicked thought struck him: What if he had left some sort of evidence at the graves? A piece of cloth, some blood, or the hole his knee made in the collapsing soil? The original sleepwalk had been several days ago, but he had no way of knowing if she had been there since then or not; this could be her first trip back. She was now probably crossing from the wild forest into the grove itself. He estimated that if she continued at her current pace, she would reach the graves in—about two minutes.

He dropped the scrap wood he had been holding and ran, grabbing his sweatshirt and bolting through the front door to the road, where he ran the two hundred plus yards to the property line. It was either that or make a run for his truck by the barn and potentially risk running into her by the path at the bend in the driveway. If she had discovered any clue that he'd been there, she might make it there pretty quickly because she might be pissed off; he couldn't chance it.

Now he crouched in the woods by the property line, looking back across the field at the house, very close to the spot he had seen her from the window…second-guessing himself. He paused, panting, wondering why he had forgotten to leave the truck parked by the road facing out, ready for a quick escape. Now he was stuck in the woods until the coast was clear. *And around here, the coast is* never *clear.* He decided to live with his decision and set up a hiding spot with a clear view of the house and barn, waiting nervously.

Within ten minutes, she emerged from the trees. Tim sunk behind the wall, feeling truly helpless. It was a good move, leaving the house just in case, but that was as far as the plan had gone. Now what? She was a hundred yards closer to the house than he was, but thankfully had not looked back, a sign that she might be unaware of his position. From this distance, he could still make out the flies that followed her. *Hundreds...if not thousands; it's a warm day.*

She stood in the middle of the meadow with the pond between her and the house, staring for more than a minute, motionless. *Was she looking for movement?* The thought made him shiver...she had watched him work the day he thought he smelled something dead in the wall...*hadn't she?* How often had she watched? He swallowed hard.

She started ahead in the tall grass, never dropping her head to watch her footing. Just before the pond she planted her left foot awkwardly and fell forward, face down, then picked herself up as if it were nothing at all, then continued. *What the hell was that?* He wondered. *A ghost that—falls down. A ghost that—falls down?*

When she reached the driveway, she took a wide right turn around the side of the house and disappeared into the barn. Tim had to stand and stretch his legs, still mostly hidden by the new leaves of a young white birch. *Where is she going?*

Several minutes passed with no more Mildred. He began to examine his surroundings and check behind him. *You never know.* Luckily she didn't show. He needed to urinate and relieved himself on the stone wall; then watched the house for two more minutes. Despite the excitement and the danger, he was beginning to feel... bored. *What now?*

No sooner had the thought entered his mind, he heard something, behind and to the left. It was a car engine and the sound of tires on gravel.

Her car buzzed past fifty yards to his left, and there was no way she would have seen him in his hiding place. He glanced at his watch: 3:22 pm. *Holly—no! She was early.*

There was nothing to do but burst out of the woods and into the meadow, running full speed in a futile attempt to intercept her, hopefully in the driveway. Holly pulled in and drove along the front of the house, turning the corner and parking behind Tim's truck. He was sucking wind, bounding over the uneven ground, hoping to remain upright. He wasn't even halfway to the pond yet.

"Holly! Holly, no! Don't go in!" he screamed. Holly didn't hear. "*Holly!*"

Oblivious to Tim's shouting, she entered the house from the side door; dangerously close to the last place he had last seen Mildred. He powered on, past the pond falling on his face near the exact spot Mildred had, mildly twisting his ankle on a clod of dirt under the grass. He decided it would be better to enter the front door and intercept her inside rather than run all the way around to the side and pursue.

He burst through the front door nearly bowling her over; Holly had made it through the house to the living room. She screamed.

"Ahhh! Oh my God, ...*oh my God.* Tim! You scared me!" she collapsed on the couch, breathing heavily.

"Sorry! Sorry! *I saw her.*" He quickly left the room while checking the downstairs rooms Holly had not yet crossed through, the first being the one he had been working on—the room by the road. To Holly, it looked like a work-in-progress; to Tim, it was a message.

The room was exactly as he had left it with one exception: On top of his toolbox lay the hatchet from the barn.

"Let's go. Follow me. We have to go now."

Holly saw the look on his face and decided she could wait for the explanation. He grabbed her hand and led her outside, around the house to the vehicles.

"Get in and go. Drive to the diner in town, and I'll explain, but go quickly. I'm going to follow you." Holly followed his unnerving instructions and got out of there as fast as possible, checking her rearview mirror to make sure he was following safely.

Fourteen minutes later, when they were safe and seated at the diner, Tim, still wild-eyed, began to catch his breath.

"What the hell was that?" she asked. "You weren't in the grove again, were you?" Her face was that of a mother correcting a disobedient child. Tim ignored the question.

"I was working in the 'end room' again today, and I looked outside and saw her out in the field heading toward the grove and the gravestones. I got a little paranoid, wondering if I might have left some evidence out there—in fact, I'm sure I must have—my blood, at the very least. I did go out there, but I also had a flashback; in it, I saw part of her headstone. Her name is Mildred Wells."

Holly's face changed from scolding to questioning.

"Not Mildred *Pike*?"

"I guess not. Anyway, the dirt over her grave was...sunken and uneven. I don't know who buried her, but they did a crappy job. My knee sank into the dirt as I read her name, so I'm sure I left that physical evidence. Plus I left blood there."

"Okay, so you saw her from the house. Why did you come running through the front door and scare the hell out of me? Were you coming from the grove?"

"No, that was earlier. I saw her and ran out of the house so she wouldn't know where I was if she came looking. I...made a judgment call when I saw her and decided the house was a bad place to be. I jogged out to the property line and hid."

She exhaled to lower her blood pressure. "What if she decided to hang out at the house all day to wait for you? Or saw your truck and decided to look for you...anywhere—until she found you?"

"I only had a second to think. And it turns out she did go to the house once she checked out the woods. But the really scary thing is that she might have been upstairs while we were in the room by the road. That hatchet—You probably thought that was just one of my tools lying around. It wasn't. She put it there."

Holly went pale. "She was in there with us?" Tim lowered his voice to a whisper so the surrounding tables wouldn't hear.

"She might have been; I'm not sure. Maybe she left. I thought you were going to run into her in the kitchen or something. That's why I barged in like that." Holly slumped back into the padded booth.

"I told you not to go in that grove. That was dangerous, and now we're definitely on her shit list."

"Yes, Holly…but it started with the roofer again. He was up there, pounding away, and I tried to get him to talk. I told him I thought he was trying to help us, and that he should stop me from going into the grove if it was the wrong thing to do."

"That's just an assumption on your part, Tim."

"I had a flashback to the sleepwalking. Everything was night time, and I was wearing the same clothes. I saw how I got all my scratches. I don't think I'm wrong—and we may not *have* a choice."

Tim went on. The ghost, Mildred, seemed to have known exactly what he had worked on that day, which was extremely unsettling. Perhaps she wasn't sure he had been to the grave and decided to leave a warning?

"So, what now?" Holly asked. "Do you really want to work in a house that has a ghost that wields a hatchet? What if you hadn't left the building and hid in the woods? Would she have killed you?"

"Here it is again: The life or death scenario. I get it. It *is* a valid question. It always comes back to this, doesn't it?"

"Of course, it does! You have your health, your daughters and, I'm not sure how you feel exactly but…I'm having fun… aren't you?"

"You know I feel the same, and I love my daughters, but here are the facts: Mildred Wells dressed my kids in nightgowns. She didn't kill anyone that night—and I know we aren't sure if it was her or Thomas Pike that changed their clothes—but I'm betting it was her. Then, she stared me down in the bedroom the next night. She could have killed me then, too, I suppose…and maybe she would have, I don't know, but…maybe not! Maybe she's just crazy. That's a little off-putting too, I know, but bottom line, I'm still alive. She also seems to care for Elmer, because she dropped the girls and me like a bad habit to go looking for him. The bottom line is, we really don't know what she wants. Hell, maybe she's just misunderstood!"

Holly frowned at Tim's current train of thought. Her instincts told her otherwise about Mildred Wells. Tim continued:

"…And then there's today. Who knows what she would have done if I had stayed in the house. Maybe she knew where I was hiding the whole time and just wanted to leave a…crazy calling card. In any event, we're back where we started with the same old dilemma: I can quit now, go bankrupt and second-guess myself for the rest of my life, or I can stick with the plan and accept the consequences."

Holly decided to sit this battle out. He had a point, but safety was definitely higher up on her list of priorities than it was on his.

"All right, Tim; but we are still going to talk about the house tonight, and the journal, and whatever else we have to so that you know. Your trips to the grove, and your dreams, and your sleepwalking, etcetera, are driving me crazy. We've got to figure this out. It doesn't seem like Henry and Annette ended up so well after all, does it?"

"I agree, don't worry," he assured her. "Oh, and one more thing—I'm not sure Mildred Wells is a ghost at all."

CHAPTER TWENTY-NINE

The Anniversary Journal

Monday evening, April 26th, 1971

Holly changed the original dinner plans, including Tim's grilled asparagus, so that they could save time and get down to business. They opted for simple take-out pizza and absolutely no wine. It was time to drag out the homework. Tim wasn't thrilled but understood. *At least I have a hot study partner,* he thought.

The two journals were side by side on the coffee table, and Holly began the "meeting."

"Well, I guess we should try to put our heads together and compare notes, and try to end this whole thing as soon as we possibly can. I read most of the first journal, and what I gathered from it is we are dealing with the same three ghosts Annette was. It's a woman that we now know is named Mildred Wells, and a little boy named Elmer Pike, and an unseen man named Thomas Pike. Annette never figured out Elmer's name, or Mildred's, so we are progressing on our own somewhat. We see Mildred regularly, and on occasion Elmer, but we never see Thomas.

"Additionally, there are a lot of things that Annette saw that we haven't yet. She talks about things she calls 'anniversaries,' where certain scenes play out annually, on specific dates. Not every date on the calendar has an 'anniversary,' however."

"That's the title of the second journal: *Anniversaries,*" Tim added.

"It is?" Holly seemed surprised. She felt a pang of guilt again, regretting the fact that they hadn't gotten around to making these journals their priority. There had been no time to even crack the new book yet. Well, actually there had been, but their adult lives had gotten in the way. "Let me see that for a second." He passed her the second journal, and she took a moment or two to skim the first few entries.

"Okay, this might be a timesaver here…this looks like stuff I have already read; it's just more organized like she recopied her notes or something. I hope I'm right about that; I haven't read the entire book obviously," Holly reported.

"Hooray for small miracles! Does that mean we can go to bed—I mean sleep now?"

"No. We haven't even been talking for even three minutes yet. Nice try. Do you want to be able to sell your house?"

"I was just joking. But honestly, I'm not much of a reader, Holly. Thank God you are. I can't thank you enough. I mean… why do you think I became a carpenter? I ain't no intellectual."

Holly ignored Tim's attempt at humor. "Well, do you need a coffee or something? Just because you aren't a 'reader' doesn't mean you shouldn't take a look. You might catch something I didn't. I'm sure you don't want Millie Wells to sabotage your nest egg, do you?" Tim didn't answer right away, seemingly lost in thought.

"Hey, I just realized something when you said her name that way. That rifle I found down by the furnace has the name 'Millie' carved into the stock."

"See? We should have sat down a week ago. When we put our heads together, it works! Thomas was killed during training exercises right here in New Hampshire while getting ready to go to the Civil War, right? And I'll bet that's probably a Civil

War-era rifle…we should check on that. Maybe he felt guilty or got sentimental while he was away and named his rifle after her." Holly was right. They were better when they put their heads together.

They did not, however, have an answer for Mildred's fall in the field that Tim had witnessed. Holly's first thought was that Mildred was a real living woman attempting to pull a Scooby Doo-type caper, *i.e.,* somebody who wanted to scare him into abandoning the property and then cash in somehow. She even classified the bank manager's son as a "for instance," but Tim corrected her immediately when he reminded her of the sickening swarm of flies that followed the woman everywhere she went. There was just no explanation for her fall in the field, at least not yet.

"Okay, where was I…anniversaries?" Holly continued checking her notes. "Right. According to the journal, there is some crazy stuff that happens around here every year. For instance, there is a funeral march of sorts that goes on, and Mildred is the only one who shows up. It took Annette a few years and a whole lot of thinking to figure it out. She says if you listen closely, you can hear the horses and everything, but you can't see them. And there's a boat on the pond at some point and a bunch of other things that we should be ready for. Maybe if we know where the ghosts will be, we can avoid them."

"Yeah, or on the other hand, maybe we can piece together the whole story. Who was the funeral for…did she say?"

"I'm not sure—the book didn't say. I was guessing it was for Thomas."

"Annette was alone in the house…what, four years?

"Three and a half or four; something like that."

"Well, are all four years' worth of 'funeral march' anniversaries covered in the first journal?"

"No, I don't think so, but give me a second, and I'll double-check." Holly thumbed through the pages until she found the entry for the funeral march on May 17, 1966. She skimmed the passage, which was about two pages long. Then she flipped through the book looking for May 17, 1967.

"Nope, …this journal entry is only about the funeral march on May 17, 1966. In fact, this whole 'Journal #1' *only* documents Annette's first year. This book goes as far as March 1967. Good observation. The second journal is more of a compilation of observations, sorted by date."

"So…I'm confused. If all of the entries from the first journal are all from just one year, how did you know there are 'anniversaries'?"

"The last page explains it. It was as if she returned to the book as an afterthought and left us a note. It says that several things in the journal happen every year. She goes on and on, making it sound important." Holly flipped to near the back of the book and showed Tim. The last two pages that had writing on them were written in red ink.

> *VERY IMPORTANT: To whomever this journal finds, be warned that many of the events written here repeat themselves on an annual basis. I suggest that you take note of exactly where the events take place to avoid any encounters for which you may not be prepared. As I write this, I live in fear of the woman that roams the property; I do not know her name yet, but be careful. She has not harmed me but my intuition…and experience—tells me to stay clear. Use this journal to plan your days! Any time a ghost interacts with another ghost for something important or memorable would be an anniversary. Also, some anniversaries are "celebrated" alone. Any time a ghost interacts with a human being, perhaps YOU… would NOT be repeated or celebrated the following year.*
>
> *If you have read this journal, you know about the woman and the other two entities with which I am dealing. The activity has increased significantly recently. I see visions*

on an almost weekly basis. I will write more as I learn more, just in case I alone am unable to finish the job and rid the property of their presence. Perhaps someone (you, the reader) will need to follow my work.

"'Almost weekly basis'? Good Lord, I see ghosts almost daily!" Tim complained.

"That is strange. Maybe the ghosts took it easy on Annette so she wouldn't leave; either that or she made a lot of progress with them, and they've grown impatient during your turn."

"Yeah, well I could just leave, too. They'd better be patient…! And who is this 'they' to which you're referring? Do you think all of them want this mystery solved? I don't. I think Thomas wants us to solve it, and maybe Elmer, but Mildred—she might be content to leave things as is. She's the one that destroyed the town hall records I think, for example."

"You're right. We've learned a couple of things since I finished the journal. I read it with a certain mindset, but things have changed since then, and we should definitely separate the ghosts and their motives now. I agree. Thomas is the one that wants this all figured out, and Mildred is the one that likes things as-is. Elmer…I'm not sure. Maybe he's caught in between."

"Is he? Why does Mom have to chase him, then? Annette said she never saw the two of them together, and neither have we. And Thomas is never seen with anyone; in fact, he's not even seen *at all.*"

Holly paused in thought. "His gravestone isn't with the rest of the family in the grove, either… maybe he's not able to…interact… because they aren't buried together? Some supernatural law we know nothing about? Oh, and she did put 'Mildred Wells'…not *Pike*, on her own headstone…or…somebody did, I guess. That can't be good." Holly paused, and Tim sat pondering.

"It's overwhelming…but I feel better now that we're comparing notes, you were right. We don't have all the answers yet, but we're moving forward, I think—but as to your point about their relationship—maybe Thomas is hiding from her. I sure as hell know *that* feeling, and I wouldn't blame him."

Holly picked up the second "Anniversaries" journal again. Yes, this was the next logical step; attempting to organize everything so her work could be followed if need be. The handwriting was neater as if Annette were preparing for this type of scenario; it was set up perfectly as a calendar of events for whoever reads it. If you wanted to know what might happen on October 14th, for example, you would simply turn to the desired date.

She opened both books to January entries and started reading. Journal #1 was a plain-and-simple diary. Not only was it about ghost sightings, but most of the entries were personal thoughts and theories, how Annette's day had gone, days where nothing at all happened and others when she simply missed Henry or went to the grocery store. Journal #2 was all about boiling down her diary into a set of instructions. *A very practical and forward-thinking person*, Holly noted.

Holly turned the pages in Journal #1 until she got to a sighting, which happened to be January 23rd, 1966, the day Annette woke up to find her journal on her chest after she had left it in the turret the night before. Holly then found the same page in Journal #2. The page was much neater than the page in Journal #1, and under the header "January 23" were three short paragraphs divided by lines that Annette had drawn to separate the years. The first paragraph had a sub-header "1966"; the second had a sub-header "1967", and so on.

> Sunday, January 23rd, 1966
> *This was the morning I woke with my journal placed on my chest after I had unmistakably left it in the turret the night before. I believe it was placed on my person by Thomas Pike as a message to me to follow my idea of solving the ghostly occurrences going on in this house.*

<u>*Monday, January 23rd, 1967*</u>
No sightings today. No reason to repeat this day as an "anniversary" because it was an interaction between Thomas and me, and not something the ghosts would remember and "celebrate" as a milestone in their lives. Not part of the history I am trying to uncover.

<u>*Tuesday, January 23rd, 1968*</u>
Same.

Then she flipped ahead to April 20th, which was just a few days ago. "Tim…what did we…or just you…see ghost-wise on Tuesday the 20th?" Tim sat on the couch, bleary-eyed. April 20th wasn't even a week ago, and yet it seemed like ancient history.

"Tuesday? My gosh…all the days are running together. That would have been my third full day here…um… That was the day I followed the boy into the grove."

"Oh yeah, right." She shot Tim a disapproving glance, remembering his recklessness. She skimmed the page Annette had written for April 20th.

<u>*Wednesday, April 20th, 1966*</u>
No sightings.

<u>*Thursday, April 20th, 1967*</u>
Volunteering every Thursday at the nursing home, no sightings that evening.

<u>*Saturday, April 20th, 1968*</u>
Same.

"Okay, nothing happened that day that anybody knows about. Lucky Annette." Holly read through the rest of the previous week. No "anniversaries" to speak of. Annette hadn't seen any ghosts at all. She flipped forward until she saw a date with something more than "no sightings" listed and stopped on Monday, April 25, 1966.

Monday, April 25th, 1966
Today I woke to a banging noise out by the barn. It was the only sound on the farm and was very loud. I warily made my way through the house, stopping in the turret to see if I could get a look at somebody from that vantage point, but no luck. From there, I descended the stairs and went out the side door right in front of the barn. I was unable to get a look at the other side of the barn roof due to the proximity to the forest, and I dared not call out to whoever might be up there. I guess that the barn was built in April and this was some sort of memory of such a momentous occasion.

Tuesday, April 25th, 1967
No sightings, although I was out most of the day volunteering at the nursing home. I was feeling lonely and went in as an unscheduled extra.

Thursday, April 25th, 1968
Thursdays: Nursing home all day.

Holly's pulse quickened with the recognition of an anniversary she and Tim had already experienced. It didn't seem like much of an "anniversary," but perhaps somebody (Thomas) had fond memories of it and enjoyed...*roofing*...every year. Perhaps building his house had gone down as one of the best times in his life.

"All right, now we're getting somewhere. What day did you hear the roofing guy on the barn? Not today, but the first time. Was it the 25th?"

She looked up from the journal and across the room to Tim, who had fallen asleep sitting up. *Well, meeting adjourned*, she thought. The poor guy was burning the candle at both ends.

Between kids, construction, dating, ghosts and now journal homework, he was being pulled in every which direction. Even if she woke him he wouldn't absorb any more of this time-jumping confusing journal mess tonight. She would fill him in tomorrow morning before he set foot on the property. To help set him up, she flipped ahead to April 27th, which was tomorrow's date.

> *Wednesday, April 27th, 1966*
> *The mother was seen in a small rowboat on the pond. She remained almost motionless except for the drifting of the boat. It went on until I grew tired of watching! I actually let down my guard and started some of the menial tasks on my to-do list, checking back every few minutes or so. I'm not sure how long it took but roughly half an hour in I went to check on her and she was gone. For the next hour, I lived in fear that she would pop up behind me or something, but that was it for the day. She was gone.*
>
> *Thursday, April 27th, 1967*
> *Volunteering at the nursing home every Thursday.*
>
> *Saturday, April 27th, 1968*
> *No sightings.*

Holly let out a small sigh of relief, relaxing because tomorrow's anniversary schedule was relatively light. Annette did seem to leave more than a few holes in her history, however, …how would she know if a ghost had shown up if she wasn't even home? Apparently Annette had enjoyed a busy adult life, too.

It was an odd thing to be saying that Tim might "only" be seeing Mildred in a boat on the pond tomorrow, but after the past few days, a little boat ride sounded like a day off. And they had learned so much. A week ago, they might have walked down to the pond to ask her what she was doing there; now they knew better.

In today's reality, a sighting was routine; you just had to hope this was not one of those days they wanted to take a closer look.

She closed the book and set it on the table by the door. Then she put the wine glasses in the dishwasher and shut off the kitchen lights. She showered and brushed, all the while letting Tim sleep on the couch in the position she had left him; sitting up. Only at the last minute did she wake him to come to bed, forgiving the fact that he hadn't showered. She would not be requesting his services tonight to let him sleep, and truth be told she was exhausted as well. It had been another stressful day in a succession of stressful days.

She clicked off her night table lamp and kissed Tim goodnight. He had done a zombie-like walk into the bedroom and had barely been able to undress. Her eyes remained open for a few minutes in the darkness. She was relieved that tomorrow seemed safe enough to let him go back to the house alone, but there was something bothering her she couldn't quite put her finger on. After racking her brain for a minute or two, she had to force herself to let it go or else risk trading a good night's sleep for a bout of insomnia.

She woke seven hours later with the same lingering, incomplete feeling, still unable to identify the reason why. Was it related to the ghost situation? Or perhaps it was something as simple as forgetting to pay a bill. It just wasn't coming, so she put it out of her mind once again to brief Tim on what she had learned about today's "forecast."

"Keep an eye on the pond today. Annette saw the mother in a rowboat on one of her years here."

"Only one of her years? What happened in the other years?" Tim asked.

"One year she was at the nursing home, and the other year says 'no sightings.' I don't think I understand it, either. I was wondering if she was out of the house for part of the day, or had a poor recollection as she backfilled her journal after taking a few days off. Here, take a look." She opened the book and turned it around so he could read. Tim was still waking up and had barely made a dent in his coffee.

"That's weird. I don't get it, either. How is this supposed to help? Did she mean to write 'nursing home, no sightings' on the last one? Or does it mean she was home and there were no sightings at all? Anyway, I'll be all right. I never go near the pond anyway, not even on my grove trips."

This riled Holly a tiny bit. "Yeah, well don't go *there,* either! Not today, and not any day until we get our heads around this! Don't go macho on me!" Tim smiled and winked; pleased, he had been able to stir up a little emotion so easily. She cared, and it was a nice feeling.

"I won't. I didn't say I was going to the grove, I just said 'on my grove trips'! I don't have time anyway. I'm so behind. I'm thinking of calling Johnny up here just to put my mind at ease. I'll check and see if he can spare a day in between the paying projects we have lined up. Speaking of that, I also need to be a salesman sometime soon to keep the money train rolling so I can *pay* Johnny! Ugh. I have so much to do. It's...overwhelming sometimes." He shook his head.

Holly could see that Tim had plenty on his mind, yet she still felt they needed to talk more...daily—about The ghost problem. Tim falling asleep sitting up was time they could not spare, but she couldn't blame him. "What are you doing tonight?" she asked.

"Well, I was hoping to hang with you again, of course...! Are you sending me back to Ghost Haven or something?"

Holly grinned, having stirred up a little emotion of her own.

"How about we do the same thing we did last night...just take it easy? I'll get takeout or something, so there isn't a whole lot of prep or cleanup, and then we'll finish our conversation about your house and your visitors? Tim...something is bothering me; I'm not sure what it is. I feel like I'm forgetting something, and I need you to help me figure it out. I thought it might be that Annette spent a lot of time at the nursing home and she might have missed a lot of sightings...but....that doesn't feel like it."

"Something about the house is bothering you, you mean?"

"Maybe. I'm not sure. We're so busy, and there is so much to talk about, we are falling behind on comparing notes, and that could be dangerous. Especially since we're—and I mean mostly you—are behind on sleep."

"Well, in that case, Holly, let me check my schedule. Um...yes, I am free tonight, and I look forward to pizza and ghost stories. Maybe I'll be able to tell you about the rowboat episode, too!"

Holly wanted to laugh, but Tim's last line clipped all humor out of his joke. She went from looking forward to their evening together to the feeling of unease that had haunted her since last night.

"Be careful today. And take pictures if you can. Take my agency's Nikon. We use it to photograph houses for sale, so please be careful and don't break it. It's not going to zoom in very much, but I don't care. Don't walk any closer to the pond to try and get a better shot or anything; it's not worth it."

Tim took the camera and looked closer at the Nikon "F" model. She was right; the 50mm lens would offer little or no zoom capabilities, and the pond, being a good seventy-five to one hundred feet away from the house meant that you might be able to see a boat with a person in it, but definitely no facial details or the ability to identify them. In any case, it was a decent idea and couldn't hurt.

"Okay, I'll stay away from the pond. And I'll try to take a picture, but I'm lousy with cameras—no promises on quality. And, I have a question for you; if I call my worker Johnny up here for tomorrow night, would that be all right with you? I'm not even sure he'll want to come. I told him about our ghosts, and I was surprised to find out that he's had some experience with at least one: his grandmother. I don't know any of the details, however."

"No, I don't have any problems with that, as long as he's okay on the fold-out couch… But, you're going to tell him everything first, right? I mean that he could be in danger? You've got to give him every chance to back out, Tim. Does he have a family? Wife, kids?"

"Yeah, he's got a wife and kids. I'll make sure he knows everything. That's why I said I wasn't sure if he would come up or not. I plan to use his skills for the majority of the sunlight hours. No early mornings or late afternoons or anything close to darkness."

"Maybe his grandmother story can help us, too. All right, well, keep me posted if he says yes. I'll stop at the grocery store and pick up some things." They finished breakfast, cleaned up, and left for work. Tim followed her until the intersection where left meant Sanborn and right meant downtown Laconia. When she turned, he waved to her through his Plexiglas patchwork repair job window, which was still on his ever growing to-do list.

Holly waved, smiling as she did. Over the next half mile, her smile transformed to a furrowed brow with a slight frown. This *tip-of-the-tongue* type problem was bugging the hell out of her. Little did she know, but in less than twelve hours, she would have her answer, and it was all because of Annette's anniversary journal.

CHAPTER THIRTY
Cornered

Tuesday, April 27th, 1971

Tim cruised down Lancaster Hill Road, preparing for the first glance of his property coming up on the right. First, he would pass the field and then the pond, but he didn't want to pass the pond at all if there might be a boat on the water. Slowing to twenty miles per hour, he craned his neck to try and get the perfect viewing angle out the truck window and over the stone wall. It was difficult; the angle was bad, and the pond itself was ringed with high cattail weeds that further limited visibility.

Looks like...no boat, no Mildred...no anything. Good. He pulled around the house to his customary parking spot in front of the barn, but then reminded himself to turn around and face the road. He got out, did the obligatory scouting, and from there made a quick stop in the turret to see if there had been any correspondence (there hadn't).

From there, he went to the room at the end of the house. As he entered the room, he recalled his last time here; he and Holly had left suddenly because of the hatchet-message-threat left on top of his toolbox. A chill went up his spine:

It was gone.

Upset at the thought of Mildred's tool of choice being out there, free and available for her use, he dropped everything and went out to the barn, the most likely place it would be. He stepped through the doorway and past the point the sunlight reached and opened the drawer to the workbench; there it lay, in the same position he had found it the day the girls were hiding on him in the hayloft. He took it and locked it in the toolbox in the bed of his truck.

After that, he went back to the room at the end of the house and retrieved the necessary tools and materials needed for today's project and brought them upstairs to the guest room across from the master bedroom.

He chose this room for today's project because it had the best straight-on view of the pond. There were two maples that grew along the stone wall running between the front lawn and the pond itself, but the two trees were far enough apart as to afford a wide-open view of the water which rippled in the gentle breeze as he gazed out at it. *It looks better than it smells*, he noted. Then he set to work with his crowbar, once again demolishing the old wall with the intent to rebuild and fortify it with modern materials.

The noisy part of the job was this first step, and he had it all torn out in less than an hour. He took short breaks often to test the air for the scent of death and walk the hallway to the top of the stairs to see if Mildred might be lurking. The thought of being watched again was not a comforting one. The work went swiftly, but every nail and old board that the crowbar pried out seemed to release its own individual whine or growl, and he wondered if it might attract unwanted attention.

This room was the sunniest in the house, but the day was gray. Clouds in the distance threatened to bring some of the famous April Showers about which everyone loved to complain. *April showers bring May flowers, but what do May flowers bring?*

"Pilgrims," he whispered out loud. Mayflowers bring pilgrims. Good one, Tim. Good joke. Everybody in New England knows that, or, at least they should. The whole country should know that joke, for that matter.

He was surprised to realize that he was actually getting bored. There were no in-betweens in this house. Either you were terrified while you worked, or you were bored—the ghosts got you both ways. *Darn you ghosts for not showing up today and leaving me bored,* he thought. *Now that's ironic.*

Under normal circumstances on a job like this, Tim would bring a radio and attempt to tune into the local station to help pass the time. Sometimes it was an AM radio station that played Top 40 hits, or if he was lucky, he might catch a Red Sox game. This job site was different, however, in that he didn't want to be distracted. He didn't want to be "deaf" to the sounds that the house made—and it made plenty. Even the false alarms were scary.

There were the countless cracking noises, as the day came up to temperature after a cold night. There was also the occasional scampering squirrel either on the roof, or, (hopefully not) inside the crawlspaces. Occasionally two or three noises would happen in succession, which Tim took to naming "false footsteps." Not only did they raise the hair on his arms, but they stopped work for several minutes as he paused to check things out thoroughly. All the while, Tim shot glances at the pond, with the real estate agency's camera sitting on the windowsill in the hallway waiting for its photo op safely out of the range of his construction dust. Noon came and went.

At around 12:30 he took a break and went downstairs to call Johnny. He had almost forgotten to make the call at all. It was Tuesday, and he knew Johnny must be working on the Mills' kitchen down in Topsfield. Mrs. Mills picked up on the second ring, and after Tim had made small talk for a few minutes, making sure things were going to her satisfaction, she passed the phone to Johnny.

"How are things down there, Johnny? Ahead of schedule as usual?"

"Yeah, hey, I was going to call you tonight. I'm done here after today, or at least as done as I can be until Mrs. Mills' exhaust vent arrives. When is that coming?"

This particular exhaust vent was a thorn in Tim's side. The manufacturer had sent it to the wrong address, and the result was a work stoppage, pissing off Mrs. Mills and delaying his payday. "It's coming on Friday now. What a pain in the ass. I told them I'll just order from China direct next time if they can't get the shipping straight—this is the second time with them. Give me a break; I always speak to some guy named Larry, and Larry doesn't know his ass from his elbow."

"I know that dude. He's terrible. I always ask to speak to someone else," Johnny retorted. "So what do you want me to do?"

"That's why I'm calling, Johnny. I wanted to ask you—, and I completely understand if you aren't up for it, but if you could come up and help me, I might be able to catch up a little bit here."

"Is Holly slowing you down, boss?" Tim could hear Johnny's grin through the telephone line; never one to miss an opportunity to bust some balls. The two of them shared the same sense of humor, and when they worked together, would swap playful barbs all day long, provided the customers were out of earshot.

"Uh…ha ha…I hear you smiling, my friend, and you're right, that's part of it. That's a pretty good chunk, in fact. But it's not the whole deal—and I need to tell you about it."

Johnny could tell Tim wasn't playing today for some reason. There was a lack of gutter humor, which was fine with him because Mrs. Mills was one room away, most likely listening to his conversation. She was a stay-at-home rich housewife who employed a cleaning lady and spent a good amount of time reading romance novels…but had little patience. Johnny continued: "So… is this about the other thing you were talking about the last time I saw you, correct?"

Tim could tell that Johnny was not in a position to speak

freely. Mrs. Mills wouldn't even allow a radio on her job site, and he knew all about her close tabs on the work-in-progress. "Yeah, it's about the ghosts. I see them every damn day. We even have a couple of journals now that we uh…'found,' that tell us when some of the things are going to happen. The previous owner of the house wrote them."

"Did she give them to you? Or is she…let me guess. She's uh… not around anymore, right?"

"Right. She's dead; died in her sleep at the ripe old age of sixty. And I know what you're thinking, and that fact never sat well with me, either." *Sixty years old and "natural causes." Give me a break.*

"Anyway, Johnny, we have actually been…physically touched by these ghosts; or by one of them anyway, I'm not sure. I couldn't even move, man. I'm serious. I was pressed back into my truck seat like a pancake. So was Holly, so it's not just me going crazy. You can ask her."

"Well, what the heck are you still doing up there, then? If it's not safe, just leave, man! It's not worth it!"

Here we go again. It's just not that easy, Johnny.

Johnny had lowered his voice drastically, so Mrs. Mills wouldn't hear the content of the phone call but knew that his whispers would most certainly piss her off and she would soon come to the kitchen to pretend to get a snack.

"I… I don't think he was trying to hurt me. Maybe he was trying to help—I'm not sure, to be honest."

"*He*? Like you know this guy? How's that? How does holding your body immobile help you?" Johnny asked.

"Yeah, look, I know it sounds crazy, especially when you've only heard as much as I've told you…but…never mind, I can't tell you over the phone. I can tell you more when you get here."

Mrs. Mills showed up in the kitchen at that moment and pretended she was looking for a box of crackers in the cupboard. "Uh, Tim, I'm going to clean up here, give Mrs. Mills back her kitchen for now and get ready for Friday when the exhaust fan comes. I'll be up tomorrow morning first thing, just give me the address again, and I'll go buy a map of New Hampshire."

"Hey listen, Johnny, no pressure, you don't have to do this, I would understand..."

"No, don't worry about it, I'll be up there by eight o'clock, and we'll go from there. I have to go. I don't think Mrs. Mills knew that the exhaust fan was coming Friday; thanks for letting me break the news to her, old friend. I'll explain it all. Oh, and Chief...if you happen to talk to my wife between now and tomorrow, like she calls you or something, for whatever reason, do not mention the *pollen count* up there if you know what I mean. She wouldn't want me to have an *allergy attack*. Understand?"

"Right; don't tell your wife about the ghosts. I got it."

Just before they hung up, Tim heard Mrs. Mills say "Friday?!" and he was thankful to have such a capable employee as Johnny. Not only could Johnny outwork anyone he'd ever met, but he was also great with the customers. In all the times he had let Johnny do the talking, he had never been disappointed with the way the situation had been handled. Right now, it was nice not to have to add Mrs. Mills to his list of problems.

He placed the telephone back into its cradle and walked over to the front window to look down at the pond. It was still overcast, and the surface of the pond was a dull gray, but it was also free of boats, so he was happy, albeit confused. *Fine by me*, he thought. *But what's up with your journal, Annette?*

At that moment, something caught the corner of his eye. He turned quickly, looking through the house from the living room to the breakfast area; whatever it was, it was gone, but the hairs on the back of his neck confirmed what his eyes had missed.

Quietly he backed away from the front window to avoid being visible to whoever might be in the kitchen. Then he huddled against the wall and listened.

He heard the sound of something boiling and a knife against a cutting board. *Click click click.*

He was no longer alone in the house.

His thoughts went immediately to Annette's diary, more specifically the entry where she said that she was suspicious of the "woman ghost"...and to stay away. *It had to be Mildred in there right now.*

He decided against peering around the corner to the dining room, never mind the kitchen. His heart pumped harder than any of his trips to the grove. This was different; this time someone came to visit *him. Where's the damn boat? What the hell is THIS episode going to be? Why, why, why have we gotten this so wrong?*

All bets were off. He decided to escape as soon as the opportunity presented itself—*if* he could hope to be so lucky. He backpedaled, stepping carefully, trying to remember the floorboards that made noises. His plan of escape was through the front door at the bottom of the stairs, and he was nearly halfway there. He took another careful step backward, never turning his back.

Her voice disrupted his train of thought.

She was crying; an odd, low sob broken up by long pauses as she drew her next breath. To call it sadness was an understatement; this was anguish. During the pauses, the house went silent except for the boiling pot. The chopping had stopped.

Tim waited seemingly forever between wails, beginning to sweat, bracing for the next round of lament. The realization she had a knife was not lost on him, and once again, he realized he was caught unprepared with no weapon of any sort.

Another full-on wail broke the silence; a cry that could have been heard past the pond, in Tim's estimation. It was the loudest thing he had heard in *many* days. Unconsciously he raised his hands to his ears.

She had moved closer, he guessed, but how close or for what purpose he couldn't be sure; he wanted nothing more than to leave and leave now...anything to avoid hearing the next shriek. He held his breath, ready to make a break for it.

Then; a loud crash in the kitchen; and another...and another;

dishes were breaking—or rather, being smashed. A high-pitched scream filled the air, infinitely worse than the wailing. Sorrow had turned to anger, and Tim wanted no part. The scream tailed off as her breath ran out, followed by a guttural groan as she inhaled… reloading. It might have been a wild animal in his kitchen if he didn't know better.

Tim began to shake; the first few members of her personal swarm were beginning to cross over into the living room, and he knew the stench would soon follow. He was cornered, backed almost into the office behind the living room, cut off from his truck entirely. Even if he decided to go diving through the office window into the back yard, he would have to run around the entire building. *This could be curtains.*

Another dish smashed, but it sounded different this time; it might have been a window. Tim's eyes darted left then right, eyeing the front door, calculating distance, about to run directly through her field of vision. *If she wants me, I'm done. I'll be dead before I get to the door.* Her fury, her noise, and her presence were unlike anything he had ever felt or heard.

The gray sky outside darkened suddenly as if a storm was imminent, and just before Tim sprang, the front door swung open.

On the front step stood Elmer, looking just as glassy-eyed as Tim had remembered. The dark clouds hung behind as if they had brought him. He looked directly at Tim, a finger pressed against his mouth. *Silence.*

He raised his left hand in a *stop* gesture, and Tim's mouth dropped. He would have to trust him. The screaming continued, more and more frantic; sobs, shrieks, and rasping whines pushed from twisted vocal cords. The shattering of plates continued, along with the crashing of pots and pans as they struck floor, ceiling, and walls. Tim watched the boy intently, clearly distraught that the balance of his life was up to the dead thing in the doorway. Elmer remained still, *perhaps because this doesn't really matter to him*, Tim presumed cynically.

On the table to his left, the telephone rang.

The piercing ring startled Tim and caught the attention of the banshee in the kitchen. Everything stopped; no more screaming, wailing, or smashing. The dead boy lowered his hands, and the only noise in the house was the buzz of flies that cared only about their next warm landing spot. The pressure heightened as Tim watched the two doorways.

CHAPTER THIRTY-ONE

The Four Aprils

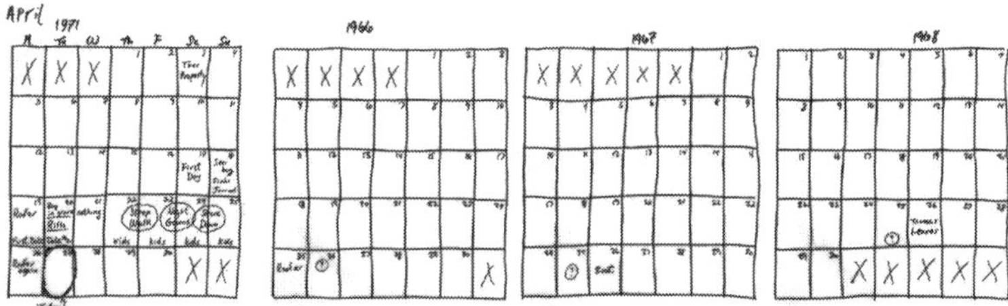

Tuesday, April 27th, 1971 (Laconia)

Holly parked in her usual spot at Depot Realty. It was named that because the building the business was housed in used to be an actual railroad depot. The owner had bought the building and paid to have it moved on a tractor-trailer truck up the road away from the tracks. The outside looked quaint, but Holly hated the cramped quarters her office afforded. As she removed her key from the ignition, she realized she couldn't remember one detail of the morning commute. The *thing* that was bothering her (and had been bothering her since breakfast) continued to elude her. It was almost there, and then it wasn't.

She dropped her bag and her day planner on the desk and sat down to plot out not only her day but also the whole week. Evenings with Tim were certainly fun, but they had definitely cut into her prep time, not that it wasn't a good problem to have. A big part of life was learning to handle the unexpected, and this was good practice. Besides, she didn't want her life to be all about work. She had thrown herself into her career after the breakup with Tony, and it wasn't long before she realized that work was work and it would always be there—and it wasn't very fulfilling.

She kept a rolling to-do list, and yesterday's was still taped to the light on her desk. She took it down, grabbed a new piece of paper from her pad, and recopied the items that did not get crossed off. Then she opened up her monthly planner and copied some of her upcoming tasks, duties, and things that just needed to be done regularly, like grocery shopping. On top of all this importance-wise was her *call list*, which was also consistently updated and maintained. Today there were eight phone calls to be made, two showings and thankfully, a signing.

Fifteen minutes later, Holly sat back in her chair, the day's plan finished and ready to go. Phone calls usually started at ten o'clock; a little rule she lived by to reduce anxiety. Planning downtime was just as important as planning uptime. There was a time for phone calls, and there was a time to do *everything but* phone calls. Holly hated phone calls, so she sat back and enjoyed the peace.

In a daze but deep in thought, she glanced at her bulletin board, which had a twelve-month "Depot Realty" calendar pinned to it. She didn't really use this particular calendar, preferring her day planner instead, but it had been given to her (and everyone in the agency) at the office Christmas party by her boss, Marty Dubois. The annual calendar was the only holiday "bonus" that Marty ever gave, and he was infamous for it. It earned him several nicknames around the office, "the Frugal Frenchman" being the kindest.

Holly noticed that April was almost over and she hadn't yet flipped the page from March, so she pulled the pushpins and corrected it. She stared at the stark pages, devoid of any handwritten notes like many of her coworkers had on theirs—*brown-noses that they were.* The picture on the upper page was of a covered bridge that was more than an hour from Laconia. Marty wasn't selective with his calendars. *Scenes from the Lakes Region would have been more appropriate,* she thought.

She began to daydream and yawned as she continued to stare at the world's most boring calendar. There were only three holidays printed on the entire month of April; the first was April Fool's Day, the second was Passover, and the third was Easter, which had already come and gone on April 11th. Holly was somewhat of a "lapsed Catholic" and hadn't realized she had missed it, something her mother would not be proud of if she ever realized it. *Easter*, she thought. *So hard to keep track of...it's on a different day every year.*

All at once it hit her; and she stood up, processing the realization. The "thing" that was bothering her was not something forgotten, but something she hadn't thought completely through. She needed to get her hands on some old calendars as soon as possible.

On her way to the library, she wondered what the best way to look up old calendars might be. There were encyclopedias, but where to start? Or she could just go to the microfilm, or microfiche, or whatever they called it and go through some old newspapers. As soon as she arrived and situated herself in front of the microfilm reader, the thought occurred to her that Annette may have at one time sat in this very chair as she worked on her journal. The term "same page" popped into her mind, and she couldn't help but shake her head at the irony.

Holly opened a blank notepad, and on the first page drew herself an empty calendar with seven boxes across and five boxes down. Then she traced the same blank calendar three more times. When she was finished, she wrote April 1971 at the top of the first, April 1966 at the top of the second; then did the same for the years 1967 and 1968. 1971 was *present-day* for her and Tim, and 1966-68 were the *Annette years.*

Next, she filled in the days of the week from Monday to Sunday. She just wasn't a "Sunday-Saturday" person because she enjoyed her weekends and hated seeing Saturday and Sunday separated by all of those workdays.

Then she inserted the first roll of film into the machine: *Sanborn Crier, 1966*. Scrolling to April, she grabbed the first date she saw: Friday, April 1. *One down*, she thought and began filling out her blank 1966 calendar with the correct dates.

April 1, 1966, was a Friday, so she placed large Xs in the first Monday-through-Thursday boxes, followed by a small "1" in the upper right-hand corner of the first Friday box. From there she continued numbering until she got to April 30th. She did the same for all of the other years, popping in the appropriate film roll for each of the years to figure out which days the dates fell on. She could have just started 1967 one day later and so forth, but with leap years and such she didn't want to take the chance of getting something this important wrong. She just didn't have the mental clarity to figure out leap years right now. *I'm too damn tired*.

When all of the blank calendars had their days and dates in order, she opened Annette's Anniversary Journal to April and began writing abbreviated notes for all of the occurrences.

To save time, and for Tim's safety, she began with the current week: the fourth full week in April. Beginning on Monday, April 25, 1966, she re-read the same journal entry she had the previous night:

> *Monday, April 25th, 1966*
> *Today I woke to a banging noise out by the barn. It was the only sound on the farm and was very loud. I warily made my way through the house, stopping in the turret to see if I could get a look at somebody from that vantage point, but no luck. From there, I descended the stairs and went out the side door right in front of the barn. I was unable to get*

a look at the other side of the barn roof due to the proximity to the forest, and I dared not call out to whoever might be up there. I guess that the barn was built in April and this was some sort of pleasant memory of such a momentous occasion.

Tuesday, April 25th, 1967
No sightings, although I was out most of the day volunteering at the nursing home. I was feeling lonely and went in as an unscheduled extra.

Thursday, April 25th, 1968
My normal day at the nursing home; I volunteer every Thursday.

On the 1966 calendar, in the Monday, April 25 box, she wrote "ROOFER." She flipped the page to 1967, and in the Tuesday, April 25 box, she wrote a small question mark in pencil, because Annette wasn't home for some part of the day and might have missed something. Then she flipped the page to 1968, and in the Thursday, April 25 box wrote another question mark for the same reason. After that, she continued to April 26th.

What she saw written on the page gave her a funny feeling, very similar to the feeling she had this morning. Her pulse quickened, and she told herself not to panic, but silent alarms went off in her head. She needed to think clearly and wrap her mind around this.

Tuesday, April 26, 1966
Volunteered all day at the nursing home.

Wednesday, April 26, 1967
As expected, the mother was again seen in a small rowboat on the pond. It was an identical replay of last

year. No moving, no nothing—just drifting, then a sudden disappearance after I looked away. No further sightings this day.

Friday, April 26, 1968

A very upsetting day! The mother went berserk with emotion…it was so loud; I can't get her screaming out of my head. Thank God she didn't see me. I was upstairs making the bed. A loud howl came from the living room below and nearly scared me to death. I jumped out of my skin and let out a scream of my own that I muffled immediately. She was VERY close.

I waited in silence for a moment, praying she didn't hear me. A second later she wailed again, and despite the bloodcurdling volume, I felt some relief; she either hadn't heard me or didn't care. I heard her footsteps as she ran through the house downstairs, sobbing. She left through the front porch, bursting through both doors, and I'm surprised neither one came off their hinges.

She stood in the middle of the driveway facing away from the road; hands held out straight as if attempting to keep someone back or impede their progress.

She appears …DEAD for lack of a better word, and I'm sure that seems obvious to the reader, being that she is a ghost, but I mean to say that she looks like a corpse. Her motions are odd, slightly stiff and jerky, and her face has a blank expression despite the obvious emotion expressed by the noises she makes. She is a terrible sight! She is covered in flies—visible flies.

There were no clear words that I could make out...about the closest she came to being intelligible was something resembling "no"...but it might as well have been another language...or from another world. I have never heard anything like it, and I hope I never do again.

As she stood, holding back something I could not see, her body visibly moved to the side, as if someone was there... or as if she had choreographed it. She moved violently; could she throw herself around like that? Perhaps she can channel energy from the fateful day Thomas left her for the war.

I think it was a reenactment of the morning he left. If I'm right, that will place the year in 1861, I believe. Thomas Pike died May 12, 1861, during training exercises.

The ordeal in the driveway ended when she collapsed near the road in defeat, sobbing heavily. Eventually, she stood and slow-walked around the building toward the barn. The whole ordeal was highly disturbing.

What are the five stages of grief? Anger, sorrow, depression—I can't remember them all (I knew the list very well right after Henry died). Some of the ones I have written here might be wrong, but I know the last one is "acceptance"...and I am sure this woman has NOT accepted her fate. Her emotions are powerful; she is angry. She is the epitome of unrest.

I hope you find this journal and can avoid this day. I may pay a visit to the nursing home after this writing to do some good work and be with some living people for a while.

April 26th is a very busy day, Holly thought; *and always different.* She began to jot down abbreviations for Annette's journal entries. Tim heard the so-called "ROOFER" on April 26, 1971. Annette saw a "BOAT" on that date in 1967 and "THOMAS LEAVES" in 1968. She was beginning to understand what she hadn't until today; "Anniversary Journal" was a misnomer in some ways; Annette's attempt to organize the ghost activities, while much appreciated, was imperfect.

An "anniversary," such as a birthday or a wedding date, is the same date every year. A person born on August 8th celebrates their birthday every year on August 8th. Easter and Passover are a different type of annual happening, calculated using the vernal equinox and falling on different dates every year—but Holly was guessing that this whole ghost problem worked more like—*Thanksgiving.* Thanksgiving is always the fourth Thursday in November. Annette had not crafted her Anniversary Journal this way; she did it by *date,* and it wasn't about the date. It was about the *day of the week or the month.*

Holly was a visual learner and needed to see the information written out on a calendar, or in this case, calendars. The first thing she did was fill out Tim's experiences to the best of her ability in the 1971 calendar. There were a couple of days that he ran into the "roofer," there was the kids' visitation, the sleepwalking, the nightgowns, the stare-down in the bedroom, a couple of trips to the grove…but not all of these would be considered official "anniversaries" because as Annette had said:

> *"No reason to repeat this day as an 'anniversary' because it was an interaction between Thomas and me, and not something the ghosts would remember and 'celebrate' as a milestone in their lives."*

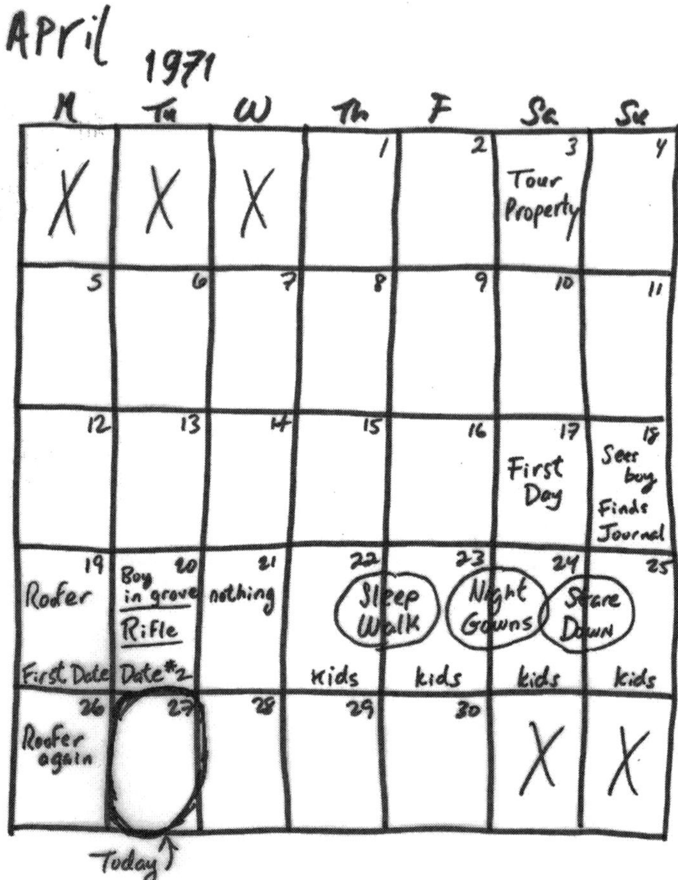

After she had finished the 1971 calendar, all she had to do was transfer Annette's somewhat confusing work, and then they would have a pretty good idea of when these "anniversaries" would actually happen in 1971. Working quickly, she filled in the April 26th entries on the 1966, 1967 and 1968 pages.

Next, Holly gathered and stacked the four calendars together and held them up to the fluorescent bulbs on the ceiling above. From this viewpoint, she could read her notes through all four pages. *The fourth week in April for all four years could be viewed at the same time.*

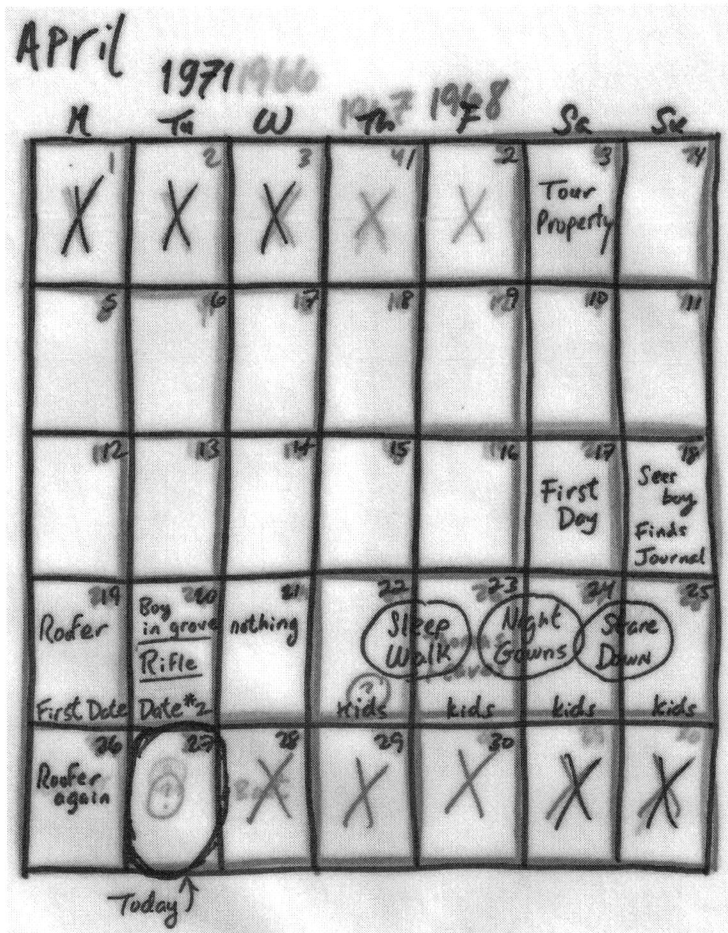

But then she caught something disturbing. The fourth week of 1968 did not line up with the fourth week of the other three years; in fact, none of the weeks of *April 1968* lined up with the other three Aprils.

April 1st, 1968 was a Monday and Holly had simply used the first available Monday square on her hand-drawn calendar. In the other three years, April started on a Thursday (1971), a Friday (1966) and a Saturday (1967), so most of the first week of those three calendars was crossed off *as the end of March.*

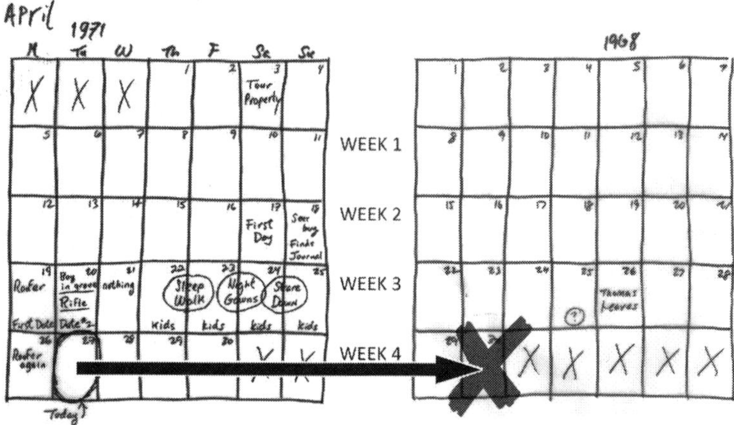

She had to *offset* the 1968 calendar in the stack so that the four weeks of all four Aprils would align.

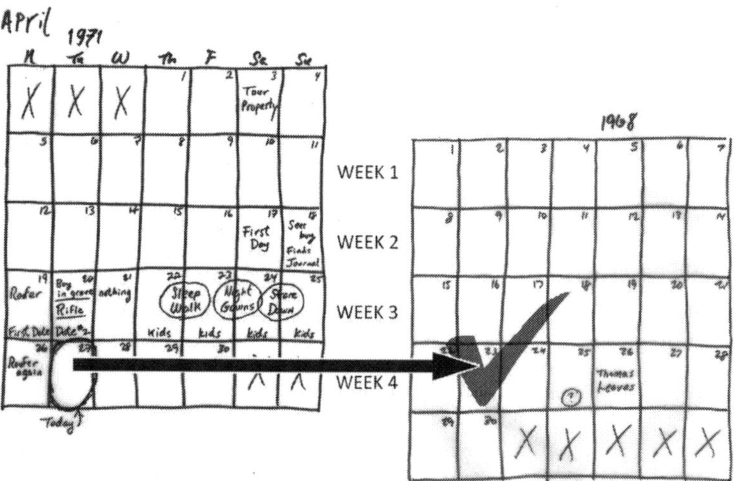

Monday, April 26, 1971, said "ROOFER" on it. Looking through the page, she could also see the word "ROOFER" through the pages on the 1966 calendar.

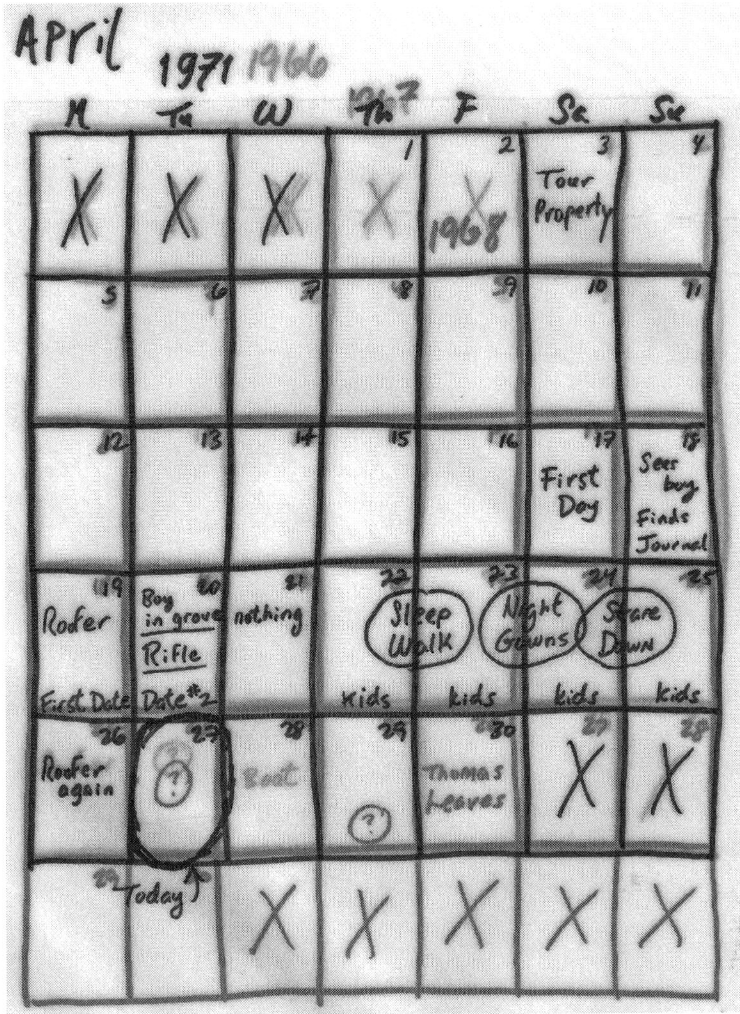

Tuesday, April 27, 1971, was the fourth Tuesday of the month and *today's* date; which made it *the most important date of her life*—and Tim's as well. It was blank because, well, they hadn't lived through this day yet. What had happened on this date on Annette's watch? Holly was a bit surprised to see two question marks, slightly offset from each other as they shone through the backlit pages. Those were the two days, in different years, that Annette had not been home to observe because she had volunteered at the nursing home. Why only two question marks, and no notes from the remaining Annette year, April 1968? Holly felt her stomach sink. *Oh no.*

Today, April 27th, 1971…was the same day as *April 23*rd, 1968.

She hadn't even looked at Annette's April 23rd entries yet because she had considered them *in the past—as in, last week*—and therefore no danger to Tim until next year—but she had miscalculated. Suddenly, April 23rd, 1968 scared her. She couldn't flip back through the Anniversary Journal fast enough. She frowned as she arrived at the page and saw that it included an extra-long piece of paper folded up; Annette needed more space to write it all down.

> *<u>Tuesday, April 23rd, 1968</u>*
> *Awful, awful day! I was upstairs changing the bedsheets when a cacophony of crying and screaming, followed by crashing dishes and pots and pans, came from the kitchen. I know that this house is haunted, and whoever was making the racket is not of this world, so I stayed upstairs. The…sorrows, I will call them…went on for several minutes, and the gloom in the woman's voice was the most depressing thing I have ever heard.*
>
> *At one point, I heard her moving away from the kitchen approaching the staircase, which terrified me, but I was relieved to hear the porch door open. She left in a rage, a hatchet in her grasp, walking briskly to the pond. I hid behind the curtain, watching.*
>
> *It was then that I saw two Canada geese near the water; we get them here all the time. They were grazing near the pond as they always do. She was quiet upon approach, like a hunter…no longer wailing uncontrollably as she had*

been moments before. I realized her intent and turned away—and then I felt a hand on my shoulder which startled me mightily. I was forced back around, made to watch just who this woman really was when she was at her worst.

The grasp on my shoulder was firm, but not violently so. I could not see Thomas, but I'm sure it was him. I have never seen him in any shape or form or from any distance, and this is only the second time I have been close enough to have been "touched" that I know of. I pray it never happens again.

Dismally I witnessed the woman slaughter the two beautiful creatures by cutting their heads off against the stone wall. She picked them up by their feet as they died; wings flapping as their nervous systems shut down slowly. She stood there, arms out to her sides; a headless goose suspended from each hand, spraying blood everywhere. It was all over the geese, the grass—and her. Hands, face, and dress—she didn't care. It was the messiest, most unnecessary act I have ever witnessed, and I am somewhat of a farmer myself and no stranger to putting meat on the table.

The look on her nearly emotionless face…wasn't anguish anymore. It was a small measure of vengeance. I will have to refer to my notes, but this is my third April logging these happenings, and I have never seen this happen. I have seen the day that I call "THOMAS LEAVES" before, but this…tops them all.

I'm guessing based on my timeline and her emotions before today's slaughter that this must have been the day he broke the news to her that he would be leaving soon. "THOMAS LEAVES" happens three days from now.

He must have left with naïve thoughts of returning safely, but we know how that worked out.

That was all Holly had time for; she would have to read the rest later. Tim could be in trouble if all this were going down today. She quickly refolded the extra-long journal entry back into the book and ran downstairs to the payphone, dialing Tim frantically. The phone at the house rang once and then disconnected suddenly. She dropped another dime and dialed again, this time getting a busy signal. In a panic, she bolted out the library door, down the steps to the parking lot and took off for Lancaster Hill Road.

CHAPTER THIRTY-TWO

Something's Cooking

Tim froze after silencing the noisy living room phone. Everything in the kitchen stopped; no more screaming, wailing, or smashing. The dead person in the kitchen had also heard it and was most likely on her way. Thinking quickly, Tim picked the receiver back up before it could ring again, then left it on the table as he unplugged the phone from the wall.

Only the flies disturbed the silence as she drifted from the kitchen to the dining room, listening for the intruder who had disrupted her dark ritual. Tim took his eyes off the doorway just long enough to look to the boy, who was still outside on the steps, motionless; staring.

Suddenly and unexpectedly, Tim heard a door open followed by a slam and then, another door and another slam. Mildred had left the house through the front porch. *What the hell?*

He was still standing by the disabled phone. Three seconds later, he saw Mildred through the living room curtains walking down to the pond. He crouched down in case she decided to turn back; then looked again to the front door, but it was closed. The boy was gone.

Unsure of what to do, Tim peeked around the corner into the dining room. From here, he could see into part of the kitchen;

it looked like a bomb had gone off. He crossed the dining room quickly and peered into the kitchen itself; the floor was completely covered in broken dishware, pots and pans, and all of the windows had been smashed out—a pot boiled on the stove.

Blood was everywhere...splattered over absolutely everything; walls, countertops, floors—even the ceiling.

Blood....and *feathers.*

Feathers?

He gagged; not sure if it was the remnants of her stench or the contents of the boiling pot filling the room. Using his foot, he swept the broken glass aside and stepped in to turn the stove off.

The cutting board was piled high with...*meat.* It was an incredible quantity; way too much for a small family like the Pikes. There was so much piled high that some had spilled onto the floor. Tim stepped forward to take a closer look and saw it *move.* He jumped back; the light was bad, and his eyes were blurred. He was tired and confused...perhaps hallucinating. At least he hoped he was.

The pile Mildred had been working on resembled stuffing, giblets, gizzards and such...and it was rancid. It crawled with maggots; some that had escaped her blade and others that writhed somewhat faster, in pieces. The pot bubbled red and spattered on the stovetop. The heads and feet of two geese collided and bounced in the crimson broth. *What in God's name...?*

He had seen enough; after a gallant try, it was no longer worth it to be here. It was time to abandon the plan, *money be damned,* but first, he must escape safely. He crouched again and peered out the broken windows looking down toward the pond. There was no sign of Mildred, at least that he could see. Was it...over? Even if it was, Tim had just now accepted the fact that there would be another incident tomorrow and the next day...and the next, and it was all too much. The house was unlivable, ...and he was too tired to care anymore.

Tell people it's haunted. Take the loss. Buy something smaller;

refurbish that. Winterize lakeside cabins and make them year-round houses. You'll get there; it will just take longer. Now get out before you lose absolutely everything.

He left through the side door, again forgetting where he had parked: *Around front—FUCK.* As if on cue, he heard a car engine. Picking up the pace, he raced around the corner cautiously. It was Holly. The phone had rung about fifteen minutes ago; it must have been her.

She had already exited the vehicle and was nowhere to be seen. The porch door slammed shut in front of Tim. At first, he was unsure if it was Holly's doing, or worse, Mildred's; but regardless of who shut it, he didn't want Holly in the kitchen. Rather than try to chase her, he sprinted back the way he came in through the side door to head her off.

Tim bolted through the carriage house and into the breakfast area. Holly was already there in the threshold to the dining room, mouth aghast. He was too late to spare her the gore, yet was silently thankful that he wouldn't have to explain it all later. Breathing through the sleeve of her jacket, Holly spoke first:

"Tim, I figured it out. There won't be a boat on the pond today. I'll explain it later. She's actually supposed to be closer than that. It's dangerous to be here. This whole kitchen mess is part of it. Let's go; please...*right now.*"

"Okay. I'm completely done." He tiptoed carefully through the blood, being careful not to slip. "Look," he pointed to the broken windows. "She left the stove on, too. I *have* to leave. She'll probably burn the house down, anyway."

Holly looked out past his pointing finger, out the broken window and stiffened.

"Tim...she's outside."

It had started to rain. Holly crouched quickly, hoping to remain unnoticed. Mildred was very close—just outside on the upper lawn, directly in between the house and the driveway. She was covered in blood, which was slowly being washed away. The flies were gone. She stood still, seemingly searching the windows. Two more dead geese lay in a heap at her feet. Tim knelt quickly and moved closer to Holly.

Mildred's head rolled left, right, up and down. The odd adjustments recalled the night she visited Tim and the girls in the guest room. Her shoulders rocked, and her arms followed, and it was then that Holly noticed the glint of the hatchet.

Holly grabbed Tim's arm, looked him in the eye and gestured. Mildred seemed as unpredictable as ever, her blank stare still studying what appeared to be the entire front of the house. Tim saw the hatchet dripping blood and rainwater and began to crawl under the windowsill along the wall, leading her away through the broken shards toward the living room and the front door. It seemed a much safer place to be than the room Mildred had been cooking in. *How did she get into my truck to get her hatchet?*

When they made it into the living room, he peeked ever so slightly up around the curtain. From here, Mildred would be very close; no more than fifteen feet away.

Mildred had not moved; she stood outside in the same spot near the cars, panting slightly, clothes stuck to her body, looking deranged.

Just before he began to fade back from the window, her head turned. For a second, their eyes seemed to lock…as far as he could tell. *Had she seen the curtain? Olivia, Vivian…I love you both.*

"She's looking at me," he whispered.

Holly still huddled under the window looking up, studying Tim's face for a reaction. His emotions determined hers, and she didn't like the feeling. Tim held her hand.

She's looking at him. I can't see anything. It can't end this way.

She rolled quietly over and stood in the corner, feeling the options returning. The turtle had righted itself. Tim stood up with her.

"I think she's coming," he said anxiously.

Holly opened the curtain wide and looked out. Mildred addressed Holly's bravery and turned her shoulders to face them.

"She's blocking the vehicles, and she still has the hatchet," Tim muttered.

Mildred Wells moved in long trudging steps, back slightly humped, arms swinging, white knuckles on the hatchet. She climbed the slope of the lawn and headed for the porch door.

"Coming left," Holly said as she instinctively took two steps to the right, toward the stairs. Tim reacted the same way but stopped when he heard a noise like thunder coming down from the bedrooms. He grabbed Holly's arm and pulled her back, raising a finger to his lips. They backpedaled to the office doorway and waited, grievously no longer able to see Mildred.

BUMP bump, BUMP bump, BUMP bump, BUMP bump; it was the boy. They couldn't see the stairs themselves; only the front door, which opened itself wide; then, a blur as the boy ran out into the rain, flagging his mother's attention. Mildred changed course, forgetting all about reentering the house.

Her body language spoke volumes as she opened her arms and dropped to one knee. The boy considered her gesture teasingly but did not approach. Instead, he turned and walked past the dead geese toward the pond. Halfway there he checked back over his shoulder. Mildred stood as still as a hunter considering her prey, then followed steadily behind him, her dress soaked and hanging, being careful not to pursue too quickly, lest he spook like a deer… as he always did.

Tim and Holly remained frozen in the back of the living room, happy to be forgotten, if at least for a moment. Once Mildred had passed the pond, they wasted no time rushing through the downpour for their cars, speeding down Lancaster Hill Road at their first opportunity. Before they cleared the property line, they saw little Elmer break into a run and turn into the woods heading toward the grove. They could guess the story by now: he would never let his mother catch him.

Mildred slowed to a stop just past the pond and watched him disappear into the trees. He was gone again, and the tenants had escaped; the tenants who seemed to be becoming more and more intrusive. She liked the house to be maintained, but why must they all wander so close to her affairs? The threat they posed was making her—uncomfortable again. She needed more time to persuade him; more time to repair their lives and start again… and when she got her chance he would understand that Mother was sorry…*very* sorry.

The last thing Tim saw in his rearview mirror was Mildred's head as she turned her attention from the woods back to his taillights, and it chilled his blood. He attempted to tell himself that it didn't really matter, anyway; he was all but done with the house. All he had to do was pick up his tools, and it would be over.

As the house blurred in the rainy rear window, he furrowed his brow, concerned. He spoke aloud to himself as Holly led him home in her car.

"Just for your tools, right? Who the hell do you think you're kidding?"

CHAPTER THIRTY-THREE

Don't Jump the Gun

Tuesday, April 27th, 1971
(same day) Back at Holly's house

Tim pulled into Holly's driveway and parked behind her. The temporary Plexiglas window had leaked once the skies had opened up, but that was the last thing on his mind. He got out of his truck and quickly examined the toolbox built into the bed of his truck; the lock was still in place—it hadn't been broken open—*and yet she got in there.* Getting wet, he ran through the rain to the open front door where Holly waited, holding it open. As soon as they were inside, he grabbed her and held her. They stayed that way for several seconds without speaking. Finally, he asked:

"How are you doing?"

"Uh…shocked, or shaken, I guess. It's hard to put into words. That was bad. That was dangerous."

Tim decided to prolong his denial.

"Yeah. I've decided that I'm done with the house. I'll take the loss. I'll give full disclosure to potential buyers; I'll tell 'em the house is haunted, and then I'll sell to the first guy that doesn't believe me."

"Wait, no...Hold on, Tim. Not yet. You might want to take a look at what I figured out in the library today. Annette's 'anniversary journal' has a major flaw that makes it confusing and hard to use." Tim listened begrudgingly, looking like a man that didn't want to be convinced.

"Holly... Like you said; 'today was dangerous'... Now you've figured out a clue. Is following your hunch through and going any further worth the risk? I mean, we're not just haunted; one of our ghosts carries a hatchet."

"Uh, well, it is pretty scary when you put it that way, but I feel pretty confident, at least about what I learned about the anniversaries. The hatchet is clearly—an issue—but maybe we can work around it, avoid it. Let me get this out: You've seen her three times now, right? I mean, not counting the times she was just walking through the field? There was our first date, where we think Thomas held us back, and then there was the night she looked in on you and the girls sleeping, and then today's *cooking show.*

"Today was definitely in Annette's book, but...the way it's laid out is confusing. I think I've figured that part out. The night she was upstairs pacing around while we were down in the truck might be in it too, I haven't had time to check; the same thing with the stare-down in the guest bedroom. We can check now, though. I'm telling you, I'm on to something."

"Holly, I want to believe you, but I'm just...burnt, I guess. I mean, visitation is going to be here again before we know it, which makes me think; what if today's 'cooking show' as you call it, had been the same day my daughters were making pancakes? I couldn't live with myself. It's like a clichéd horror movie. I don't want to be the dumbass that doesn't leave. It seems like it's time to go."

Holly had to admit that he had a point. Despite today's discoveries in the library, there were still many potentially dangerous holes in Annette's journals. The books could not be relied on anywhere near one hundred percent. She chimed in one last time:

"All I'm saying is, don't jump the gun. It's 2:15 pm. We have the rest of the day to map it all out, talk about it and reassess. Johnny is coming up tonight too, correct? We can bring him up to speed. You said he had a ghost situation with his grandmother, right? So he won't think we're nuts. He'll have an open mind—a fresh perspective."

"Oh shit, I need to call him. I don't want him showing up at the house while we're not there. Give me a minute; otherwise, I might have to intercept him before he gets to the driveway." Tim called Mrs. Mills' residence, and of course, she answered. She probably even answered on the kitchen phone while watching him work. The good news was that Johnny hadn't left yet.

"Johnny, don't go to my house—I'm not going to be there when you arrive. Let me give you Holly's address; got a pencil?" Tim relayed the information but left out the part that he might have given up on the house. As soon as he hung up, Holly pulled out her calendars along with the two journals to share her new theory.

"Let me show you what I'm talking about."

She shared what she had learned in the library. She also showed Tim Annette's take on *today's* happenings back in 1968.

"Wow, that's spot-on," he commented.

"Yeah, and I've only had time to figure out a few days. Think about it, Tim...you know we haven't done our due diligence with the materials at our disposal. We're flying blind without studying these journals front to back, and it's dangerous to go in unprepared, and it wastes your work time. You could get so much more done if you knew she wasn't going to show up on a given day, and vice-versa."

She had a point. If Mildred was going to be hanging around on a given day, he shouldn't even go. Drive down to Massachusetts and line up some work on that day; stop going against the grain.

"All right, let's take a look. What else does Annette have to say?" Holly found where she had left off at the library before leaving to rescue Tim; it was the aftermath of the so-called "freak-out" or "cooking show," and read aloud:

"I remained at the window under Thomas's grasp, his hand on my shoulder until the woman walked back from the pond covered in blood. She wore a smirk as if she would enjoy his reaction to seeing her that way.

He let my shoulder go after that, and I was free, but I had questions. I ran into my bedroom and grabbed an empty journal that I had yet to write in. Turning to a random page in the middle of the book, I wrote "YES," and flipping about fifty pages forward, I wrote "NO." I then closed the book and brought it with me back into the guest room across the hall. Knowing that the woman might still be downstairs, I held the book in my hands, up to the air and whispered:

"Thomas, is she angry that you are leaving for the war? The answer you want to say is written in this book."

And then I set the journal on the guest bed and peered out the window to see if she was still outside. The two geese were in a pile on the grass, but she was nowhere to be seen. It took twenty minutes for me to slowly sneak downstairs to see if she might be inside the house, but it seemed safe. She had apparently gone; anniversary over, thank God.

I picked the geese up by the feet to bring them to the compost near the barn. The poor birds had left a gruesome trail of blood across the driveway, down the lawn, and to the pond. I would have to look at that for a few days until nature cleaned it up for me.

As I dropped the bodies on the pile, I turned back to the house. It was still daylight, but something caught my eye. Up in one of the turret windows facing me (done this way on purpose, I believe), was a lit candle.

I sighed, and walked steadily but not hurriedly back into the house through the side door and up the stairs to the turret. I knew what I would find.

My nearly empty journal of just two words was open to the word "YES."

The ghost woman's reenactment of the anniversary was chilling, to say the least; in fact, they all are. She is angry, crazy, and perhaps even evil (or some combination of the three), and that is the reason for her unrest...that and the fact that her son eludes her. I don't think I could help her even if I wanted to. She seems dangerous; I know I've said that before.

As for Thomas; I think he remains unseen because he doesn't want her to know he's here. She haunts this place, but Thomas? He wants something else.

And the boy...I know very little about him, and that might make sense; he may not know how to communicate what he wants, or even know what he wants at all. All I know is, he doesn't want Mommy.

Who is the ghost woman (besides being Thomas's wife)? Or who was she, I mean to say? The town records were smudged by her, I must assume. She must have a history, and a family with a history as well. I will ask some of the older friends of mine at the nursing home. There wasn't much of anything in the microfilm when I looked at 1860–1863 unless I missed something. Lord knows it is worth another shot.

As I mentioned before, I feel like a prisoner now; a prisoner who wants to help even though it is so very hard on me. At times I am terrified, but I'm not afraid of dying, so ultimately I think I'm going to stick around, but I'm hoping Thomas would let me leave if the situation became too much. I think, however, that I sense desperation from him and my needs may not come first. I have no idea what sort of man he is or was. He might be dangerous, too, for all I know.

Another important thing that happened today: I confirmed that Thomas could communicate using my "flip book" idea. He has turned the pages of my books twice now. I should have thought to do it sooner, but I will use my "yes/no" journal and fill it up with words that might be useful and maybe communication will improve.

And...as I have written several times; I pray this is not the first time you have read this:

My <u>Anniversary Journal</u> has a flaw. Anniversaries do not go by calendar date. Just because it happened on the 23rd for me doesn't mean it will happen on the 23rd for you. I haven't had time to recopy the book.

For this particular date, watch for these occurrences on the <u>fourth Tuesday in April!</u>

"What the hell! What does she mean 'I pray this is not the first time you have read this'? We've read a decent chunk of her stuff!" Tim griped.

"No, we haven't. This is what I've been telling you; we need to get caught up on these journals! Her warnings must be in the last quarter of the first journal, and all through the Anniversary

Journal. We just haven't done our homework—and our professor is a dead man; a freaking *ghost!* He's not messing around, Tim."

"He only gave it to us forty-eight hours ago!"

"Yeah, and I bet Thomas Pike is worried that your life isn't fair. I dare you to try and convince him."

CHAPTER THIRTY-FOUR

Johnny Arrives

Tuesday, April 27th, 1971 (Evening)

Johnny had arranged things with his wife so that he could head up to Sanborn and sleep overnight. This way, he and Tim could start early and put in a marathon workday to catch Tim up. What Johnny didn't know was that he was being called up solely for the ghostly experience he had with his grandmother. Tim didn't want to put anyone in danger, Johnny especially, so further construction on the house was on hold.

Tim had asked him to come up early, before dinner, which was somewhat of a surprise to Johnny; now, he would miss dinner with his family. Maria, Johnny's wife, wasn't happy with the news, but she knew Tim, and liked him, so she decided not to protest, *this one time*. Johnny knocked off work at Mrs. Mills' house about half an hour early, claiming that his daughter had a school play that night that he had to get ready. Mrs. Mills would probably not have liked to hear that he was leaving early to have dinner with Tim. If she had known, she would stew over it, wind herself into a tizzy, and explode in Tim's ear the very next day. The mishandled exhaust fan shipment was bad enough.

Holly's plan for the evening was to spend some time

transcribing Annette's anniversaries into her new calendar. This way, when Johnny arrived for the big huddle, she would have a sort of presentation to give when that part of the conversation came up. The other part of Holly's plan was to delegate dinner duties to Tim.

"Pick whatever you want to cook, but keep it simple, so you're not in the kitchen too long; Johnny won't be up here every night, and let's make the most of his time."

Tim noticed that Holly was confident and all business. She seemed motivated, and that was good because he was discouraged. Hopefully, her confidence would rub off on him at some point. He decided on creamy chicken marsala for dinner; then headed out to buy some beer, wine, pasta, chicken, Alfredo sauce, and of course, mushrooms.

Holly began transcribing. She had bought a pad of tracing paper to make seeing through several pages of calendars much easier than holding everything up to the light. The puzzle pieces began to come together, and this sparked her enthusiasm. Tim arrived home and, thinking ahead, seasoned the chicken and mushrooms and precooked the pasta, putting everything in the fridge until dinner when he would simply reheat the pasta in a pot of boiling water, and the rest in a sauté pan. Taking his mind off the ghosts and having fun in the kitchen was a nice mental break.

Johnny arrived at around six o'clock. Holly and Tim were just barely ready to greet him after an impromptu afternoon delight; leaving the bathroom just in time to answer the door. Johnny gave Tim the eyeball as he smelled the shampoo and saw the damp hair.

"Half day for you, Chief? How many nails did you hit today? Couple dozen?" Just like that, Johnny started the ball-busting. Each man would brag that they had outworked the other on any given day and God forbid one of them took a day off that the other did not, it was fodder for weeks that would not soon be forgotten. Tim's truck had broken down a few years back that made him miss a half-day which began a Ford versus Chevy sub-argument that continued to this day. On another occasion, Johnny cut himself on a table saw, which would have kept the average man out of work for a week, but Tim never let him forget the one day he missed. They were very respectful about family commitments, however. Some things were off-limits.

Tim sighed. "Ah, here we go. Already ragging on me and he hasn't even had a beer yet. Holly, this is Johnny, and Johnny, this is Holly. Honey, if you believe everything this guy says you might break up with me, so put a heavy bullshit filter on anything that comes out of his mouth. He's actually a pretty good guy, though, if you don't care about personality."

Johnny ignored Tim's snarky retort but gave him a quick bro-hug as he stepped inside. "Pleased to meet you, Holly," he stated as he shook her hand. "Wow, smells good in here! You aren't cooking for him, are you? Just get a dog dish and leave it over there by the fridge."

"No, no…he cooks for me!" Holly replied.

Johnny stopped everything and stared at Tim as if he didn't recognize him, then slowly smiled the shit-eating grin that only a buddy could. His eyes said it all because his mouth could not, at least in the presence of a lady: *Henpecked, to put it nicely.*

"That's right, that's right—a real man cooks, Johnny. This is the seventies. Women's Lib. Equal rights. Macho is dead!" Tim knew Johnny would be a semi-gentleman in front of Holly, but also knew he would exact revenge later. Tim had never cooked for Sheila, as far as Johnny knew—this was a complete departure from the boss he thought he knew so well. Johnny looked as if he could burst out laughing any second but kept his composure… for the time being.

"What are you drinking, buddy? We have beer, and we have red wine." Johnny surprised Tim when he opted for the wine. Johnny took a seat on one end of the couch and Holly the other; Tim pulled a chair over from the table to form a triangle. Johnny started the conversation.

"So...how are things up here? I mean, I know you're running behind, but how're things in general?" He didn't want to be the first person to raise the subject of ghosts; he wasn't sure how much Holly knew. Tim paused for a half-second and exhaled, letting off pressure. *And here, ...we...go.*

"Johnny...I'm not going to lie to you. I told you briefly on the phone, and Holly knows everything first-hand. It's a real shit show up here. We see things every day, *including* today. In fact, today was the worst day. I left the house early this afternoon because—well I mean *we* left the house early because we had a close call—a dangerously close call. I think I might be done with the house; in fact, I'm pretty sure I am. I'm not going to ask you to help me over there. Today there was even—a woman with a hatchet."

Johnny's brow furrowed, and he frowned. He looked over at Holly, who sat straight-faced, and met her eyes. *Nobody was joking here.*

"Holly knows everything and has seen her fair share, so you can speak freely. Today was the worst by far. Chopped up maggots, dead geese, blood—and I don't mean a few drops. Johnny...it was everywhere. It was disgusting. The *smell...*"

"Whoa, whoa, whoa...start over." Johnny said. "Where's the ghost at this point? Forget that, just start from the beginning. The very beginning. Like, *Day One* beginning."

"We got the anniversary wrong. We were following the journal, um—*journals,* left by Annette, the previous owner, and..." Holly paused for a second, realizing that Johnny was right; the story was easier to digest if you heard it from the beginning. "He's right... we have to start over. This story builds. Does he know about the journals, or anniversaries, or anything?" Tim looked at Johnny because he didn't remember exactly what he'd told him.

"Yeah, I know there are ghosts, and there are journals, and that's about it," Johnny reported. Holly recognized where they were and picked up the story. First, she explained what an 'anniversary' was, according to Annette. She went on to explain her first date with Tim and the choking feeling in the truck. Tim filled in on parts of the story when Holly wasn't there, such as the nights the girls were over and the mysterious "roofer."

Johnny asked questions periodically to clarify certain situations. Over the next half hour, Tim and Holly recounted the last ten days starting with the tour of the property up until today's happenings, finishing with the noisy day in the kitchen, the boy at the front door, and the mad dash to escape. Johnny went to the table, grabbed the wine bottle, and refilled everyone's glasses. He let it all sink in and then looked at Holly for her two cents.

"What's today? April 27th? And you moved in when?" he asked.

"My first day was the 18th," Tim replied.

"Wow...all that in...ten days. That's heavy-duty. Well, my first reaction is that this man-ghost, the unseen one—Thomas... he's the quarterback here, and you're working for him. He's using the journals as ways to communicate with you. It's not like you *found* a stack of journals and went from there...he is putting them in strategic places. He even left one lying open on top of Allison."

"Annette," Holly corrected.

"Oh, right, Annette. And this Annette did a lot of legwork for you. And she lived there for many years with little or no ghost activity—just the woman ghost and the kid ghost from time to time, and never together. I'm guessing the reason that house went from *zero to sixty* so to speak, was that Thomas took notice of Annette's research; either that or realized that Annette might be tough or weird enough—to stick around and not run off scared. He saw an opportunity."

"You mean like...he saw she was interested in the sightings, and when she started writing stuff down, he helped her along?" Tim questioned.

"Yeah, don't quote me on anything, because like I said I'm no expert and I'm talking myself through it for the first time as well; just throwing thoughts out there. No offense but you guys look tired—holding it together, but also tired. Boss, what would you have done without this lady helping you out? That's a very cool thing." Johnny tipped an invisible cap in Holly's direction.

"But I guess I'm the 'fresh perspective' guy here. If you've already figured something out and feel I'm going down the wrong path, stop me. Where was I...oh yeah, I remember.

"Uh...Thomas sees Annette investigating things and decides to help. Maybe the death of Annette's husband had something to do with it. Annette was hurting, just like Thomas...*is*. Kindred spirits, no pun intended. And...he even protects her when the ghost lady Mildred is around because...let's face it, after today's happenings, you *know* she's insane. Cooking bugs and shit on your stove—Pardon my French, but that's fucked up."

Tim chuckled at Johnny's offbeat take on what happened today in the kitchen because the majority of the day had been so dire and he needed to laugh. He took another sip of wine, beginning to feel the effects; his stomach was empty, and he would start cooking very soon.

Holly spoke up: "Do you think he was helping us too, on our first date? The night in the truck? I had been thinking it was her that 'choked' us...but she was alone upstairs, walking around doing whatever...pacing I guess...maybe Annette has some notes on what she was doing, but we didn't seem to have her attention."

"Could have been," Johnny answered.

"That little kid has saved me twice, too," noted Tim, back to being serious. "He showed up today and got her attention, and he also started running around downstairs the night that she looked in on the girls and me. Are we being helped?"

"Well, I wouldn't assume that you're safe or whatever. Thomas and the kid might be working in their own best interest. Annette and her husband are dead, right? What was his name—Henry?"

"Yes, well, as far as we know Henry appeared to have died from a heart attack by the barn, but Annette's death was suspicious, in my opinion."

Johnny disagreed somewhat. "I'm betting Henry's death was

suspicious, too. I don't believe he just dropped dead, or she died in her sleep or whatever. Maybe it's time for me to tell you about my grandmother…and my experiences with a ghost." He stood up and began to pace slowly.

"I was…eleven years old or so, and my grandmother was sick with cancer. We would visit her in the hospital, almost daily. She was in there for a long time too, like it must have been a couple of months. Anyway, being a kid, I had always assumed that Grandma and Grandpa were that cute old couple that feeds pigeons together on park benches; boy, was I wrong.

"One day, I was visiting Grandma in the hospital with my mom after school, and my grandfather walked in behind us while we were sitting with her. Grandma's mood turned sour as soon as she saw him. We had been having a normal chat, and when he walked through the doorway, her eyes turned …*black*—huge pupils and shit. I don't know if I was the only one to see it, but it really scared me. She looked mean. I had never noticed her like that before that day, but Grandpa pretended not to notice and started acting, and I mean he started acting like an actor.

"He seemed so fake and…well, full of shit, but he sounded scared or intimidated to me, kind of like how I felt at the time. It really changed the whole mood of the room, and I wanted to leave the bedside to let him get closer to her, but Grandma quietly grabbed my hand and pulled me in so that he couldn't get close. He didn't seem to mind, either; he just hung back and made small talk with my mom.

"I had no choice but to look straight at her; I couldn't even turn around comfortably to address my mom and grandpa. She stared up at him with those dark eyes like she hated his guts, and when he and my mom were out of things to say, he turned to my grandma and said: 'How are you feeling today, Isabella?'…and then…I'll never forget her face or her words—I had a front-row seat to this shit—she said:

'I'm not done with you yet, you motherfucker.'

"She didn't raise her voice or anything. But it was terrifying. I mean, she *hated* him. I had never heard her swear before, not ever. And I still have not used that swear to this day...it reminds me of her—of the *real* grandma, not the sweet faking little old lady. It gives me the creeps."

"Oh my God, what did your mom do?" asked Holly.

"Wait, I'm not finished. My mom didn't have time to do anything, because right after Grandma said that, her head rose off the pillow a good three inches like she was starting to do a sit-up, and then she hung there and started moaning. She squeezed my hand really tight, and it hurt, but I just stared...and—she let out this big moaning breath like she was in pain, and then her head fell back to the pillow...dead. My mom had to help me pry my hand out of hers. It fucked me up big time. I had nightmares for weeks straight—no, months. It was definitely months."

Tim and Holly sat there in amazement, at a loss for words. Johnny noticed he had a captivated audience.

"But that isn't the half of it. Several hours later, after a long car ride home and a dinner that I barely touched, I asked my mom if Grandma really hated Grandpa. My mom's eyes were red; she had been trying to hide that she had been crying. Obviously, the death of her mother was upsetting, but the three of us had heard her last words and that just, well, it was a hell of a way to go, especially for my mom. She probably had nightmares longer than I did."

"Where did your grandfather go after that happened?" asked Holly.

"Mom tried to comfort him and get him to come over and stay with us, but he wouldn't go. I found out later that he had a girlfriend and he just wanted to get back to her."

"Oh shit, that's why Grandma was pissed off," said Tim.

"Right. And that's how my mom answered my question, too. She told me that he had done a bad thing and had started seeing another woman, and Grandma knew all about it. It made me feel weird. It didn't really break my heart…it was more like I had been tricked. You want to think your grandparents are the cheesy couple holding hands, but then you realize they're just like everyone else. It was such a shock. I never looked at him the same way again."

"Okay, so not to rush your story, but obviously she becomes a ghost soon, right? What happened?"

"Yeah. Not a week later, my mom tells me that Grandpa's girlfriend died and that he was going to come live with us. I didn't know how to feel about that because I didn't know how to feel about Grandpa anymore, plus he sounded so different the last time I saw him, that day in the hospital—I felt like I didn't know him anymore.

So the guest room becomes his room, and of course, he's not happy to be there, and two nights later I wake up, and I hear all sorts of screaming. Mom and Dad are up, and they're in the guest room—I mean Grandpa's room, which was right next to mine. I was scared, so I stayed in bed listening. My first eleven years with him were so great, and the last two weeks, I didn't want anything to do with him. Anyway, he starts talking to my parents.

'It was *her*; she was right here, right in my face! She killed Dorothy, and now she's going to kill me!' he said.

'No, no, no… Dad, stop it! Please keep your voice down, Johnny is sleeping, and you're going to scare him. You must have had a bad dream, Mom is dead, and you were there. You saw her die in the hospital.'

'Of course, I know she's dead. That's the point! I saw the whole thing. I saw the murder. I told you that, I told the police that, and nobody fucking believes me!'

'Dad…shhh… You've got to be quieter—and watch your mouth, please! I don't want Johnny to wake up and be afraid. You…you did this. It's all those guilty feelings eating you up. Please…this is hard on all of us, myself included. It sounds like you need to talk to someone, and that someone can't be me. We can look into that tomorrow.'

'I don't want to fucking talk to anyone! I'm going to *die*! I'm going to be dead in the room right next to Johnny's, and you're not even listening! And you don't want him to be the one to find me; I promise you that.'

Then my father spoke up: 'That's enough, Luis. I can move your room downstairs if you like but if you want to live upstairs with us, where there is carpeting, and bathrooms, you're going to have to knock it off. Keep your mouth shut. We have an eleven-year-old. We took you in because you are family, but I can't let you destroy the happiness here. Not that I believe a word of what you're saying, but even if what you say is true, you asked for it. Now think about your grandson in the next room and if you think you're going to die, just do it quietly.' Dad was pissed.

He didn't believe my grandfather's story, but I think what he said shamed the old man into being quiet. Grandpa didn't say a word the rest of the night, or the night after."

"Why didn't they just put him in a nursing home or something?" asked Holly.

"I'm not really sure, but I know we didn't have much money, and my family was always close-knit, kind of *take-care-of-their-own* types."

"This doesn't end well," Holly made the statement nervously in anticipation of the rest of Johnny's story.

"No, you *know* it doesn't." Johnny took a long drink of wine and put the glass down. "On the third night after Grandpa's meltdown, I woke up to….*noises*. At first, I thought I was dreaming, and it sort of sounded like the fan in grandpa's room was vibrating or something. I had to pee anyway so I got up and decided to see if I could reposition the fan a little bit or something to stop the noise. His bedroom door was ajar, and I pushed it open slowly.

Grandma was standing over the bed, except it didn't completely remind me of her. She hunched over him like she was…working on something, but I couldn't see very well from the doorway, so very stupidly I stepped into the room to Grandma's left. She was shoving a rolled-up newspaper down his throat, and I mean really jamming it in there; back and forth, putting her weight into it—not at *all* like a weak old lady. I had never seen her move that way—she was always so gentle.

Grandpa was...already gone, or at least I hope he was. His arms were down at his sides, open wide like he had tried to fight and then just lost badly. A gurgling came from his throat, and I'm not sure if he was still making it or if it was the sound of the rolled-up newspaper thrashing his wet throat. It was disgusting, really nasty. And then she saw me, and dropped what she was doing, turned my way and smirked...pretending to act all dainty again...like a grandmother. Then she winked.

I peed myself right there, and she saw that and reached back and pulled the newspaper out of his mouth. His throat made a noise like air escaping a...deflating raft or something—and he went still. She dropped the newspaper on the floor put her finger up to her lips to shush me, opened the closet door and just left through it like it was some sort of emergency exit. I never went in that closet again."

Both Tim and Holly sat quietly with their mouths open. Johnny continued.

"I turned right around, wet pajamas and all, and went into my parents' room to tell them I thought something was wrong with grandpa because ...I had heard noises. While they rushed into his bedroom, I walked stunned back into my bedroom and changed into clean pj's. I didn't want to have to explain anything I had seen; I just wanted to forget. They found him dead, of course, but the cause of death was ruled a heart attack.

I never mentioned Grandma's ghost to my parents. I even went back into the room when the ambulance arrived to see what he looked like and...you'd think his mouth would be all newspaper ink, and the newspaper itself would be there all crumpled and wet with saliva, but the scene didn't look like that at all. The murder had been covered up somehow; how I don't know. I can't help you with 'ghost physics,' sorry. Some things just can't be explained, I guess.

An old man had a heart attack, and that was good enough for everybody. People that didn't know about his affair thought it was even romantic that they had died just a week apart like he couldn't live without her or something, but I knew better. And I never said anything just in case Grandma was listening."

Holly's living room remained quiet for a few seconds as they waited to see if Johnny had more. In a way, they didn't want it to be over; not only was it entertaining, but they hadn't heard much yet that would help them solve their Mildred problem.

"Wow," said Tim. He looked over at Holly who looked as if she had become part of the couch, head pushed back into the cushion, fingers gripping the soft arm. Johnny stood up again to stretch his legs and shake out his nerves.

"Did she ever come back? Did you have to figure out how to get rid of her?" Tim asked.

"No, boss. I think she handled it herself. A double murder and she was ready to go."

"So you're saying you couldn't even take care of your own ghost situation then?" Tim took the opportunity to bust some balls and lighten the mood.

"Screw you, man! I was *eleven!* You haven't figured out yours, either!" They poked at each other like brothers.

Holly remained serious. "Now I think that Henry and Annette were murdered." Tim's teasing grin disappeared, and he stowed the jokes.

"Just kidding, Johnny; this kind of thing is too risky to solve. I'm not going to chance it. I'm still selling the place," added Tim.

"You can't sell the place," countered Johnny. "It's unethical. You're a better man than that."

"Hey, full disclosure. I'll tell them it's haunted and then it's up to them."

"Who's going to sell it for you? Holly, will you be the listing agent? Do you have the heart to do that, even with 'full disclosure'? And what does 'full disclosure' mean, Tim? Are you going to tell them that you saw blood boiling on the stove and a woman in your bedroom who sometimes wields a hatchet? Or are you just going to say it's 'haunted'? There's a big difference there. You know you can't go into such detail, or it will *never* sell. And at the very least you'd be embarrassed because you'd sound crazy. I know you, man. Why don't you just wreck the existing building? Too expensive?"

"Exactly."

Dammit, why had he invited Johnny? He wasn't hearing what he wanted, and Johnny was right on all counts. "What the hell do you want me to do, Johnny? What would *you* do?"

"Well, first of all, don't lose your shit just because of my story. And second; please, could you start that dinner, because I've got a buzz from this wine and my empty stomach! Then we can take it from there. Panic never helps. I mean, what makes you think Thomas Pike is going to let you stop, anyway?" The wine had loosened Johnny's lips enough to drop the last thought like a horse turd.

"What the hell do you mean by that?" Holly asked nervously.

"Well, it's just a thought, but remember how you told me that Thomas hadn't bothered the Smiths for most of the time they lived there? And then Annette got motivated and started to make progress, and all of a sudden clues started popping up, and physical contact was made?"

"Yeah," said Tim.

"And then you told me how infrequent Annette's contacts with the ghosts were compared to yours? I mean, you've got shit happening *every day*. You've been here only about a week, and you've found two journals up in the turret, complete with lit candles to light your way. It's like you're on his freaking *mailing list!* Do you think he's not invested in this? When did Thomas die?"

"Um…1861," said Holly.

"1861. So he's been waiting, like *a hundred and ten years* for this. I'd say you've been recruited. He may be protecting you from Mildred, but it might be for his own selfish reasons. He might not even be a good guy, and you should consider that."

Johnny's words were a cold slap to Tim's "new life" sense of independence and freedom. It now occurred to him that even if he left the house on Lancaster Hill Road that he could be followed and hounded, perhaps even killed, if he didn't help out. Johnny's grandmother had died in the hospital, yet killed the grandfather at Johnny's house and the mistress at Johnny's grandfather's house. *They can travel.*

Tim stood up suddenly, looking ten years older and made his way to the adjoining kitchen to arrange the *quick-cook system* (his name for it) that he had been so proud of just a few hours ago. Now he wasn't even hungry—more like sick to his stomach. He filled a pot of water and turned on the burner, then got out the large sauté pan and all of the neatly organized Tupperware containers full of different foods and portions, some pre-cooked and some kept fresh until the last minute. Holly set the table and refilled the glasses. Tim might have declined the wine but because of Johnny's new downer of a theory decided—*screw it.*

While Tim cooked, Holly gathered Annette's journals and her calendar project, which had turned out to be much trickier to construct than she had imagined. There were several times that she had to tear up and start over. She silently forgave Annette for the layout of the Anniversary Journal; it had been an excellent first effort and would still serve as a valuable tool for filling out the calendar once it was all set up correctly. Johnny made a trip to the bathroom and returned with a thought:

"Hey, boss… Don't let it get you down. I imagine this guy Thomas has a plan, or he wouldn't be…*directing.* That means there could be an answer, I think. You just have to remember to stay alive no matter what his plan is. Maybe the two goals; yours and his, are not mutually exclusive. Maybe you can both win. I mean, why would you *have* to die for his family to be put to rest? You weren't even around when they were alive, or when their problems began."

"Okay, let's speculate then; what does Thomas Pike want from me?"

Johnny started: "Well, you said that he's invisible, and the other ghosts are not. That's strange. They're from the same family after all, right?"

"Right."

"And we might assume that husband and wife are never together, even if we ignore the fact that he's invisible? What I mean is; when you see her, do you get the feeling that he is right there with her? Working with her, etcetera?"

"No, we do not get the feeling that they are ever together. And she's always chasing the kid, and the kid doesn't seem to want to be caught, either. That little guy can *run.* He blows her away; it's not even close. As far as the kid and the father ever being together...I'm not really sure. I can't say either way," said Tim.

"And she's crazy. Chops up worms and toads in your kitchen."

Tim laughed. "Stop embellishing! It was 'only' maggots. No snakes, no toads, spiders, etcetera." Holly chuckled at the table while she prepared her notes.

"So, what happened to the kid?" Johnny asked.

Tim turned and looked at Holly. They both blinked. Had they not thought of this yet? Or had they already talked about it? "Dammit, I feel like *I'm* one hundred years old. Holly, do you remember what happened to the kid? I'm so tired. I don't remember anything anymore."

"We do *not* know what happened to the little boy for sure, but it can't be good. She's weird...I don't like her, and I don't trust her. I don't want to be there when that part is solved. He died early, after all, right? I know I'm going to be upset."

Johnny picked up on Holly's thoughts: "So...something bad

happened to the boy…and she did it. That would make a lot of sense."

"I don't know…I just don't think she was a healthy human being. If I recall, Annette thought the boy was in a state of 'unrest' because he might have been murdered. As far as Dad being mad at Mom…yes, that makes sense."

"Okay then, here's a question for you: Does Mom know Dad is around? He's invisible, right? Doesn't show himself? They're never seen together, blah, blah, blah—Is this the reason why he is invisible?"

Tim and Holly looked at each other once again, trying to turn their two overtired brains into one.

"Probably," said Tim, feeling stupid that Johnny was already on top of everything. Holly nodded in agreement.

"Is this stuff you've already thought of? Are we making progress right now, or am I just catching up?" Johnny asked.

"This is pretty good, Johnny. We're both frazzled, to say the least. I'm burnt—just burnt out. I don't think I have the ability to think outside the box right now. It's been a very busy ten days." He winked at Holly as he said it.

Johnny seemed encouraged by the positive feedback. "Do I detect *hope*?"

Tim dunked precooked pasta into a pot of boiling water as he tossed a mixture of chicken, mushrooms, Marsala wine and Alfredo sauce in a frying pan. "I'm with you, man. Thanks for coming—seriously."

The night progressed. It was closing in on nine o'clock, and dinner was ready. Holly opened another bottle of wine and guessed that the three of them would soon lose focus and say goodnight to the productive part of the evening. That was all well and good. They deserved a break, and besides, they had made a lot of progress.

After they ate, Holly showed them her calendar. When it was finally finished, it would hold every known incident as recorded by Annette, boiled down and posted on an April 1971 calendar, and when that was done, she would begin work on May. It provided a forecast of annual events, but did not include random sightings; in other words, the ghosts could pop up on any given day, but on *anniversaries*, you could count on them to be in a specific place, most likely reliving their tortured past.

April 1971

M	Tu	W	Th	F	Sa	Su
X	X	X	1	2	3 Tour Property	4
5	6	7	8	9	10	11
12	13	14	15	16	17 First Day	18 Sees boy Finds Journal
19 Roofer First Date	20 Boy in grove Rifle Date #2	21 nothing	22 Sleep Walk kids	23 Night Gowns kids	24 Stare Down kids	25 kids
26 Roofer again	27 Mildred "Cooks"	28 Boat	29	30 Thomas Leaves	X	X

Today

"Can I see that?" asked Tim.

"Why, boss? I thought you were selling the place?" ribbed Johnny. Tim gave him the evil eye and went right to April 28th.

April 28th, 1971 was the same day (fourth Wednesday in April) as:

April 27th, 1966,

April 26th, 1967 and

April 24th, 1968, so Annette's journal was exasperatingly familiar:

> *Wednesday, April 27, 1966*
>
> *The mother was seen in a small rowboat on the pond. She remained almost motionless except for the drifting of the boat. It went on until I grew tired of watching! I actually let down my guard and started some of the menial tasks on my to-do list, checking back every few minutes or so. I'm not sure how long it took, but roughly a half-hour in I went to check on her and she was gone. For the next hour, I lived in fear that she would pop up behind me or something, but that was it for the day. She was gone.*

Tim erupted, just a bit. "What the hell? That's what I was expecting today! Instead, I got a blood-sprayed kitchen and a woman with a hatchet. Holly…are you sure?"

"Yeah, I'm sure. Annette's journal confused me, and I knew it did, I just didn't know why. Then I figured it out and dropped everything to save your bacon. I'm certain this time. She saw the same thing on the same day in 1967, too. The same day in 1968 is actually May 1st, but I went and checked it. All three match."

Johnny spoke up: "Okay then, chief; that means I'm coming with you tomorrow. Let's get up early and get some things done and get you back on track. Good meeting?"

Tim wasn't sure how it happened, but Johnny had taken control of the night, …and in a way, Tim's destiny. What a great friend.

"Good meeting," he echoed.

"Good meeting," agreed Holly.

Just when Tim thought he was out, they dragged him back in.

CHAPTER THIRTY-FIVE

Holly's Day, Part One

Wednesday, April 28th, 1971

While Tim and Johnny went to work on the house, Holly called in sick and stayed home to work on her calendar project. After the incident with the hatchet, it was time…no…it was *past* time to *make* time and review all of the clues they had been given. No more excuses; they were now playing with their lives. Truth be told, she was also excited to *organize* everything and skip her boring phone calls.

The calendar for April 1971 was nearly finished; she just needed to look at tomorrow, April 29th because she knew that Friday, April 30th would be "Thomas Leaves." After that, she would begin May. She also wanted to be near the phone for Tim, reminding him that she wanted to be updated on any happenings.

The first task was to finish reading Annette's original journal. It had only been eight days since she knew it existed, and when you factored in normal distractions like work and child visitation time passed quickly, but there could be no more excuses; they might be *out of time* if they put it off any longer.

Tomorrow was once again *the most important day of their lives.* She scoured the journals for any and all information and…came up empty. Like April 21st, Annette had been busy on that day; out at the nursing home or elsewhere. The journal was a virtual dead-end. Tim would not be impressed with the forecast, but it wasn't the calendar's fault. She read on.

Apparently, Annette had asked around in the nursing home about her house and its history. She found a patient named Martha Simmons, whose family came from one of the first houses on Lancaster Hill Road, close to Route 3 and the town of Franklin.

This part of Annette's journal was written as a series of interviews, which made the reading very boring. Holly had to guess that the interviews had been recorded on audiotape and then transcribed by hand into the journal. Thinking ahead to her recap meeting with Tim (they would be nightly from here on out), she pulled out her notepad and began to summarize Annette's unedited dialog with the patient in the nursing home.

Martha Simmons was ninety-six years old, and her mother Emma had been a schoolmate of Elmer Pike's, who was more commonly known to Holly and Tim as the *ghost boy*. According to Annette's research, Martha's grandmother Elizabeth and family were very upset when the boy went missing in 1862, about a year after his father had been killed in training exercises for the Civil War.

Elizabeth had met Mildred—*Pike* (as she was known then) several times and disliked her intensely. Her excuse was that Mildred came from a disreputable family in Salem, Massachusetts. This information was just a smokescreen; however; the truth was that Elizabeth was jealous of Mildred. Thomas Pike was a handsome young man and the pride of Sanborn. Many of the homegrown lady folk were hopeful that one day they might be *Mrs. Thomas Pike*. To say that young Elizabeth LeBlanc was one of those hopefuls would be an understatement.

Mildred won the contest. She showed up suddenly and out of nowhere; just an orphan at sixteen years of age, marrying Thomas just two years later. Elizabeth, exasperated by all the time she had wasted, found a mousy consolation prize by the name of Frederick Simmons soon after, and they had a baby girl named Emma just after Elmer Pike was born.

Elizabeth's obsession with the Pikes continued, however, as she found it impossible not to keep jealous tabs on her neighbors down the road. She was a gossipmonger extraordinaire, and it was widely known around town that she was very bitter and wanted the marriage to fail more than anything.

She began to keep a scrapbook.

According to Martha Simmons, she would write about how she felt daily, and she would detail encounters and run-ins she had with either Thomas, Mildred, or both. Her husband Frederick, far from being an alpha-male, did as he was told, remaining indifferent about his wife's dark hobby.

As Holly read on, she gathered that Martha's recollection of the scrapbook (which had become a sort of family heirloom) included a newspaper clipping that Thomas Pike would be joining the 5th New Hampshire Infantry of the Union Army sometime just before the Civil War began. It also featured a copy of his obituary.

Elizabeth quit on the scrapbook after Thomas's death; there was no one left to covet, after all. The book collected dust on the shelf, and she thought once or twice about throwing it away. An undetermined amount of time later (Holly couldn't tell from the notes), Elizabeth's father George, who was a police captain in Sanborn, was called to the Pike house because something terrible had happened to little Elmer.

For reasons…unproven, the story was never a big splash in the local press. All they could gather was that the boy was simply found dead on the property. Elizabeth, of course, suspected Mildred immediately of murder and a cover-up, questioning out loud to anyone who would listen about the timing. It seemed all too convenient to Elizabeth that a recently widowed woman might be suddenly completely free to find new romance without the baggage of a child.

The funeral services for the boy were private affairs; no wake or burial for the general public, and strangely, an obituary never appeared in the newspaper. These facts inspired Elizabeth to dust off the scrapbook once again and continue collecting her poisonous thoughts.

She learned through her father that he had suspicions about Mildred and her relationship with the Chief of Police, Abner Wallace. Chief Wallace was a single man, having lost his wife to pneumonia several years back. Once or twice, Captain George had witnessed Mildred stop by the Police Station at odd hours, never talking to anyone but the Chief.

Chief Wallace died when he fell off a ladder at his home in late 1862. Captain George discreetly checked on Mildred's whereabouts on the day of Abner's death but could not find a reason to pursue his hunch; and since he may have been the only person to suspect that they were "keeping company," he said nothing. Elizabeth wrote it all down, wondering if Chief Wallace had exerted his influence on Jacob Callan, the editor of the *Sanborn Crier*, to keep things as quiet as possible for his secret "grieving" girlfriend.

After the death of the Chief, things at the Pike estate got even quieter. What had once been a happy homestead, with an adorable young family seen plowing the fields and tending to animals, was now overgrown and unkempt. The Christmas tree farm, where people from the area would flock right after Thanksgiving every year, had gone to seed. Even Lancaster Hill Road itself seemed darker as the life and joy of the Pike house dried up and soured the rural pass.

Elizabeth decided she could not let things rest. She renewed her obsessions so emphatically that even her granddaughter Martha could remember some of the rants. Frederick Simmons, as passive as he was, began to complain that her negative energy was taking away from their daughter and their "happy" home, but his concerns were pushed aside as she rambled down the road to full-blown-conspiracy-theory.

She wrote long meandering opinions in the scrapbook and drew pictures and diagrams, frequently repeating herself, unable to shake her emotions even though everyone else had moved on. She raved about the death of little Elmer and how unfair it was to the entire town that he was here one day, and gone the next, and what a pity it was that they all didn't get a chance to say goodbye.

She conjured up a theory that he was never buried; that Mildred had him stuffed and kept him inside, moving him from sofa to bed and bed to sofa, day after day. Elizabeth went so far that nobody believed her anymore.

And then one day in December (the year was not written in Annette's journal), Elizabeth Simmons went missing.

This made the newspapers, and everyone searched for the daughter of the police captain, the loving mother of Emma and loving wife of Frederick. Emma was the one that alerted the authorities. She had come home from school on December 2nd and could not find her mother. The entire town opened their hearts and doors to the effort, despite their true feelings that Elizabeth had lost a screw or two somewhere along the way and might have actually asked for her problems.

Mildred Pike had, after all, been one of the more benevolent townspeople during the crisis, donating her time and volunteering in the search, allowing anyone and everyone to search her property. She was, after all, an orphan herself and understood little Emma's pain. She had also mentioned that she hoped poor Elizabeth hadn't "become deranged," which struck Captain George as odd.

It was the first time since Thomas Pike's death that Mildred had been so social and outgoing, even though she still wore mostly black clothing as if her grieving was not over. Even so, as he watched her, he felt suspicious. With this in mind he saw to it that her property was searched completely; he even walked most of the twenty-three acres himself before all was said and done.

Elizabeth's body—what was left of it—was found in early May of 1863 in the woods just across the road from the Pike estate.

By then she was just scattered bones and hair spread across half an acre, as the coyotes had discovered her at some point during the winter. Mildred was not even questioned, as it had nothing to do with her property, and she had been so helpful and involved with the search last fall. George also didn't want to give her the opportunity to call his daughter "deranged" again.

Holly put down the journal, sat back, and took a breath, reflecting on Annette's good work. *She could have been a reporter.* The big take was that Elizabeth's *feud* with Mildred (for lack of a better word) had become a family legend and had been passed down the generations with great care, and simmering anger.

CHAPTER THIRTY-SIX

The Boat on the Pond

Wednesday, April 28th, 1971

Tim and Johnny arrived at the house just before seven o'clock. Tim parked at the end of the driveway, facing nose-out for safety. As soon as he stepped out of the truck, Tim noticed the kitchen windows.

"Son of a bitch."

Johnny got a little spooked and looked around wildly.

"What? What is it?"

"The kitchen windows… I—I don't know; I thought that

everything would be 'reset' today as if nothing had happened. Look at those windows. Oh my God…now she's haunting my wallet, too!" Everything was as they had left it yesterday. Every single window in the kitchen was smashed out, and it obviously was wide open all night. Hopefully, nothing got in.

Before moving any closer, Tim gave a basic tour from right where they stood, gesturing and pointing. He showed Johnny the pond (where today's main event would supposedly happen), the field beyond, the woods, and the house itself, room by room, window by window. He delivered a brief synopsis of everything that happened behind those windows before they even touched the doorknob. When he was done, they walked around the side of the house to the barn, which looked the same as ever.

"So, where does that path go?"

Tim turned and looked at the skinny path that disappeared into the trees.

"Eventually you end up in the grove."

"Want to take me up there?" asked Johnny.

"Hell no. Not now, and hopefully not ever. We don't know where she is right now."

"Well haven't you been up there two or three times?"

"Yeah, but that was before yesterday. That's ground zero for bad shit. I'm not taking any more chances…after yesterday I didn't even think I'd be back today at all. It's terrible, Johnny. The smell, the flies…she's scary, man. She's dangerous."

"I may be naïve, boss, but I think I'm kind of putting some faith in my Thomas Pike theory… He wants something, and he'll protect you, at least until he gets it!"

"No, just get to work. If I have to pull rank, I will, because this isn't fooling around time. I need to get back on track. And listen, don't be a hero and try something on your own," he added hypocritically.

"You're the boss." Johnny left it at that. Tim took him in the side door where they paused at the sliding door.

"Are you ready for this?" Tim asked. "It's going to be gross in there." Johnny nodded, and Tim opened the slider.

It smelled bad…but it was bad *goose*, not bad *Mildred*, and Tim was thankful for that. Johnny wrinkled his nose as both men remained silent. As they rounded the counter separating the breakfast area from the kitchen, it was all there, just as Tim and Holly had left it: piles of broken glass, dishes, the pot on the stove, the feathers, the blood-sprayed walls and the drying, congealed pile of meat. Everything that had been red yesterday was now brown, and there were flies, although not part of Mildred's entourage. Luckily it didn't appear as though any animals had gotten in to eat the mess. *It might have killed them if they did*, Tim thought.

Tim poked his head into the dining room and looked around, then jogged to the end of the house. When he got there, he held his finger to his lips and waved Johnny through. Together they checked out the upstairs; the house was empty. They stood in the guest room looking out at the pond.

Johnny broke the brief silence. "We never finished our talk last night. We never got into Thomas Pike's end game…his ultimate goal, the thing that will set you free."

"Welcome to my world. The days aren't long enough, you're old, you get tired, and you never finish your to-do list. What are you talking about?"

"Fix that attitude, boss. What I was saying is: how many graves are out there—in the grove?"

"Two."

"So that's…let me guess…Mildred and the kid then, right? Thomas is buried somewhere else?"

"Yeah, …right… I mean, he *is* buried elsewhere, I know that—and I suppose you're right about the other two."

"Maybe the guy, Thomas—just wants to be buried with them…or…maybe not with…*them*. Maybe just with the kid, you know—kick the old lady out."

Tim stared at the pond, considering Johnny's last point. A smile came to his face.

"I bet you're right."

He turned to face Johnny. "That's got to be it. I don't want to inflate your ego to any bigger than it already is, but I think you're right! What do we do? Move the kid or move her? Shit, there's Thomas too…" The thought trailed off, and Tim's brief excitement ended as he realized how overwhelming the task at hand would be.

"I'm not sure about that yet…I just got here last night, you know; been here about twelve or thirteen hours. I can't solve it all for you in the blink of an eye."

Tim rolled his eyes. He was still blown away by the revelation and ignored Johnny's sarcasm.

"By the way, Boss, you haven't done hardly *anything* to this place! How much of that would you attribute to the ghost, and how much is because you're rolling out the red carpet for Holly?"

"None of your business; and don't forget that it's Sheila's fault, too. She sabotaged last Thursday. That's ten percent of my time right off the top." The manly banter died down quickly as the two men went back downstairs to clean up the kitchen as best they could, throwing the goose meat into the trees around the side of the barn. The kitchen windows would have to wait; new ones had to be ordered, and it would take a day. He made some measurements and some phone calls and got it all lined up.

When they were done in the kitchen, Johnny set himself to work in the master bedroom, and Tim continued his project in the guest room across the hall, directly in front of the pond. Holly's Nikon was still on the windowsill in the hallway between the two rooms; sitting in the same place he left it yesterday. Tim thought it would be a good idea to call Holly and share Johnny's idea… his…full-blown *epiphany*, really, that perhaps Thomas' end-game was to be buried with his son.

In odd moments, the house would make noises. Sometimes it came from one of the bedrooms in the back of the house, and sometimes it came from downstairs. Johnny would poke his face around the doorjamb to check the staircase and then look across the hall to silently ask Tim if he had heard the same thing. If Tim were making noise at the time and didn't hear it, Johnny would catch his attention to notify him with hand signals that he'd heard something. Johnny became tenser the longer nothing happened, and Tim noticed he was sweating more than he usually did.

"Hey boss, I'm kind of getting nervous…I mean, you see ghosts every day here, right? That means I'm probably going to see one—or two. I keep looking out the window. This is kind of nerve-wracking."

"That's because you're still a virgin. It's much different when you're a real man, and you see them all the time."

"It's not my first time, bro. Remem…" Johnny cut himself off, hoping Tim didn't follow what he had been about to say. Tim stopped what he was doing, put down his tools, and swaggered into the doorway of the master bedroom.

"Oh, yeah, right. I do remember. You're not a virgin anymore because your grandma was your first."

Johnny flipped him another bird then bit his own finger as if to curse himself, head down with a smile, admitting he messed up. Tim burst into exaggerated laughter just to make it last a bit longer. The men worked steadily until noon. At that point, they broke out the coolers and had some sandwiches. They sat on their toolboxes in the guestroom, and every few minutes, one of them would peek over the windowsill at the pond. Tim retrieved the Nikon and kept it close. Half the day was gone; it would have to happen soon.

Suddenly Tim spoke in a whisper like a hunter that had just seen a deer.

"*Hey…hey…hey…here she comes.*" Johnny laid down his tools quietly and crept low into the guest bedroom. Tim knelt on the floor in front of one of the windows, and Johnny did the same.

Out on the water drifted a small rowboat. Mildred sat in it, very still. She wore a sunbonnet; her face completely obscured from where they watched. She had chosen the seat at the front of the boat, away from the oars, which were lying inside the boat. A basket was on the seat next to her, and there were two fishing poles over the side.

Johnny was spellbound and spoke in short excited whispers: "Oh my God, there she is. She's so creepy, man! She doesn't even move! What's she doing? Can you see her face? I can't see her face." Tim picked up the camera and snapped approximately five pictures, realizing that there would be no perfect shot; without a zoom lens, she was just too far away. Maybe the developer could blow it up in the darkroom; he didn't know a lick about photography, so he put the camera down and just watched.

"No, I can't see her face. She doesn't usually wear that hat. This is weird. That pond barely fits a rowboat. And she has a picnic basket, all to herself. There are *two* fishing poles. Is she... with someone?"

"You mean like the day Dad is supposed to leave, but she's the only actor on the stage? Yeah, maybe... Maybe it's supposed to be the kid. I don't think a man would get in a boat to fish in that pond. I mean, I could cast my line clear across from one side to another. I wouldn't need a boat."

"She's sitting at the front of the boat; she didn't do the rowing, obviously. It's nearly impossible from that seat, and the oars aren't even next to her."

They stopped speculating and watched. The boat drifted, never reaching shore...back and forth aimlessly. Mildred never moved, not once; just sat like a statue. After fifteen minutes, Johnny had to reposition his knees and turned his back to the pond to face the back of the room. Tim wanted to do the same but didn't think it wise to take eyes off of her. He closed his toolbox, turned it on its side lengthwise, and took a seat about five feet back from the window.

"In one of the journal entries, Annette talks about the anniversary of Thomas Pike leaving to go fight in the Civil War.

According to Holly's new calendar, it's supposed to happen for us this Friday. As you know, Mildred didn't want him to go, and followed him to the road, hysterical."

"So…it's just her? No props or anything?"

"We'll see…maybe. I wonder if I should skip it. Annette says she does it all by herself—a one-woman show. It was realistic enough so she could figure out what was happening. Like right now, we're looking at a boat that should have two people in it, but it's just her, and we know she's supposed to be fishing with the kid. This could be proof that they hate her guts. They don't want to take part."

"Riiight." Johnny let the thought drift away and turned back to the pond. Both men had taken their eyes off of it for a brief second. Johnny panicked. "Boss?"

Tim stood up casually. Holly's calendar had worked. Paired with Annette's journal, they might now be able to predict where Millie might be at certain times. That could come in handy if they were going to start moving some graves soon. A nervous twinge in his gut raised his blood pressure; *am I really up for this?* He scanned the entire property through the window to be sure Mildred wasn't wandering nearby, then relaxed somewhat.

"I think it's over." Johnny looked over the railing to check the stairs anyway.

"Hey, are we in danger? I didn't see where she went, did you? Is she coming here? Is she in the house, maybe?"

"Annette had three years logged for this particular date, and she didn't mention anything about her coming back to the house, so I'm not too worried, but I'm not going to let down my guard yet either, just in case."

"So how does Thomas figure? How does he get in touch with you? Remind me."

"Well, one night I sleepwalked to the gravestones, another night I had a dream, sometimes I'll find a journal in the turret… stuff like that."

"That sleepwalking has to be upsetting, man. Holly didn't see you leaving?"

"No, I was sleeping alone. I had the girls, and we didn't want to introduce them to Holly yet. The next night I literally tied myself to the floor!"

"That time you went out, though; you left the girls alone in the house? That's scary."

"I know that's part of the reason I quit on the house until you showed up and talked me out of it. Thanks very much…*I think*. And you know they woke up in old-fashioned nightgowns one morning too…"

"Yeah, that can't happen again. When is next visitation?"

"Nine days away."

"That'll be here before you know it. Let's hope we figure this shit out before then. Otherwise, you're going to have to introduce the girls to Holly, or I'm going to have to come up and 'help with construction' on the weekend. Maria is not going to like that."

"Don't even think about it, Johnny. Thank you, though. I appreciate it. You're always there for me." Tim rambled a bit as he pretended to inspect the living room wall, slightly choked up.

"Have you thought about hiring a psychic, or having a séance or whatever? I mean, I don't believe in that crap but…" Johnny asked.

"Uh…no, I don't believe in that either. Sheila did. She used to have her palm read every so often. Maybe that's part of the reason I'm against it. It's all so vague."

"The Bible says it's crap, too." Johnny was a very religious man.

"Yeah, I know. It's like a horoscope. Those are good enough reasons for me to skip the psychics."

"Where does Holly stand on the matter?"

"Uh…I'll ask, I guess. Or maybe I should just let her come up with it on her own, if she ever does, like if we run out of options. It might just slow things down. We're already communicating with Thomas, right?"

After yesterday's kitchen calamity, it was nice to feel a bit of success. The calendar had worked. Tim went downstairs and called Holly to congratulate her, promising dirty things as a reward. The two men worked at a more relaxed pace until seven o'clock…a full twelve-hour day. Tim made up at least a day, if not more of production that he had lost.

Sunset would be at around seven-thirty, and Johnny let it be known that he would prefer to be home for dinner if it was at all possible. Tim understood and didn't push the issue or start any razzing largely since he too did not wish to tempt fate after the sun went down, and he appreciated all that Johnny had brought to the table. His clear thinking alone was invaluable.

The two men hugged, and Johnny loaded up his tools, jumped in his truck and hit the road. Tim wondered if he would need to be bailed out again before this was all over.

CHAPTER THIRTY-SEVEN
A Complete Blank

April 28th, 1971 (Evening)

There was a lot of talk at dinner. Johnny's breakthrough that Thomas might want to be buried with his son was at the top of the list. Tim raved about Holly's calendar. Today had been spot-on, and they now had another tool in the toolbox to help figure it all out. Tim, of course, also recounted every detail of seeing Mildred in the boat. Holly, in turn brought Tim up to speed on Annette's nursing home connection, Martha Simmons, and all the work her grandmother Elizabeth had apparently put into some sort of scrapbook.

Tim had a random thought: "How did Mildred die? Is that still a mystery?"

"Good question. We don't know, and I really don't have much of Annette's journals left to read."

Tim sat back, deep in thought as the room went quiet. Holly decided to brighten the mood.

"Well, in other news, I filled in my calendar for April and May…so now we're good for another month or so if we can make it that long. If we get through May, I'll be sure and figure June nice and early, or at least until the anniversaries stop happening.

If they do stop…maybe we won't get the random drop-ins, either. Maybe they'll just be gone—*at peace.*

"Can you imagine that? Honey, I'll take every bit of good news I can at this point. Thanks for skipping work today to do that—now here's the million-dollar question: What does the calendar say about tomorrow?" Holly's enthusiasm drained from her face as Tim pulled the plug on the good news conversation. She looked down at the paper.

"Well, here's tonight's buzzkill. Annette volunteered most Thursdays, and when I say most Thursdays, that includes the four that pertain to tomorrow. Tomorrow is nothing but a big question mark." Tim took the news in stride even though he was visibly affected by it. It had been a very good day, and he wasn't ready to get off the confidence train. Holly continued:

"I'm sorry. I don't like it, either. Is Johnny going to help you again?"

"No. Johnny has to finish up at Mrs. Mills' house. She's one of only three active clients I have right now. He may be freed up in two or three days but tomorrow is a no go." Holly frowned.

"Well, in that case, I have more good news for you; I'm free to come and help you tomorrow."

Tim put down his chicken wing. "Are you sure? Are you going to get in trouble at work? It would be very macho for me to say 'you don't have to do that,' you know…"

Holly smiled. "I'll be okay at work, and I can spare another day to make sure you're safe."

Tim stood up, came over to her chair, and hugged her. "You just made my night. What's the matter, you don't put your faith in Thomas Pike watching my back?"

"That's not good enough; not after Mildred slaughtered those geese in front of us and ended up all covered in blood—not to mention the hatchet. I can't get that image out of my head." He kissed her, and they remained entwined for several minutes.

Tim checked his watch: A quarter 'til midnight. It seemed

like a week ago that he and Johnny had pulled into the driveway and saw the smashed kitchen windows. "Honey...I need to sleep. Please...come to bed with me."

"Sleep? You only put in a twelve-hour day today. Go shower, and I'll be right in." He ambled out of the room, smiling. Holly gathered the half-empty cartons of Chinese food and put them in the fridge, then followed.

CHAPTER THIRTY-EIGHT

Special Delivery

April 29th, 1971: (2:17 A.M.)

Holly woke with a start to the sound of her doorbell. It rang once, disrupting the silence of the early morning. She looked at her bedside clock radio: 2:17 A.M. *Who the hell?* Tim was sound asleep, dead tired from the extended paranormal-infused workday, not to mention Holly's after-hours obligations.

She nudged him hard. Nobody had ever rung her doorbell at this time of night—in fact, she couldn't remember the last time anyone had used her doorbell at all. Thank goodness Tim was here; *two people are better than one*, she thought.

Tim snapped to attention, and together, they approached the front door; it was just beginning to rain. The windows around the door were small, and there were no good angles from which to get a clear look outside unless the person that rang the bell wanted to be seen. Holly grabbed two kitchen knives and handed one to Tim as he turned on the outside light and released the bolt to open the door. Before opening the glass storm door, he craned his neck to the left and right, trying to see the perimeter; *no one there.* He opened it and stepped out cautiously.

Something shifted under his foot, and he jumped back, scaring

Holly, but it was only a photo album of some sort, just starting to catch the rain. He took one last look around, picked it up and went back in, locking the door.

Holly took one look at the slightly damp book and knew exactly what it was. She took it and thumbed through the pages to be sure. It was Elizabeth Simmons' scrapbook.

"How did this get…*here*? How did he know that I read that part of Annette's journal? I did all that *in my own house!* Was he looking over my shoulder at the exact page I was on? Tim, this is *the scrapbook* that Elizabeth Simmons wrote."

"Johnny was right; they can travel. Congratulations, he likes you too. We're both in the club."

"That's not funny."

"Well, this is proof he knows who we are and can go wherever he wants…"

How unsettling, she thought, putting the scrapbook on the table and opening it. As Annette had reported, "The Scrapbook" was started by Elizabeth Simmons and began as a sort of catty, immature crush-piece on Thomas Pike that evolved into a diatribe against Mildred Wells, the mysterious orphan who showed up out of the blue and stole his heart.

The book was thicker than Holly had imagined. Annette's notes concerning the scrapbook had been in interview form, apparently taken from recordings of Martha Simmons. If the majority (or potentially all) of the information in Annette's journal was taken *only* from Martha's recollections and not the scrapbook itself, then this special delivery might potentially hold a treasure trove of discoveries.

"Remember how I said I was going to help you tomorrow, Tim?"

"Yeah, let me guess. Now you're staying home to read."

"Close. I'm still going with you, but I'm not going to help, at least with construction. I'll read it there."

"Oh, good, you had me worried there. You were probably just

going to be in my way, anyway. Your new plan is even better." She punched his arm, and they left the scrapbook on the table and went back to bed.

Tomorrow was already here.

CHAPTER THIRTY-NINE

The Power of Two

April 29th, 1971 (5:39 A.M.)

It took Tim about a half-hour to fall back asleep, but it took Holly much longer since the privacy of her home had been violated. It took her until 5:18 am, and shortly after that the dream started.

They dreamt separately but simultaneously: it commenced with Mildred walking through a cemetery, on her way to the back row of stones just before a forest's edge. *Not Lancaster Hill Road*, Tim noted.

He floated, bodiless in the dream with a bird's eye view. It was a small cemetery, no more than a hundred or so graves. He looked back to the entrance, at the wrought iron gate, and there it was in bold letters: *Tower Hill.*

This was Mildred from years back, still alive, visiting Thomas, although it was hard to tell as yet how long he had been gone. She wore her customary dark farm dress, but didn't wear dark because she was truly mourning; it was for appearance only, as well as her color of choice. She brought nothing to the grave; no flowers, no bible—and that came as no surprise to either of them.

Mildred made her way across the neglected lawn and approached the last row where she arrived at Thomas's grave; the man that had introduced special happiness to her life that she had never before felt. A man who helped heal many of the wounds inflicted by her upbringing and then betrayed it all by leaving her with his offspring albatross. She didn't sit, kneel or pray; but stood defiantly over where his chest would be and looked straight down.

"Are you there, Thomas? I hope so. I hope you are trapped, with nothing to do but watch. If for some reason, you are resting peacefully—well, there is no justice in the world. But I choose to believe there is. I choose to believe you can hear me. I hang my hat on that hope.

I was finally happy…and you knew that. *We* were happy…but you had to leave us to so selfishly '*serve.*' I told you I could not be alone. I told you I would not do well alone in my head. Don't think for a second that the company of a child is a sufficient substitute until you try it yourself. But we know now that will never happen.

"You abandoned us in search of selfish glory. The irony is that you don't even deserve to be buried here…next to other soldiers who actually *served*; you didn't even make it to battle, which is so embarrassing to explain to people *over* and *over*, but I still do—every single time I'm asked, thank you very much.

"I tell them the truth. I tell them you died in an idiotic bayonet duel with a fellow trainee. It wasn't even a real fight, just clownery. You were fucking around if we're honest. I heard tell there was drinking…and that you were the life of the party. How ironic… And then you somehow managed to end up on the wrong end of your own bayonet. I hope it was painful for you, and by painful, I mean embarrassing; because it is embarrassing for all of us.

"I buried you on Tower Hill because I want you to be alone… to *think*…and *think some more*…just like you made me do. It's not healthy to be alone in your head for too long; if you don't believe me, ask Elmer. It's *overwhelming.*

"I'm not sure if you saw it or not, but yesterday…I put him down. He was never the same without you, and he really wasn't dealing with it very well. I feel I did us all a favor. You should not be surprised, and don't think for a second that you do not share in the blame.

"I will be cleared of suspicion shortly, so don't waste your energy dwelling, but I came here to tell you that he will not be laid to rest with you. He will be on the property with me when my time comes, which could be soon. Why do you think I put you here in this *veterans* cemetery? Because you're a war hero? Ha ha…sadly, no.

"I'm not sure yet about myself…I…I'm not feeling well. The things that were embedded within me are sometimes too much. You knew all this, however." Mildred lifted her palms and pressed them into her eyes, rubbing deeply, as if her inner turmoil were suddenly more important than the conversation.

"Elmer will be with me, and…you won't…but here is something—his hat. He wore it in the boat. I fished it out when it was all over and decided it should be yours."

Her shoulders pulled back in defiance as if the headstone was Thomas himself. She tossed it at the ground and took a step back; inhaling deeply, finishing by spitting directly between his first and last name, then watching the saliva drip into his date of birth. She turned, having delivered the vengeful yet somehow unsatisfying last word, and then walked out the front gate. Her shoulders hunched, and her head slumped. *Her anger is eating her alive*, thought Holly.

It was quiet for nearly half a minute as the dream continued. Tim and Holly wondered individually why they were left there floating to stare at an empty cemetery.

Then, from the woods behind the stones came the boy.

Elmer, newly deceased, meandered toward his father's grave and circled to face it. He dropped to all fours and ran the fingers of his right hand through the grass as if overjoyed to have finally found this place that his mother had purposefully never shown him. After stroking the grass, he crawled forward, picked up his cap and wiped the saliva from the headstone. When it was finally clean he tossed the cap aside, erasing whatever pain his mother had just inflicted. *I found you, Dad*, he seemed to say.

Holly wondered where Thomas was and why he didn't appear. Thomas was long dead, and now, so was Elmer. Where was the happy reunion between father and son? Tim had similar thoughts. Maybe it was because the boy was not yet buried? There was no way of knowing—*ghost physics.*

Holly finished the thought: Perhaps Thomas was playing the long game, hiding from everyone, including his son, very patiently—until the right time to properly fix Mildred.

Elmer hugged the headstone, talking to it with words too soft to hear. He lay on his back and stretched out over the grave as if sharing a hammock with his father. He spent nearly half an hour there, then abruptly sat up and walked back into the woods.

Mildred would never know how much her unnecessary and vindictive speech had cost her.

CHAPTER FORTY

The Horse's Mouth

April 29th, 1971 (6:15 A.M.)

"What a bitch," said Holly, her first words of the morning.

"Yeah, she messed up, though. The kid followed her. She didn't even realize."

"Did she kill him? Is that what I heard her say?"

"Thank you, Thomas. Message received."

CHAPTER FORTY-ONE

Deeper into the Scrapbook

April 29th, 1971 (7:21 A.M.)

As they pulled into the driveway on Lancaster Hill Road, Holly felt the aura of the house more than ever; the stories—the history. She knew this place, and it was possible it even knew her. She was aware that several people had been found dead here over the years, and that some were even buried on the property. Also not to be forgotten was the fact that somebody that had once lived here now knew where *she* lived.

Holly wondered: Why bother to look for the ghosts anymore? Why be so guarded? Whatever will be, will be, and they were bound to cross paths again sooner or later. Both she and Tim were exhausted to the point of carelessness. Despite her current mood, Holly made sure that their first stop was to the barn where Tim found the old hatchet; once again magically back in its drawer. She put it in her handbag.

He set up a workspace in the dining room between the kitchen and living room. The porch partially blocked the view of the yard, so visibility was not optimal for Tim. Because of this, Holly sat in a chair directly in front of the first window in the living room. From there, she was not only close to him, but she could see past the pond and into the field, and also to her left through the kitchen into the breakfast area.

Tim started his noisy work, and Holly opened the scrapbook and began to read. She still had some of Annette's first journal left but figured that good old Thomas and his urgent midnight delivery might want this read first. It was difficult to concentrate, however, because she couldn't stop checking her surroundings despite her "what does it matter" attitude upon arrival.

She would read a sentence and then look out to the pond and field. After that, she looked behind her while listening to her right (the front door and the upstairs). Finally, she gave double the attention to the breakfast area, figuring that was Tim's back. She repeated this cycle nearly fifty times.

The scrapbook began as Annette had described it. It appeared to be written by a young girl (Elizabeth) with a crush that quickly turned cold when she didn't land her Prince Charming (Thomas). It continued with his death while training for the war then went on to the suspicious death of his son Elmer, and the doubly suspicious death of the Chief of Police.

Holly dug deeply into the ramblings of the aging Elizabeth Simmons; a woman who married but obviously settled for second best once Mildred had claimed her supposed birthright, and continued to obsess over the young couple for years to come. It was obvious by her erratic writing style that she was a bit of a loon. She wrote for hours on end, frequently without punctuation or noticing that there were lines on the paper to keep the sentences straight. Elizabeth's writing would get smaller and smaller at times, for no apparent reason other than what Holly guessed was a change of mood. The book was eighty percent rambling jealousy.

Near the end of Elizabeth's section (and before Emma took over writing duties), Holly was surprised to read that she had begun sneaking onto the Pike property after dark to "get a closer look." She would "go exploring," sometimes long after everyone had gone to bed, and would spend some of her early morning hours peering through the windows of the formerly Pike...but now *Wells* house. Apparently she wandered the old grove but never found the gravestones, simply remarking that her father used to buy their Christmas trees there when she was a child and that Mildred had spoiled *that too* for the whole town by closing the Christmas tree farm and letting the grove grow wild.

Elizabeth's chapters ended due to her untimely death, but the scrapbook didn't end there. Emma, Elizabeth's daughter (mother of Martha), and onetime classmate of Elmer Pike took over the writing.

Emma's first entry picked up about a month after her mother had gone missing. She suspected Mildred immediately and hounded Grandpa George the police captain to do something about it, but he said he couldn't, which prompted Emma to say a few things to him that she shouldn't have, earning her a slap across the face. Grandpa George added insult to injury in the heat of the moment, reminding Emma that the "whole town knew your mother was crazy" and that "sneaking around at all hours of the night was no way to live." It became clear to Emma that the death of her mother had brought relief for some in her own family and she alone would have to be the one to expose Mildred Wells and bring her to justice.

When Elizabeth's remains were found "just barely" off the Pike property, Emma scribbled over twenty pages (much like her mother in her prime) about how much she hated Mildred and how she knew she had killed again. Emma had commiserated with her mother the day the news broke about Elmer; both knew in their hearts that Mildred must somehow be guilty. Elizabeth's death was the same thing, just much closer to home.

Desperate for a strategy, Emma weighed her options. She decided she was not (*yet*, at least) crazy enough to go trespassing at night. Grandpa George's police connection was no help, either; he was more of a brick wall since the slap; "the case is closed" was all he would give her. So she decided to take a different angle.

One weekend in June of 1863, Emma announced to the family that she would be taking a leisure trip to Boston, and she would be going alone.

Nobody really cared, as the whole family was as odd and as self-absorbed as she was. What Emma didn't tell them was that her trip to Boston was really a trip to Salem, Massachusetts, Mildred's hometown. She traveled by coach, and as soon as she arrived started digging for information at the town hall, researching Mildred, her family, and their property. Disappointedly there wasn't much to discover, but she took a lot of notes then spent part of the day visiting the neighborhood Mildred supposedly grew up in, which strangely enough (or maybe not so strange after all) was in a part of town called Gallows Hill.

Gallows Hill was the spot in 1692 where women accused of witchcraft were hanged in public, but Emma knew some of the histories of Salem before even buying her ticket. She was secretly hoping to find out that Mildred was the descendant of a witch or part of a witch family; but what she didn't know was that the Salem Witch Trials were just a hoax started by schoolgirls, and that innocent people, not real witches, had been hanged. That wouldn't have stopped her, anyway. Ironically she had started a proverbial witch hunt of her own.

She felt in her bones that Mildred, using a spell, had lured poor Elizabeth out of the house in the middle of the night to murder her. She felt that if she could learn all there was to know about witches that one day she could convince the Sanborn police that they had one right here in town.

Emma finished her day in the library, then stayed overnight in a small hotel near the Jonathan Corwin "Witch House." When she woke the next morning, she went straight back to the library and city hall for more research. Emma was now hot on the trail of the entire Wells family tree. She started with the obvious by looking up the names of the women executed for witchcraft to see if any of them were named Wells, or had ever been named Wells, but unfortunately no, things were not that convenient. Another half-day later she had learned the backgrounds of all of the ill-fated women, with still no linkage to Mildred. Then a thought occurred to her: What if not all of the women associated with witchcraft had been executed?

Emma rubbed her eyes. They were red and irritated, and she had a headache. Maybe she should have listened to her doctor and gotten those ugly spectacles that made her look older than she wanted to. Frustration set in, and she was tired, still no closer to proving that Mildred Wells was into *Wicca*. Defeated, she logged her final thoughts on the Salem trip in the scrapbook, packed her things and left town the next morning, somehow more obsessed and wound up than she had been when she arrived. The failure made her angry. In the coach on the way home, her thoughts turned from Mildred to poor Elmer, the sweet boy she had sat behind in third grade.

He was in class one day, then gone the next. She went from seeing him every day to never again. He was handsome, too, like his father. Perhaps Mildred had killed her future husband!

...but why *never again*?

What had her mother Elizabeth written about the details of his death? Her memory was not clear on the subject, being that she was so young when it happened, so she opened the scrapbook right there in the coach and re-read of the events that had occurred back when she was only eight. She knew that Mildred had not-so-surprisingly been the only one on scene at the time of death, but what about the funeral? What happened there? Perhaps she could visit his grave and learn more.

The wheels in her mind began to turn, and the fire in her belly blazed anew when she read her mother's rants on the mini-scandal, and the outright injustice that *private* services had been held for poor little Elmer. Elizabeth wrote that the entire town should have been able to grieve for the little boy, not just the self-serving mother who surely killed him one way or another. If it wasn't murder, it was at the very least gross negligence. Emma bought every word, agreeing completely with her deceased mother.

Services were held on the Wells property. Perhaps that's what mother was doing on their land, thought Emma. She was looking for the gravesite, and then, on one of those excursions, got a little too close and was murdered, just like…well, just like some other people that came into contact with Mildred Wells, like the Chief of Police. Emma was still not ready to go searching in the woods by lantern-light for a grave all by herself, but she did have other ideas.

She arrived home from Salem mid-evening and went straight to bed, exchanging only the bare minimum of pleasantries with her father. Grandpa George had gone to bed early, and that was fine with her; she was not in the mood for the questions an ex-cop would be sure to ask. It was part of his nature and extremely annoying. The next morning she went to the Barker Funeral Home.

Simon Barker was the director of his namesake funeral home and had been the person contacted by Mildred Wells soon after her son had been found dead. Now Emma sat across a large desk from him in his office on the second floor. He had a curious, although annoyingly understanding look on his face, a face that came from years of consoling customers, a face that came with the profession.

"What can I do for you, Ms. Simmons? How is your family?" Simon Barker had his finger almost literally on the pulse of Sanborn and was responsible for over ninety percent of the town's burial services. Elizabeth Simmons' funeral had fallen into the ten percent that did not request his services, and he was not quick to forget. Emma caught the drift almost immediately—the almost imperceptible condescension, holding a grudge that his business had been shunned, most likely because Mildred Wells was a client. Elizabeth had made damn sure to pinpoint specific funeral arrangements when she revised her will.

"Yes, we're all healthy for now, thank you, Mr. Barker, thank you for asking. The reason for my visit today is not about my family, however…but it is sentimental. I recently took a trip to Boston, and as you know, it is a rather long ride. For whatever reason, as soon as I left Sanborn, I began to reminisce about my childhood classmate Elmer Pike. We were *best* friends"—she exaggerated this last point—"and you know, one day he was there, just like every other, and then…suddenly he was gone. I guess I never really got over it, and who knows—I think he might be the reason I am unmarried to this day."

Simon Barker hid a smirk with the skill of a politician, a veteran of hundreds of services that called for a somber but "understanding" stone face: The face that told customers *I'm sorry for your loss, but we'll take good care of your loved one.*

Just like her mother, he thought. Borderline crazy and as nosy as the day is long, not to mention they both had crushes on Pikes. Here it comes.

"Oh, yes, what a pity. That one goes back several years and still stings. A tragic loss—Elmer was so young. I'm sorry to hear that you're still feeling the pain."

"Thank you, Mr. Barker, I appreciate it, I really do, and I'll get to the point. The reason for my visit is that I thought I would like to visit him—you know, visit his grave. Also to pay respects to his father as well, perhaps bring some flowers, and tidy them up if they need it—say some prayers and such—but I was young when Elmer died and—I don't know where they are buried."

"Ah, that's very sweet of you. I can help direct you to Thomas Pike's grave; he is located at the Tower Hill Cemetery. We did not perform the services for that funeral because he was cared for by a fine establishment near Concord where he passed, but I do remember Ms. Wells informing me of his location. As for Master Elmer, I'm afraid you will need permission to visit his grave; it is on private land, you see."

"Private land? Wh…? Oh…I'm sorry…I assumed they would have been buried together. Is…is Elmer's grave on the Pike, I mean, Wells property then? I'm sorry, I'm a bit surprised. I didn't realize..."

"Well, I'm not at liberty to say exactly where Master Pike is buried, but I can tell you that you will have to speak with his mother for permission." Barker knew that if he confirmed that Elmer was on Pike property, then the daughter might follow in her mother's footsteps and take it upon herself to trespass. He wanted no blemish on his professional record that he had been anything less than discreet with any Pike family secrets, or *anyone's* family secrets for that matter.

"They primarily bury veterans at Tower Hill. There are civilian graves up there, but they are older than the Civil War. That's primarily why they are separate, so I was told. Elmer would not have been allowed to be buried there, as he wasn't old enough to have served. And due to the nature of Elmer's death, Mrs. Pi—Wells requested the utmost...discretion. I'm sorry, but I hope you understand—in the name of professional courtesy, of course. I'm afraid I am unable to help you at this time."

Barker lied through half of his speech, remaining calm while dismissing the Simmons family as pure country trash. Everyone knew they were a near-inbred family of gossips, several generations deep, but most importantly, they were just not...*customers.* He surmised that Emma would never have the guts to ask Mildred Wells the whereabouts of her son's grave. The tension between the two families was well known, especially after Elizabeth's mysterious death.

Barker was semi-relieved when Emma Simmons became apologetic and seemingly embarrassed. That reduced the possibility of a visit from Ms. Wells if the Simmons girl went knocking. Any compromises with discretion, whether real or imagined, was bad business. Perhaps the girl was not as obnoxious as her mother had been, *may God have mercy on her soul, of course.* Emma thanked him for his time and let herself out. He watched her walk through the front path and down the street from his office window. *Rabble-rouser.*

CHAPTER FORTY-TWO

The Monumental Mason

Simon Barker hoped that Emma Simmons would give up on her quest to visit Elmer Pike's grave. Barker, like the rest of the town, knew the Simmons' family reputation as gossipmongers and suspected that Emma might have ulterior motives. The girl's mother had died looking for trouble, but it still wasn't enough to convince Emma to mind her own business.

Barker was right; Emma was not finished. She was surprised that the boy was not buried with his father, so for an hour or two, she gave pause; after all, she was not about to go knocking on Mildred Wells' door. But the busybody in her kept the wheels turning, and it was Mr. Barker's sickeningly fake air of caring and discretion that helped push her onward. With this in mind, she decided to pay a visit to Samuel Taylor of Taylor Memorials over in Belmont.

Sam Taylor didn't have to put a face on for his customers. He was usually covered in dust, right in the middle of cutting a memorial for someone or perhaps making granite steps for new construction. He was a working-class man with rough hands and a blunt way about him, which was basically the opposite of the greasy Simon Barker. Emma stood in the doorway of his shop and waited ten minutes for him to finish a cut before calling his attention.

"Mr. Taylor, hello…I'm Emma Simmons. My mother was Elizabeth Simmons; I'm not sure if you remember but…"

"Yes, I do, in fact. I know…I'm sorry; I *knew* your mother from my school days. I was very sorry to have to make her stone. It was very tragic how your mom left us. That's the thing about making memorials; it takes so long to make one, you think about every word, and you can't help but think about the person it's for… especially if you knew them. Most people think we crank these out like writing a postcard, but with these old tools…hammers… chisels…there's plenty of time to think." He gestured to his workbench, which was covered by old-fashioned looking hand tools. Mr. Taylor was near the last of a dying breed and couldn't justify the cost of buying modern state-of-the-art saws; besides that, they would probably just slow him down.

Emma continued: "Well, thank you. I appreciate that, Mr. Taylor, and thank you for helping my mother. I…I'm here for a different reason, however; do you mind if I ask you about my old classmate, Elmer Pike?"

"Another tragedy. You're young, and you've felt some pretty painful passings already, haven't you? Poor girl—Of course you can ask. What's on your mind?"

"Well, first of all, just so I understand; you deliver the gravestones to the gravesites, is that right?"

"Yes, that's right."

"Okay, good…I…I was hoping to visit Elmer and fix things up, tidy the grave and such, pay my respects—but I don't know where he and his father are buried. I was just a girl when he died." Emma pretended she didn't know that the two graves were not together and purposefully left out that she had already visited Simon Barker and didn't get the answers she wanted to hear.

"Darling, they're in two different graveyards, but it was wrong to do it that way if you ask me. She must have hated his guts for leaving. Some men hear the call, though…they can't say no to duty…or country. Thomas Pike is up at Tower Hill."

"The veterans cemetery?" Emma asked.

"No, not just veterans. Some are veterans, and some are civilians. Sanborn doesn't have many veterans, after all. It's just a small town."

"I heard the only people buried there that weren't veterans died before the Civil War."

"Nope. The entire Walton family is up there. They have a whole family plot up there with room for several more. None of them ever even saw a uniform, never mind a war."

Emma scowled. Simon Barker had lied to her, and in her mind, there was a conspiracy going on in Sanborn—or a cover-up, or something. *Mother was right about everything—and most likely murdered for it.* None of this was necessarily true, but she could not convince her Simmons family blood otherwise.

"So where was Elmer buried?"

"On the property, in the last row of the old Christmas tree farm. You can't even see the grove from the road anymore. It's gone wild; overgrown."

Emma was slowly processing the information, trying to think of more questions before Mr. Taylor lost interest in her visit and decided to get back to work.

"So...you made both of the stones...and..."

"I made all three," he offered teasingly.

"Three? Why thr—"

"She wanted hers done, too, at the same time as her son's. Thomas's was made a few years before, of course. She's a real planner, that Mildred—a real piece of work. Cold fish. I never liked her, not at all. She had me make her headstone with her maiden name on it, and it made me feel funny. *Mildred Wells.* I did a lot of thinking while I carved those two stones..."

Emma was captivated. "Yes, I knew her maiden name was Wells, but *I had no idea* she had it engraved on her stone! She was from Salem, Massachusetts—You know—*that* Wells family." Emma acted as if she had actually heard of a notorious Wells family from Salem to see if Samuel Taylor had ever heard anything of such a family.

"Never heard of them," he said. Emma forged ahead despite her disappointment.

"Mr. Taylor, tell me the thoughts that ran through your mind as you chiseled Mildred Wells' name into her headstone. What were you thinking? You've got my curiosity!" It was as if Mr. Taylor had been waiting for Emma…or any of the Simmons family with the gossip gene, to come walking into his shop. Or maybe he was of the same ilk—kindred spirits, having a chat. He continued:

"Well, she *did* use her maiden name. And she wanted it in bold letters, which was different from Elmer's stone. So they're next to each other, but they don't even match. I think it was just a big 'F You' to the Pike name if you'll excuse my language. That can't say much about their relationship if you ask me. I remember them, too…they *were* a happy family. Good-looking, too. You'd see them in town, and there was just no doubt that life was good; it was right there on their faces. Then the war started, and he got the fever—the *call of duty*. That just never goes over well with women, and who can blame them? And then, a little time goes by, and some say she got lonely. *Angry* lonely—and the little boy—your friend Elmer…became the metaphorical whipping boy. She wasn't enjoying the single mother life, and he might have looked a little too much like his father, which…might have cost him his life in the end, if you ask me."

"You're saying she murdered her son?"

"That was the rumor, although nobody could prove anything, of course, or she would have been put away. Oh, they investigated it. Your grandfather was a part of it too if I recall correctly—but it was kept quiet. You didn't *read* anything about the investigation; some say because she ended up banging the editor of the paper, excuse my language…but people talked about it. The grapevine was buzzing, and buzzing good. She got off scot-free if you ask me."

"So you think she did it then?"

"I do. And you will too when I tell you what she had written on little Elmer's headstone." Taylor loved the drama and paused, waiting for her to ask. Emma was almost speechless with anticipation.

"Uhm…oh, go on, go on!"

"It said:

HERE LIES
ELMER PIKE
ABANDONED BY HIS FATHER,
SUFFERER OF HIS MOTHER'S BROKEN HEART."

"*Sufferer of his mother's broken heart*? What is that supposed to mean? Is that a kind of double meaning thing?"

"Well…I thought about that for a long time, *several* times, too. I'll explain: First, I thought about it the entire time it took me to engrave the words. So, for that particular sentence, you're talking about a quarter of a day. My thinking at the time was that it sounded like a part of a riddle or a poem or something. I had to take her at face value at that point, meaning something like, 'the kid was sad because his mother was sad.'

"And then, I get wind that the police are doing a routine investigation, which struck me as weird; I mean, this lady's name is involved in the only two suspicious deaths in Sanborn in the last forty years. That is one hell of a coincidence if you ask me.

"Now, where was I? Oh, so I'm done engraving her so-called poem, but I'm still thinking about the words. I start reading that sentence as if the kid suffered because his mom took it out on him, and I've got to say, I felt sick to my stomach after that. Pretty soon, I couldn't read the sentence any other way. I couldn't un-see it that way.

"The worst part is, I'm one of very few people to have seen what was written at all. If the public knew what she had ordered, they'd probably show up at her front door with pitchforks, but most people don't know…and will never know what's on that stone. It's on *her* land!"

"She dated the police chief too, right?" Emma asked.

"Oh, more than just the chief. He died as well, come to think of it, but Mildred wasn't investigated that time. She went on a bit of a tear…sexually, I mean. She dated the editor of the *Crier* too as I told you—and there were others, but none that come to mind right away. I don't know too many details, but there was lots of talk in those days; lots of ugly, dirty, evil talk."

"And you never felt the need to tell everybody what she had you write?"

"After sleeping with the chief of police and the editor of the newspaper, amongst others? Spread more rumors? No. I need to make a living too, so I decided to mind my own business. She gave me the creeps, anyway. I wanted her out of my shop three minutes after she walked in. She was bad news; you could feel it in the air like a switch got flipped when her husband left. I didn't want her to come back here. I still look over at the door at random times when I'm alone in the shop, and it's because I'm thinking of her."

Emma silently agreed that the vision of Mildred Wells in one's doorway would be upsetting, to say the least.

"So, go back…she had *her* headstone made at the same time as Elmer's? What did it say?"

"Oh, yes. Yes, she did indeed, and I'll never forget what it said. It was the meanest thing I ever carved in stone, not including Elmer's. It also ended cryptically. I wasn't sure what she meant with the last line. I almost didn't do the job, but she threatened to take her business elsewhere—and, well, I suppose I needed the money at the time. I hope God doesn't punish me for helping her post her hate, or revenge or whatever the hell you want to call it."

"Please, tell me…what did it say?"

"I will. It said:

HERE LIES
MILDRED WELLS
BORN: OCTOBER 6, 1836
FORSAKEN BY HER HUSBAND
FATED TO SUFFER THE SINS OF HER BLOOD

...and that's not all. Down at the bottom, she wanted some sort of hoodoo or something—a half-warning. It said:

LEAVE US BE"

Emma stood stunned and said nothing.

"You want to know the weirdest part of the whole thing? Something I didn't realize right away until I had already taken a chisel to it? She didn't ask me to leave a spot for her date of death. I brought it up before she paid, and she just told me it wasn't important."

"Where did you deliver that stone?" she asked.

"I set it up right next to Elmer's. To sum it up, she arranged to be buried with her son who many around town think she killed, meanwhile leaving Thomas—*the pride of Sanborn and Civil War volunteer*—up there all alone on Tower Hill. If you ask me, it doesn't get much colder than that."

"Mr. Taylor, can I ask you one more thing?"

"Well, of course you can. Ask me anything you like."

"Did you think she was crazy?"

Samuel Taylor took a minute to ponder. "Well, I can see how some people would think that, but I've looked her in the eyes, and a lot is going on in there. She read me like a book. No, I don't think she's crazy. But I do think she's *evil*."

CHAPTER FORTY-THREE

Mystery Date Revealed

Holly sighed and closed the scrapbook, digesting the newest pieces of the puzzle. The book ended there; the last several pages left blank. It wasn't hard to wager a guess as to why; Emma had undoubtedly followed perilously in her mother's footsteps in one way or another.

So Mildred had her headstone made at the same time as her son's, Holly brooded. She was angry and planned the whole thing out, but of course, it wasn't enough to solve her problems...she's still walking around. She stood up to tell Tim what she had just read.

Tim's circular saw whined loudly in the dining room as she waited for his next pause. In the meantime, she stretched her legs and checked the surroundings. Walking to the bottom of the stairs, she looked up, listening carefully. It was quiet up there; in fact, it was quiet everywhere except for Tim's work in the other room. She almost started up but thought better of it, remembering that this place was not safe to explore. Putting too much space between them was probably not a good idea; so she turned back to the living room.

She ducked her head as she passed the first window and looked out past the lawn to the pond. Mildred was there...floating motionless...

again...

...in the boat.

Holly's heartbeat picked up as she sidestepped her way quickly into the dining room to unplug Tim's saw. It took him a half-second to realize that she wasn't joking, and he scrambled to his feet as she motioned frantically, finger pressed to lips. They knelt in front of the living room window and watched.

At first, it seemed to be a replay of the day before; the woman, a couple of fishing rods, and the oars resting on the edge of the boat. She wore the same hat, but the dress was different; today's was darker than yesterday's, and Holly had to wonder, as tension built in the air if that was intentional or not. The boat drifted slowly on the still pond, nearly stationary, allowing the breeze to choose the direction.

A few minutes later, the boat wobbled and rocked as if unsteady, and Mildred Wells, remaining seated picked up one of the oars and jabbed it into the air near the front of the boat.

A large splash disrupted the surface underneath the airborne oar, and she leaped like a cat to the bow. Leaning over the edge she plunged both arms into the water, hat still in place—face inches from the surface—body prone across both seats.

Bubbles erupted and sputtered from under the surface between her arms.

Elmer's murder.

Mildred wrapped her long fingers around his small shoulders and locked her arms straight, keeping them a measured foot beneath the surface.

Elmer opened his eyes in shock, seeing only a blur of his mother's face in the atmosphere above. He kicked hard and pulled at her wrists, trying to break free to no avail. Mother's formerly loving arms now held him for the purpose of betrayal. His eyes, partially obscured by the increasingly cloudy water narrowed as he quit the fight prematurely and accepted his fate. He relaxed completely and rebelliously to spend the last twenty seconds of his life, staring directly into his mother's eyes.

Mildred was surprised by the ice in his veins—*just like his father*—but put it out of her mind as she prepared to carry through with her morbid task and then mask the crime. She would have peace, Thomas Pike be damned.

Pondside, immediately after the murder, Elmer's eyes remained open, seemingly following her as she worked to fix the scene. She double-checked the boat for signs of foul play and made sure everything was ready for police inspection.

It took forty minutes for the authorities to arrive, but to Mildred, it felt like a month.

If he would only stop staring.

CHAPTER FORTY-FOUR

Mother's Little Helper

Tim and Holly stared in silence, dumbstruck. Tim felt sick to his stomach, and Holly started to cry.

"Oh, my God—I—wasn't ready for that... She's...she's..."

Tim's heart sank as the mismatch between mother and son played out. He didn't know how to comment; there were no words. The day should never come, he thought, when one witnessed the death of a child. Annette was very fortunate to have missed *this* horrific anniversary. He even wondered if Thomas had spared her this heartbreaking day to save it for fresh legs by the names of Tim and Holly. He had, after all, waited over one hundred years; time was an entirely different concept for him. All that mattered was the result.

Holly broke down in full sobs and buried her face in Tim's shoulder. He held her close, keeping both eyes on the pond. Mildred stood on the bank and rolled up her wet sleeves. They had seen her jump into the pond and drag Elmer's invisible body to shore. Now she grabbed her head and rotated her neck as if to crack it or relieve stress. The deed was done, and the aftermath was selfishly detached.

Two minutes passed; enough time for Tim to recover from the shock and begin to calculate escape. Holly gathered herself, yet refused to look, trusting in Tim to relay any relevant information going on behind her. Before Tim could formulate, Mildred left everything behind at the pond and ambled toward the house.

Tim braced immediately, staying low, and silently guided Holly to the back of the room. Mildred tottered as she ambled up the lawn, as if in a stupor. From their immediate right, footsteps descended the stairs again:

Footsteps, and the sound of dripping water.

The boy reached the bottom and peered around the doorjamb into the room. Holly shrunk against the back wall but didn't make a sound, terrified. Tim stood frozen. The boy's face was pale white and soaking wet. His hair clung to his head as if he had just been fished out of the pond, which, in a way—he had. They could smell the pond from where they stood.

His eyes were lifeless and unblinking. He lifted his arm and opened his hand, signaling for them to remain where they were. A puddle expanded on the floor beneath the boy's feet—a lone dragonfly landed on his shoulder, then took off again. *It's all about the pond for poor Elmer*, thought Tim. Holly wondered why there weren't swarms of flies around him like there were around Mildred.

Mildred reached the driveway and seemed to regain clarity, staring blank-faced into the living room. Tim wondered frightfully if they had been discovered. He looked back to Elmer, a boy...more than a hundred years old; yet eternally only eight. He remained still, hand still raised, pond water puddle growing. Then Mildred changed direction for the barn.

They crept silently to the window and watched her anxiously until she disappeared around the corner. Three silent seconds later, Elmer dropped his hand and ran upstairs. The front door opened by itself just beyond his puddle, revealing the truck in the driveway. Tim whispered a thank-you as they rushed out. Holly jumped into Tim's truck, visibly upset. Tim started the truck while looking back over his shoulder; no sign of Mildred.

He popped the truck into gear. They split the maples at the end of the driveway and sped down Lancaster Hill road as fast as the bumps and grooves would let them. Holly watched the house until it was lost in the trees.

CHAPTER FORTY-FIVE
Tomorrow's Forecast

No one had much of an appetite that night at Holly's house. It came as no real surprise that the boy had been murdered by his mother, yet witnessing the atrocity was far more painful than they could have ever imagined. It was one thing to hear the facts, but another to see it happen in real-time.

"I think the reason we only see *her* in these reenactments and not Thomas or the boy is they would never participate, and she knows it." Holly broke the long silence.

"I agree with that," said Tim. "But she chases him every time like she wants to make things right, I'm guessing. Why would she replay the murder for him, then?"

"Because she's selfish and crazy. Doesn't even know it's not the right thing to do. Too self-absorbed. I know a lot of people like that."

"You know a lot of people that murdered their children? Eww."

"Shut up! You know what I mean. She chases the boy every time she hears him or sees him, correct? She feels guilty, and he wants nothing to do with her. She went the selfish route and killed him so she could—I don't know, start over, or just get laid, but then—*I love it*—the kid haunts her, avoids her; drives her crazy. He doesn't want anything to do with her except torment her."

Tim nodded in agreement. Her perceptions rang true; Holly was on a roll.

"So Elmer haunted her after she drowned him, while she was still alive...but how does she end up? What happened to Mildred? How'd she die? Why didn't Annette figure this out? She was here for three years with Mildred, and she never figured this out? Wasn't it in the microfilm at the library? Or she just never looked? Did you read anything about this?" he asked.

"The scrapbook alleged that Mildred was *with*...sexually... the editor of the *Sanborn Crier* at one point. That might keep a lid on a lot of things. I'm guessing Emma Simmons took all that information from the headstone maker and went trespassing like her foolish mother had...looking for the graves. That probably didn't end well. That's my guess, anyway. The scrapbook ends abruptly. We could look that stuff up tomorrow I suppose or ask around, but I'm pretty sure the answer won't really help, no matter what it is. The short answer to your question of what happened to Mildred is—I still don't know."

"Mildred...she's racked up quite the body count. There's Elmer, Elizabeth Simmons and maybe even Emma Simmons. Add to that the possibilities of Henry Smith, the Chief of Police, and Annette herself—and that's potentially six, but at the very least, one that we know of for sure. We saw it with our own eyes."

Holly shifted in her chair after a moment of silence. "I'm still sick about what we saw. I can't stop thinking about it." Tim moved behind her and grabbed her shoulders, kneading.

"You should stay home tomorrow. Call in sick again. What's the forecast on the calendar you made? What depressing, grisly scene will we be running into tomorrow?" Holly pulled her papers from the growing stack of journals and scrapbooks and took a look at tomorrow, April 30th, 1971, which was actually the fifth Friday of the month. Counting backward from Thanksgiving, it corresponded with April 26th, 1861; the day Thomas left the family to go to war:

The day that started it all.

"Oh, no. It's the day Thomas left the family. That means Mildred will be wailing across the front lawn at some point. It was the year before the murder we just saw. That's too close to the house, Tim. It's dangerous. You shouldn't go." Tim appeared disappointed that the ghosts would once again interrupt his real-world financial problems.

"Shit. This woman is all up in my business—and I mean literally. She's killing my investment, Holly. I'm so ready to say goodbye to her." Tim looked up at the ceiling in mock confrontation: "Thomas…what else do we need to know? This is your story; you're the narrator. I admire your patience, but I'm losing mine—and maybe my shirt, too, if we don't fix this soon. Annette got you started; we've picked up the baton—so now, what, short of dying for the cause and financial ruin—can we do for you? Make it a win/win deal, or I'm out of here. One hand washes the other, or you can just kill me now…I'm very near the end of my rope anyway, and I mean it."

"If it were only that easy," offered Holly. "He won't just answer you; I'd bet my life. Everything is cryptic. Journals, scrapbooks, calendars—they can't use a pen…dreams…sleepwalking…it's exhausting."

"It is. *Did you hear that, Thomas!?* We're sick of this. Can't take any more! Holly, how about if I wake up early, then I can get some work done and get out of there around the time she shows up? Do we know what time of day she comes?"

"No, we don't. Annette was sporadic with her 'times.' Tim, I really don't want you to go—not tomorrow. Let's be smart about this. *Six* people, remember. You're not going to be number seven."

Tim wanted to continue the rant but held back. "Fine. You're right; it's too dangerous. Maybe I'll drive down to Massachusetts and help Johnny, which might free him up the following day to come and help me again."

"Good idea. Looking ahead—there's nothing on the calendar

for May 1st, but that doesn't necessarily mean we're off the hook; Annette has missed things before, like today, for instance…but tomorrow is a certainty that Mildred will be there and should be avoided."

They didn't even have dinner. Tim ended up snacking anxiously on some potato chips before bed, but Holly's appetite didn't return until the next day.

CHAPTER FORTY-SIX

The End of Journal #1

Friday, April 30th, 1971

Holly was sleepy but knew she couldn't rest until she finished Annette's first journal. She was within shouting distance so to speak, and if she could keep her eyes open long enough, the reward would be a clear conscience; the satisfaction that she had done all that was asked of her. If Thomas Pike still had problems after that, she could shout back in defiance just as Tim had this afternoon, but until then she just didn't feel she had done her job.

She picked up the readings in Annette's journal just after the nursing home interview chapters with Martha Simmons. The "interview style" was over thank goodness, and once again Holly was happy to see that Annette's familiar (and much more readable) diary-style continued.

> *Saturday, April 27th, 1968*
> *Last night I had a very intense dream.*
>
> *I dreamt I saw Mildred (now that I know her name), but...*
> *she was not dead, at least not as I have come to know her.*
> *She did not have the pale, lifeless skin I am used to seeing.*

She had color in her cheeks and life in her eyes, ...and most importantly, ...no flies.

She was alone in the turret as I watched from somewhere above, third-person style. She sat in the window, staring out at the pond and the field beyond. There was nothing with her to while away her time, like a book or knitting basket; instead, she brooded, lost in thought.

I watched her sit there for several minutes when she stood suddenly, hands balled into fists. Outside, not fifty yards down the lawn; the little boy Elmer (I know his name, too) her son, broke the surface of the pond, coming OUT of the water. His eyes were already fixed on the turret—as if he had been watching her from beneath the surface. He waded slowly out onto dry land and stood there for at least ten seconds, looking right at her. When he seemed satisfied, he turned back around, wading slowly into the stagnant water, disappearing in a trail of bubbles.

The woman began sobbing, I'm not sure if it was out of regret, guilt or frustration but it was certainly shock at the very least, and she ran out of the house to the pond. I believe she intended to follow the boy directly into the water, but when she got close enough, she reconsidered, realizing the folly of her efforts...or the danger. I think she could smell the death and the algae, and hear the frogs and the bugs. She sobered and walked back up to the house, her brow knitted in worry. Perhaps it was the realization that starting over had not gone as planned and the consequences could go on virtually forever.

Sunday, April 28th, 1968
Last night was apparently "Chapter Two" of yesterday's

dream! In fact, I'm not sure if it was really a dream (once again) or if I was awake witnessing some sort of replay. I woke in the middle of the night (at least I think I did) and sat up in bed; I had heard the front door opening downstairs. I got up quietly, my pulse racing, and peeked around the doorjamb into the hallway; Mildred was at the top of the stairs looking down at the door, which was out of my line of sight. I backed up ever so slowly and carefully so as not to be seen. She was in her nightgown and had a terrified look on her face. When I saw this, I knew this was the same Mildred I had seen in my previous "dream." She was still alive, not yet a ghost, being haunted by her dead son.

She took three steps down the stairs and paused; then I heard small footsteps mixed with the sound of splashing water as they entered the house through the front door. From there, I believe they headed away toward the kitchen. I lost audible track of them. Mildred bolted down the stairs and called out, "Elmer!"

As soon as I could no longer see her, I moved to the top of the stairs. She had disappeared to other parts of the house. I stood there for a minute or two and listened carefully.

Hearing nothing for so long a time, I began to wonder if it was over. I knew I could not tolerate just going back to my room like a sitting duck, so I descended the stairs as quietly as I could. Before I reached the bottom I took a careful peek around the corner toward the breakfast area, looking down through the dark house. Mildred was in the kitchen facing the opposite direction, white nightgown brightened by the moonlight coming through the window. She was talking softly. I perked my ears, but my positioning was wrong. I was doing too much leaning, and my neck was craning, so I repositioned letting my right foot touch the ground floor.

My foot set in something cold—a puddle. I peered down and realized that several square feet of floor were soaked by a reflective sheen that continued in a dripping path through to the kitchen. It smelled like a swamp.

From my new position, I could hear more clearly. I couldn't see him behind her, but it was clear that she was talking with Elmer. She knelt:

"Elmer, I was angry…"

"Where's Daddy?"

"Elmer, he's gone. He left us…that's wh-"

"I want Daddy."

"He's not coming, dear. I told you, he left us, but we can…"

"No. I don't want you. I want DADDY!"

I must say that this last 'Daddy' was abnormally loud; I jumped out of my skin. It echoed through the house. I nearly went back upstairs. For a second I wasn't sure if there wasn't someone else in the kitchen or what, but it was him, and Mildred, began to lose her patience, despite facing what was clearly a ghost. Back from the dead or not, she didn't want to give him control of the situation. She stood up and loomed over the boy as if to attempt to intimidate him; this, after she had murdered him. So strange.

"HE'S DEAD. HE LEFT US. HE LEFT YOU. I'm not going to stand here and LISTEN to this! Get out! Get out of here! Go back to the grove! There's NOBODY for you out there. Come back when you're ready to pay me some respect!"

Her arms were stiff at her sides as she shook and screamed. I wondered how she found the gall to scream at a ghost that she was directly responsible for creating. Elmer was clearly not her little boy anymore; he was...an entity, from God knows where (the bottom of the pond certainly, but potentially a place much darker). It seemed irrational, but then again, so is murdering your child. Either she knew more about the afterlife than I thought, or it was just another sign of lunacy.

I still could not see the boy from my position or his initial reaction. There was a silence for two seconds, and then he spoke again:

"I'll look again tomorrow."

Mildred relaxed her arms and shoulders as if the boy was no longer in the room. I quickly and quietly made my way back up the stairs before she turned. As I reached the top, a disturbing thought crossed my mind: Would she be returning, nightgown and all, to the same bedroom I slept in?

But then I awoke from the dream, very thankful that I would never learn the answer. Even so...I am sleepless... and afraid.

Monday, April 29th, 1968
Chapter three, …apparently.

The boy came back again last night, and I got to see it from Mildred's perspective. There's no possible way that these are just random dreams I am experiencing. They are too straightforward; not illogical as most dreams are. I feel as though I am being shown these dreams. Is it Thomas? It can't be Mildred; why would she want her crime (and its retribution) exposed? Hers is certainly no success story.

Yes, it must be Thomas, finishing the telling of this tragedy, to be followed by some sort of request (or demand) or favor from me.

I "woke" (from the dream) in the middle of the night to the sensation of water splashing my face. When I opened my eyes, the boy stood next to my bed, directly in my face. I nearly jumped out of my skin, backing off, up against the headboard pulling the sheets and blankets with me. The odor was there, again, the funk of the pond. I looked down at the sleeve of my nightgown and realized that…it was not my sleeve at all; it was Mildred's. I was dreaming through her eyes.

"Elmer…" I said…with Mildred's voice, still coming to the realization that this scene had happened years ago and that none of the decisions to be made would be mine.

"Elmer…Why are you back? I told you to go. Are you back to apologize? What do you want? And don't say…"

"Where is Daddy?" he rebelled.

My (Mildred's) hand went to my chest to cover my pounding heart. My legs scissored, moving me toward the opposite edge of the bed. I stood there, heart racing. The boy stared, blank-faced, and I was cornered.

"Get out. I told you to get out until you could show some respect, and I am telling you again. Get out, and do not come back. Go back to the grove, but…wait for me. Stay in the grove for a little while longer, and I will be with you—very soon."

"No. I can't find Daddy."

It was apparent the boy was not listening or could give a damn about Mildred's agenda, and she angrily came to this realization then and there. In a huff, she flipped off her nightgown and threw on her working dress, which had been left in a pile at the foot of the bed. She left the room, marched through the house and headed for the barn.

As I (she) trudged through the dining room, she turned back checking to see if the boy followed. He did…slowly and deliberately. He seemed to be…smirking if I had to guess—unless I was misinterpreting things. Mildred grabbed a lantern and a shovel from the barn and marched up the path to the grove.

When she got to the little family-plot-for-two, she placed the lantern in front of the small headstone and began throwing shovelfuls off to the side in a specific pile. The boy had seemingly not followed; perhaps left behind in the dark or perhaps just disappeared, like last night. Mildred looked back down the dark row of spruce in between each shovelful. Nothing. Good.

I heard a hollow thump as the spade struck something wooden, then took a last look down the row. There he was, just in range of the lantern, barely illuminated, watching, now soaked as if he had just left the pond.

A taunt. This gave Mildred pause. She drove the shovel into the spruce needles and let it stand as she wiped her forehead with the back of her sleeve and addressed him.

"I can move you, you know. I'll put you in the middle of the woods, off the property, and you can spend forever alone if you don't change your attitude. I won't even mark your grave. Better yet, I can split you up and bury you all over the state. You don't want that, do you? Make your choice. You can have that, or you can be next to me when I die, and be with me forever. I told you why I did what I did. I was angry. He left us, and he's gone for good, resting selfishly at peace all by himself. He's not coming back for you; he left us both, and he left for good! Now, what's it going to be?"

The boy remained motionless in the shadows for a moment and then took four steps forward, into the light. He passed me (as Mildred), walked over to the half dug up grave and sat on the edge of the headstone as if to spectate; expecting her to dig more. After a moment of pacing and thought, she spitefully snatched the spade from its hold and began returning the pile of dirt to the top of the boy's coffin.

"On second thought, you aren't going anywhere."

And then I woke up.

It's getting so that I begin to dread bedtime at around

noon. The anticipation is very draining, not to mention terrifying. The suspense is just…too intense.

Tuesday, April 30th, 1968
As I write this, I am crying. My heart has been re-broken. These dreams are terribly, terribly cruel. I don't know that I can do this much longer. I may have to abandon the property, our home—our pride and joy—sell it…or just leave the farm empty for a while, as I…I don't know. If Thomas is the one showing me all this, why is he so cruel?

The reason I am crying, the horror I witnessed-I saw my beloved Henry murdered last night! And the way he died was just so…unfair…it was like a lamb to the slaughter. I don't even understand how it happened. What I witnessed has no logical connection to the way I previously understood his death. They were up in the grove, so I'm guessing he was after a Christmas tree. She said nothing as he tried to make conversation, but approached him reaching out with her hand…then it seemed like all she did was touch his face…and he went down. That's exactly what it was—a lamb to the slaughter. They were so far from the lawn outside the barn where I found him dead. I have no idea how she got him there.

The graphic details, the mental picture I now carry with me—I wish I could erase them from my mind. Damn you, Thomas Pike! You showed me far too much, I don't care how much you're hurting or how angry you are, there are limits. You aren't the only one who has lost someone.

And you, Mildred…I don't think you even know about my journals because you're too ignorant and wrapped up in your own sick way…but—Who are you? And where do you come from, other than Salem, Massachusetts, the 'witch capital' of the whole world? I don't believe in witches, but maybe I should reconsider, because it wasn't long ago that I didn't believe in ghosts, either. I will take a look into your family tree, and figure it out, for whatever good it will do me.

You killed my Henry. You must have killed your son, too, it's obvious; you must be stopped. Despite my anger at your husband, I will work with him to do whatever it takes to get you off of my property; I don't care if you had a hand in building this place: it's mine now.

Wednesday, May 1st, 1968
Last night's dream was not even a dream; it was a sleepwalk. The action is hot and heavy this week. Something must be up. Something might happen soon.

I woke up in the grove with a flashlight and a shovel, right in front of Elmer's grave, and I read the disgusting epitaphs. What does it all mean? What was I supposed to do, exhume the body? And if I did, then…what? I'm so confused, scared, and drained. I dropped everything and ran out of the grove immediately. All the grove reminds me of now is the death of my Henry.

Maybe I'll take this to the police and tell them about my dreams…but that would sound ludicrous; I certainly wouldn't believe me.

Thomas, am I supposed to exhume your son and rebury him next to you, across town? How am I supposed to do that, a single woman with a station wagon? It must be illegal, if not immoral, and I will need to talk to the police or at least a funeral home first. Let it be known that if I am refused at any step of the process, I am done here, and I WILL abandon the property.

For anyone that might read these writings: I am going to ask Thomas for clarification tonight. I'll write some more full-page word choices in my "flip book" journal like I did when I figured out his name. I think I'll put "MOVE" and "BOY" across two pages, and maybe "MOVE" and "WOMAN" across two more, and, "MOVE" and "ME" (Thomas), on the next two, then "GUESS" and "AGAIN" across two more, maybe "NO" and "POLICE" and "YES" and "POLICE"...and finally (wishful thinking), "DO" and "NOTHING". I'll get back to you tomorrow if he responds.

Holly turned the page, still about twenty pages or so from the end of the journal, but that was it; there was nothing else written. It was the end of *all* of the reading materials for that matter: *Journal 1*, the *Anniversary Journal,* and the *scrapbook*. The first journal's abrupt ending reminded Holly of the ending of the scrapbook. *She must have died just after this.*

Holly lamented the fact that Henry's death was officially another Mildred Murder. She looked over at Tim, who snored softly next to her. Even though she was bursting at the seams to tell him, she let him sleep. They weren't going to the house anyway, and they needed, collectively, as much sleep as they could get. It was better to have at least one person rested than none. Hopefully, rest would help to avoid potentially fatal mistakes.

With nothing to read, she let her head fall back into the pillow. So much bad news: Elmer and Henry...for sure murdered by Mildred. Emma and Annette, "missing" suspiciously. *Natural causes, my ass.*

It took her only twenty minutes to fall asleep.

CHAPTER FORTY-SEVEN

The First Dream

April 30th, 1971 (1:09 A.M.)

Two hours later, another dream began. Just like Annette's final days, the dreams were coming more and more frequently. Hopefully it wouldn't end for them as it had for her.

In it, Annette sat in the turret just after sundown and finished what would be her final journal entry. She closed the book and left it on the desk in the middle of the room, then headed down to the car; it was off to the nursing home for a Tuesday evening shift. She exited the side door with keys in hand, checking her surroundings carefully as always before opening the car door.

Mildred stood in the corner of the driveway, just off the path that led to the grove. In her right hand, she held the spade that Annette had carelessly left at the graves when she woke from her sleepwalk.

Annette scowled, as thoughts went immediately to Henry's death, the love of her life. She became angry as well as afraid. *This is it,* thought Annette, as she placed her purse and car keys on the hood of the car and squared her shoulders, preparing to confront the woman that killed her husband.

She realized full well that this might be the end, but like

many adults, she had reached a tipping point; the only thing left to do was fight. *When you've got nothing, you've got nothing to lose.* Her anger burned as she took a step forward. How cowardly it had been for Mildred to cover it all up as though Henry had a heart attack, leaving him to grow eternally colder on the lawn by the barn. Annette was so tired of everything, especially all of the tedious dreams.

"You're afraid of things too, aren't you, Mildred? You're afraid we're going to figure this all out, and we'll move your bones, or maybe Elmer's. Which would be worse? You were afraid that my Henry would call the police and your family plot would be discovered, revisited, and perhaps exposed. You didn't want people to know what you had written on those headstones. You thought it would all be private forever, am I right?" Annette took one more step forward as if to show her she wasn't afraid, but of course, she was. She stopped just fifteen feet away from the dead woman with the shovel.

Her courage took a hit, however, as she caught the smell of death. It was not the odor of a hundred-year-old body but much worse; it was the scent of a person dead for perhaps a week...*mid-rot.*

Mildred stood quietly, emotionless. It was hard to read her features in this light, but she did hear the buzz of flies as they swarmed and crawled over their hostess.

This could not be a ghost, could it? Weren't ghosts supposed to do things like pass through walls and doors, and make the temperature drop?

These thoughts would have to wait. It had been a terrible mistake to drop the spade at the grave, and it had been an even bigger mistake to attempt to confront this supernatural murderess in front of her.

Annette's next words tumbled out; stripped of all power and confidence.

"You know...we will figure this all out...We will figure you out and—and we will be rid of you. I'm not afraid."

Mildred said nothing but brought the head of the shovel up slowly with both hands.

Annette took a moment to consider the fact that Thomas Pike was as far as she knew, still free to work in the background; Mildred may not know he was even around. Perhaps he would have better luck going forward—with the next people. *God help them, and God help me.*

"We will get you. The work has begun. Even Elmer is against you, and if I can..."

With tremendous force, Mildred swung the spade like a bat, letting go at the last second. It hit Annette just above her collarbone, and she collapsed, mortally wounded by the sharp weapon.

Mildred walked over to Annette's body and finished the job with her bare hands. Using the powers forced upon her by her evil forebears, she disguised the damage and effortlessly threw the body over her shoulder; she would leave it in the master bedroom for its eventual discovery.

She would have the place to herself at least until then; perhaps she could find Elmer during that period, and she wouldn't have to even bother with whoever came next.

CHAPTER FORTY-EIGHT

Intermission

April 30th, 1971 (1:16 A.M.)

They woke with a start.

"Oh! Oh my God, ...oh my God Tim, I just saw..."

"Annette is dead. Mildred killed her...I know...it was... awful." The sheets were soaked with sweat, both sides of the bed, all from an eight-minute dream. Tim grabbed Holly, and they hugged, still catching their breath.

"She's...evil. We can't deal with her, Tim. She's dead! And she's strong! And apparently she's fucking magic too because she can disguise the murders!"

Tim realized there weren't many options. "I hate to say it, Holly, but I don't think we have a choice. The scrapbook was delivered *here*, to your house, right? And ...we have simultaneous dreams...*regularly!* Let's calm down and relax a minute; don't panic."

He was right. There weren't any alternatives. They had become wrapped up in the lives of the Pike family in less than two weeks—just like that, and there was nothing they could do about it. She put her face in her hands and cried silently for a few seconds, fighting her frustrations, hiding it as much as possible. Things were beginning to spin out of control, and the pace the last few days had been relentless.

"Hold on, wait right here. I've got an idea." Tim left the room, and Holly heard him open the outside door. He came back in a minute later holding a bottle of Jack Daniel's.

"Where was that, out in the bushes?" she asked.

"Nope, I had it behind the seat in my truck."

"Oh, that's better! The police love that—driving around with whiskey behind your seat. Has it been opened?"

"Uh, maybe once, but I wasn't driving at the time…just a completed job…you know, mini-celebration about a month back. Come on; it will relax you. I'm going to pour you a nightcap."

"No, Tim, I don't want to have a hangover tomorrow…I'm exhausted. I need to sleep!"

"*One drink* will not give you a hangover. This will help you sleep. I'll get a glass." He went to the kitchen and returned a few seconds later. "Fair warning, it will burn your throat a little bit, but it will…put things into perspective."

She took the glass and did the shot, complete with a prerequisite grimace. She was not a whiskey person…but the temporary discomfort broke the tension, if but for a moment.

Tim spoke first. "The only thing we can do now is catch up on sleep—no decisions right now…just sleep. Okay?"

"All right; good enough. Worrying does nothing to strengthen tomorrow. It only ruins today."

"Wow, that's beautiful…did you write that?" he asked.

"No, of course, I didn't write that. Whoa…I feel it already."

"It's because you're tired. Now just lay back and relax. Here, read this magazine and try to enjoy it. Don't think, and we'll try to figure it all out tomorrow."

"Fine, thank you. I will."

Tim got back in bed, and within ten minutes she dropped the magazine, fast asleep. Tim picked it up and put it on his nightstand and shut off the lights. He'd better try and follow her; tomorrow was shaping up to be a hell of a day.

Thomas allowed them a four-hour nap, and then the next dream began.

CHAPTER FORTY-NINE

The Next Dream, Part One

Mildred was in bed on Lancaster Hill Road, and she was not alone. The Chief of Police, Abner Wallace, was with her and they were enjoying some adult time. The new couple was rounding third base when Elmer's footsteps furiously pounded the floorboards of the hallway outside the bedroom. The chief nearly jumped out of his skin as he grabbed his pistol and charged out of the bedroom stark naked, ready to confront whoever had dared interrupt his first attempt at sex in more than a year.

As he drew his gun and left the bedroom, it didn't take long for him to realize that it was no burglar that had interrupted his good time. The Pike boy, the same one that he and his officers had pulled from the pond nearly two months previously, was staring at him from the end of the hallway, soaking wet. There was no question as to who he was, or of the Chief's mental state of mind; he had only had two glasses of wine, which was about six behind his usual pace. He slowed it down big-time tonight to avoid scaring off his new love interest.

Despite no previous encounters with the paranormal, he realized immediately that this would be a first for him. He made absolutely no attempt to convince himself the boy was alive; the child stared at him plainly as if they had met…and they had; that day at the pond. Three seconds later, the Chief started a puddle of his own around his bare feet. And then things got *really* strange. Mildred poked her head out into the hallway.

"Leave us! Get out of here, Elmer. You're just like your father! Stubborn! Go! Let me go on with my life!" It was Mildred, seemingly...*accustomed to* this type of intrusion, and at the same time unafraid of the corpse just outside her bedroom. *I am thinking with the wrong head. What have I gotten myself into?*

Elmer ran down the stairs, dripping as he went, coitus interrupted; mission accomplished.

"Come back to bed," said Mildred, and the Chief looked at her, aghast. He finally understood what his crude drunk of a father had taught him years ago growing up. Dad would speak ill of certain women even in front of his mother, all-too-candidly. He called them *bad pussy*. And here she was. Thirty-seven years later, he finally understood his father's warning. *Thank you, Father; now help me out of this.*

The Thomas-guided dream faded to black, but it wasn't over; it was on to the next segment.

The forest was bare except for the pines and spruce, which kept their needles year-round. The path to the grove was leaf-free, however, as Mildred had been busy plowing through them over the last two days, back and forth with wheelbarrows full of cargo. Elmer had been very unforgiving over the past year; and so—*conniving*. He attacked her fragile relationships at their most vulnerable moments, just when she thought she might be back on track.

First had been the Chief, then the editor, and then the lawyer. Elmer seemed to leave the dalliances alone, knowing they would never last, but as soon as a relationship was off of the ground and began to feel hopeful...he would sabotage it. She knew deep down he would never stop; he would never forgive her for what she had done and for starting over. He was a lot like her, after all.

The little nuisance also figured out her agenda; she should not have installed both headstones at the same time. Now that Elmer was dead, he knew the plan. She woke one night in her bedroom to the familiar dripping sound; not just a drip-at-a-time pace from a faucet, but more like a sopping towel being carried down a corridor. She left the bed, preparing to scold him again but as she peered out and down the hallway, he was already downstairs. He left the same mess he always did—a twenty-foot wet path warping the floorboards.

She followed him downstairs, unafraid and cursing. Where did he go this time, back to the cellar to bang his drum? She would burn the damn thing and put an end to the noise. No… the footsteps did not go to the cellar; they went up. *I told you to stay out of that turret; you'll soak the ceiling!* Mildred climbed the stairs, stepping in puddles as she went, calling his name.

But he wasn't up there. *He planned this.* On the desk were a lit candle and a small pile of papers—ablaze. It had just started burning; hardly a threat to do any lasting damage to anything, let alone the house. She easily beat the flame out with a book. *Stay out of my papers! What do you want with them anyway?*

She looked closer: It was her most recent last will and testament; in it, specific instructions regarding burial arrangements. *Stay out of my papers! What does an eight-year-old, living or dead, know about legal p—*

Thomas?

She straightened up and tightened her lips, scowling. *Is this you?… Yes…I believe it is you.*

Almost! Very clever Thomas! Now I know I will need—to rethink some things.

Now she had an Elmer problem, the boy dashing every solid chance at new romance—*and could Thomas be back?* Was it possible that after all this time he was never really gone? Did he know about the incident at the pond? Could they be working against her? Together, digging into her life and personal business?

If it was true, she could not let him interfere. She had a plan in place, and Thomas was not a part of it; she might have to make adjustments.

The dream faded for a moment, but Tim and Holly slept on.

CHAPTER FIFTY

The Next Dream, Part Two

April 30th, 1971 (5:33 A.M.)

The darkness opened up again in the dream, allowing them to see. The path came to an end, and the grove began. Tim and Holly floated, observing unseen. Mildred had been busy; the dirt was piled high on one side of her grave. On the other side of the freshly dug hole was Elmer's grave, now a year old.

The latest wheelbarrow out to the gravesite had been considerably lighter than preceding loads. This time it was only blankets and pillows. On a previous trip, she had managed to get her mattress out there. With a long knife, she ripped them all open and dumped the feathers and fluff into the hole. She also scattered hay, woodchips, and her dangerously flammable formal dress. Across the hole she laid several planks and doused them with kerosene, leaving one plank-width at the bottom of the grave uncovered; just enough space to crawl down through as soon as she was done constructing. It took her another half day to move the large pile of rocks and dirt back on top of the planks, which, in the end, barely held the weight—*almost done now.*

It was such a strange set of circumstances; she couldn't just ask somebody to bury her once she had committed suicide.

The traditional way of doing things, like leaving a last will and testament, was in jeopardy with Thomas looking to sabotage the paperwork after she was gone. And was it really Thomas, or just Elmer digging into her papers? Thomas or Elmer, it didn't matter. She would take no chances.

Very soon they would all be back on a level playing field, and she would take back control of the whole mess. Elmer would learn to forgive her; eternity was a long time, and she could be very persuasive. Once she was equal, she could...arrange things and ensure that Thomas would be out of their lives forever.

When the pyre was finished, she squeezed through the gap between the boards at the foot of the grave and nested herself deeply into the bed of feathers and shavings. It was dark there beneath the bowed planks; the near ton of soil tested the boards already; never mind after they caught fire. She propped the quarter stick of candle into a pile of wood chips on her chest and lit it. Then she pulled out the kitchen knife she had used on the mattress and without hesitation opened her wrists. As she adjusted to the initial shock, she began to count the heartbeats until her final sleep. She guessed the final number would be somewhere between sixty and one hundred.

As the light-headedness washed over, she was sure of one thing; she would be back. There would be no rest. This trait ran in the family, the family she tried to leave. Even if she wanted to leave it all behind, she wasn't sure it was an option, but...she didn't want rest anyway. She didn't want *rest,* and she didn't want *peace.*

The plan was in action. Thomas was...*wherever he was,* it didn't matter. If he were still around she would deal with that soon, right after she was buried next to her boy.

Mildred closed her eyes for a moment as she began to feel the final warmth, but opened them again to take a last look at the candle. *Final minute.*

Her eyes closed for the final time as the flame met the feathers. The feathers, in turn, lit the flammable dress made of crinoline, then the shavings, the hay, the wood chips, and the kindling. The pine planks, already stressed under the weight of the dirt and stones, caught fire and collapsed according to plan. The fire was largely snuffed by the soil and completely burned out three minutes later.

Mildred was buried.

CHAPTER FIFTY-ONE

Message Received

April 30th, 1971 (5:39 A.M.)

Tim woke suddenly, and it was still dark out. The dream was over, and Holly was already sitting up.

"You saw that?" he asked.

"Yes. Oh my God…who the hell is this woman? How did she think this up? What a *sicko!*"

"I think we've been given all of the facts now. Mildred couldn't trust that her last will would be carried out because Thomas would mess with it, so she took care of it herself. I…I hate to say this, but I think it's my turn now."

"What are you talking about?" she asked.

"A few hours ago, I shouted out loud that I wanted Thomas Pike to tell me what he needs me to do. Well, he answered. It's exactly like Johnny said: he wants to be buried with his son. I'm not sure whether they can't be together until they lie next to each other, or if he needs to get rid of her before he shows himself to the kid, but either way, bodies need to be moved, and she's got to go. On top of that, as we already know, we don't have a choice."

Holly hung her head, reluctant but unable to dispute the logic.

Without saying a word, she got out of bed and left the room. She came back a minute later with her calendar.

"We've been wrapped up in this whole ghost problem for only two weeks, but it seems like a lifetime. I'm looking at my calendar from today through next week because I can't possibly take any more than that. TODAY is our best chance to do what we have to do while she is busy. She's doing that 'Thomas goes to war' ritual. There's no other major time-distracting anniversary in the near future."

Tim wasn't surprised a bit that the workload would get harder before it got easier, but that was all well and good. He wanted to get on with his life, even if it meant risking it. Maybe he was the chosen one to solve the Mildred problem, or maybe he was just the next man up; who knew? Leaving the property was no choice at all. On top of the financial ruin, he would most likely be followed—and haunted—forced to reconsider. He accepted his situation; the direction was clear. He had no further questions and sure as hell didn't need another dream to teach him anything.

CHAPTER FIFTY-TWO
Family Reunion

April 30th, 1971, 7:30 A.M.

There was no more sleep for Tim and Holly; instead, they made their plans and prepared for what they hoped would be the end game. It was an overcast day with scattered showers—not the best and brightest day to go digging in the woods, but it could have been worse. They left early, surprising the manager of Aubuchon Hardware in Franklin as he arrived to open the store. All of Tim's tools were "trapped" in the house, and he wasn't about to chance getting caught attempting to fetch them. They bought two spades, a rake, a pickaxe, some trowels, a hammer, a crowbar, some burlap bags, a tarp and a bag of cement.

Once the pickup was loaded, they set off for Sanborn. As they approached the house, Tim slowed the truck and pulled over into the gulley just before the property line. He and Holly got out and made their way covertly by the cover of woods, walking parallel to the meadow between the trees toward the grove. When they reached the corner of the field, they chose a secluded spot and waited anxiously. Annette had not noted a time in her journals, but their best guess was that a soldier would not have left for combat training late in the day. Fortunately only thirty-five minutes after their arrival, Mildred came running out the side door of the house, begging an imaginary Thomas to stay home and not join the Union Army.

They hurried through the wild forest toward the grove; the clock had started, and time was now a factor. The beginning of the anniversary was their cue that Mildred would not be at the graves for a while, but it did not promise them all the time in the world. Mildred would be busy for roughly half an hour, which was their agreed-upon best guess. Unfortunately, Tim thought they would need at least a full hour to dig everybody up; they had to hope that Mildred's next move would not be to return to the grove immediately after the anniversary.

Hopefully, she had other places to be and people to haunt… but deep down they knew she didn't. They rushed through the grove cutting across the aisles until they arrived at the point of Mildred's Revenge: her two grave family plot.

The canopy of trees made the grove seem almost cave-like, and the scattered showers were somewhat blocked by their cover. Tim began digging energetically at Mildred's grave, and Holly started on Elmer's. He noticed immediately that, just like his sleepwalk, the ground was uneven. He quickly ran into a deep layer of ashes that turned his boots and shovel black. There would be no coffin, so he looked for her bones…whenever he wasn't looking over his shoulder. Was the anniversary over yet? He checked his watch; only fifteen minutes gone.

He pulled chunks of plank charred by fire out of the soil along with several large rocks, casting them in all directions; there would be no reason to fill in the grave when they were done. The plan was to remove every one of Mildred's bones, cast them in a bucket of cement, and drop it off of a tall bridge somewhere far from here. Somewhere where ghosts don't seem as scary, like Boston Harbor, or the Tappan Zee Bridge; anywhere, in fact, away from the secluded farmhouses and collapsing barns of northern New England, which seemed tailor-made for chilling supernatural encounters.

He was making good progress after twenty minutes and looked over at Holly who was also at least a foot deep and likely to hit the boy's coffin soon. Tim worriedly began to wonder where all the bones were; he hadn't seen a one as yet. He switched to the edge rake and hastily sifted through the grave itself and the pile of dirt to his right; still no bones. Then he heard some good news; the *thunk* of shovel on wood...Holly had struck Elmer's coffin.

Suddenly encouraged after having no success himself, he jumped over to the other grave to help the progress. When space got tight, and shovels began to unintentionally clang, he asked Holly to try and see if she might have better luck finding Mildred's bones. As the half-hour mark passed he had trenches on all four sides of the coffin but realized it was much bulkier than he had anticipated...so he made a decision.

"What are you going to do? Wait, are you... You're not opening it, are you?" Holly was aghast. This was a major change of plans. She looked at Tim, who was clearly stressed and dripping sweat. Veins bulged in his neck as he spoke:

"The half-hour is up. She's done down at the house for all we know, and this could come to an end any minute. I'm freaking out—I don't know about you. It's going to take me another half hour to dig this coffin out, never mind pull it out. It's bigger than we thought. Elmer's coming out right here."

Holly looked down the long corridor of trees to check for Mildred, then quickly stepped into the next aisle over to check it as well. "All right, just hurry."

"Have you found anything with the rake?" he asked her.

"No. Did her bones burn up, or something? I thought the fire went out almost immediately..."

"No, they couldn't have burned. Keep trying; I'm almost done here."

Tim pulled out the new crowbar and began to work on the coffin's seal as quietly as possible. Within a minute, he was able to get his fingers inside the lid and pull up with both hands. One of the nails squealed in protest and Tim cursed under his breath as he turned to look down the aisle once again. With still no Mildred in sight, he finished the job.

Poor little murdered Elmer was dressed in farmer's overalls; apparently Mother Mildred wasn't sorry enough to bury him in his Sunday best. He was little more than a skeleton with hair, the bones almost in perfect order; only his jawbone seemed out of place; he appeared to be eternally yawning. Tim felt for the boy and silently thanked him for saving his bacon more than once.

"Don't worry, kid, we're going to get you out of here and back with your dad," he whispered. Starting with the skull, he carefully placed it in one of the burlap bags; then grabbed the spinal cord, which quickly fell apart. He realized that he didn't have time to treat every bone with tender loving care, and verbally apologized to Elmer as he scooped the boy's remains from the coffin by the handful. When he had gathered everything, he left the bag on the ground and grabbed a spade hurriedly to help Holly continue the search for the remains of Mildred Wells.

"Anything?"

"No! How deep was this hole anyway? Tim…I hate to say this…*is she even* in *here?* Emma Simmons wrote that she thought Mildred was a witch, and I'm wondering now myself. I never believed in…witches, but I don't know what to believe anymore…" Tim stared blankly, deciding to save Holly's disturbing thought for later.

"Let me back in the hole, and you rake what I dig." He jumped into the grave, which was now almost three feet deep. Tim knew the old phrase "six feet under," but he also knew that most graves didn't go that deep. He learned this as a boy when his uncle died. His father explained that most states only require eighteen to twenty-four inches of soil on top of a casket or body; and when adding the depth of the coffin, that meant that as little as four feet of depth was common.

Mildred had dug her own grave, and Tim couldn't remember

from the dream if he had gotten a good look inside the hole to gauge the depth. *There's no way she went down six feet,* he assured himself. Plus, they had already dug through a layer of ashes and burnt feathers, the things Mildred had surrounded herself with. They were several inches below that now into another layer of just plain dirt—and still no bones.

"Tim…stop…stop…stop. She's here." Holly gripped the rake like a security blanket. Tim misunderstood and looked down at the end of Holly's rake as if perhaps she had found one of Mildred's bones. The rake was still, but there were no bones. Tim followed the handle of the rake up to Holly's face which—was locked on something down at the other end of the row. A chill ran up his back, and his heart picked up as he turned to face his expected guest. His mouth went dry.

Mildred leered forty yards down the aisle, as still as a gargoyle; he wondered how long she had been watching but decided quickly this detail didn't matter. She was within striking distance, leaving them little chance of escape. Her face was grim and sallow, her eyes ringed with black circles.

"What do we do? What do we do?" Holly whispered the words rapid-fire.

"Wait, wait a minute…" It was a request to buy *time* more than anything. Tim needed it right now, but Mildred didn't afford them much. She walked stiffly, and as she did, the hatchet Holly had stuck in her handbag just the other day slid down out of her sleeve and into her right hand. He decided to try words to slow her approach as she drew near.

"Mildred…*stop.* I want you gone. You're a murderer, and we're going to move your son. You've been here too long."

Holly looked at Tim as if he had two heads. *That was the plan?*

Mildred took one more step and stopped. She swayed slightly, and Tim gripped the spade in his hands. He was knee-deep in her grave and was about to step up and out to deal with her on her level.

Suddenly the hatchet fell out of her hand to the forest floor.

No shit, he thought.

"*Tim!*" it was Holly.

"There's someone behind you."

He turned to see the bottom of a boot as it crashed into his nose and jaw. Stars exploded, and the lights went out as he fell limply, hands instinctively rising in a powerless and late attempt to guard his head. He collapsed against the wall of the grave in a lifeless heap.

It happened so fast Holly had trouble understanding the situation. A tall man with a beard was suddenly behind them; if she hadn't looked back as Tim addressed Mildred, she wouldn't even have known he was there.

Tim crumpled in a heap down into the hole. The tall stranger dressed in farm clothes held a long rifle with a bayonet and spun it around to point the blade where his victim had just fallen. He looked at Holly for a brief moment, and she noticed that his eyes were blue. He dropped his gaze after less than a second and stepped down into the grave, raising his arms, and the rifle… above his head.

At that moment, she realized that the man was Thomas Pike.

He thrust both arms downward, and drew the rifle back up instantly, finishing the kill. Holly screamed.

"No! *Why?*"

Like that, Tim was gone. Holly wailed in disbelief. Johnny was right—Thomas Pike had used them for his own selfish reasons.

With Tim disposed of, Holly was the odd man out, to put it mildly. Thomas turned his attention to her as he pulled out a handkerchief and wiped the blood from his bayonet. Holly spun her head quickly to look back at Mildred; the original threat…for the first time in several seconds. Thankfully Mildred could have cared less for Holly, and only had eyes for Thomas.

She was smiling.

Holly had but a split-second to decide whether to run or

fight and chose the only real option. She ran for help…more, specifically the phone in Tim's house, and she could only pray the ghosts would be gone by the time the ambulance arrived. If she had stayed she would have ended up dead; on the wrong end of Thomas's bloody bayonet—*as Tim did*—or perhaps bashed by Mildred's hatchet.

She ran as fast as she could, cutting across the rows of spruce, crying as she went, arbitrarily cutting across rows and running down aisles to shake potential pursuers.

Thomas Pike stood in his wife's grave and looked down at his victim. He hadn't served in the Union Army long enough to be fitted for dress blues. The overalls and white button-up shirt he wore now were the clothes he had worn the day he left for training. He propped the butt of his Springfield rifle on the edge of the grave and used it as a crutch to step over the body up to Mildred's level.

When he arrived at her eyes, he dropped the rifle and relaxed his arms. Hopefully terminating the intruder's efforts to move the graves would be seen as a sign of good faith. Mildred had been angry for a long time; she should speak first. He waited with the patience of a dead man, and for a moment, time didn't matter. Surely she would need to vent, and there would be much to discuss, but he sensed only confusion.

Mildred was overwhelmed; overcome. Perhaps it was because she had been alone inside her head for so many years…bouncing the lonely thoughts around; inventing poisonous tangents, upon tangents—upon tangents.

She hadn't seen his rifle since the funeral. At the time the monogram only riled her; *what good will that do me*? Now here it was again, next to him on the ground…*"Millie"* on the stock. She couldn't help but see it in a different light. She had also forgotten how tall he was. Above all, he had prevented the graves from being robbed gallantly; but where had he been for the last hundred years? Had he been watching? *Did he know about…?*

Thomas turned his head, whistling loudly into the forest air.

Within seconds Elmer appeared at the end of the row. The boy hesitated, clearly anxious to see his father for the first time in a century, but he was clearly reluctant to allow his mother to get near, after all she had done.

Mildred's head spun upon Elmer's entrance, and her knees bent slightly as if to invite approach—if he would only reciprocate somehow. *Are you ready to forgive and put the past behind you?*

Elmer didn't budge but looked to his father. Mildred turned to Thomas, slightly perturbed that she needed to wait for his blessing to be with her son. She had always hated their bond but had no choice now but to stow her feelings and let this special moment play out.

Thomas paused and slowly extended his hand to her. Mildred looked down at it; he should admit he was wrong first, and admit that leaving her had contributed to…the mistakes.

Her upbringing; her parents—Thomas was the only one who heard the stories about from what and where she had come. Her thoughts were dark and unbearable when she was alone. The years with Thomas had been the most…*normal.* He should have realized how *lost* he had left her. Suddenly, here he was; back again…about to apologize and make things right again, as she always felt he should have. *One hundred and ten years.* She didn't even know he existed anymore. *Where were you, Thomas?*

With her hand in his, she felt these pressures dissolve. The insanity, the anger…was slipping away; seeped back into the ground beneath her feet. Perhaps she could be happy now—*again*; she could rest. *Anger only drains you.* Thomas embraced her, hugging devotedly. Did he know everything? Was this his first reunion with Elmer too? Only minutes ago she was poised to raise the hatchet, and now she didn't care if it sank into the forest floor; none of this mattered. *Goodbye, rot…flies…pain.*

There was one more thing she needed; Elmer's forgiveness. She let Thomas's hand go gently and turned to Elmer kneeling, arms open. She glanced at Thomas before she knelt, seeking his influence and his support. The boy looked to his father, and Thomas nodded. With the green light given, he slowly walked the thirty yards into his mother's arms, *the perfect ending to the perfect day.*

The family embraced in the last aisle hand-in-hand, and Thomas led them toward the end of the row, together for the first time in a long, long time. Before they reached the end, Thomas pointed into the deepest part of the wild woods, suggesting a destination. As a family, they vanished into the dark, wet, wild of the forest, and away from the artificial order of the grove.

CHAPTER FIFTY-THREE

Bones

When he could no longer hear the crunching of spruce needles, Tim opened his eyes and moved his neck which had been jammed into the corner of the grave. From what he could remember, he had been kicked in the head and then fell backward into the hole.

He hit his head hard when he landed, making back-to-back concussions; boot to head and head to ground. Instinctively he raised his hands somewhere during the fracas before Thomas jumped into the pit bayonet first. He took the blade through his palm, perfectly between the bones. It hurt, but it was the head trauma that was more serious. The bleeding, although substantial, was superficial. There would be no lasting damage.

If Thomas had wanted him dead, he would have been dead. If the bayonet had missed its intended mark, it would have taken little effort to remove the blade and finish the job, perhaps through his head or his heart. *He had to make it look real.*

Tim stood up and collected himself. He wiped his palm on his jeans and inspected the wound. The blood disappeared for a quick second then appeared again on the edge of the wound, teetering, and beginning a new stream. He would be fine. He had experienced worse while on the job.

Thinking quickly he grabbed the spade and the burlap sack of Elmer's bones and ran for the house to find Holly. Perhaps she went for the telephone, or just hoofed it down the road to town. She couldn't have taken the truck; he had the keys in his front pocket; a major flaw in their early morning planning.

He jogged at three-quarters speed down the path watching for anything but trusting that Thomas would occupy Mildred long enough to get the bones off-site. He called out for Holly, hoping to save some time. She heard him and ran out the front door carrying a book, clearly amazed and overjoyed that he was alive. She had been crying, and Tim held up his bloody hand.

"I'm all right. It was a fake-out. Thomas didn't want to kill me; he had to make it look good. I didn't see where they all went, but I think he's at least buying us time. I've got Elmer right here in this bag; we've got to go. What's that?" He pointed to the book.

"Never mind right now, Tim, please get me the hell out of here. I don't know for sure myself yet. Please please please, let's *GO!*"

It took them another full minute to get to the truck that they had left in the gully at the side of the road. When they got there, Holly insisted on driving so that he could care for his hand. Tim wanted to go straight to Tower Hill Cemetery, but she took him in the opposite direction toward town so that he could get some peroxide and fresh bandages at the drug store. When the pharmacy didn't happen to have any gardening gloves, she drove all the way to Franklin again to buy them at the hardware store.

CHAPTER FIFTY-FOUR

Reanimated

Mildred followed Thomas and Elmer into the forest, her ancient anger now a distant memory. Eternal rest had begun, or at least the will to allow it had, which was a brand new feeling for her; peaceful more than anything. The forest suddenly darkened as if storm clouds had rolled in, followed by a warming comfort and a sensation that her family was near, sharing the same feelings—*and that it would last forever.* It was like a warm bath or a warm bed; loneliness was gone, and her lifelong torment might have never happened. It was the feeling of catharsis and love. She could let go and forgive them now, and certainly, they forgave her too.

Thomas held her hand and smiled. She had a sense that he knew what *she had done* but at the same time, understood, and had forgiven. Perhaps he shared in the blame. Perhaps he knew that whatever happened while they were alive was ancient history and no longer important. *Relief...*

She looked down at Elmer, who still chose to walk much closer to his father, but occasionally looked her way—a small step in the right direction. He would come around. She would talk to him and explain things, and he would eventually understand. If where they were going felt this good, she could wait forever for him to change his mind.

Abruptly her sense of well being was interrupted by a violent shock. The comfort ebbed, the warmth grew colder; and a twinge of pain returned to the base of her neck. The comfort of the peaceful shadows gave way to cracks of blinding light. Panicking slightly, she reached out; searching for Thomas and Elmer, but couldn't find them. She waited to feel *their* searching hands as if there might have been a temporary disconnection, and the reunion would continue. Hopefully, they would find her and come to her rescue as a loving family should.

But the covers had been ripped off of the bed. They didn't search her out at all. *Far worse,* they had *abandoned* her. *Betrayed* her! Anxieties flashed, and the earthy discomfort that so recently went numb was back, fresh and alive like an exposed nerve.

When she was completely lucid and clear of the comforting fog, she found herself in a heap at the bottom of her own grave. The trespasser's body was gone, and her worst nightmare came true; the mess that they had created was everywhere; the dirt, the rocks...and Elmer's coffin.

Where are his fucking bones?

She had been played the fool. Thomas had lied. His promise of forgiveness and reconciliation was *deception*. Everyone knew... everyone! Including Elmer...and the bitch she had killed with the spade. She recalled Annette's last words:

"We will get you. The work has begun. Even Elmer is against you, and if I can..."

Years. For *years (!)* they had been plotting...and planning. The rage seethed in her reanimated heart.

Elmer was gone—*forever*, she could sense it; Thomas had *stolen* him. He would not be back, and she would never get to teach him another lesson. *You win, Thomas. You win. Selfish bastard. Are you happy now? You got me twice. Twice!*

Mildred hung her head in final, unmitigated defeat. Why hadn't it worked? What gave him the power to filter her out... to rest in peace and leave her behind? She was alone again, as the lonely teenage years before she met him; after she had escaped in search of a normal life; before parenthood. How he had tricked her today, she could not yet comprehend, but she would look back, and figure it out; *study*, so she would *know* in the end. He had been so calculating…sneaky…*patient*; much more patient than the day he heard the egotistical call of duty. He couldn't leave her fast enough back then.

The man and the woman from the house were complicit as well. They knew exactly what they were doing. They were working with Thomas. How coordinated was the whole ordeal? How naïve—she should have killed the whole family that night in the guest room, never mind the foolish fantasy of having daughters.

Perhaps, though…perhaps Thomas had figured out the incomplete theories that she had not. She had told him years back of her upbringing, and the black rituals and rites that were a large part of her childhood. Back then, she believed she would never learn what they had done to her at those gatherings, and she didn't want to know; preferring to forget it all and start over.

She had also questioned her own—*state*—back on the day of her suicide. The fire burned in her grave and collapsed the boards. As expected, she passed out due to blood loss, so she missed the fire and the collapse, and she did indeed *die*…but it was not like she planned.

Hours after the grave fell in she awoke, pressed beneath the weight of the stones and the dirt. She was surprised to be…*alive(?)*, pinned beneath the surface, crushed and unable to move. Her neck was broken. Had the suicide failed? She wanted the lights to go out forever, but it was not to be; a soul as altered and angry as hers was not fit for rest. Mildred was born the child of parents practicing the dark arts; the odds of eternal rest would forever be slim.

The weight of the burial did not bring pain, nor was it capable of killing a person already dead; what it did do was give her time to think. She lay trapped; the claustrophobia maddening; with no choice but to wiggle her fingers, and slowly dig for two straight days until she clawed her way out. She emerged charred and *rotting*. Once above ground, she began a search for Elmer. They were on equal ground again. When she found him, she would teach him a lesson for haunting her.

The boy proved to be stubborn like his father, eluding her—punishing her. Why was he so much faster than she was? Had she known then that there would never be reconciliation, she would not have given him her attention…the little swine.

CHAPTER FIFTY-FIVE

More Bones

It was near midday when they arrived at Tower Hill. The clouds hung low, threatening to open up and make a mess of things. Holly parked the truck a half-mile away in the Sanborn Central School parking lot to disguise their presence. Tim set to work on Thomas's grave and did his best to roll the grass up like a carpet (in four pieces) for the final cover-up. They laid the tarp they had bought that morning on the side of the grave to throw the dirt on. Tim had only grabbed one of the shovels on his way out of the grove, so the work went slower than planned. Holly insisted on frequent turns digging because of Tim's injured hand.

They struck Thomas's coffin approximately twenty minutes later and put his bones in the same sack, along with Elmer. It didn't matter that they were mixed…that was the plan; father and son, together, forever.

They covered their tracks this time, not leaving the mess they had in the grove; replacing every last speck of dirt on the tarp. As carefully as possible, they replaced the rolls of grass, making the grave look *almost* as if it had not been disturbed. Nobody came to this cemetery anyway; at least it didn't look like it. In a year it would look as good as…old.

"What now?" asked Holly.

"I need a woodstove. I don't want these bones ever moved again...and...we never found Mildred's bones, so...I'm guessing if I don't cremate what we have now, it could be sabotaged. If we get caught, we're probably going to jail, so it can't be just any woodstove."

"Well, I have a woodstove, but what about a campfire or a torch or something? It would be kind of weird knowing that I burned human bones in my living room. What if they decide to stay and start haunting my place?"

"So, do you think...I mean, is it too soon to go back and..." he began even though he knew the answer.

"To go back to YOUR house? Uh, YES it is too soon. I am *not* going back to your house right now. We have no idea where Thomas took her. And, honestly, it would be nearly impossible to call that house home *ever*. The drowning in the pond, the graves—Oh, Tim...*I'm so sorry*, it's such a mess."

"First things first; forget the woodstove. Let's go to Sears."

CHAPTER FIFTY-SIX

Cremation

Tim and Holly walked out of the Sears store with a small hand crank meat grinder. Then they went to the supermarket and got a case of beer and things for dinner. At Holly's place, Tim assembled the meat grinder and lit her ex-boyfriend's grill, throwing the bones of Thomas and Elmer onto the flames to further dry and weaken them. The fire would not be hot enough to turn the bones to ash, and that's where the meat grinder came in. His hand throbbed, and he hoped to be done with the scattering of the ashes soon so he could see a doctor.

Holly, for the first time that day, had time to pull out the book that had been left in the turret. She had fled the horrible scene in the grove, leaving Tim crumpled in the open grave. In hysterics she escaped and ran to the house, hoping to use the telephone. As soon as she left the path in the corner of the driveway, she saw them; a trail of candles before her, one not six feet away, then three more leading to the side door, and of course, one burning in the turret window.

Fuck you, Thomas Pike. She headed in through the porch, the closest door to the living room telephone. When she got there, the phone was in the middle of the room, receiver far from the cradle, the cord ripped from the wall.

"You bastard!" she screamed and stood up straight to gather her strength and head to the place she had been summoned, the turret. The whole situation was out of her hands; there was nothing she could do but *trust* or *die*...or both. Tim had gone on and on with stories about having nothing to lose, and his divorce, and so on, and at this moment, she finally understood. "If you want me, take me. Kill me quick!"

What had been left was a library book: a volume from an encyclopedia. It had been left open to a specific page—a passage on the term *revenant*. A revenant was a person who had returned from the grave with their original body, taken from the French word "returning"—a dead person walking, and *not a ghost*. A reanimated corpse.

And that explains the flies, thought Holly.

By the time Tim regained consciousness and met her at the house, the trail of candles had vanished.

CHAPTER FIFTY-SEVEN

Final Plan

Two hours later, Tim shut the grill down and let the bones cool. Then he doubled up some burlap bags and pulverized them with a hammer for a good half hour, followed by two passes through the meat grinder; he felt like a serial killer. When all was said and done, he filled one of Holly's old vases with the ground bones of Thomas Pike and his son, Elmer. It was six o'clock.

"Come on, let's get these 'gentlemen' off your property. Maybe after this, they'll be gone and leave us alone." As he got into the passenger side, his eye caught the bag of cement in the bed of the pickup. The intention had been to mix Mildred's bones in a bucket and dump it off of a bridge somewhere far away, but there sat the bag, unused; a grim reminder that perhaps they couldn't let their guards down yet—or maybe ever.

There were no bones. There were no bones. There were no bones.

"Yeah, we'll drop these guys off...but I don't feel so confident about Mildred, the Revenant. Did Thomas take care of her, or what? What are we going back to? I mean, he left us a *warning* in the turret, or at least that's what I think it was. You could say it was just an explanation, but...I'm skeptical. He told us what she is to warn us. If she was gone for good...why even bother?"

Holly was silent, which was an acknowledgment that he had

a point, but it was also a denial, in that they should just take what they were given for now; bury Thomas and Elmer first, then worry about Mildred later. *Let's not get ahead of ourselves.*

"Where are we taking them?" she asked as they drove north.

"Thomas and Elmer? I'm going to take them to a place that I enjoyed until about a year ago…up until my divorce. I'm done with it now because it will only make me think of—my previous life. I like where my new life is going, so…they can have it. It's nice there." Holly was touched; Tim was a romantic.

"Where is this magic place Sheila ruined for you?"

"Lake Kanasatka. We had a cottage—and it was fun while it lasted, but I'm going to let these guys have it. I don't really want to see *them* again, either. I'm going to very respectfully pour them into the lake from someone's borrowed rowboat. I'll just steal it for twenty minutes and hope nobody notices."

"What if it's locked up?"

"I've got a set of bolt cutters in the back of the truck. I'll leave them twenty bucks to make up for it."

"Ooh, what a bad boy. You break allllll the rules," Holly teased.

"That's me… Yeah, that's me. I even cremated some people today."

Holly laughed.

CHAPTER FIFTY-EIGHT

Lake Kanasatka

"Why do you think it took Thomas so many years to…*wake up?*" asked Holly. They were the only boat out on the lake, most of the cabins on the shore still winterized, empty until Memorial Day or even the Fourth of July.

"Probably because there *wasn't even a plan* for many years, I'm guessing? He was a slave to the 'talent' available. Maybe some of the people that owned the house were just not right for the job: Weak, unable to communicate, flighty—who knows? Then he saw Annette pick up the baton and…she inspired him. We didn't have much choice; he was already motivated so he—*persuaded* us to finish.

"He couldn't move the graves; just part of the ghost physics I'll never fully understand. I mean, he could choke you, or kick you in the head, or stab you with a bayonet, but write with a pen or move a grave? For that, you need helpers." Holly laughed.

After a good scan of the shoreline for whistle-blowers, Tim opened the burlap bag and poured the powdered mixture of Thomas and Elmer out into the water. Like a good Christian, he said a short prayer and made the sign of the cross. Holly, the lapsed Catholic, did the same. He dunked the burlap bag in the lake and rinsed it out, filled it with rocks they found on the shore, and let it sink.

How does that feel, Tom? Tim wondered.

CHAPTER FIFTY-NINE

Some patience of her own

It would be too easy to stalk them or hide in the house. No, these...*mutts*...killing them quickly would not be satisfying enough; this called for creativity. They, after all, were part of a plan that took years to hatch; she could wait, too—for inspiration. This would take some time and some thinking.

She paced the woods, keeping her distance from the house on purpose; letting the emotions settle so the brain could plan properly. She was alone now, and would most likely be forever. There was much to process, and much she still didn't understand. She wasn't even completely sure of who she was.

Her childhood: What exactly had they done to her? The potions, the spells, the chanting—Why was she so different from Thomas and Elmer? *They* had crossed, yet she had been denied. Was Thomas aware this would happen? Was he always there...waiting for his opportunity...for more than a hundred years? If he was—*well played* Thomas; she would never underestimate anyone ever again.

She needed gratification, something smart and rewarding. There had to be more creative options to consider than a couple of quick murders...The trespassers were relatively young and had many natural years left—*plenty of time.*

But even that was thinking small, and she knew it.

CHAPTER SIXTY
Open House

October 7th, 1972

Holly was relieved to finally host an open house on Lancaster Hill Road. Tim had returned (very bravely) and finished the refurbishment, with Johnny's help, in a little more than a year. Their work was fast, efficient, beautiful, and most importantly, uninterrupted. The housing market was favorable, and it seemed like Tim was about to score a well deserved financial victory.

A good crowd arrived that Saturday; close to twenty people in fact, but Holly was skeptical as to how many were qualified buyers when she saw a policeman in full uniform. His nametag read SIMMONS, and she drew the connection immediately. *A policeman like his grandfather, and nosy like the Simmons ladies. The apple doesn't fall too far from the tree. I know who you are.* Was it his grandfather that was the cop? Or great-grandfather? She couldn't recall. Maybe it was even great-great-grandfather. It didn't matter—Simmons was finally able to gawk at the entire "Wells property" and its infamous past without it being trespassing. Holly shrugged it off. Today was a good day; let him gawk—but she would keep a close eye on him nonetheless.

She had already shown the house twice and given the complete spiel—and both couples had submitted bids. Tim was not there—house owners were typically not on-site during showings—but he would be very pleased with the news. There would be two more private showings later in the week before they would select a winning bid. Things were looking up in so many words, but she couldn't wait for the day to be over so she could get the hell off this godforsaken property.

She avoided areas like the pond and the grove, announcing to potential buyers that they were free to check things out on their own if they chose to do so; she just hung back and pointed people in the right directions. The kitchen and the turret were also painful for her, but Tim had done such a wonderful job on the interior that it was almost easy to pretend that what had happened in there occurred someplace else.

She waited on the front lawn for her latest guests to return from the outskirts. One couple ambled through the field, past the pond area and straight through the spot that Mildred had slaughtered the geese. When they passed the stone wall and arrived at Holly's little lemonade tent, she turned to them, composed herself and prepared to answer questions.

"It's beautiful, isn't it? Romantic, even?" Holly spoke of the grove the way she used to feel; her current opinion would not be ideal for her sales pitch.

"Yes…it is, and very peaceful. I can see myself taking walks up there to de-stress after work," the woman commented.

"Yes, perfect; and with the sunset? Wow…"

Tim had rototilled the entire gravesite; and to cover up the excavation, Tim planted what he called a "forest garden." Now if Simmons or anyone else got nosy there would be an explanation for the turned soil. No one needed to know there had ever been any graves out there; not many people had even known to begin with. The two headstones were removed and were now smashed into pieces, miles away at the bottom of a lake in North Andover, Massachusetts, where Tim's parents used to walk their dog.

Her conscience was clear, for the most part. She didn't feel guilty for not disclosing every detail of what they had witnessed—and the ones they knew about but had missed. They hadn't seen a thing since the family reunion in the grove; not one sighting. Thomas had, in the end, seemingly done his part; Mildred wasn't even "stealing blueberries" anymore.

Thinking back, Holly remembered how damn hard it was to get everything to this moment. Communication with Thomas had been difficult, and the obstacles to success were downright life-threatening; she was even beginning to forget how the hell they got it all done. Perhaps her brain was naturally helping her to forget because it was just too much to bear. The whole ordeal had happened in approximately two weeks, but it had felt much longer.

Now they were in the home stretch. The house was finished and finally up for sale; the bids were rolling in. It wouldn't be long now, and they could move on to bigger and better things. *I'll move to Florida with Tim, maybe; if I can convince him—and we can start over down there. Do they have ghosts down there? If there are, how could they possibly be scary? It just seems so sunny and happy there—at least the way I picture it—*

"Excuse me...Holly, was it? I have a question if you don't mind." It was one of the potential buyers coming out of the house to meet her on the lawn.

Holly turned. "Mrs. Wallace. Yes, how can I help you?"

"How close are the nearest neighbors? I don't recall seeing even one other house on this road, except right at the beginning," she asked.

"Those *are* the closest neighbors. The Simmons family, I believe. There are actually three houses down that driveway. There's a policeman here right now looking at the house; it says 'Simmons' on his nametag. He might know more than I do, but it is very private here, and you should not be bothered by neighbors at all. There's plenty of New Hampshire peace, quiet, and fresh air."

"And you said the whole meadow comes with the property, correct? All the way to the trees?"

"That's right. You get the meadow, the pond, the house, the barn and a big chunk of woods, including the grove—twenty-three acres in all. You can even tap your maples right here in the front yard if you want to make homemade syrup."

"No close neighbors? Okay, well—who do you suppose that lady is—out near the corner of the field? She's been standing and staring at the house since I arrived. That was forty-five minutes ago. First, she was over there…and then she moved over there. It's creepy, isn't it? I mean, as you said, it's not even her land!"

THE END of Book One

Turn the page for an excerpt from
Dead Woman Scorned:
The Patience of a Dead Man—Book Two

EXCERPT FROM

Dead Woman Scorned:
The Patience of a Dead Man—Book Two

October 1971—One year before the Open House

Tim Russell banged his palm against the steering wheel in frustration—he'd forgotten his wallet. He wondered for a second if he really needed it before tomorrow, then looked at the gas gauge—near empty. Not even enough gas to make it to Holly's house in Laconia. He stepped on the brake and pulled over to the side of the dirt road to make a U-turn, then hesitated.

It shouldn't be a problem—to simply turn around, drive the quarter-mile back, walk into the house and retrieve the wallet—but it was undeniably *harrowing*, even though their struggles with the murderous Mildred Wells were over. They'd beaten her, and she'd been taken away weeks ago, but even so, Tim's stress level was off the charts as he worked alone each day, watching over his shoulder, restoring the old house as fast as he possibly could.

He looked back before making the turn, his heart picking back up to the level it had maintained the entire day. *Here I go—I'm going back in*, he thought, as he postponed thoughts of the cold beer waiting for him at the convenience store a mile down the road. *Best to hit and run*. He stepped on the gas and made the turn, never taking his eyes off of the house and, more specifically, the turret, his designated office space during the reconstruction—the room where he'd left his wallet.

Rip that band-aid he thought, as the truck climbed the small hill up the driveway. Quickly and carefully, he pulled around to the side of the house, then backed up and parked in front of the porch, facing the road. Now he had the shortest path inside the house to the turret and the shortest path to the road once he was back in the truck. Annoyingly, he had to kill the engine because the house keys were on the same damned ring—something he would remedy tomorrow with a quick stop at the hardware store.

He jogged up to the door and inserted the key as quickly and quietly as possible. His actions were nothing like the words he used to soothe Holly. She worried about him each and every day as he worked alone, and he did his best to persuade her that it was a "totally different place now"—Mildred was gone, and it "seemed as if she'd never been there." Holly didn't believe a word. She hated the house now—it would never be the same for her, no matter what work he did to disguise it.

In seconds he was inside the front porch, opening the front door, faking as though there was nothing to be afraid of. Once inside, he noticed that it seemed very dark in the kitchen. It was late May, and the longest day of the year would be here in less than a month. Sunset should be at around 8 pm today, with the twilight keeping things well lit for another half-hour at least. *Strange.* He turned to look out the kitchen window.

It was pitch black outside, and his truck was already gone.

In a panic, he spun for the porch, deep down, becoming aware that forgetting his wallet was the greatest mistake of his life. The smell hit him right then, and he wondered why he hadn't noticed it sooner. The front door was closed and locked, even though he'd left it open on purpose. He grabbed the knob and began to work it when three flies landed on his hand and wrist. *No. She must be close.* Tim turned to the dark dining room to protect his back. She stood in the far corner, motionless.

She knew he'd forgotten the wallet. She knew he'd be back, and then she set the trap.

Buy now on Amazon
https://www.amazon.com/dp/B081FWZLRG/

For Josi, Karil, Ed, Addison and Olivia
Very special thanks to Scott Reid

Michael Clark was raised in New Hampshire and lived in the house *The Patience of a Dead Man* is based on. The bats of the barn really circled the rafters all day and there actually was a man-made grove hidden in the forest. He now lives in Massachusetts with his wife Josi and his dog Bubba. If you enjoyed this book, please consider reading

Dead Woman Scorned:
The Patience of a Dead Man—Book Two.

Follow:
https://www.michaelclarkbooks.com/
https://www.facebook.com/michaelclarkbooks/
Twitter: @MIKEclarkbooks
Instagram: @michaelclarkbooks
Reddit: u/michaelclarkbooks

ONE LAST THING...

If you enjoyed this book, I'd be very grateful if you'd post a short review on Amazon. I read all the reviews personally and your input could very well influence future books.

Thank you!
–Mike

Made in the USA
Columbia, SC
07 January 2020